ADVENTURES IN TIME

ADVENTURES IN TIME

by Andre Norton

THE TIME TRADERS
THE DEFIANT AGENTS
KEY OUT OF TIME

THE TIME TRADERS

CONTENTS

CHAPTER 1

To anyone who glanced casually inside the detention room the young man sitting there did not seem very formidable. In height he might have been a little above average, but not enough to make him noticeable. His brown hair was cropped conservatively; his unlined boy's face was not one to be remembered—unless one was observant enough to note those light-gray eyes and catch a chilling, measuring expression showing now and then for an instant in their depths.

Neatly and inconspicuously dressed, in this last quarter of the twentieth century his like was to be found on any street of the city ten floors below—to all outward appearances. But that other person under the protective coloring so assiduously cultivated could touch heights of encased and controlled fury which Murdock himself did not understand and was only just learning to use as a weapon against a world he had always found hostile.

He was aware, though he gave no sign of it, that a guard was watching him. The cop on duty was an old hand—he probably expected some reaction other than passive acceptance from the prisoner. But he was not going to get it. The law had Ross sewed up tight this time. Why didn't they get about the business of shipping him off? Why had he had that afternoon session with the skull thumper? Ross had been on the defensive then, and he had not liked it. He had given to the other's questions all the attention his shrewd mind could muster, but a faint, very faint, apprehension still clung to the memory of that meeting.

The door of the detention room opened. Ross did not turn his head, but the guard cleared his throat as if their hour of mutual silence had dried his vocal cords. "On your feet, Murdock! The judge wants to see you."

Ross rose smoothly, with every muscle under fluid control. It never paid to talk back, to allow any sign of defiance to show. He would go through the motions as if he were a bad little boy who had realized his errors. It was a meek-and-mild act that had paid off more than once in Ross's checkered past. So he faced the man seated behind the desk in the other room with an uncertain, diffident smile, standing with boyish awkwardness, respectfully waiting for the other to speak first.

Judge Ord Rawle. It was his rotten luck to pull old Eagle Beak on his case. Well, he would simply have to take it when the old boy dished it out. Not that he had to remain stuck with it later....

"You have a bad record, young man."

Ross allowed his smile to fade; his shoulders slumped. But under concealing lids his eyes showed an instant of cold defiance.

"Yes, sir," he agreed in a voice carefully cultivated to shake convincingly about the edges. Then suddenly all Ross's pleasure in the skill of his act was wiped away. Judge Rawle was not alone; that blasted skull thumper was sitting there, watching the prisoner with the same keenness he had shown the other day.

"A very bad record for the few years you have had to make it." Eagle Beak was staring at him, too, but without the same look of penetration, luckily for Ross. "By rights, you should be turned over to the new Rehabilitation Service...."

Ross froze inside. That was the "treatment," icy rumors of which had spread throughout his particular world. For the second time since he had entered the room his self-confidence was jarred. Then he clung with a degree of hope to the phrasing of that last sentence.

"Instead, I have been authorized to offer you a choice, Murdock. One which I shall state—and on record—I do not in the least approve."

Ross's twinge of fear faded. If the judge didn't like it, there must be something in it to the advantage of Ross Murdock. He'd grab it for sure!

"There is a government project in need of volunteers. It seems that you have tested out as possible material for this assignment. If you sign for it, the law will consider the time spent on it as part of your sentence. Thus you may aid the country which you have heretofore disgraced—"

"And if I refuse, I go to this rehabilitation. Is that right, sir?"

"I certainly consider you a fit candidate for rehabilitation. Your record—" He shuffled through the papers on his desk.

"I choose to volunteer for the project, sir."

The judge snorted and pushed all the papers into a folder. He spoke to a man waiting in the shadows. "Here then is your volunteer, Major."

Ross bottled in his relief. He was over the first hump. And since his luck had held so far, he might be about to win all the way....

The man Judge Rawle called "Major" moved into the light. At the first glance Ross, to his hidden annoyance, found himself uneasy. To face up to

Eagle Beak was all part of the game. But somehow he sensed one did not play such games with this man.

"Thank you, your honor. We will be on our way at once. This weather is not very promising."

Before he realized what was happening, Ross found himself walking meekly to the door. He considered trying to give the major the slip when they left the building, losing himself in a storm-darkened city. But they did not take the elevator downstairs. Instead, they climbed two or three flights up the emergency stairs. And to his humiliation Ross found himself panting and slowing, while the other man, who must have been a good dozen years his senior, showed no signs of discomfort.

They came out into the snow on the roof, and the major flashed a torch skyward, guiding in a dark shadow which touched down before them. A helicopter! For the first time Ross began to doubt the wisdom of his choice.

"On your way, Murdock!" The voice was impersonal enough, but that very impersonality got under one's skin.

Bundled into the machine between the silent major and an equally quiet pilot in uniform, Ross was lifted over the city, whose ways he knew as well as he knew the lines on his own palm, into the unknown he was already beginning to regard dubiously. The lighted streets and buildings, their outlines softened by the soft wet snow, fell out of sight. Now they could mark the outer highways. Ross refused to ask any questions. He could take this silent treatment; he *had* taken a lot of tougher things in the past.

The patches of light disappeared, and the country opened out. The plane banked. Ross, with all the familiar landmarks of his world gone, could not have said if they were headed north or south. But moments later not even the thick curtain of snowflakes could blot out the pattern of red lights on the ground, and the helicopter settled down.

"Come on!"

For the second time Ross obeyed. He stood shivering, engulfed in a miniature blizzard. His clothing, protection enough in the city, did little good against the push of the wind. A hand gripped his upper arm, and he was drawn forward to a low building. A door banged and Ross and his companion came into a region of light and very welcome heat.

"Sit down—over there!"

Too bewildered to resent orders, Ross sat. There were other men in the room. One, wearing a queer suit of padded clothing, a bulbous headgear hooked over his arm, was reading a paper. The major crossed to speak to him and after they conferred for a moment, the major beckoned Ross with a crooked finger. Ross trailed the officer into an inner room lined with lockers.

From one of the lockers the major pulled a suit like the pilot's, and began to measure it against Ross. "All right," he snapped. "Climb into this! We haven't all night."

Ross climbed into the suit. As soon as he fastened the last zipper his companion jammed one of the domed helmets on his head. The pilot looked in the door. "We'd better scramble, Kelgarries, or we may be grounded for the duration!"

They hurried back to the flying field. If the helicopter had been a surprising mode of travel, this new machine was something straight out of the future—a needle-slim ship poised on fins, its sharp nose lifting vertically into the heavens. There was a scaffolding along one side, which the pilot scaled to enter the ship.

Unwillingly, Ross climbed the same ladder and found that he must wedge himself in on his back, his knees hunched up almost under his chin. To make it worse, cramped as those quarters were, he had to share them with the major. A transparent hood snapped down and was secured, sealing them in.

During his short lifetime Ross had often been afraid, bitterly afraid. He had fought to toughen his mind and body against such fears. But what he experienced now was no ordinary fear; it was panic so strong that it made him feel sick. To be shut in this small place with the knowledge that he had no control over his immediate future brought him face to face with every terror he had ever known, all of them combined into one horrible whole.

How long does a nightmare last? A moment? An hour? Ross could not time his. But at last the weight of a giant hand clamped down on his chest, and he fought for breath until the world exploded about him.

He came back to consciousness slowly. For a second he thought he was blind. Then he began to sort out one shade of grayish light from another. Finally, Ross became aware that he no longer rested on his back, but was slumped in a seat. The world about him was wrung with a vibration that beat in turn through his body.

Ross Murdock had remained at liberty as long as he had because he was able to analyze a situation quickly. Seldom in the past five years had he been at a loss to deal with any challenging person or action. Now he was aware that he was on the defensive and was being kept there. He stared into the dark and thought hard and furiously. He was convinced that everything that was happening to him this day was designed with only one end in view—to shake his self-confidence and make him pliable. Why?

Ross had an enduring belief in his own abilities and he also possessed a kind of shrewd understanding seldom granted to one so young. He knew that while Murdock was important to Murdock, he was none too important in the scheme of things as a whole. He had a record—a record so bad that Rawle might easily have thrown the book at him. But it differed in one important way from that of many of his fellows; until now he had been able to beat most of the raps. Ross believed this was largely because he had always worked alone and taken pains to plan a job in advance.

Why now had Ross Murdock become so important to someone that they would do all this to shake him? He was a volunteer—for what? To be a guinea pig for some bug they wanted to learn how to kill cheaply and easily? They'd been in a big hurry to push him off base. Using the silent treatment, this rushing around in planes, they were really working to keep him groggy. So, all right, he'd give them a groggy boy all set up for their job, whatever it was. Only, was his act good enough to fool the major? Ross had a hunch that it might not be, and that really hurt.

It was deep night now. Either they had flown out of the path of the storm or were above it. There were stars shining through the cover of the cockpit, but no moon.

Ross's formal education was sketchy, but in his own fashion he had acquired a range of knowledge which would have surprised many of the authorities who had had to deal with him. All the wealth of a big city library had been his to explore, and he had spent much time there, soaking up facts in many odd branches of learning. Facts were very useful things. On at least three occasions assorted scraps of knowledge had preserved Ross's freedom, once, perhaps his life.

Now he tried to fit together the scattered facts he knew about his present situation into some proper pattern. He was inside some new type of super-super atomjet, a machine so advanced in design that it would not have been used for anything that was not an important mission. Which meant that Ross Murdock had become necessary to someone, somewhere. Knowing that fact should give him a slight edge in the future, and he might well need such an edge. He'd just have to wait, play dumb, and use his eyes and ears.

At the rate they were shooting along they ought to be out of the country in a couple of hours. Didn't the Government have bases half over the world to keep the "cold peace"? Well, there was nothing for it. To be planted abroad someplace might interfere with plans for escape, but he'd handle that detail when he was forced to face it.

Then suddenly Ross was on his back once more, the giant hand digging into his chest and middle. This time there were no lights on the ground to guide them in. Ross had no intimation that they had reached their destination until they set down with a jar which snapped his teeth together.

The major wriggled out, and Ross was able to stretch his cramped body. But the other's hand was already on his shoulder, urging him along. Ross crawled free and clung dizzily to a ladderlike disembarking structure.

Below there were no lights, only an expanse of open snow. Men were moving across that blank area, gathering at the foot of the ladder. Ross was hungry and very tired. If the major wanted to play games, he hoped that such action could wait until the next morning.

In the meantime he must learn where "here" was. If he had a chance to run, he wanted to know the surrounding territory. But that hand was on his arm, drawing him along toward a door that stood half-open. As far as Ross could see, it led to the interior of a hillock of snow. Either the storm or men had done a very good cover-up job, and somehow Ross knew the camouflage was intentional.

That was Ross's introduction to the base, and after his arrival his view of the installation was extremely limited. One day was spent in undergoing the most searching physical he had ever experienced. And after the doctors had poked and pried he was faced by a series of other tests no one bothered to explain. Thereafter he was introduced to solitary, that is, confined to his own company in a cell-like room with a bunk that was more comfortable than it looked and an announcer in a corner of the ceiling. So far he had been told exactly nothing. And so far he had asked no questions, stubbornly keeping up his end of what he believed to be a tug of wills. At the moment, safely alone and lying flat on his bunk he eyed the announcer, a very dangerous young man and one who refused to yield an inch.

"Now hear this...." The voice transmitted through that grill was metallic, but its rasp held overtones of Kelgarries' voice. Ross's lips tightened. He had explored every inch of the walls and knew that there was no trace of the door which had admitted him. With only his bare hands to work with he could not break out, and his only clothes were the shirt, sturdy slacks, and a pair of soft-soled moccasins that they had given him.

"... to identify ..." droned the voice. Ross realized that he must have missed something, not that it mattered. He was almost determined not to play along any more.

There was a click, signifying that Kelgarries was through braying. But the customary silence did not close in again. Instead, Ross heard a clear, sweet trilling which he vaguely associated with a bird. His acquaintance with all feathered life was limited to city sparrows and plump park pigeons, neither of which raised their voices in song, but surely those sounds were bird notes. Ross glanced from the mike in the ceiling to the opposite wall and what he saw there made him sit up, with the instant response of an alerted fighter.

For the wall was no longer there! Instead, there was a sharp slope of ground cutting down from peaks where the dark green of fir trees ran close to the snow line. Patches of snow clung to the earth in sheltered places, and the scent of those pines was in Ross's nostrils, real as the wind touching him with its chill.

He shivered as a howl sounded loudly and echoed, bearing the age-old warning of a wolf pack, hungry and a-hunt. Ross had never heard that sound before, but his human heritage subconsciously recognized it for what it was—death on four feet. Similarly, he was able to identify the gray shadows slinking about the nearest trees, and his hands balled into fists as he looked wildly about him for some weapon.

The bunk was under him and three of the four walls of the room enclosed him like a cave. But one of those gray skulkers had raised its head and was looking directly at him, its reddish eyes alight. Ross ripped the top blanket off the bunk with a half-formed idea of snapping it at the animal when it sprang.

Stiff-legged, the beast advanced, a guttural growl sounding deep in its throat. To Ross the animal, larger than any dog he had even seen and twice as vicious, was a monster. He had the blanket ready before he realized that the wolf was not watching him after all, and that its attention was focused on a point out of his line of vision.

The wolfs muzzle wrinkled in a snarl, revealing long yellow-white teeth. There was a singing twang, and the animal leaped into the air, fell back, and rolled on the ground, biting despairingly at a shaft protruding from just behind its ribs. It howled again, and blood broke from its mouth.

Ross was beyond surprise now. He pulled himself together and got up, to walk steadily toward the dying wolf. And he wasn't in the least amazed when his outstretched hands flattened against an unseen barrier. Slowly, he swept his hands right and left, sure that he was touching the wall of his cell. Yet his eyes told him he was on a mountain side, and every sight, sound, and smell was making it real to him.

Puzzled, he thought a moment and then, finding an explanation that satisfied him, he nodded once and went back to sit at ease on his bunk. This must be some superior form of TV that included odors, the illusion of wind, and other fancy touches to make it more vivid. The total effect was so convincing that Ross had to keep reminding himself that it was all just a picture.

The wolf was dead. Its pack mates had fled into the brush, but since the picture remained, Ross decided that the show was not yet over. He could still hear a click of sound, and he waited for the next bit of action. But the reason for his viewing it still eluded him.

A man came into view, crossing before Ross. He stooped to examine the dead wolf, catching it by the tail and hoisting its hindquarters off the ground. Comparing the beast's size with the hunter's, Ross saw that he had not been wrong in his estimation of the animal's unusually large dimensions. The man shouted over his shoulder, his words distinct enough, but unintelligible to Ross.

The stranger was oddly dressed—too lightly dressed if one judged the climate by the frequent snow patches and the biting cold. A strip of coarse cloth, extending from his armpit to about four inches above the knee, was wound about his body and pulled in at the waist by a belt. The belt, far more ornate than the cumbersome wrapping, was made of many small chains linking metal plates and supported a long dagger which hung straight in front. The man also wore a round blue cloak, now swept back on his shoulders to free his bare arms, which was fastened by a large pin under his chin. His footgear, which extended above his calves, was made of animal hide, still bearing patches of shaggy hair. His face was beardless, though a shadowy line along his chin suggested that he had not shaved that particular day. A fur cap concealed most of his dark-brown hair.

Was he an Indian? No, for although his skin was tanned, it was as fair as Ross's under that weathering. And his clothing did not resemble any Indian apparel Ross had ever seen. Yet, in spite of his primitive trappings, the man had such an aura of authority, of self-confidence, and competence that it was clear he was top dog in his own section of the world.

Soon another man, dressed much like the first, but with a rust-brown cloak, came along, pulling behind him two very reluctant donkeys, whose eyes rolled fearfully at sight of the dead wolf. Both animals wore packs lashed on their backs by ropes of twisted hide. Then another man came along, with another brace of donkeys. Finally, a fourth man, wearing skins for covering and with a mat of beard on his cheeks and chin, appeared. His uncovered head, a bush of uncombed flaxen hair, shone whitish as he knelt beside the dead beast, a knife with a dull-gray blade in his hand, and set to work skinning the wolf with appreciable skill. Three more pairs of donkeys, all heavily laden, were led past the scene before he finished his task. Finally, he rolled the bloody skin into a bundle and gave the flayed body a kick before he ran lightly after the disappearing train of pack animals.

CHAPTER 2

Ross, absorbed in the scene before him, was not prepared for the sudden and complete darkness which blotted out not only the action but the light in his own room as well.

"What—?" His startled voice rang loudly in his ears, too loudly, for all sound had been wiped out with the light. The faint swish of the ventilating system, of which he had not been actively aware until it had disappeared, was also missing. A trace of the same panic he had known in the cockpit of the atomjet tingled along his nerves. But this time he could meet the unknown with action.

Ross slowly moved through the dark, his hands outstretched before him to ward off contact with the wall. He was determined that somehow he would discover the hidden door, escape from this dark cell....

There! His palm struck flat against a smooth surface. He swept out his hand—and suddenly it passed over emptiness. Ross explored by touch. There *was* a door and now it was open. For a moment he hesitated, upset by a nagging little fear that if he stepped through he would be out on the hillside with the wolves.

"That's stupid!" Again he spoke aloud. And, just because he did feel uneasy, he moved. All the frustrations of the past hours built up in him a raging desire to do something—anything—just so long as it was what *he* wanted to do and not at another's orders.

Nevertheless, Ross continued to move slowly, for the space beyond that open door was as deep and dark a pit as the room he left. To squeeze along one wall, using an outstretched arm as a guide, was the best procedure, he decided.

A few feet farther on, his shoulder slipped from the surface and he half tumbled into another open door. But there was the wall again, and he clung to it thankfully. Another door ... Ross paused, trying to catch some faint sound, the slightest hint that he was not alone in this blindman's maze. But without even air currents to stir it, the blackness itself took on a thick solidity which encased him as a congealing jelly.

The wall ended. Ross kept his left hand on it, flailed out with his right, and felt his nails scrape across another surface. The space separating the two surfaces was wider than any doorway. Was it a cross-corridor? He was about to make a wider arm sweep when he heard a sound. He was not alone.

Ross went back to the wall, flattening himself against it, trying to control the volume of his own breathing in order to catch the slightest whisper of the other noise. He discovered that lack of sight can confuse the ear. He could not identify those clicks, the wisp of fluttering sound that might be air displaced by the opening of another door.

Finally, he detected something moving at floor level. Someone or something must be creeping, not walking, toward him. Ross pushed back around the corner. It never occurred to him to challenge that crawler. There was an element of danger in this strange encounter in the dark; it was not meant to be a meeting between fellow explorers.

The sound of crawling was not steady. There were long pauses, and Ross became convinced that each rest was punctuated by heavy breathing as if the crawler was finding progress a great and exhausting effort. He fought the picture that persisted in his imagination—that of a wolf snuffling along the blacked-out hall. Caution suggested a quick retreat, but Ross's urge to rebellion held him where he was, crouching, straining to see what crept toward him.

Suddenly there was a blinding flare of light, and Ross's hands went to cover his dazzled eyes. And he heard a despairing, choked exclamation from near to floor level. The same steady light that normally filled hall and room was bright again. Ross found himself standing at the juncture of two corridors—momentarily, he was absurdly pleased that he had deduced that correctly—and the crawler—?

A man—at least the figure was a two-legged, two-armed body reasonably human in outline—was lying several yards away. But the body was so wrapped in bandages and the head so totally muffled, that it lacked all identity. For that reason it was the more startling.

One of the mittened hands moved slightly, raising the body from the ground so it could squirm forward an inch or so. Before Ross could move, a man came running into the corridor from the far end. Murdock recognized Major Kelgarries. He wet his lips as the major went down on his knees beside the creature on the floor.

"Hardy! Hardy!" That voice, which carried the snap of command whenever it was addressed to Ross, was now warmly human. "Hardy, man!" The major's hands were on the bandaged body, lifting it, easing the head and shoulders back against his arm. "It's all right, Hardy. You're back—safe. This is the base, Hardy." He spoke slowly, soothingly, with the steadiness one would use to comfort a frightened child.

Those mittened paws which had beat feebly into the air fell onto the bandage-wreathed chest. "Back—safe—" The voice from behind the face mask was a rusty croak.

"Back, safe," the major assured him.

"Dark—dark all around again—" protested the croak.

"Just a power failure, man. Everything's all right now. We'll get you into bed."

The mitten pawed again until it touched Kelgarries' arm; then it flexed a little as if the hand under it was trying to grip.

"Safe—?"

"You bet you are!" The major's tone carried firm reassurance. Now Kelgarries looked up at Ross as if he knew the other had been there all the time.

"Murdock, get down to the end room. Call Dr. Farrell!"

"Yes, sir!" The "sir" came so automatically that Ross had already reached the end room before he realized he had used it.

Nobody explained matters to Ross Murdock. The bandaged Hardy was claimed by the doctor and two attendants and carried away, the major walking beside the stretcher, still holding one of the mittened hands in his. Ross hesitated, sure he was not supposed to follow, but not ready either to explore farther or return to his own room. The sight of Hardy, whoever he might be, had radically changed Ross's conception of the project he had too speedily volunteered to join.

That what they did here was important, Ross had never doubted. That it was dangerous, he had early suspected. But his awareness had been an abstract concept of danger, not connected with such concrete evidence as Hardy crawling through the dark. From the first, Ross had nursed vague plans for escape; now he knew he must get out of this place lest he end up a twin for Hardy.

"Murdock?"

Having heard no warning sound from behind, Ross whirled, ready to use his fists, his only weapons. But he did not face the major, or any of the other taciturn men he knew held positions of authority. The newcomer's brown skin was startling against the neutral shade of the walls. His hair and brows were only a few shades darker; but the general sameness of color was relieved by the vivid blue of his eyes.

Expressionless, the dark stranger stood quietly, his arms hanging loosely by his sides, studying Ross, as if the younger man was some problem he had been assigned to solve. When he spoke, his voice was a monotone lacking any modulation of feeling.

"I am Ashe." He introduced himself baldly; he might have been saying "This is a table and that is a chair."

Ross's quick temper took spark from the other's indifference. "All right—so you're Ashe!" He strove to make a challenge of it. "And what is that supposed to mean?"

But the other did not rise to the bait. He shrugged. "For the time being we have been partnered—"

"Partnered for what?" demanded Ross, controlling his temper.

"We work in pairs here. The machine sorts us ..." he answered briefly and consulted his wrist watch. "Mess call soon."

Ashe had already turned away, and Ross could not stand the other's lack of interest. While Murdock refused to ask questions of the major or any others on that side of the fence, surely he could get some information from a fellow "volunteer."

"What is this place, anyway?" he asked.

The other glanced back over his shoulder. "Operation Retrograde."

Ross swallowed his anger. "Okay, but what do they do here? Listen, I just saw a fellow who'd been banged up as if he'd been in a concrete mixer, creeping along this hall. What sort of work do they do here? And what do we have to do?"

To his amazement Ashe smiled, at least his lips quirked faintly. "Hardy got under your skin, eh? Well, we have our percentage of failures. They are as few as it's humanly possible to make, and they give us every advantage that can be worked out for us—"

"Failures at what?"

"Operation Retrograde."

Somewhere down the hall a buzzer gave a muted whirr.

"That's mess call. And I'm hungry, even if you're not." Ashe walked away as if Ross Murdock had ceased to exist.

But Ross Murdock did exist, and to him that was an important fact. As he trailed along behind Ashe he determined that he was going to continue to exist, in one piece and unharmed, Operation Retrograde or no Operation Retrograde. And he was going to pry a few enlightening answers out of somebody very soon.

To his surprise he found Ashe waiting for him at the door of a room from which came the sound of voices and a subdued clatter of trays and tableware.

"Not many in tonight," Ashe commented in a take-it-or-leave-it tone. "It's been a busy week."

The room was rather sparsely occupied. Five tables were empty, while the men gathered at the remaining two. Ross counted ten men, either already eating or coming back from a serving hatch with well-filled trays. All of them were dressed in slacks, shirt, and moccasins like himself—the outfit seemed to be a sort of undress uniform—and six of them were ordinary in physical appearance. The other four differed so radically that Ross could barely conceal his amazement.

Since their fellows accepted them without comment, Ross silently stole glances at them as he waited behind Ashe for a tray. One pair were clearly Oriental; they were small, lean men with thin brackets of long black mustache on either side of their mobile mouths. Yet he had caught a word or two of their conversation, and they spoke his own language with the facility of the native born. In addition to the mustaches, each wore a blue tattoo mark on the forehead and others of the same design on the backs of their agile hands.

The second duo were even more fantastic. The color of their flaxen hair was normal, but they wore it in braids long enough to swing across their powerful shoulders, a fashion unlike any Ross had ever seen. Yet any suggestion of effeminacy certainly did not survive beyond the first glance at their ruggedly masculine features.

"Gordon!" One of the braided giants swung halfway around from the table to halt Ashe as he came down the aisle with his tray. "When did you get back? And where is Sanford?"

One of the Orientals laid down the spoon with which he had been vigorously stirring his coffee and asked with real concern, "Another loss?"

Ashe shook his head. "Just reassignment. Sandy's holding down Outpost Gog and doing well." He grinned and his face came to life with an expression of impish humor Ross would not have believed possible. "He'll end up with a million or two if he doesn't watch out. He takes to trade as if he were born with a beaker in his fist."

The Oriental laughed and then glanced at Ross. "Your new partner, Ashe?"

Some of the animation disappeared from Ashe's brown face; he was noncommittal again. "Temporary assignment. This is Murdock." The introduction was flat enough to daunt Ross. "Hodaki, Feng," he indicated the two Easterners with a nod as he put down his tray. "Jansen, Van Wyke." That accounted for the blonds.

"Ashe!" A man arose at the other table and came to stand beside theirs. Thin, with a dark, narrow face and restless eyes, he was much younger than the others, younger and not so well controlled. He might answer questions if there was something in it for him, Ross decided, and filed the thought away.

"Well, Kurt?" Ashe's recognition was as dampening as it could be, and Ross's estimation of the younger man went up a fraction when the snub appeared to have no effect upon him.

"Did you hear about Hardy?"

Feng looked as if he were about to speak, and Van Wyke frowned. Ashe made a deliberate process of chewing and swallowing before he replied. "Naturally." His tone reduced whatever had happened to Hardy to a matter-of-fact proceeding far removed from Kurt's implied melodrama.

"He's smashed up ... kaput...." Kurt's accent, slight in the beginning, was thickening. "Tortured...."

Ashe regarded him levelly. "You aren't on Hardy's run, are you?"

Still Kurt refused to be quashed. "Of course, I'm not! You know the run I am in training for. But that is not saying that such can not happen as well on my run, or yours, or yours!" He pointed a stabbing finger at Feng and then at the blond men.

"You can fall out of bed and break your neck, too, if your number comes up that way," observed Jansen. "Go cry on Millaird's shoulder if it hurts you that much. You were told the score at your briefing. You know why you were picked...."

Ross caught a faint glance aimed at him by Ashe. He was still totally in the dark, but he would not try to pry any information from this crowd. Maybe part of their training was this hush-hush business. He would wait and see, until he could get Kurt aside and do a little pumping. Meanwhile he ate stolidly and tried to cover up his interest in the conversation.

"Then you are going to keep on saying 'Yes, sir,' 'No, sir,' to every order here—?"

Hodaki slammed his tattooed hand on the table. "Why this foolishness, Kurt? You well know how and why we are picked for runs. Hardy had the deck stacked against him through no fault of the project. That has happened before; it will happen again—"

"Which is what I have been saying! Do you wish it to happen to you? Pretty games those tribesmen on your run play with their prisoners, do they not?"

"Oh, shut up!" Jansen got to his feet. Since he loomed at least five inches above Kurt and probably could have broken him in two over one massive knee, his order was one to be considered. "If you have any complaints, go make them to Millaird. And, little man"—he poked a massive forefinger into Kurt's chest—"wait until you make that first run of yours before you sound off so loudly. No one is sent out without every ounce of preparation he can take. But we can't set up luck in advance, and Hardy was unlucky. That's that. We got him back, and that was lucky for him. He'd be the first to tell you so." He stretched. "I'm for a game—Ashe? Hodaki?"

"Always so energetic," murmured Ashe, but he nodded as did the small Oriental.

Feng smiled at Ross. "Always these three try to beat each other, and so far all the contests are draws. But we hope ... yes, we have hopes...."

So Ross had no chance to speak to Kurt. Instead, he was drawn into the knot of men who, having finished their meal, entered a small arena with a half circle of spectator seats at one side and a space for contestants at the other. What followed absorbed Ross as completely as the earlier scene of the wolf killing. This too was a fight, but not a physical struggle. All three contenders were not only unlike in body, but as Ross speedily came to understand, they were also unlike in their mental approach to any problem.

They seated themselves crosslegged at the three points of a triangle. Then Ashe looked from the tall blond to the small Oriental. "Territory?" he asked crisply.

"Inland plains!" That came almost in chorus, and each man, looking at his opponent, began to laugh.

Ashe himself chuckled. "Trying to be smart tonight, boys?" he inquired. "All right, plains it is."

He brought his hand down on the floor before him, and to Ross's astonishment the area around the players darkened and the floor became a stretch of miniature countryside. Grassy plains rippled under the wind of a fair day.

"Red!"

"Blue!"

"Yellow!"

The choices came quickly from the dusk masking the players. And upon those orders points of the designated color came into being as small lights.

"Red—caravan!" Ross recognized Jansen's boom.

"Blue—raiders!" Hodaki's choice was only an instant behind.

"Yellow—unknown factor."

Ross was sure that sigh came from Jansen. "Is the unknown factor a natural phenomenon?"

"No—tribe on the march."

"Ah!" Hodaki was considering that. Ross could picture his shrug.

The game began. Ross had heard of chess, of war games played with miniature armies or ships, of games on paper which demand from the players a quick wit and a trained memory. This game, however, was all those combined, and more. As his imagination came to life the moving points of light were transformed into the raiders, the merchants' caravan, the tribe on the march. There was ingenious deployment, a battle, a retreat, a small victory here, to be followed by a bigger defeat there. The game might have gone on for hours. The men about him muttered, taking sides and arguing heatedly in voices low enough not to drown out the moves called by the players. Ross was thrilled when the red traders avoided a very cleverly laid ambush, and indignant when the tribe was forced to withdraw or the caravan lost points. It was the most fascinating game he had ever seen, and he realized that the three men ordering those moves were all masters of strategy. Their respective skills checkmated each other so equally that an outright win was far away.

Then Jansen laughed, and the red line of the caravan gathered in a tight knot. "Camped at a spring," he announced, "but with plenty of sentries out." Red sparks showed briefly beyond that center core. "And they'll have to stay there for all of me. We could keep this up till doomsday, and nobody would crack."

"No"—Hodaki contradicted him—"someday one of you will make a little mistake and then—"

"And then whatever bully boys you're running will clobber us?" asked Jansen. "That'll be the day! Anyway, truce for now."

"Granted!"

The lights of the arena went on and the plains vanished into a dark, tiled floor. "Any time you want a return engagement it'll be fine with me," said Ashe, getting up.

Jansen grinned. "Put that off for a month or so, Gordon. We push into time tomorrow. Take care of yourselves, you two. I don't want to have to break in another set of players when I come back."

Ross, finding it difficult to shake off the illusion which had held him entranced, felt a slight touch on his shoulder and glanced up. Kurt stood behind him, apparently intent upon Jansen and Hodaki as they argued over some point of the game.

"See you tonight." The boy's lips hardly moved, a trick Ross knew from his own past. Yes, he *would* see Kurt tonight, or whenever he could. He was going to learn what it was this odd company seemed determined to keep as their own private secret.

CHAPTER 3

Ross stood cautiously against the wall of his darkened room, his head turned toward the slightly open door. A slight shuffling sound had awakened him, and he was now as ready as a cat before her spring. But he did not hurl himself at the figure now easing the door farther open. He waited until the visitor was approaching the bunk before he slid along the wall, closing the door and putting his shoulders against it.

"What's the pitch?" Ross demanded in a whisper.

There was a ragged breath, maybe two, then a little laugh out of the dark. "You are ready?" The visitor's accent left no doubt as to his identity. Kurt was paying him the promised visit.

"Did you think that I wouldn't be?"

"No." The dim figure sat without invitation on the edge of the bunk. "I would not be here otherwise, Murdock. You are plenty ... have plenty on the ball. You see, I have heard things about you. Like me, you were tricked into this game. Tell me, is it not true that you saw Hardy tonight."

"You hear a lot, don't you?" Ross was noncommittal.

"I hear, I see, I learn more than these big mouths, like the major with all his do's and don'ts. That I can tell you! You saw Hardy. Do *you* want to be a Hardy?"

"Is there any danger of that?"

"Danger!" Kurt snorted. "Danger—you have not yet known the meaning of danger, little man. Not until now. I ask you again, do you want to end like Hardy? They have not yet looped you in with all their big talk. That is why I came here tonight. If you know what is good for you, Murdock, you will make a break before they tape you—"

"Tape me?"

Kurt's laugh was full of anger, not amusement. "Oh, yes. They have many tricks here. They are big brains, eggheads, all of them with their favorite gadgets. They put you through a machine to get you registered on a tape. Then, my boy, you cannot get outside the base without ringing all the alarms! Neat, eh? So if you want to make a break, you must try it before they tape you."

Ross did not trust Kurt, but he was listening to him attentively. The other's argument sounded convincing to one whose general ignorance of science led him to be as fearful of the whole field as his ancestors had been of black magic. As all his generation, he was conditioned to believe that all kinds of weird inventions were entirely possible and probable—usually to be produced in some dim future, but perhaps today.

"They must have you taped," Ross pointed out.

Kurt laughed again, but this time he was amused. "They believe that they have. Only they are not as smart as they believe, the major and the rest, including Millaird! No, I have a fighting chance to get out of this place, only I cannot do it alone. That is why I have been waiting for them to bring in a new guy I could get to before they had him pinned down for good. You are tough, Murdock. I saw your record, and I'm betting that you did not come here with the intention of staying. So—here is your chance to go along with one who knows the ropes. You will not have such a good one again."

The longer Kurt talked, the more convincing he was. Ross lost a few of his suspicions. It was true that he had come prepared to run at the first possible opportunity, and if Kurt had everything planned, so much the better. Of course, it was possible that Kurt was a stool pigeon, leading him on as a test. But that was a chance Ross would have to take.

"Look here, Murdock, maybe you think it's easy to break out of here. Do you know where we are, boy? We're near enough to the North Pole as makes no difference! Are you going to leg it back some hundreds of miles through thick ice and snow? A nice jaunt if you make it. I do not think that you can—not without plans and a partner who knows what he is about."

"And how *do* we go? Steal one of those atomjets? I'm no pilot—are you?"

"They have other things besides a-j's here. This place is strictly hush-hush. Even the a-j's do not set down too often for fear they will be tracked by radar. Where have you been, boy? Don't you know the Reds are circling around up here? These fellows watch for Red activity, and the Reds watch them. They play it under the table on both sides. We get our supplies overland by cats—"

"Cats?"

"Snow sleds, like tractors," the other answered impatiently. "Our stuff is dumped miles to the south, and the cats go down once a month to bring it back. There's no trick to driving a cat, and they tear off the miles—"

"How many miles to the south?" inquired Ross skeptically. Granted Kurt was speaking the truth, travel over an arctic wilderness in a stolen machine was risky, to say the least. Ross had only a very vague idea of the polar regions, but he was sure that they could easily swallow up the unwary forever.

"Maybe only a hundred or so, boy. But I have more than one plan, and I'm willing to risk *my* neck. Do you think I intend to start out blind?"

There was that, of course. Ross had early sized up his visitor as one who was first of all interested in his own welfare. He wouldn't risk his neck without a definite plan in mind.

"Well, what do you say, Murdock? Are you with me or not?"

"I'll take some time to chew it over—"

"Time is what you do not have, boy. Tomorrow they will tape you. Then—no over the wall for you."

"Suppose you tell me your trick for fooling the tape," Ross countered.

"That I cannot do, seeing as how it lies in the way my brain is put together. Do you think I can break open my skull and hand you a piece of what is inside? No, you jump with me tonight or else I must wait to grab the next one who lands here."

Kurt stood up. His last words were spoken matter-of-factly, and Ross believed he meant exactly what he said. But Ross hesitated. He wanted to try for freedom, a desire fed by his suspicions of what was going on here. He neither liked nor trusted Kurt, but he thought he understood him—better than he understood Ashe or the others. Also, with Kurt he was sure he could hold his own; it would be the kind of struggle he had experienced before.

"Tonight...." he repeated slowly.

"Yes, tonight!" There was new eagerness in Kurt's voice, for he sensed that the other was wavering. "I have been preparing for a long time, but there must be two of us. We have to take turns driving the cat. There can be no rest until we are far to the south. I tell you it will be easy. There are food caches arranged along the route for emergencies. I have a map marked to show where they are. Are you coming?"

When Ross did not answer at once the other moved closer to him.

"Remember Hardy? He was not the first, and he will not be the last. They use us up fast here. That is why they brought you so quickly. I tell you, it is better to take your chance with me than on a run."

"And what is a run?"

"So they have not yet briefed you? Well, a run is a little jaunt back into history—not nice comfortable history such as you learned out of a book

when you were a little kid. No, you are dropped back into some savage
time before history—"

"That's impossible!"

"Yes? You saw those two big blond boys tonight, did you not? Why do
you suppose they sport those braids? Because they are taking a little trip
into the time when he-men wore braids, and carried axes big enough to
crack a man open! And Hodaki and his partner.... Ever hear of the Tartars?
Maybe you have not, but once they nearly overran most of Europe."

Ross swallowed. He now knew where he had seen braids pictured on
warriors—the Vikings! And Tartars, yes, that movie about someone named
Khan, Genghis Khan! But to return into the past was impossible.

Yet, he remembered the picture he had watched today with the wolf
slayer and the shaggy-haired man who wore skins. Neither of these was of
his own world! Could Kurt be telling the truth? Ross's vivid memory of the
scene he had witnessed made Kurt's story more convincing.

"Suppose you get sent back to a time where they do not like strangers,"
Kurt continued. "Then you are in for it. That is what happened to Hardy.
And it is not good—not good at all!"

"But why?"

Kurt snorted. "*That* they do not tell you until just before you take your
first run. I do not want to know why. But I do know that I am not going
to be sent into any wilderness where a savage may run a spear through me
just to prove something or other for Major John Kelgarries, or for Millaird
either. I will try my plan first."

The urgency in Kurt's protest carried Ross past the wavering point. He,
too, would try the cat. He was only familiar with this time and world; he
had no desire to be sent into another one.

Once Ross had made his decision, Kurt hurried him into action. Kurt's
knowledge of the secret procedures at the base proved excellent. Twice
they were halted by locked doors, but only momentarily, for Kurt had a
tiny gadget, concealed in the palm of his hand, which had only to be held
over a latch to open a recalcitrant door.

There was enough light in the corridors to give them easy passage, but
the rooms were dark, and twice Kurt had to lead Ross by the hand,
avoiding furniture or installations with the surety of one who had practiced
that same route often. Murdock's opinion of his companion's ability

underwent several upward revisions during that tour, and he began to believe that he was really in luck to have found such a partner.

In the last room, Ross willingly followed Kurt's orders to put on the fur clothing Kurt passed to him. The fit was not exact, but he surmised that Kurt had chosen as well as possible. A final door opened, and they stepped out into the polar night of winter. Kurt's mittened hand grasped Ross's, pulling him along. Together, they pushed back the door of a hangar shed to get at their escape vehicle.

The cat was a strange machine, but Ross was given no time to study it. He was shoved into the cockpit, a bubble covering settled down over them, closing them in, and the engine came to life under Kurt's urging. The cat must be traveling at its best pace, Ross thought. Yet the crawl which took them away from the mounded snow covering the base seemed hardly better than a man could make afoot.

For a short time Kurt headed straight away from the starting point, but Ross soon heard him counting slowly to himself as if he were timing something. At the count of twenty the cat swung to the right and made a wide half circle which was copied at the next count of twenty by a similar sweep in the opposite direction. After this pattern had been repeated for six turns, Ross found it difficult to guess whether they had ever returned to their first course. When Kurt stopped counting he asked, "Why the dance pattern?"

"Would you rather be scattered in little pieces all over the landscape?" the other snapped. "The base doesn't need fences two miles high to keep us in, or others out; they take other precautions. You should thank fortune we got through that first mine field without blowing...."

Ross swallowed, but he refused to let Kurt know that he was rattled. "So it isn't as easy to get away as you said?"

"Shut up!" Kurt began counting again, and Ross had some cold apprehensive moments in which to reflect upon the folly of quick decisions and wonder bleakly why he had not thought things through before he leaped.

Again they sketched a weaving pattern in the snow, but this time the arcs formed acute angles. Ross glanced now and then at the intent man at the wheel. How had Kurt managed to memorize this route? His urge to escape the base must certainly be a strong one.

Back and forth they crawled, gaining only a few yards in each of those angled strikes to right or left.

"Good thing these cats are atomic powered," Kurt commented during one of the intervals between mine fields. "We'd run out of fuel otherwise."

Ross fought down the impulse to move his feet away from any possible contact point with the engine. These machines must be safe to ride in, but the bogy of radiation was frightening. Luckily, Kurt was now back to a straight track, with no more weaving.

"We are out!" Kurt said with exultation. But he added no more than just the reassurance of their escape.

The cat crawled on. To Ross's eyes there was no trail to follow, no guideposts, yet Kurt steered ahead with confidence. A little later he pulled to a stop and said to Ross, "We have to drive turn and turn about—your turn."

Ross was dubious. "Well, I can drive a car—but this—"

"Is fool proof." Kurt caught him up. "The worst was getting through the mine fields, and we are out of that now. See here—" his hand made a shadow on the lighted instrument panel, "this will keep you straight. If you can steer a car, you can steer this. Watch!" He started up again and once more swung the cat to the left.

A light on the panel began to blink at a rate which increased rapidly as they veered farther away from their original course.

"See? You keep that light steady, and you are on course. If it begins to blink, you cast about until it steadies again. Simple enough for a baby. Take over and see."

It was hard to change places in the sealed cabin of the cat, but they were successful, and Ross took the wheel gingerly. Following Kurt's directions, he started ahead, his eyes focused on the light rather than the white expanse before him. And after a few minutes of strain he caught the hang of it. As Kurt had promised, it was very simple. After watching him for a while, his instructor gave a grunt of satisfaction and settled down for a nap.

Once the first excitement of driving the cat wore off, the operation tended to become monotonous. Ross caught himself yawning, but he kept at his post with dogged stubbornness. This had been Kurt's game all the way through—so far—and he was certainly not going to resign his first chance to show that he could be of use also. If there had only been some break in the eternal snow, some passing light or goal to be seen ahead, it would not have been so bad. Finally, every now and then, Ross had to jiggle off course just enough so that the warning blink of light would alert him and keep him from falling asleep. He was unaware that Kurt had awakened during one of those maneuvers until the other spoke. "Your own private alarm clock, Murdock? Okay, I do not quarrel with anyone who uses his head. But you had better get some shut-eye, or we will not keep rolling."

Ross was too tired to protest. They changed places, and he curled up as best he could on his small share of seat. Only now that he was free to sleep, he realized he no longer wanted to. Kurt must have thought Ross had fallen asleep, for after perhaps two miles of steady grinding along, he moved cautiously behind the wheel. Ross saw by the trace of light from the instrument panel that his companion was digging into the breast of his parka to bring out a small object which he held against the wheel of the cat with one hand, while with the other he tapped out an irregular rhythm.

To Ross the action made no sense. But he did not miss the other's sigh of relief as he restored his treasure to hiding once more, as if some difficult task was now behind him. Shortly afterward the cat ground to a stop, and Ross sat up, rubbing his eyes. "What's the matter? Engine trouble?"

Kurt had folded his arms across the wheel. "No. It is just that we are to wait here—"

"Wait? For what? Kelgarries to come along and pick us up?"

Kurt laughed. "The major? How I wish that he *would* arrive presently. What a surprise he would receive! Not two little mice to be put back into their cages, but the tiger cat, all claws and fangs!"

Ross sat up straighter. This now had the bad smell of a frame, a frame with himself planted right in the middle. He figured out the possibilities and came up with an answer which would smear Ross Murdock all over any map. If Kurt were waiting to meet friends out here, they could only be of one brand.

For most of his short life Ross had been engaged in a private war against the restrictions imposed upon him by a set of legal rules to which something within him would not conform. And he had, during those same years filled with attacks, retreats, and strategic maneuvering, formulated a code of rules by which to play his dangerous game. He had not murdered, and he would never follow the path Kurt took. To one who was supremely impatient of restraint, the methods and aims of Kurt's employers were not only impossibly fantastic and illogical—they were to be opposed to the last ounce of any man's energy.

"Your friends late?" He tried to sound casual.

"Not yet, and if you now plan to play the hero, Murdock, think better of it!" Kurt's tone held the crack of an order—that note Ross had so much disliked in the major's voice. "This is an operation which has been most carefully planned and upon which a great deal depends. No one shall spoil it for us now—"

"The Reds planted you on the project, eh?" Ross wanted to keep the other talking to give himself a chance to think. And this was one time he had to think, clearly and with speed.

"There is no need for me to tell you the sad tale of my life, Murdock. And you would doubtless find much of it boring. If you wish to continue to live—for a while, at least—you will remain quiet and do as you are told."

Kurt must be armed, for he would not be so confident unless he had a weapon he could now turn on Ross. On the other hand, if what Ross guessed were true, this *was* the time to play the hero—when there was only Kurt to handle. Better to be a dead hero than a live captive in the hands of Kurt's dear friends across the pole.

Without warning, Ross threw his body to the left, striving to pin Kurt against the driver's side of the cabin, his hands clawing at the fur ruff bordering the other's hood, trying for a throat hold. Perhaps it was Kurt's over-confidence which betrayed him and left him open to a surprise attack. He struggled hard to bring up his arm, but both his weight and Ross's held him tight. Ross caught at his wrist, noticing a gleam of metal.

They threshed about, the bulkiness of the fur clothing hampering them. Ross wondered fleetingly why the other had not made sure of him earlier. As it was he fought with all his vigor to keep Kurt immobile, to try and knock him out with a lucky blow.

In the end Kurt aided in his own defeat. When Ross relaxed somewhat, the other pushed against him, only to have Ross flinch to one side. Kurt could not stop himself, and his head cracked against the wheel of the cat. He went limp.

Ross made the most of the next few moments. He brought his belt from under his parka, twisting it around Kurt's wrists with no gentleness. Then he wriggled about, changing places with the unconscious man.

He had no idea of where to go, but he was sure he was going to get away—at the cat's top speed—from that point. And with that in mind and only a limited knowledge of how to manage the machine, Ross started up and turned in a wide circle until he was sure the cat was headed in the opposite direction.

The light which had guided them was still on. Would reversing its process take him back to the base? Lost in the immensity of the cold wilderness, he made the only choice possible and gunned the cat again.

CHAPTER 4

Once again Ross sat waiting for others to decide his future. He was as outwardly composed as he had been in Judge Rawle's chambers, but inwardly he was far more apprehensive. Out in the wilderness of the polar night he had had no chance for escape. Heading away from Kurt's rendezvous, Ross had run straight into the search party from the base, had seen in action that mechanical hound that Kurt had said they would put on the fugitives' trail—the thing which would have gone on hunting them until its metal rusted into powder. Kurt's boasted immunity to that tracker had not been as good as he had believed, though it had won them a start.

Ross did not know just how much it might count in his favor that he had been on his way back, with Kurt a prisoner in the cat. As his waiting hours wore on he began to think it might mean very little indeed. This time there was no show on the wall of his cell, nothing but time to think—too much of that—and no pleasant things to think about.

But he had learned one valuable lesson on that cold expedition. Kelgarries and the others at the base were the most formidable opponents he had ever met, and all the balance of luck and equipment lay on their side of the scales. Ross was now convinced that there could be no escape from this base. He had been impressed by Kurt's preparations, knowing that some of them were far beyond anything he himself could have devised. He did not doubt that Kurt had come here fully prepared with every ingenious device the Reds could supply.

At least Kurt's friends had had a rude welcome when they did arrive at the meeting place. Kelgarries had heard Ross out and then had sent ahead a team. Before Ross's party had reached the base there had been a blast which split the arctic night wide open. And Kurt, conscious by then, had shown his only sign of emotion when he realized what it meant.

The door to Ross's cell room clicked, and he swung his feet to the floor, sitting up on his bunk to face his future. This time he made no attempt to put on an act. He was not in the least sorry he had tried to get away. Had Kurt been on the level, it would have been a bright play. That Kurt was not, was just plain bad luck.

Kelgarries and Ashe entered, and at the sight of Ashe the taut feeling in Ross's middle loosened a bit. The major might come by himself to pass sentence, but he would not bring Ashe along if the sentence was a really harsh one.

"You got off to a bad start here, Murdock." The major sat down on the edge of the wall shelf which doubled as a table. "You're going to have a second chance, so consider yourself lucky. We know you aren't another plant of our enemies, a fact that saves your neck. Do you have anything to add to your story?"

"No, sir." He was not adding that "sir" to curry any favor; it came naturally when one answered Kelgarries.

"But you have some questions?"

Ross met that with the truth. "A lot of them."

"Why don't you ask them?"

Ross smiled thinly, an expression far removed and years older than his bashful boy's grin of the shy act. "A wise guy doesn't spill his ignorance. He uses his eyes and ears and keeps his trap shut—"

"And goes off half cocked as a result..." the major added. "I don't think you would have enjoyed the company of Kurt's paymaster."

"I didn't know about him then—not when I left here."

"Yes, and when you discovered the truth, you took steps. Why?" For the first time there was a trace of feeling in the major's voice.

"Because I don't like the line-up on his side of the fence."'

"That single fact has saved your neck this time, Murdock. Step out of line once more, and nothing will help you. But just so we won't have to worry about that, suppose you ask a few of those questions."

"How much of what Kurt fed me is the truth?" Ross blurted out. "I mean all that stuff about shooting back in time."

"All of it." The major said it so quietly that it carried complete conviction.

"But why—how—?"

"You have us on a spot, Murdock. Because of your little expedition, we have to tell you more now than we tell any of our men before the final briefing. Listen, and then forget all of it except what applies to the job at hand.

"The Reds shot up Sputnik and then Muttnik.... When—? Twenty-five years ago. We got up our answers a little later. There were a couple of spectacular crashes on the moon, then that space station that didn't stay in orbit, after that—stalemate. In the past quarter century we've had no voyages into space, nothing that was prophesied. Too many bugs, too many costly failures. Finally we began to get hints of something big, bigger than any football roaming the heavens.

"Any discovery in science comes about by steps. It can be traced back through those steps by another scientist. But suppose you were confronted by a result which apparently had been produced without any preliminaries. What would be your guess concerning it?"

Ross stared at the major. Although he didn't see what all this had to do with time-jumping, he sensed that Kelgarries was waiting for a serious answer, that somehow Ross would be judged by his reply.

"Either that the steps were kept strictly secret," he said slowly, "or that the result didn't rightfully belong to the man who said he discovered it."

For the first time the major regarded him with approval. "Suppose this discovery was vital to your life—what would you do?"

"Try to find the source!"

"There you have it! Within the past five years our friends across the way have come up with three such discoveries. One we were able to trace, duplicate, and use, with a few refinements of our own. The other two remain rootless; yet they are linked with the first. We are now attempting to solve that problem, and the time grows late. For some reason, though the Reds now have their super, super gadgets, they are not yet ready to use them. Sometimes the things work, and sometimes they fail. Everything points to the fact that the Reds are now experimenting with discoveries which are not basically their own—"

"Where did they get them? From another world?" Ross's imagination came to life. Had a successful space voyage been kept secret? Had there been contact made with another intelligent race?

"In a way it's another world, but the world of time—not space. Seven years ago we got a man out of East Berlin. He was almost dead, but he lived long enough to record on tape some amazing data, so wild it was almost dismissed as the ravings of delirium. But that was after Sputnik, and we didn't dare disregard any hints from the other side of the Iron Curtain. So the recording was turned over to our scientists, who proved it had a core of truth.

"Time travel has been written up in fiction; it has been discussed otherwise as an impossibility. Then we discover that the Reds have it working—"

"You mean, they go into the future and bring back machines to use now."

The major shook his head. "Not the future, the past."

Was this an elaborate joke? Somewhat heatedly Ross snapped out the answer to that. "Look here, I know I haven't the education of your big brains, but I do know that the farther back you go into history the simpler things are. We ride in cars; only a hundred years ago men drove horses. We have guns; go back a little and you'll find them waving swords and shooting guys with bows and arrows—those that don't wear tin plate on them to stop being punctured—"

"Only they were, after all," commented Ashe. "Look at Agincourt, m'lad, and remember what arrows did to the French knights in armor."

Ross disregarded the interruption. "Anyway"—he stuck doggedly to his point—"the farther back you go, the simpler things are. How are the Reds going to find anything in history we can't beat today?"

"That is a point which has baffled us for several years now," the major returned. "Only it is not *how* they are going to find it, but *where*. Because somewhere in the past of this world they have contacted a civilization able to produce weapons and ideas so advanced as to baffle our experts. We have to find that source and either mine it ourselves or close it off. As yet we're still trying to find it."

Ross shook his head. "It must be a long way back. Those guys who discover tombs and dig up old cities—couldn't they give you some hints? Wouldn't a civilization like that have left something we could find today?"

"It depends," Ashe remarked, "upon the type of civilization. The Egyptians built in stone, grandly. They used tools and weapons of copper, bronze, and stone, and they were considerate enough to operate in a dry climate which preserved relics well. The cities of the Fertile Crescent built in mud brick and used stone, copper, and bronze tools. They also chose a portion of the world where climate was a factor in keeping their memory green.

"The Greeks built in stone, wrote their books, kept their history to bequeath it to their successors, and so did the Romans. And on this side of the ocean the Incas, the Mayas, the unknown races before them, and the Aztecs of Mexico all built in stone and worked in metal. And stone and metal survive. But what if there had been an early people who used plastics and brittle alloys, who had no desire to build permanent buildings, whose tools and artifacts were meant to wear out quickly, perhaps for economic reasons? What would they leave us—considering, perhaps, that an ice age had intervened between their time and ours, with glaciers to grind into dust what little they did possess?

"There is evidence that the poles of our world have changed and that this northern region was once close to being tropical. Any catastrophe violent enough to bring about a switch in the poles of this planet might well have wiped out all traces of a civilization, no matter how superior. We have good reason to believe that such a people must have existed, but we must find them.

"And Ashe is a convert from the skeptics—" the major slipped down from his perch on the wall shelf—"he is an archaeologist, one of your tomb discoverers, and knows what he is talking about. We must do our hunting in time earlier than the first pyramid, earlier than the first group of farmers who settled by the Tigris River. But we have to let the enemy guide us to it. That's where you come in."

"Why me?"

"That is a question to which our psychologists are still trying to find the answer, my young friend. It seems that the majority of the people of the several nations linked together in this project have become too civilized. The reactions of most men to given sets of circumstances have become set in regular patterns and they cannot break that conditioning, or if personal danger forces them to change those patterns, they are afterward so adrift they cannot function at their highest potential. Teach a man to kill, as in war, and then you have to recondition him later.

"But during these same wars we also develop another type. He is the born commando, the secret agent, the expendable man who lives on action. There are not many of this kind, and they are potent weapons. In peacetime that particular collection of emotions, nerve, and skills becomes a menace to the very society he has fought to preserve during a war. He is pressured by the peaceful environment into becoming a criminal or a misfit.

"The men we send out from here to explore the past are not only given the best training we can possibly supply for them, but they are all of the type once heralded as the frontiersman. History is sentimental about that type—when he is safely dead—but the present finds him difficult to live with. Our time agents are misfits in the modern world because their inherited abilities are born out of season now. They must be young enough and possess a certain brand of intelligence to take the stiff training and to adapt, and they must pass our tests. Do you understand?"

Ross nodded. "You want crooks because they are crooks—"

"No, not because they are crooks, but because they are misfits in their time and place. Don't, I beg of you, Murdock, think that we are operating a penal institution here. You would never have been recruited if you hadn't tested out to suit us. But the man who may be labeled murderer in his own period might rank as a hero in another, an extreme example, but true. When we train a man he not only can survive in the period to which he is sent, but he can also pass as a native born in that era—"

"What about Hardy?"

The major gazed into space. "There is no operation which is foolproof. We have never said that we don't run into trouble or that there is no danger in this. We have to deal with both natives of different times, and if we are lucky and hit a hot run, with the Reds. They suspect that we are casting about, hunting their trail. They managed to plant Kurt Vogel on us. He had an almost perfect cover and conditioning. Now you have it straight, Murdock. You satisfy our tests, and you'll be given a chance to say yes or no before your first run. If you say no and refuse duty, it means you must become an exile and stay here. No man who has gone through our training can return to normal life; there is too much chance of his being picked up and sweated by the opposition."

"Never?"

The major shrugged. "This may be a long-term operation. We hope not, but there is no way of telling now. You will be in exile until we either find what we want or fail entirely. That is the last card I have to lay on the table." He stretched. "You're slated for training tomorrow. Think it over and then let us know your answer when the time comes. Meanwhile, you are to be teamed with Ashe, who will see to putting you through the course."

It was a big hunk to swallow, but once down, Ross found it digestible. The training opened up a whole new world to him. Judo and wrestling were easy enough to absorb, and he thoroughly enjoyed the workouts. But the patient hours of archery practice, the strict instruction in the use of a long-bladed bronze dagger were more demanding. The mastering of one new language and then another, the intensive drill in unfamiliar social customs, the memorizing of strict taboos and ethics were difficult. Ross learned to keep records in knots on hide thongs and was inducted into the art of primitive bargaining and trade. He came to understand the worth of a cross-shaped tin ingot compared to a string of amber beads and some well-cured white furs. He now understood why he had been shown a traders' caravan during that first encounter with the purpose behind Operation Retrograde.

During the training days his feeling toward Ashe changed materially. A man could not work so closely with another and continue to resent his attitude; either he blew up entirely, or he learned to adjust. His awe at Ashe's vast amount of practical knowledge, freely offered to serve his own blundering ignorance, created a respect for the man which might have become friendship, had Ashe ever relaxed his own shield of impersonal efficiency. Ross did not try to breach the barrier between them mainly because he was sure that the reason for it was the fact that he was a "volunteer." It gave him an odd new feeling he avoided trying to analyze. He had always had a kind of pride in his record; now he had begun to wish sometimes that it was a record of a different type.

Men came and went. Hodaki and his partner disappeared, as did Jansen and his. One lost track of time within that underground warren which was the base. Ross gradually discovered that the whole establishment covered a large area under an external crust of ice and snow. There were laboratories, a well-appointed hospital, armories which stocked weapons usually seen only in museums, but which here were free of any signs of age, and ready for use. There were libraries with mile upon mile of tape recordings as well as films. Ross could not understand everything he heard and saw, but he soaked up all he could so that once or twice, when drifting off to sleep at night, he thought of himself as a sponge which had nearly reached its total limit of absorption.

He learned to wear naturally the clumsy kilt-tunic he had seen on the wolf slayer, to shave with practiced assurance, using a leaf-shaped bronze razor, to eat strange food until he relished the taste. Making lesson time serve a double duty, he lay under sunlamps while listening to tape recordings, until his skin darkened to a weathered hue resembling Ashe's. There was always talk to listen to, important talk which he was afraid to miss.

"Bronze." Ashe weighed a dagger in his hand one day. Its hilt, made of dark horn studded with an intricate pattern of tiny golden nail heads, had a gleam not unlike that of the blade. "Do you know, Murdock, that bronze can be tougher than steel? If it wasn't that iron is so much more plentiful and easier to work, we might never have come out of the Bronze Age? Iron is cheaper and easier found, and when the first smith learned to work it, an end came to one way of life, a beginning to another.

"Yes, bronze is important to us here, and so are the men who worked it. Smiths were sacred in the old days. We know that they made a secret of their trade which overrode the bounds of district, tribe, and race. A smith was welcome in any village, his person safe on the road. In fact, the roads themselves were under the protection of the gods; there was peace on them for all wayfarers. The land was wide then, and it was empty. The tribes were few and small, and there was plenty of room for the hunter, the farmer, the trader. Life was not such a scramble of man against man, but rather of man against nature—"

"No wars?" asked Ross. "Then why the bow-and-dagger drill?"

"Wars were small affairs, disputes between family clans or tribes. As for the bow, there were formidable things in the forests—giant animals, wolves, wild boars—"

"Cave bears?"

Ashe sighed with weary patience. "Get it through your head, Murdock, that history is much longer than you seem to think. Cave bears and the use of bronze weapons do not overlap. No, you will have to go back maybe several thousand years earlier and then hunt your bear with a flint-tipped spear in your hand if you are fool enough to try it."

"Or take a rifle with you." Ross made a suggestion he had longed to voice for some time.

Ashe rounded on him swiftly, and Ross knew him well enough now to realize that he was seriously displeased.

"That is just what you don't do, Murdock, not from this base, as you well know by now. You take no weapon from here which is not designed for the period in which your run lies. Just as you do not become embroiled while on that run in any action which might influence the course of history."

Ross went on polishing the blade he held. "What would happen if someone did break that rule?"

Ashe put down the dagger he had been playing with. "We don't know—we just don't know. So far we have operated in the fringe territory, keeping away from any district with a history which we can trace accurately. Maybe some day—" his eyes were on a wall of weapon racks he plainly did not see—"maybe some day we can stand and watch the rise of the pyramids, witness the march of Alexander's armies.... But not yet. We stay away from history, and we are sure that the Reds are doing the same. It has become the old problem once presented by the atom bomb. Nobody wants to upset the balance and take the consequences. Let us find their outpost and we'll withdraw our men from all the other runs at once."

"What makes everyone so sure that they have an outpost somewhere? Couldn't they be working right at the main source, sir?"

"They could, but for some reason they are not. As for how we know that much, it's information received." Ashe smiled thinly. "No, the source is much farther back in time than their halfway post. But if we find that, then we can trail them. So we plant men in suitable eras and hope for the best. That's a good weapon you have there, Murdock. Are you willing to wear it in earnest?"

The inflection in that question caught Ross's full attention. His gray eyes met those blue ones. This was it—at long last.

"Right away?"

Ashe picked up a belt of bronze plates strung together with chains, a twin to that Ross had seen worn by the wolf slayer. He held it out to the younger man. "You can take your trial run any time—tomorrow."

Ross drew a deeper breath. "Where—to when?"

"An island which will later be Britain. When? About two thousand B.C. Beaker traders were beginning to open their stations there. This is your graduation exercise, Murdock."

Ross fitted the blade he had been polishing into the wooden sheath on the belt. "If you say I can do it, I'm willing to try."

He caught that glance Ashe shot at him, but he could not read its meaning. Annoyance? Impatience? He was still puzzling over it when the other turned abruptly and left him alone.

CHAPTER 5

He might have said yes, but that didn't mean, Ross discovered, that he was to be shipped off at once to early Britain. Ashe's "tomorrow" proved to be several days later. The cover was that of a Beaker trader, and Ross's impersonation was checked again and again by experts, making sure that the last detail was correct and that no suspicion of a tribesman, no mistake on Ross's part would betray him.

The Beaker people were an excellent choice for infiltration. They were not a closely knit clan, suspicious of strangers and alert to any deviation from the norm, as more race-conscious tribes might be. For they lived by trade, leaving to Ross's own time the mark of their far-flung "empire" in the beakers found in graves scattered in clusters of a handful or so from the Rhineland to Spain, and from the Balkans to Britain.

They did not depend only upon the taboo of the trade road for their safety, for the Beakermen were master bowmen. A roving people, they pushed into new territory to establish posts, living amicably among peoples with far different customs—the Downs farmers, horse herders, shore-side fisherfolk.

With Ashe, Ross passed a last inspection. Their hair had not grown long enough to require braiding, but they did have enough to hold it back from their faces with hide headbands. The kilt-tunics of coarse material, duplicating samples brought from the past, were harsh to the skin and poorly fitting. But the workmanship of their link-and-plate bronze belts, the sleek bow guards strapped to their wrists, and the bows themselves approached fine art. Ashe's round cloak was the blue of a master trader, and he wore wealth in a necklace of polished wolf's teeth alternating with amber beads. Ross's more modest position in the tribe was indicated not only by his red-brown cloak, but by the fact that his personal jewelry consisted only of a copper bracelet and a cloak pin with a jet head.

He had no idea how the time transition was to be made, nor how one might step from the polar regions of the Western Hemisphere to the island of Britain lying off the Eastern. And it was a complicated business as he discovered.

The transition itself was a fairly simple, though disturbing, process. One walked a short corridor and stood for an instant on a plate while the light centered there curled about in a solid core, shutting one off from floor and wall. Ross gasped for breath as the air was sucked out of his lungs. He experienced a moment of deathly sickness with the sensation of being lost in nothingness. Then he breathed again and looked through the dying wall of light to where Ashe waited.

Quick and easy as the trip through time had been, the journey to Britain was something else. There could be only one transfer point if the secret was to be preserved. But men from that point must be moved swiftly and secretly to their appointed stations. Ross, knowing the strict rules concerning the transportation of objects from one time to another, wondered how that travel could be effected. After all, they could not spend months, or even years, getting across continents and seas.

The answer was ingenious. Three days after they had stepped through the barrier of time at the outpost, Ross and Ashe balanced on the rounded back of a whale. It was a whale which would deceive anyone who did not test its hide with a harpoon, and whalers with harpoons large enough to trouble such a monster were yet well in the future.

Ashe slid a dugout into the water, and Ross climbed into that unsteady craft, holding it against the side of the disguised sub until his partner joined him. The day, misty and drizzling, made the shore they aimed for a half-seen line across the water. With a shiver born of more than cold, Ross dipped his paddle and helped Ashe send their crude boat toward that half-hidden strip of land.

There was no real dawn; the sky lightened somewhat, but the drizzle continued. Green patches showed among the winter-denuded trees back from the beach, but the countryside facing them gave an impression of untamed wilderness. Ross knew from his briefing that the whole of Britain was as yet only sparsely settled. The first wave of hunter-fishers to establish villages had been joined by other invaders who built massive tombs and had an elaborate religion. Small village-forts had been linked from hill to hill by trackways. There were "factories," which turned out in bulk such fine flint weapons and tools that a thriving industry was in full operation, not yet having been superseded by the metal imported by the Beaker merchants. Bronze was still so rare and costly that only the head man of a village could hope to own one of the long daggers. Even the arrowheads in Ross's quiver were chipped of flint.

They drew the dugout well up onto the shore and ran it into a shallow depression in the bank, heaping stones and brush about for its concealment. Then Ashe intently surveyed the surrounding country, seeking a landmark.

"Inland from here...." Ashe used the language of the Beakermen, and Ross knew that from now on he must not only live as a trader, but also think as one. All other memories must be buried under the false one he had learned; he must be interested in the present rate of exchange and the chance for profit. The two men were on their way to Outpost Gog, where Ashe's first partner, the redoubtable Sanford, was playing his role so well.

The rain squished in their hide boots, made sodden strings of their cloaks, plastered their woven caps to their thick mats of hair. Yet Ashe bore steadily on across the land with the certainty of one following a marked trail. His self-confidence was rewarded within the first half mile when they came out upon one of the link trackways, its beaten surface testifying to constant use.

Here Ashe turned eastward, stepping up the pace to a ground-covering trot. The peace of the road held—at least by day. By night only the most hardened and desperate outlaws would brave the harmful spirits roving in the dark.

All the lore that had been pounded into him at the base began to make some sense to Ross as he followed his guide, sniffing strange wet smells from the brush, the trees, and the damp earth; piecing together in his mind what he had been taught and what he now saw for himself, until it made a tight pattern.

The track they were following sloped slightly upward, and a change in the wind brought to them a sour odor, blanking out all normal scents. Ashe halted so suddenly that Ross almost plowed into him. But he was alerted by the older man's attitude.

Something had been burned! Ross drew in a deep lungful of the smell and then wished that he had not. It was wood—burned wood—and something else. Since this was not possibly normal, he was prepared for the way Ashe melted into cover in the brush.

They worked their way, sometimes crawling on their bellies, through the wet stands of dead grass, taking full advantage of all cover. They crouched at the top of the hill while Ashe parted the prickly branches of an evergreen bush to make them a window.

The black patch left by the fire, which had come from a ruin above, had spread downhill on the opposite side of the valley. Charred posts still stood like lone teeth in a skull to mark what must have once been one of the stockade walls of a post. But all they now guarded was a desolation from which came that overpowering stench.

"Our post?" Ross asked in a whisper.

Ashe nodded. He was studying the scene with an intent absorption which, Ross knew, would impress every important detail upon his mind. That the place had been burned was clear from the first. But why and by whom was a problem vital to the two lurking in the brush.

It took them almost an hour to cross the valley—an hour of hiding, casting about, searching. They had made a complete circle of the destroyed post and Ashe stood in the shadow of a copse, rubbing clots of mud from his hands and frowning up at the charred posts.

"They weren't rushed. Or if they were, the attackers covered their trail afterward—" Ross ventured.

The older man shook his head. "Tribesmen would not have muddled a trail if they had won. No, this was no regular attack. There have been no signs of a war party coming or leaving."

"Then what?" demanded Ross.

"Lightning for one thing—and we'd better hope it was that. Or—" Ashe's blue eyes were very cold and bleak, as cold and bleak as the countryside about them.

"Or—?" Ross dared to prompt him.

"Or we have made contact with the Reds in the wrong way!"

Ross's hand instinctively went to the dagger at his belt. Little help a dagger would be in an unequal struggle like this! They were only two in a thin web of men strung out through centuries of time with orders to seek out that which did not fit properly into the pattern of the past: to locate the enemy wherever in history or prehistory he had gone to earth. Had the Reds been searching, too, and was this first disaster their victory?

The time traders had their evidence when they at last ventured into what had been the heart of Outpost Gog. Ross, inexperienced as he was in such matters, could not mistake the signs of the explosion. There was a crater on the crown of the hill, and Ashe stood apart from it, eying the fragments about them—scorched wood, blackened stone.

"The Reds?"

"It must have been. This damage was done by explosives."

It was clear why Outpost Gog could not report the disaster. The attack had destroyed their one link with the post on this time level; the concealed communicator had gone up with the blast.

"Eleven—" Ashe's finger tapped on the ornate buckle of his wide belt. "We have about ten days to stick it out," he added, "and it seems we may be able to use them to better advantage than just letting you learn how it feels to walk about some four thousand years before you were born. We have to find out—if we can—what happened here and why!"

Ross gazed at the mess. "Dig?" he asked.

"Some digging is indicated."

So they dug. Finally, black with charcoal smudges and sick with the evidences of death they had chanced upon, they collapsed on the cleanest spot they could find.

"They must have hit at night," Ashe said slowly. "Only at that time would they find everyone here. Men don't trust a night filled with ghosts, and our agents conform to local custom as usual. All of the post people could be erased with one bomb at night."

All except two of them had been true Beaker traders, including women and children. No Beaker trading post was large, and this one was unusually small. The attacker had wiped out some twenty people, eighteen of them innocent victims.

"How long ago?" Ross wanted to know.

"Maybe two days. And this attack came without any warning, or Sandy would have sent a message. He had no suspicions at all; his last reports were all routine, which means that if they were on to him—and they must have been, judging by the results—he was not even aware of it."

"What do we do now?"

Ashe looked at him. "We wash—no—" he corrected himself—"we don't! We go to Nodren's village. We are frightened, grief-stricken. We have found our kinsmen dead under strange circumstances. We ask questions of one to whom I am known as an inhabitant of this post."

So, covered with dirt, they walked along the trackway toward the neighboring village with a weariness they did not have to counterfeit.

The dog sighted or perhaps scented them first. It was a rough-coated beast, showing its fangs with a wolflike ferocity. But it was smaller than a wolf, and it barked between its warning snarls. Ashe brought his bow from beneath the shelter of his cloak and held it ready.

"Ho, one comes to speak with Nodren—Nodren of the Hill!"

Only the dog snapped and snarled. Ashe rubbed his forearm across his face, the gesture of a weary and heartsick man, smearing the ash and grime into an awesome mask.

"Who speaks to Nodren—?" There was a different twist to the pronunciation of some words, but Ross was able to understand.

"One who has hunted with him and feasted with him. The one who gave into his hand the friendship gift of the ever-sharp knife. It is Assha of the traders—"

"Go far from us, man of ill luck. You who are hunted by the evil spirits." The last was a shrill cry.

Ashe remained where he was, facing into the bushes which hid the tribesman.

"Who speaks for Nodren yet not with the voice of Nodren?" he demanded. "This is Assha who asks. We have drunk blood together and faced the white wolf and the wild boar in their fury. Nodren lets not others speak for him, for Nodren is a man and a chief!"

"And you are cursed!" A stone flew through the air, striking a rain pool and spattering mud on Ashe's boots. "Go and take your evil with you!"

"Is it from the hand of Nodren or Nodren's young men that doom came upon those of my blood? Have war arrows passed between the place of the traders and the town of Nodren? Is that why you hide in the shadows so that I, Assha, cannot look upon the face of one who speaks boldly and throws stones?"

"No war arrows between us, trader. *We* do not provoke the spirits of the hills. No fire comes from the sky at night to eat us up with a noise of many thunders. Lurgha speaks in such thunders; Lurgha's hand smites with such fire. You have the Wrath of Lurgha upon you, trader! Keep away from us lest Lurgha's wrath fall upon us also."

Lurgha was the local storm god, Ross recalled. The sound of thunder and fire coming out of the sky at night—the bomb! Perhaps the very method of attack on the post would defeat Ashe's attempt to learn anything from these neighbors. The superstitions of the people would lead them to shun both the site of the post and Ashe himself as cursed and taboo.

"If the Wrath of Lurgha had struck at Assha, would Assha still live to walk upon this road?" Ashe prodded the ground with the tip of his bowstave. "Yet Assha walks, as you see him; Assha talks, as you hear him. It is ridiculous to answer him with the nonsense of little children—"

"Spirits so walk and talk to unlucky men," retorted the man in hiding. "It may be the spirit of Assha who does so now—"

Ashe made a sudden leap. There was a flurry of action behind the bush screen and he reappeared, dragging into the gray light of the rainy day a wriggling captive, whom he bumped without ceremony onto the beaten earth of the road.

The man was bearded, wearing his thick mop of black hair in a round topknot secured by a hide loop. He wore a skin tunic, now in considerable disarray, which was held in place with a woven, tasseled belt.

"Ho, so it is Lal of the Quick Tongue who speaks so loudly of spirits and the Wrath of Lurgha!" Ashe studied his captive. "Now, Lal, since you speak for Nodren—which I believe will greatly surprise him—you will continue to tell me of this Wrath of Lurgha from the night skies and what has happened to Sanfra, who was my brother, and those others of my kin. I am Assha, and you know of the wrath of Assha and how it ate up Twist-tooth, the outlaw, when he came in with his evil men. The Wrath of Lurgha is hot, but so too is the wrath of Assha." Ashe contorted his face in such a way that Lal squirmed and looked away. When the tribesman spoke, all his former authority and bluster had gone.

"Assha knows that I am as his dog. Let him not turn upon me his swift-cutting big knife, nor the arrows from his lightning bow. It was the Wrath of Lurgha which smote the place on the hill, first the thunder of his fist meeting the earth, and then the fire which he breathed upon those whom he would slay—"

"And this you saw with your own eyes, Lal?"

The shaggy head shook an emphatic negative. "Assha knows that Lal is no chief who can stand and look upon the wonders of Lurgha's might and keep his eyes in his head. Nodren himself saw this wonder—"

"And if Lurgha came in the night, when all men keep to their homes and leave the outer world to the restless spirits, how did Nodren see his coming?"

Lal crouched lower to the ground, his eyes darting to the bushes and the freedom they promised, then back to Ashe's firmly planted boots.

"I am not a chief, Assha. How could I know in what way or for what reason Nodren saw the coming of Lurgha—?"

"Fool!" A second voice, that of a woman, spat the word from the brush which fringed the roadway. "Speak to Assha with a straight tongue. If he is a spirit, he will know that you do not tell him the truth. And if he has been spared by Lurgha...." She showed her wonderment with a hiss of indrawn breath.

So urged, Lal mumbled sullenly, "It is said that there came a message for one to witness the Wrath of Lurgha in its descent upon the outlanders so that Nodren and the men of Nodren would truly know that the traders were cursed, and should be put to the spear should they come here again—"

"This message—how was it brought? Did the voice of Lurgha sound in Nodren's ear alone, or came it by the tongue of some man?"

"Ahee!" Lal lay flat on the ground, his hands over his ears.

"Lal is a fool and fears his own shadow as it skips before him on a sunny day!" Out of the bushes stepped a young woman, obviously of some importance in her own group. Walking with a proud stride, her eyes boldly met Ashe's. A shining disk hung about her neck on a thong, and another decorated the woven belt of her cloth tunic. Her hair was bound in a thread net fastened with jet pins.

"I greet Cassca, who is the First Sower." There was a formal note in Ashe's voice. "But why should Cassca hide from Assha?"

"There has been death on your hill, Assha—" she sniffed—"you smell of it now—Lurgha's death. Those who come from that hill may well be some who no longer walk in their bodies." Cassca placed her fingers momentarily on Ashe's outstretched palm before she nodded. "No spirit are you, Assha, for all know that a spirit is solid to the eye, but not to the touch. So it would seem that you were not burned up by Lurgha, after all."

"This matter of a message from Lurgha—" he prompted.

"It came out of the empty air in the hearing not only of Nodren, but also of Hangor, Effar, and myself, Cassca. For we stood at that time near the Old Place...." She made a curious gesture with the fingers of her right hand. "It will soon be the time of sowing, and though Lurgha brings sun and rain to feed the grain, yet it is in the Great Mother that the seed lies. Upon her business only women may go into the Inner Circle." She gestured again. "But as we met to make the first sacrifice there came music out of the air such as we have never heard, voices singing like birds in a strange tongue." Her face assumed an awesome expression. "Afterward a voice said that Lurgha was angered with the hill of the men-from-afar and that in the night he would send his Wrath against them, and that Nodren must witness this thing so that he could see what Lurgha did to those he would punish. So it was done by Nodren. And there was a sound in the air—"

"What kind of a sound?" Ashe asked quietly.

"Nodren said it was a hum and there was the dark shadow of Lurgha's bird between him and the stars. Then came the smiting of the hill with thunder and lightning, and Nodren fled, for the Wrath of Lurgha is a fearsome thing. Now do the people come to the Great Mother's Place with many fine offerings that she may stand between them and that Wrath."

"Assha thanks Cassca, who is the handmaiden of the Great Mother. May the sowing prosper and the reaping be good this year!" Ashe said finally, ignoring Lal, who still groveled on the road.

"You go from this place, Assha?" she asked. "For though I stand under the protecting hand of the Mother and so do not fear, yet there are others who will raise their spears against you for the honor of Lurgha."

"We go, and again thanks be to you, Cassca."

He turned back the way they had come, and Ross fell in beside him as the woman watched them out of sight.

CHAPTER 6

"That bird of Lurgha's—" said Ross, once they were out of sight of Cassca and Lal, "could it have been a plane?"

"Sounds like it," snapped his companion. "If the Reds have done their work efficiently, and there's no reason to suppose otherwise, then there is no use in contacting either Dorhta's town or Munga's. The same announcement concerning the Wrath of Lurgha was probably made there—to their good purpose, not ours."

"Cassca didn't seem to be overly impressed with Lurgha's curse, not as much as the man was."

"She is the closest thing to a priestess that this tribe knows, and she serves a goddess older and more powerful than Lurgha—the Mother Earth, the Great Mother, goddess of fertility and growth. Nodren's people believe that unless Cassca performs her mysteries and sows part of the first field in the spring there won't be any harvest. Consequently, she is secure in her office and doesn't fear the Wrath of Lurgha too much. These people are now changing from one type of worship to another, but some of Cassca's beliefs will persist clear down to our day, taking on the coating of 'magic' and a lot of other enameling along the way."

Ashe had been talking as a man talks to cover up furious thinking. Now he paused again and turned toward the sea. "We have to stick it out somewhere until the sub comes to pick us up. We'll need shelter."

"Will the tribesmen be after us?"

"They may well be. Let the right men get to talking up a holy extermination of those upon whom the Wrath of Lurgha has fallen and we could be in for plenty of trouble. Some of those men are trained hunters and trackers, and the Reds may have planted an agent to report the return of anyone to our post. Just now we're about the most important time travelers out, for we know the Reds have appeared on this line. They must have a large post here, too, or they couldn't have sent a plane on that raid. You can't build a time transport large enough to take through a considerable amount of material. Everything used by us in this age has to be assembled on this side, and the use of all machines is limited to where they can not be seen by any natives. Luckily large sections of this world are mostly wilderness and unpopulated in the areas where we operate the base posts. So if the Reds have a plane, it was put together here, and that means a big post somewhere." Again Ashe was thinking aloud as he pushed ahead of Ross into the fringes of a wood. "Sandy and I scouted this territory pretty well last spring. There is a cave about half a mile to the west; it will shelter us for tonight."

Ashe's plans would probably have been easily accomplished if the cave had been unoccupied. Without incident they came down into a hollow through which trickled a small stream, its banks laced with a thin edging of ice. Under Ashe's direction Ross collected an armload of firewood. He was no woodsman and his prolonged exposure to the chilling drizzle made him eager for even the very rough shelter of a cave, so eager that he plunged forward carelessly. His foot came down on a slippery patch of mud, sending him sprawling on his face. There was a growl, and a white bulk rushed him. The cloak, rucked up about his throat and shoulders, then saved his life, for only stout cloth was caught between those fangs.

With a startled cry, Ross rolled as he might have to escape a man's attack, struggling to unsheath his dagger. A white-hot flash of pain scored his upper arm. The breath was driven out of him as a fight raged over his prone body; he heard grunts, snarls, and was severely pommeled. Then he was free as the bodies broke away. Shaken, he got to his knees. A short distance away the fight was still in progress. He saw Ashe straddle the body of a huge white wolf, his legs clamped about the animal's haunches, his hooked arm under the beast's head, forcing it up and back while his dagger rose and sank twice in the underparts of the heaving body.

Ross held his own weapon ready. He leaped from a half crouch, and his dagger sank cleanly home behind the short ribs. One of their blows must have reached the animal's heart. With an almost human cry the wolf stiffened convulsively. Then it was still. Ashe squatted near it, methodically driving his dagger into the moist soil to clean the blade.

A red rivulet trickled down his thigh where the lower edge of his kilt-tunic had been ripped up to the link belt. He was breathing hard, but otherwise he was as composed as always. "These sometimes hunt in pairs at this season," he observed. "Be ready with your bow—"

Ross strung his with the cord he had been keeping dry within the breast folds of his tunic. He fitted an arrow to the string, grateful to be a passable marksman. The slash on his arm smarted in protest as he moved, and he noted that Ashe did not try to get up.

"A bad one?" Ross indicated the blood now thickening into a stream along Ashe's thigh.

Ashe pulled away the torn tunic and exposed a nasty looking gash on the outside of his hip. He pressed his palm against the gaping wound and motioned Ross to scout ahead. "See if the cave is clear. We can't do anything until we know that."

Reluctantly Ross followed the stream until he found the cave, a snug-looking place with an overhang to keep it dry. The unpleasant smell of a lair hung about its mouth. He chose a stone from the stream, chucked it into the dark opening, and waited. The stone rattled as it struck an inner wall, but there was no other sound. A second stone from a different angle followed the first, with the same results. Ross was now certain that the cave was unoccupied. Once they were inside with a fire going at the entrance, they could hope to keep it free of intruders. A little heartened, he cast about a bit upstream and then turned back to where he had left Ashe.

"No male?" the other greeted him. "This is a female, and she was close to whelping—" He nudged the white wolf with his toe. His hands held a pad of rags against his hip, and his face was shaded with pain.

"Nothing in the cave anyway. Let's see about this...." Ross laid aside the bow and kneeled to examine Ashe's thigh wound. His own slash was more of a smarting graze, but this tear was deep and ugly.

"Second plate—belt—" Ashe got the words out between set teeth, and Ross clicked open the hidden recess in the other's bronze belt to bring out a small packet. Ashe made a wry face as he swallowed three of the pills within. Ross mashed another pill onto the bandage he prepared, and when the last cumbersome fold was secure Ashe relaxed.

"Let us hope that works," he commented a little bleakly. "Now come here where I can get my hands on you and let me see your scratch. Animal bites can be a nasty business."

Bandaged in turn, with the bitterness of the anti-septo pill on his tongue, Ross helped Ashe limp upstream to the cave. He left the older man outside while he cleaned up the floor of the cave and then made his companion as comfortable as he could on a bed of bracken. The fire Ross had longed for was built. They stripped off their sodden clothing and hung it to dry. Ross wrapped a bird he had shot in clay and tucked it under the hot coals to be roasted.

They had surely had bad luck, he thought, but they were now undercover, had a fire, and food of a sort. His arm ached, sharp pain shooting from fingers to elbow when he moved it. Though Ashe made no complaint, Ross gauged that the older man's discomfort was far worse than his own, and he carefully hid all signs of his own twinges.

They ate the bird, saltless, and with their fingers. Ross savored each greasy bite, licking his hands clean afterward while Ashe lay back on the improvised bed, his face gaunt in the half light of the fire.

"We are about five miles from the sea here. There is no way of raising our base now that Sandy's installation is gone. I'll have to lay up, since I can't risk any more loss of blood. And you're not too good in the woods—"

Ross accepted that valuation with a new humbleness. He was only too well aware that if it had not been for Ashe, he and not the white wolf would have died down in the valley. Yet a strange shyness kept him from trying to put his thanks into words. The only kind of amends he could make for the other's hurt was to provide hands, feet, and strength for the man who did know what to do and how to do it.

"We'll have to hunt—" he ventured.

"Deer," Ashe caught him up. "But the marsh at the mouth of this stream provides a better hunting ground than inland. If the wolf laired here very long, she has already frightened away any large game. It isn't the matter of food which bothers me—"

"It is being tied up here," Ross filled in for him with some daring. "But look here, I'll take orders. This is your territory, and I'm green at the game. You tell me what to do, and I'll do it the best that I can." He glanced up to find Ashe surveying him intently, but as usual there was no readable expression on the other's brown face.

"The first thing to do is get the wolf's hide," Ashe said briskly. "Then bury the carcass. You'd better drag it up here to work on it. If her mate is hanging around, he might try to jump you."

Why Ashe should think it necessary to acquire the wolf skin puzzled Ross, but he asked no questions. His skinning task took four times as long and was far from being the neat job the shock-haired man of the record tape had accomplished. Ross had to wash himself off in the stream before piling stones over the corpse in temporary burial. When he pulled his bloody burden back to the cave, Ashe lay with his eyes closed. Ross thankfully sat on his own pile of bracken and tried not to notice the throbbing ache in his arm.

He must have fallen asleep, for when he roused it was to see Ashe crawl over to mend the dying fire from their store of wood. Ross, angry at himself, beat the other to the task.

"Get back," he said roughly. "This is my job. I didn't mean to fail."

Surprisingly, Ashe settled back without a word, leaving Ross to sit by the fire, a fire he was very glad to have a moment or so later when a wailing howl sounded down-wind. If this was not the white wolf's mate, then it was another of her kin who prowled the upper reaches of the small valley.

The next day, having provided Ashe with a supply of firewood, Ross went to try his luck in the marsh. The thick drizzle which had hung over the land the day before was gone, and he faced a clear, bright morning, though the breeze had an icy snap. But it was a good morning to be alive and out in the open, and Ross's spirits rose.

He tried to put to use all the woodlore he had learned at the base. But it was one thing to learn something academically and another to put that learning into practice. He was uncomfortably certain that Ashe would not have found his showing very good.

The marsh was a series of pools between rank growths of leafless willows and coarse tufts of grass, with hillocks of firmer soil rising like islands. Ross, approaching with caution, was glad of it, for from one of those hillocks arose a trail of white smoke, and he saw a black blot which was probably a rude hut. Why one should choose to live in the midst of such country he could not guess, though it might be merely the temporary camp of some hunter.

Ross also saw thousands of birds feeding greedily on the dried seed of the marsh grasses, paddling in the pools, and setting up a clamor to drive a man mad. They did not seem in the least disturbed by that distant camper.

Ross had reason to be proud of his marksmanship that morning. He had in his quiver perhaps half a dozen of the lighter shafts made for shooting birds. In place of the finely chipped and wickedly barbed flint points used for heavier game, these were tipped with needle-sharp, light bone heads. He had a string of four birds looped together by their feet within almost as many minutes. For the flocks rose in their first alarm only to settle again to feast.

Then he knocked over a hare—a fat giant of its race—that stared at him brazenly from a tussock. The hare kicked back into a pool in its death struggle, however, and Ross was forced to leave cover to retrieve its body.

But he was alert and he stood up, dagger out and ready, to greet the man who parted the bushes to watch him.

For a long minute gray eyes stared into brown ones, and then Ross noted the other's bedraggled and tattered dress. The kilt-tunic smudged with mud, scorched and charred along one edge, was styled like his own. The fellow wore his hair fastened back with a band, unlike the topknot of the local tribesman.

Ross, his dagger still ready, broke the silence first. "I am a believer in the fire and the fashioned metal, the climbing sun, and the moving water." He repeated the recognition speech of the Beakermen.

"The fire warms by the grace of Tulden, the metal is fashioned by the mystery of the smith, the sun climbs without our aid, and who can stop the water from running?" The stranger's voice was hoarse. Now that Ross had time to examine him more closely he saw the dark bruise on his exposed shoulder, the raw red mark of a burn running across the man's broad chest. He dared to test his surmise concerning the other.

"I am of the kin of Assha. We returned to the hill—"

"Ashe!"

Not "Assha" but "Ashe!" Ross, though sure of that pronunciation, was still cautious. "You are from the hill place, where Lurgha smote with thunder and fire?"

The man slid his long legs across the log which had been his shelter. The burn across his chest was not his only brand, for Ross noticed another red stripe, puffed and fiery looking, which swelled the calf of one leg. The man studied Ross closely, and then his fingers moved in a sign which to the uninitiated native might have been one for the warding off of evil, but which to Ross was the "thumbs up" of his own age.

"Sanford?"

At that name the man shook his head. "McNeil," he named himself. "Where is Ashe?"

He might really be what he seemed, but on the other hand, he could be a Red spy. Ross had not forgotten Kurt. "What happened?" he parried one question with another.

"Bomb. The Reds must have spotted us, and we didn't have a chance. We weren't expecting any trouble. I'd been down to see about a missing burden donkey and was about halfway back up the hill when she hit. When

I came to I was all the way down the hill with part of the fort on top of me. The rest.... Well, you saw the place, didn't you?"

Ross nodded. "What are you doing here?"

McNeil spread his hands in a tired little gesture. "I tried to talk to Nodren, but they stoned me away. I knew that Ashe was coming through and hoped to reach him when he hit the beach, but I was too late. Then I figured he would pass here to make contact with the sub, so I was waiting it out until I saw you. Where is Ashe?"

It all sounded logical enough. Still, with Ashe injured, Ross was taking no chances. He pushed his dagger back into its sheath and picked up the hare. "Stay here," he told McNeil, "I'll be back—"

"But—wait! Where's Ashe, you young fool? We have to get together."

Ross went on. He was sure that the stranger was in no shape to race after him, and he would lay a muddled trail before he returned to the cave valley. If this man was a Red plant, he would have to reckon with one who had already met Kurt Vogel.

The laying of that muddled trail took time. It was past midday when Ross came back to Ashe, who was sitting up by the mouth of the cave at the fire, using his dagger to fashion a crutch out of a length of sapling. He surveyed Ross's burden with approval, but lost interest in the promise of food as soon as the other reported his meeting in the marsh.

"McNeil—chap with brown hair, brown eyes, a right eyebrow which quirks up toward his hairline when he smiles?"

"Brown hair and eyes, okay—and he didn't smile any."

"Chip broken off a front tooth—upper right?"

Ross shut his eyes to visualize the stranger. Yes, there had been a small break on a front tooth. He nodded.

"That's McNeil. Not that you didn't do right not to bring him here without being sure. What made you so watchful? Kurt?"

Again Ross nodded. "And what you said about the Reds' planting someone here to wait for us."

Ashe scratched the bristles on his chin. "Never underrate them—we don't dare do that. But the man you met is McNeil, and we'd better get him here. Can you bring him?"

"I think he's able to get about, in spite of that leg. From his story he's been stirring around."

Ashe bit absent-mindedly into a piece of hare and swore mildly when he burned his tongue. "Odd that Cassca didn't tell us about him. Unless she thought there was no use causing trouble by admitting they had driven him away. You going now?"

Ross moved around the fire. "Might as well. He didn't look too comfortable. And I'll bet he's hungry."

He took the direct route back to the marsh, but this time no thread of smoke spiraled into the air. Ross hesitated. That shelter on the small island was surely the place where McNeil had holed up. Should he try to work his way out to it now? Or had something happened to the man while he was gone?

Again that sixth sense of impending disaster, which is perhaps bred into some men, alerted Ross. Why he turned suddenly and backed against a bushy willow, he could not have explained. However, because he did so the loop of hide rope meant for his throat hit his shoulder harmlessly. It fell to the ground, and he stamped one boot down on it. Then it was the work of seconds to grasp it and give it a quick jerk. The surprised man who held the other end was brought sprawling into the open.

Ross had seen that round face before. "Lal of the town of Nodren." He found words to greet the ropeman even as his knee came up against the fellow's jaw, jarring Lal so that he dropped a flint knife. Ross kicked it into the willows. "What do you hunt here, Lal?"

"Traders!" The voice was weak, but it held heat.

The tribesman did not try to struggle against Ross's hold, and Ross, gripping him by the nape of the neck, moved through a screen of brush to a hollow. Luckily there was no water cupped there, for McNeil lay in the bottom of that dip, his arms tied tightly behind him and his ankles lashed together with no thought for the pain of his burned leg.

CHAPTER 7

Ross whirled the rope which had been meant to bring him down around Lal. He lashed the tribesman's arms tight to his body before he knelt to cut loose his fellow time traveler. Lal now huddled against the far wall of the cup, fear in every line of his small body. So apparent was this fear that Ross felt no satisfaction at turning the tables on him. Instead he felt increasingly uneasy.

"What is this all about?" he asked McNeil as he stripped off his bonds and helped him up.

McNeil massaged his wrists, took a step or two, and grimaced with pain. "Our friend seeks to be an obedient servant of Lurgha."

Ross picked up his bow. "The tribe is out to hunt us?"

"Lurgha has ordered—out of thin air again—that any traders who escaped are to be brought in and introduced to him personally at the sacrifice for the enrichment of the fields!"

The old, old gift of blood and life at the spring sowing. Ross recalled grisly details from his cram lessons. Any wandering stranger or enemy tribesman taken in a raid before that day would meet such a fate. On unlucky years when people were not available a deer or wolf might serve. But the best sacrifice of all was a man. So Lurgha had decreed—from the air—that traders were his meat? What of Ashe? Let any hunter from the village track him down.

"We have to move fast," Ross told McNeil as he took up the rope which made a leading cord for Lal. Ashe would want to question the tribesman about this second order from Lurgha.

Impatient as Ross was, he had to mend his pace to accommodate McNeil. The man from the hill post was close to the end of his strength. He had started off bravely enough, but now he wavered. Ross sent Lal ahead with a sharp push, ordering him to stay there, while he went to McNeil's aid. It was well into the afternoon before they came up the stream and saw the fire before the cave.

"Macna!" Ashe hailed Ross's companion with the native version of his name. "And Lal. But what do you here, Lal of Nodren's town?"

"Mischief." Ross helped McNeil within the cave and to the pile of brush which was his own bed. "He was hunting traders as a present for Lurgha."

"So—" Ashe turned upon the tribesman—"and by whose word did you go hunting my kinsman, Lal? Was it Nodren's? Has he forgotten the blood bond between us? For it was in the name of Lurgha himself that that bond was made—"

"Aaaah—" The tribesman squatted down against the wall where Ross had shoved him. Unable to hide his head in his arms, he brought his face down upon his knees so that only his shaggy topknot of hair was exposed. Ross realized, with stupefaction, that the little man was crying like a child, his hunched shoulders rising and falling with the force of his sobs. "Aaaah—" he wailed.

Ashe allowed him a moment or two of noisy grief and then limped over to grasp his topknot and pull up his head. Lal's eyes were screwed tightly shut, but there were tears on his cheeks, and his mouth twisted in another wail.

"Be quiet!" Ashe shook him, but not too harshly. "Have you yet felt the bite of my sharp knife? Has an arrow holed your skin? You are alive, and you could be dead. Show that you are glad you live and continue to breathe by telling us what you know, Lal."

The woman Cassca had displayed a measure of intelligence and ease at their meeting upon the road. But it was very plain that Lal was of different stuff, a simple man in whose head few ideas could find house room at one time. And to him the present was all black. Little by little they dragged the story out of him.

Lal was poor, so poor that he had never dared dream of owning for himself some of the precious things the hill traders displayed to the wealthy of Nodren's town. But he was also a follower of the Great Mother's, rather than one who made sacrifices to Lurgha. Lurgha was the god for warriors and great men; he was too high to concern himself with such as Lal.

So when Nodren reported the end of the hill post under the storm fist of Lurgha, Lal had been impressed only to a point. He was still convinced it was none of his concern, and instead he began thinking of the treasures which might lie hidden in the destroyed buildings. It occurred to him that Lurgha's Wrath had been laid upon the men who had owned them, but perhaps it would not stretch to the fine things themselves. So he had gone secretly to the hill to explore.

What he had seen there had utterly converted him to a belief in the fury of Lurgha and he had been frightened out of his simple wits, fleeing without making the search he had intended. But Lurgha had seen him there, had read his impious thoughts....

At that point Ashe interrupted the stream of Lal's story. How had Lurgha seen Lal?

Because—Lal shuddered, began to cry again, and spoke the next few sentences haltingly—that very morning when he had gone out to hunt wild fowl in the marshes Lurgha had spoken to *him*, to Lal, who was less than a flea creeping upon a worn-out fur rug.

And how had Lurgha spoken? Ashe's voice was softer, gentle.

Out of the air, even as he had spoken to Nodren, who was a chief. He said that he had seen Lal in the hill post, and so Lal was his meat. But not yet would he eat him, not if Lal served him in other ways. And he, Lal, had lain flat on the ground before the bodiless voice of Lurgha and had sworn that he would serve Lurgha to the end of his life.

Then Lurgha had told him to hunt down one of the evil traders who was hiding in the marshes, and bind him with ropes. Then he was to call the men of the village and together they would carry the prisoner to the hill where Lurgha had loosed his wrath, and there they would leave him. Later they might return and take what they found there and use it to bless the fields at sowing time, and all would be well with Nodren's village. And Lal had sworn that he would do as Lurgha bade, but now he could not. So Lurgha would eat him up—he was a man without hope.

"Yet," Ashe said even more gently, "have you not served the Great Mother all these years, giving to her a portion of the first fruits even when the yield of your one field was small?"

Lal stared at him, his woebegone face still smeared with tears. It took a second or two for the question to penetrate his fear-clouded mind. Then he nodded timidly.

"Has she not dealt with you well in return, Lal? You are a poor man, that is true. But you are not gaunt of belly, even though this is the thin season when men fast before the coming of the new harvest. The Great Mother watches over her own. And it is she who has brought you to us now. For this I say to you, Lal, and I, Assha of the traders, speak with a straight tongue. The Lurgha who struck our post, who spoke to you from the air, means you no good—"

"Aaaah!" wailed Lal. "So do I know, Assha. He is of the blackness and the wandering spirits of the dark!"

"Just so. Thus he is no kin to the mother, for she is of the light and of good things, of the new grain, and the newborn lambs for your flocks, of the maids who wed with men and bring forth sons to lift their fathers' spears, daughters to spin by the hearth and sow the yellow grain in the furrows. Lurgha's quarrel lies with us, Lal, not with Nodren nor with you. And we take upon us that quarrel." He limped into the outer air where the shadows of evening were beginning to creep across the ground.

"Hear me, Lurgha," he called into the coming night, "I am Assha of the traders, and upon myself I take your hate. Not upon Lal, nor upon Nodren, nor upon the people who live in Nodren's town, shall your wrath lie. Thus do I say it!"

Ross, noticing that Ashe concealed from Lal a wave of his hand, was prepared for some display meant to impress the tribesman. It came in a spectacular burst of green fire beyond the stream. Lal wailed again, but when that fire was followed by no other manifestation he ventured to raise his head once more.

"You have seen how Lurgha answered me, Lal. Toward me only will his wrath be turned. Now—" Ashe limped back and dragged out the white wolf skin, dropping it before Lal—"this you will give to Cassca that she may make a curtain for the Mother's home. See, it is white and so rare that the Mother will be pleased with such a fine gift. And you will tell her all that has chanced and how you believe in her powers over the powers of Lurgha, and the Mother will be well pleased with you. But you shall say nothing to the men of the village, for this quarrel is between Lurgha and Assha now and not for the meddling of others."

He unfastened the rope which bound Lal's arms. Lal reached out a hand to the wolf skin, his eyes filled with wonderment. "This is a fine thing you give me, Assha, and the Mother will be pleased, for in many years she has not had such a curtain for her secret place. Also, I am but a little man; the quarrels of great ones are not for me. Since Lurgha has accepted your words this is none of my affair. Yet I will not go back to the village for a while—with your permission, Assha. For I am a man of loose and wagging tongue and oftentimes I speak what I do not really wish to say. So if I am asked questions, I answer. If I am not there to be asked such questions, I cannot answer."

McNeil laughed, and Ashe smiled. "Well enough, Lal. Perhaps you are a wiser man than you think. But also I do not believe you should stay here."

The tribesman was already nodding. "That do I say, too, Assha. You are now facing the Wrath of Lurgha, and with that I wish no part. Thus I shall go into the marsh for a while. There are birds and hares to hunt, and I shall work upon this fine skin so that when I take it to the Mother it shall indeed be a gift worth her smiles. Now, Assha, I would go before the night comes if it pleases you."

"Go with good fortune, Lal." Ashe stood apart while the tribesman ducked his head in a shy, awkward farewell to the others, pattering out into the valley.

"What if they pick him up?" McNeil asked wearily.

"I don't think they can," Ashe returned. "And what would you do—keep him here? If we tried that, he'd scheme to escape and try to turn the tables on us. Now he'll keep away from Nodren's village and out of sight for the time being. Lal's not too bright in some ways, but he's a good hunter. If he has reason for hiding out, it'll take a better hunter to track him. At least we know now that the Reds are afraid they did not make a clean sweep here. What happened, McNeil?"

While he was telling his story in more detail both Ashe and Ross worked on his burns, making him comfortable. Then Ashe sat back as Ross prepared food.

"How did they spot the post?" Ashe rubbed his chin and frowned at the fire.

"Only way I can guess is that they picked up our post signal and pinpointed the source. That means they must have been hunting us for some time."

"No strangers about lately?"

McNeil shook his head. "Our cover wasn't broken that way. Sanford was a wonder. If I hadn't known better, I would have sworn he was born one of the Beaker folk. He had a network of informants running all the way from here into Brittany. Amazing how he was able to work without arousing any suspicions. I suppose his being a member of the smiths' guild was a big help. He could pick up a lot of news from any village where there was one at work. And I tell you," McNeil propped himself up on his elbow to exclaim more vehemently—"there wasn't a whisper of trouble from here clear across the channel and pretty far to the north. We were already sure the south was clean before we ever took cover as Beakers, especially since their clans are thick in Spain."

Ashe chewed a broiled wing reflectively. "Their permanent base with the transport *has* to be somewhere within the bounds of the territory they hold in our own time."

"They could plant it in Siberia and laugh at us," McNeil exploded. "No hope of our getting in there—"

"No." Ashe threw the stripped bone into the fire and licked grease from his fingers. "Then they would be faced with the old problem of distance. If what they are exploiting lay within their modern boundaries, we would never have tumbled to the thing in the first place. What the Reds want must lie outside their twentieth century holdings, a slender point in our favor. Therefore they will plant their shift point as close to it as they can. Our transportation problem is more difficult than theirs will ever be.

"You know why we chose the arctic for our base; it lies in a section of the world never populated by other than roving hunters. But I'll wager anything you want to name that their point is somewhere in Europe where they have people to contend with. If they are using a plane, they can't risk its being seen—"

"I don't see why not," Ross broke in. "These people couldn't possibly know what it was—Lurgha's bird—magic—"

Ashe shook his head. "They must have the interference-with-history worry as much as we have. Anything of our own time has to be hidden or disguised in such a way that the native who may stumble upon it will never know it is man-made. Our sub is a whale to all appearances. Possibly their plane is a bird, but neither can bear too close an examination. We don't know what could result from a leak of real knowledge in this or any primitive time ... how it might change history—"

"But," Ross advanced what he believed to be the best argument against that reasoning, "suppose I handed Lal a gun and taught him to use it. He couldn't duplicate the weapon—the technology required lies so far beyond this age. These people couldn't reproduce such a thing."

"True enough. On the other hand, don't belittle the ingenuity of the smiths or the native intelligence of men in any era. These tribesmen might not be able to reproduce your gun, but it would set them thinking along new lines. We might find that they would think our time right out of being. No, we dare not play tricks with the past. This is the same situation we faced immediately after the discovery of the atom bomb. Everybody raced to produce that new weapon and then sat around and shivered for fear we'd be crazy enough to use it on each other.

"The Reds have made new discoveries which we have to match, or we will go under. But back in time we have to be careful, both of us, or perhaps destroy the world we do live in."

"What do we do now?" McNeil wanted to know.

"Murdock and I came here only for a trial run. It's his test. The sub is to call for us about nine days from now."

"So if we sit tight—if we *can* sit tight—" McNeil lay down again—"they will take us out. Meanwhile we have nine days."

They spent three more days in the cave. McNeil was on his feet and impatient to leave before Ashe was able to hobble well enough to travel. Though Ross and McNeil took turns at hunting and guard duty, they saw no signs that the tribesmen were tracking them. Apparently Lal had done as he promised, withdrawing to the marsh and hiding there apart from his people.

In the gray of pre-dawn on the fourth day Ashe wakened Ross. Their fire had been buried with earth, and already the cave seemed bleak. They ate venison roasted the night before and went out into the chill of a fog. A little way down the valley McNeil joined them out of the mist from his guard post. Keeping their pace to one which favored Ashe's healing wound, they made their way inland in the direction of the track linking the villages.

Crossing that road they continued northward, the land beginning to rise under them. Far away they heard the blatting of sheep, the bark of a dog. In the fog, Ross stumbled in a shallow ditch beyond which lay a stubbled field. Ashe paused to look about him, his nostrils expanding as if he were a hound smelling out their trail.

The three went on, crossing a whole series of small, irregular fields. Ross was sure that the yield from any of these cleared strips must be scanty. The fog was thickening. Ashe pressed the pace, using his handmade crutch carefully. He gave an audible sigh of relief when they were faced at last by two stone monoliths rising like pillars. A third stone lay across them, forming a rude arch through which they saw a narrow valley running back into the hills.

Through the fog Ross could sense the eerie strangeness of the valley beyond the massive gate. He would have said that he was not superstitious, that he had merely studied these tribal beliefs as lessons; he had not accepted them. Yet now, if he had been alone, he would have avoided that place and turned aside from the valley, for that which waited within was not for him. To his secret relief Ashe paused by the arch to wait.

The older man gestured the other two into cover. Ross obeyed willingly, though the dank drops of condensing fog dripped on his cloak and wet his face as he brushed against prickly-leafed shrubs. Here were walls of evergreen plants and dwarfed pines almost as if this tunnel of year-round greenery had been planted with some purpose in mind. Once his companions had concealed themselves, Ashe called, shrill but sweetly, with a bird's rising notes. Three times he made that sound before a figure moved in the fog, the rough gray-white of its long cloak melting in the wisps of mist.

Down that green tunnel, out of the heart of the valley, the other came, a loop of cloak concealing the entire figure. It halted right in back of the arch and Ashe, making a gesture to the others to stay where they were, faced the muffled stranger.

"Hands and feet of the Mother, she who sows what may be reaped—"

"Outland stranger who is under the Wrath of Lurgha," the other mocked him in the voice of Cassca. "What do you want, outlander, that you dare to come here where no man may enter?"

"That which you know. For on the night when Lurgha came you also saw—"

Ross heard the hiss of a sharply drawn breath. "How knew you that, outlander?"

"Because you serve the Mother and you are jealous for her and her service. If Lurgha is a mighty god, you wanted to see his acts with your own eyes."

When she finally answered, there was anger as well as frustration in her voice. "And you know of my shame then, Assha. For Lurgha came—on a bird he came, and he did even as he said he would. So now the village will make offerings to Lurgha and beg his favor, and the Mother will no more have those to harken to her words and offer her the first fruits—"

"But from whence came this bird which was Lurgha, can you tell me that, she who waits upon the Mother?"

"What difference does it make from what direction Lurgha came? That does not add nor take from his power." Cassca moved beneath the arch. "Or does it in some strange way, Assha?"

"Perhaps it does. Only tell me."

She turned slowly and pointed over her right shoulder. "From that way he came, Assha. Well did I watch, knowing that I was the Mother's and that even Lurgha's thunderbolts could not eat me up. Does knowing that make Lurgha smaller in your eyes, Assha? When he has eaten up all that is yours and your kin with it?"

"Perhaps," Assha repeated. "I do not think Lurgha will come so again."

She shrugged, and the heavy cloak flapped. "That shall be as it shall be, Assha. Now go, for it is not good that any man come hither."

Cassca paced back into the heart of the green tunnel, and Ross and McNeil came out of concealment. McNeil faced in the direction she had pointed. "Northeast—" he commented thoughtfully, "the Baltic lies in that quarter."

CHAPTER 8

"... and that is about all." Ten days later Ashe, a dressing on his leg and a few of the pain lines smoothed from his face, sat on a bunk in the arctic time post nursing a mug of coffee in his hands and smiling, a little crookedly, at Nelson Millaird.

Millaird, Kelgarries, Dr. Webb, all the top brass of the project had not only come through the transfer point to meet the three from Britain but were now crammed into the room, nearly pushing Ross and McNeil through the wall. Because this was it! What they had hunted for months—years—now lay almost within their grasp.

Only Millaird, the director, did not seem so confident. A big man with a bushy thatch of coarse graying hair and a heavy, fleshy face, he did not look like a brain. Yet Ross had been on the roster long enough to know that it was Millaird's thick and hairy hands that gathered together all the loose threads of Operation Retrograde and deftly wove them into a workable pattern. Now the director leaned back in a chair which was too small for his bulk, chewing thoughtfully on a toothpick.

"So we have the first whiff of a trail," he commented without elation.

"A pretty strong lead!" Kelgarries broke in. Too excited to sit still, the major stood with his back against the door, as alert as if he were about to turn and face the enemy. "The Reds wouldn't have moved against Gog if they did not consider it a menace to them. Their big base must be in this time sector!"

"A big base," Millaird corrected. "The one we are after, no. And right now they may be switching times. Do you think they will sit here and wait for us to show up in force?" But Millaird's tone, intended to deflate, had no effect on the major.

"And just how long would it take them to dismantle a big base?" that officer countered. "At least a month. If we shoot a team in there in a hurry—"

Millaird folded his huge hands over his barrel-shaped body and laughed, without a trace of humor. "Just where do we send that team, Kelgarries? Northeast of a coastal point in Britain is a rather vague direction, to say the least. Not," he spoke to Ashe now, "that you didn't do all you could, Ashe. And you, McNeil, nothing to add?"

"No, sir. They jumped us out of the blue when Sandy thought he had every possible line tapped, every safeguard working. I don't know how they caught on to us, unless they located our beam to this post. If so, they must have been deliberately hunting us for some time, because we only used the beam as scheduled—"

"The Reds have patience and brains and probably some more of their surprise gadgets to help them. We have the patience and the brains, but not the gadgets. And time is against us. Get anything out of this, Webb?" Millaird asked the hitherto silent third member of his ruling committee.

The quiet man adjusted his glasses on the bridge of his nose, a flattish nose which did not support them very well. "Just another point to add to our surmises. I would say that they are located somewhere near the Baltic Sea. There are old trade routes there, and in our own time it is a territory closed to us. We never did know too much about that section of Europe. Their installation may be close to the Finnish border. They could disguise their modern station under half a dozen covers; that is strange country."

Millaird's hands unfolded and he produced a notebook and pen from a shirt pocket. "Won't hurt to stir up some of the present-day agents of the M.I. and the rest. They might just come up with a useful hint. So you'd say the Baltic. But that is a big slice of country."

Webb nodded. "We have one advantage—the old trade routes. In the Beaker period they are pretty well marked. The major one into that section was established for the amber trade. The country is forested, but not so heavily as it was in an earlier period. The native tribes are mostly roving hunters, and fishermen along the coast. But they have had contact with traders." He shoved his glasses back into place with a nervous gesture. "The Reds may run into trouble themselves there at this time—"

"How?" Kelgarries demanded.

"Invasion of the ax people. If they have not yet arrived, they are due very soon. They formed one of the big waves of migratory people, who flooded the country, settled there. Eventually they became the Norse or Celtic stock. We don't know whether they stamped out the native tribes they found there or assimilated them."

"That might be a nice point to have settled more definitely," McNeil commented. "It could mean the difference between getting your skull split and continuing to breathe."

"I don't think they would tangle with the traders. Evidence found today suggests that the Beaker folk simply went on about their business in spite of a change in customers," Webb returned.

"Unless they were pushed into violence." Ashe handed his empty mug to Ross. "Don't forget Lurgha's Wrath. From now on our enemies might take a very dim view of any Beaker trade posts near their property."

Webb shook his head slowly. "A wholesale attack on Beaker establishments would constitute a shift in history. The Reds won't dare that, not just on general suspicion. Remember, they are not any more eager to tinker with history than we are. No, they will watch for us. We will have to stop communication by radio—"

"We can't!" snapped Millaird vehemently. "We can cut it down, but I won't send the boys out without some means of quick communication. You lab boys put your brains to work and see what you can turn out in the way of talk boxes that they can't snoop. Time!" He drummed on his knee with his thick fingers. "It all comes back to a question of time."

"Which we do not have," Ashe observed in his usual quiet voice. "If the Reds are afraid they have been spotted, they must be dismantling their post right now, working around the clock. We'll never again have such a good chance to nail them. We must move now."

Millaird's lids drooped almost shut; he might have been napping. Kelgarries stirred restlessly by the door, and Webb's round face had settled into what looked like permanent lines of disapproval.

"Doc," Millaird spoke over his shoulder to the fourth man of his following, "what is your report?"

"Ashe must be under treatment for at least five days. McNeil's burns aren't too bad, and Murdock's slash is almost healed."

"Five days—" Millaird droned, and then flashed a glance at the major. "Personnel. We're tied down without any useful personnel. Who in processing could be switched without tangling them up entirely?"

"No one. I can recall Jansen and Van Wyke. These ax people might be a good cover for them." The momentary light in Kelgarries' eyes faded. "No, we have no proper briefing and can't get it until the tribe does appear on the map. I won't send any men in cold. Their blunders would not only endanger them but might menace the whole project."

"So that leaves us with you three," Millaird said. "We'll recall what men we can and brief them again as fast as possible. But you know how long that will take. In the meantime—"

Ashe spoke directly to Webb. "You can't pinpoint the region closer than just the Baltic?"

"We can do this much," the other answered him slowly, and with obvious reluctance. "We can send the sub cruising offshore there for the next five days. If there is any radio activity—any communication—we should be able to trace the beams. It all depends upon whether the Reds have any parties operating from their post. Flimsy—"

"But something!" Kelgarries seized upon it with the relief of one who needed action.

"And they will be waiting for just such a move on our part," Webb continued deliberately.

"All right, so they'll be watching!" the major said, about to lose his temper, "but it is about the only move we can make to back up the boys when they do go in."

He whipped around the door and was gone. Webb got up slowly. "I will work over the maps again," he told Ashe. "We haven't scouted that area, and we don't dare send a photo-plane over it now. Any trip in will be a stab in the dark."

"When you have only one road, you take it," Ashe replied. "I'll be glad to see anything you can show me, Miles."

If Ross had believed that his pre-trial-run cramming had been a rigorous business, he was soon to laugh at that estimation. Since the burden of the next jump would rest on only three of them—Ashe, McNeil, and himself—they were plunged into a whirlwind of instruction, until Ross, dazed and too tired to sleep on the third night, believed that he was more completely bewildered than indoctrinated. He said as much sourly to McNeil.

"Base has pulled back three other teams," McNeil replied. "But the men have to go to school again, and they won't be ready to come on for maybe three, four weeks. To change runs means unlearning stuff as well as learning it—"

"What about new men?"

"Don't think Kelgarries isn't out now beating the bushes for some! Only, we have to be fitted to the physical type we are supposed to represent. For instance, set a small, dark-headed pugnose among your Norse sea rovers, and he's going to be noticed—maybe remembered too well. We can't afford to take that chance. So Kelgarries had to discover men who not only look the part but are also temperamentally fitted for this job. You can't plant a fellow who thinks as a seaman—not a seaman, you understand, but one whose mind works in that pattern—among a wandering tribe of cattle herders. The protection for the man and the project lies in his being fitted into the right spot at the right time."

Ross had never really thought of that point before. Now he realized that he and Ashe and McNeil were of a common mold. All about the same height, they shared brown hair and light eyes—Ashe's blue, his own gray, and McNeil's hazel—and they were of similar build, small-boned, lean, and quick-moving. He had not seen any of the true Beakermen except on the films. But now, recalling those, he could see that the three time traders were of the same general physical type as the far-roving people they used as a cover.

It was on the morning of the fifth day while the three were studying a map Webb had produced that Kelgarries, followed at his own weighty pace by Millaird, burst in upon them.

"We have it! This time *we* have the luck! The Reds slipped. Oh, how they slipped!"

Webb watched the major, a thin little smile pulling at his pursed mouth. "Miracles sometimes do happen," he remarked. "I suppose the sub has a fix for us."

Kelgarries passed over the flimsy strip of paper he had been waving as a banner of triumph. Webb read the notation on it and bent over the map, making a mark with one of those needle-sharp pencils which seemed to grow in his breast pocket, ready for use. Then he made a second mark.

"Well, it narrows it a bit," he conceded. Ashe looked in turn and laughed.

"I would like to hear your definition of 'narrow' sometime, Miles. Remember we have to cover this on foot, and a difference of twenty miles can mean a lot."

"That mark is quite a bit in from the sea." McNeil offered his own protest when he saw the marking. "We don't know that country—"

Webb shoved his glasses back for the hundredth time that morning. "I suppose we could consider this critical, condition red," he said in such a dubious tone that he might have been begging someone to protest his statement. But no one did. Millaird was busy with the map.

"I think we do, Miles!" He looked to Ashe. "You'll parachute in. The packs with which you will be equipped are special stuff. Once you have them off sprinkle them with a powder Miles will provide and in ten minutes there won't be enough of them left for anyone to identify. We haven't but a dozen of these, and we can't throw them away except in a crisis. Find the base and rig up the detector. Your fix in this time will be easy—but it is the other end of the line we must have. Until you locate that, stick to the job. Don't communicate with us until you have it!"

"There is the possibility," Ashe pointed out, "the Reds may have more than one intermediate post. They probably have played it smart and set up a series of them to spoil a direct trace, as each would lead only to another farther back in time—"

"All right. If that proves true, just get us the next one back," Millaird returned. "From that we can trace them along if we must send in some of the boys wearing dinosaur skins later. We *have* to find their primary base, and if that hunt goes the hard way, well, we do it the hard way."

"How did you get the fix?" McNeil asked.

"One of their field parties ran into trouble and yelled for help."

"Did they get it?"

The major grinned. "What do you think? You know the rules—and the ones the Reds play by are twice as tough on their own men."

"What kind of trouble?" Ashe wanted to know.

"Some kind of a local religious dispute. We do our best with their code, but we're not a hundred per cent perfect in reading it. I gather they were playing with a local god and got their fingers burned."

"Lurgha again, eh?" Ashe smiled.

"Foolish," Webb said impatiently. "That is a silly thing to do. You were almost over the edge of prudence yourself, Gordon, with that Lurgha business. To use the Great Mother was a ticklish thing to try, and you were lucky to get out of it so easily."

"Once was enough," Ashe agreed. "Though using it may have saved our lives. But I assure you I am not starting a holy war or setting up as a prophet."

Ross had been taught something of map reading, but mentally he could not make what he saw on paper resemble the countryside. A few landmarks, if there were any outstanding ones, were all he could hope to impress upon his memory until he was actually on the ground.

Landing there according to Millaird's instruction was another experience he would not have chosen of his own accord. To jump was a matter of timing, and in the dark with a measure of rain thrown in, the action was anything but pleasant. Leaving the plane in a blind, follow-the-leader fashion, Ross found the descent into darkness one of the worst trials he had yet faced. But he did not make too bad a landing in the small parklike expanse they had chosen for their target.

Ross pulled loose his harness and chute, dragging them to what he judged to be the center of the clearing. Hearing a plaintive bray from the air, he dodged as one of the two burden asses sent to join them landed and began to kick at its trappings. The animals they had chosen were the most docile available and they had been given sedation before the jump so that now, feeling Ross's hands, the donkey stood quietly while Ross stripped it of its hanging straps.

"Rossa—" The sound of his Beaker name called through the dark brought Ross facing in the other direction.

"Here, and I have one of the donkeys."

"And I the other!" That was McNeil.

Their eyes adjusted to a gloom which was not as thick as it would be in the forest and they worked fast. Then they dragged the parachutes together in a heap. The rain would, Webb had assured them, add to the rapid destruction wrought by the chemical he had provided. Ashe shook it over the pile, and there was a faint greenish glow. Then they moved away to the woodland and made camp for the balance of the night.

So much of their whole exploit depended upon luck, and this small part had been successful. Unless some agent had been stationed to watch for their arrival Ross believed they could not be spotted.

The rest of their plan was elastic. Posing as traders who had come to open a new station, they were to stay near a river which drained a lake and then angled southward to the distant sea. They knew this section was only sparsely settled by small tribes, hardly larger than family clans. These people were generations behind the civilized level of the villagers of Britain—roving hunters who followed the sweep of game north or south with the seasons.

Along the seashore the fishermen had established more permanent holdings which were slowly becoming towns. There were perhaps a few hardy pioneer farmers on the southern fringes of the district, but the principle reason traders came to this region was to get amber and furs. The Beaker people dealt in both.

Now as the three sheltered under the wide branches of a towering pine Ashe fumbled with a pack and brought out the "beaker" which was the identifying mark of his adopted people. He measured into it a portion of the sour, stimulating drink which the traders introduced wherever they went. The cup passed from hand to hand, its taste unpleasant on the tongue, but comfortingly warm to one's middle.

They took turns keeping the watch until the gray of false dawn became the clearer light of morning. After breakfasting on flat cakes of meal, they packed the donkeys, using the same knots and cross lashing which were the mark of real Beaker traders. Their bows protected from dampness under their cloaks, they set out to find the river and their path southward.

Ashe led, Ross towed the donkeys, and McNeil brought up the rear. In the absence of a path they had to set a ragged course, keeping to the edge of the clearing until they saw the end of the lake.

"Woodsmoke," Ashe commented when they had completed two thirds of their journey. Ross sniffed and was able to smell it too. Nodding to Ashe, McNeil oozed into nothingness between the trees with an ease Murdock envied. As they waited for him to return, Ross became conscious of another life about them, one busy with its own concerns, which were in no way those of human beings, except that food and perhaps shelter were to be reckoned among them.

In Britain, Ross had known there were others of his kind about, but this was different. Here, he could have believed it if he had been told he was the first man to walk this way.

A squirrel ran out on a tree limb and surveyed the two men with curious beady eyes, then clung head down on the tree trunk to see them better. One of the donkeys tossed its head, and the squirrel was gone with a flirt of its tail. Although it was quiet, there was a hum underneath the surface which Ross tried to analyze, to identify the many small sounds which went into its making.

Perhaps because he was trying so hard, he noted the faint noise. His hand touched Ashe's arm and a slight movement of his head indicated the direction of the sound. Then, as fluidly as he had melted into the woods, McNeil returned. "Company," he said in a soft voice.

"What kind?"

"Tribesmen, but wilder than any I've seen, even on the tapes. We are certainly out on the fringes now. These people look about cave level. I don't think they've ever heard of traders."

"How many?"

"Three, maybe four families. Most of the males must be out hunting, but there're about ten children and six or seven women. I don't think they've had good luck lately by the look of them."

"Maybe their luck and ours are going to turn together," Ashe said, motioning Ross forward with the donkeys. "We will circle about them to the river and then try bartering later. But I do want to establish contact."

CHAPTER 9

"Not to be too hopeful—" McNeil rubbed his arm across his hot face—"so far, so good." After kicking from his path some of the branches Ross had lopped from the trees they had been felling, he went to help his companion roll another small log up to a shelter which was no longer temporary. If there had been any eyes other than the woodland hunters' to spy upon them, they would have seen only the usual procedure of the Beaker traders, busily constructing one of their posts.

That they were being watched by the hunters, all three were certain. That there might be other spies in the forest, they had to assume for their own safety. They might prowl at night, but in the daytime all of the time agents kept within the bounds of the roles they were acting.

Barter with the head men of the hunting clan had brought those shy people into the camp of the strangers who had such wonders to exchange for tanned deer hides and better furs. The news of the traders' arrival spread quickly during the short time they had been here, so that two other clans had sent men to watch the proceedings.

With the trade came news which the agents sifted and studied. Each of them had a list of questions to insert into their conversations with the tribesmen if and when that was possible. Although they did not share a common speech with the forest men, signs were informative and certain nouns could be quickly learned. In the meantime Ashe became friendly with the nearest and first of the clan groups they discovered, going hunting with the men as an excuse to penetrate the unknown section they must quarter in their search for the Red base.

Ross drank river water and mopped his own hot face. "If the Reds aren't traders," he mused aloud, "what *is* their cover?"

McNeil shrugged. "A hunting tribe—fishermen—"

"Where would they get the women and children?"

"The same way they get their men—recruit them in our own time. Or in the way lots of tribes grew during periods of stress."

Ross set down the water jug. "You mean, kill off the men, take over their families?" This was a cold-bloodedness he found sickening. Although he had always prided himself on his toughness, several times during his training at the project he had been confronted by things which shook his belief in his own strong stomach and nerve.

"It has been done," McNeil remarked bleakly, "hundreds of times by invaders. In this setup—small family clans, widely scattered—that move would be very easy."

"They would have to pose as farmers, not hunters," Ross pointed out. "They couldn't move a base around with them."

"All right, so they set up a farming village. Oh, I see what you mean—there isn't any village around here. Yet they are here, maybe underground."

How right their guesses were they learned that night when Ashe returned, a deer's haunch on his shoulder. Ross knew him well enough by now to sense his preoccupation. "You found something?"

"A new set of ghosts," Ashe replied with a strange little smile.

"Ghosts!" McNeil pounced upon that. "The Reds like to play the supernatural angle, don't they? First the voice of Lurgha and now ghosts. What do these ghosts do?"

"They inhabit a bit of mountainous territory southeast of here, a stretch strictly taboo for all hunters. We were following a bison track until the beast headed for the ghost country. Then Ulffa called us off in a hurry. It seems that the hunter who goes in there after his quarry never reappears, or if he does, it's in a damaged condition, blown upon by ghosts and burned to death! That's one point."

He sat down by the fire and stretched his arms wearily. "The second is a little more disturbing for us. A Beaker camp about twenty miles south of here, as far as I can judge, was exterminated just a week ago. The message was passed to me because I was thought to be a kinsman of the slain—"

McNeil sat up. "Done because they were hunting us?"

"Might well be. On the other hand, the affair may have been just one of general precaution."

"The ghosts did it?" Ross wanted to know.

"I asked that. No, it seems that strange tribesmen overran it at night."

"At night?" McNeil whistled.

"Just so." Ashe's tone was dry. "The tribes do not fight that way. Either someone slipped up in his briefing, or the Reds are overconfident and don't care about the rules. But it was the work of tribesmen, or their counterfeits. There is also a nasty rumor speeding about that the ghosts do not relish traders and that they might protest intrusions of such with penalties all around—"

"Like the Wrath of Lurgha," supplied Ross.

"There is a certain repetition in this which suggests a lot to the suspicious mind," Ashe agreed.

"I'd say no more hunting expeditions for the present," McNeil said. "It is too easy to mistake a friend for a deer and weep over his grave afterward."

"That is a thought which entered my mind several times this afternoon," Ashe agreed. "These people are deceptively simple on the surface, but their minds do not work along the same patterns as ours. We try to outwit them, but it takes only one slip to make it fatal. In the meantime, I think we'd better make this place a little more snug, and it might be well to post sentries as unobtrusively as possible."

"How about faking some signs of a ruined camp and heading into the blue ourselves?" McNeil asked. "We could strike for the ghost mountains, traveling by night, and Ulffa's crowd would think we were finished off."

"An idea to keep in mind. The point against it would be the missing bodies. It seems that the tribesmen who raided the Beaker camp left some very distasteful evidence of what happened to the camp's personnel. And those we can't produce to cover our trail."

McNeil was not yet convinced. "We might be able to fake something along that line, too—"

"We may have to fake nothing," Ross cut in softly. He was standing close to the edge of the clearing where they were building their hut, his hand on one of the saplings in the palisade they had set up so laboriously that day. Ashe was beside him in an instant.

"What is it?"

Ross's hours of listening to the sounds of the wilderness were his measuring gauge now. "That bird has never called from inland before. It is the blue one we've seen fishing for frogs along the river."

Ashe, not even glancing at the forest, went for the water jug. "Get your trail supplies," he ordered.

Their leather pouches which held enough iron rations to keep them going were always at hand. McNeil gathered them from behind the fur curtain fronting their half-finished cabin. Again the bird called, its cry piercing and covering a long distance. Ross could understand why a careless man would select it for the signal. He crossed the clearing to the donkeys' shelter, slashing through their nose halters. Probably the patient little beasts would swiftly fall victims to some forest prowlers, but at least they would have their chance to escape.

McNeil, his cloak slung about him to conceal the ration bags, picked up the leather bucket as if he were merely going down to the river for water, and came to join Ross. They believed that they were carrying it off well, that the camp must appear normal to any lurkers in the woods. But either they had made some slip or the enemy was impatient. An arrow sped out of the night to flash across the fire, and Ashe escaped death only because he had leaned forward to feed the flames. His arm swung out and sent the water in the jar hissing onto the blaze as he himself rolled in the other direction.

Ross plunged for the brush with McNeil. Lying flat on the half-frozen ground, they started to work their way to the river bank where the open area would make surprise less possible.

"Ashe?" he whispered and felt McNeil's warm breath on his cheek as he replied:

"He'll make it the other way! He's the best we have for this sort of job."

They made a worm's progress, twice lying, with dagger in hand, while they listened to a faint rustle which betrayed the passing of one of the attackers. Both times Ross was tempted to rise and try to cut off the stranger, but he fought down the impulse. He had learned a control of himself that would have been impossible for him a few months earlier.

The glimmer of the river was pale through the clumps of bushes which sometimes grew into the flood. In this country winter still clung tenaciously in shadowy places with cups of leftover snow, and there was a bite in the wind and water. Ross rose to his knees with an involuntary gasp as a scream cut through the night. He wrenched around toward the camp, only to feel McNeil's hand clamp on his forearm.

"That was a donkey," whispered McNeil urgently. "Come on, let's go down to that ford we discovered!"

They turned south, daring now to trot, half bent to the ground. The river was swollen with spring floods which were only now beginning to subside, but two days earlier they had noticed a sandbar at one spot. By crossing that shelf across the bed, they might hope to put water between them and the unknown enemy tonight. It would give them a breathing space, even though Ross privately shrank from the thought of plowing into the stream.

He had seen good-sized trees swirling along in the current only yesterday. And to make such a dash in the dark....

From McNeil's throat burst a startling sound which Ross had last heard in Britain—the questing howl of a hunting wolf. The cry was answered seconds later from downstream.

"Ashe!"

They worked their way along the edge of the water with continued care, until they came upon Ashe at last, so much a part of his background that Ross started when the lump he had taken for a bush hunched forward to join them. Together they made the river crossing and turned south again to head for the mountains. It was then that disaster struck.

Ross heard no birdcall warning this time. Though he was on guard, he never sensed the approach of the man who struck him down from behind. One moment he had been trailing McNeil and Ashe; the next moment was black nothingness.

He was aware of a throb of pain which carried throughout his body and then localized in his head. Forcing open his eyes, the dazzle of light was like a spear point striking directly into his head, intensifying his pain to agony. He brought his hand up to his face and felt stickiness there.

"Assha—" He believed he called that aloud, but he did not even hear his own voice. They were in a valley; a wolf had attacked him out of the bushes. Wolf? No, the wolf was dead, but then it came alive again to howl on a river bank.

Ross forced his eyes open once more, enduring the pain of beams he recognized as sunshine. He turned his head to avoid the glare. It was hard to focus, but he fought to steady himself. There was some reason why it was necessary to move, to get away. But away from what and where? When Ross tried to think he could only see muddled pictures which had no connection.

Then a moving object crossed his very narrow field of vision, passing between him and a thing he knew was a tree trunk. A four-footed creature with a red tongue hanging from its jaws. It came toward him stiff-legged, growling low in its throat, and sniffed at his body before barking in short excited bursts of sound.

The noise hurt his head so much that Ross closed his eyes. Then a shock of icy liquid thrown into his face aroused him to make a feeble protest and he saw, hanging over him in a strange upside-down way, a bearded face which he knew from the past.

Hands were laid on him and the roughness with which he was moved sent Ross spiraling back into the dark once again. When he aroused for the second time it was night and the pain in his head was dulled. He put out his hands and discovered that he lay on a pile of fur robes, and was covered by one.

"Assha—" Again he tried that name. But it was not Assha who came in answer to his feeble call. The woman who knelt beside him with a horn cup in her hand had neatly braided hair in which gray strands showed silver by firelight. Ross knew he had seen her before, but again where and when eluded him. She slipped a sturdy arm under his head and raised him while the world whirled about. The edge of the horn cup was pressed to his lips, and he drank bitter stuff which burned in his throat and lit a fire in his insides. Then he was left to himself once again and in spite of his pain and bewilderment he slept.

How many days he lay in the camp of Ulffa, tended by the chief's head wife, Ross found it hard to reckon. It was Frigga who had argued the tribe into caring for a man they believed almost dead when they found him, and who nursed Ross back to life with knowledge acquired through half a hundred exchanges between those wise women who were the doctors and priestesses of these roaming peoples.

Why Frigga had bothered with the injured stranger at all Ross learned when he was able to sit up and marshal his bewildered thoughts into some sort of order. The matriarch of the tribe thirsted for knowledge. That same urge which had led her to certain experiments with herbs, had made her consider Ross a challenge to her healing skill. When she knew that he would live she determined to learn from him all he had to give.

Ulffa and the men of the tribe might have eyed the metal weapons of the traders with awe and avid desire, but Frigga wanted more than trade goods. She wanted the secret of the making of such cloth as the strangers wore, everything she could learn of their lives and the lands through which they had come. She plied Ross with endless questions which he answered as best he could, for he lay in an odd dreamy state where only the present had any reality. The past was dim and far away, and while he was now and then dimly aware that he had something to do, he forgot it easily.

The chief and his men prowled the half-built station after the attackers had withdrawn, bringing back with them a handful of loot—a bronze razor, two skinning knives, some fishhooks, a length of cloth which Frigga appropriated. Ross eyed this spoil indifferently, making no claim upon it. His interest in everything about him was often blanked out by headaches which kept him limp on his bed, uncaring and stupid for hours or even full days.

He gathered that the tribe had been living in fear of an attack from the same raiders who had wiped out the trading post. But at last their scouts returned with the information that the enemy had gone south.

There was one change of which Ross was not aware but which might have startled both Ashe and McNeil. Ross Murdock had indeed died under that blow which had left him unconscious beside the river. The young man whom Frigga had drawn back to sense and a slow recovery was Rossa of the Beaker people. This same Rossa nursed a hot desire for vengeance against those who had struck him down and captured his kinsmen, a feeling which the family tribe who had rescued him could well understand.

There was the same old urgency pushing him to try his strength now, to keep to his feet even when they were unsteady. His bow was gone, but Ross spent hours fashioning another, and he traded his copper bracelet for the best dozen arrows in Ulffa's camp. The jet pin from his cloak he presented to Frigga with all his gratitude.

Now that his strength was coming back he could not rest easy in the camp. He was ready to leave, even though the gashes on his head were still tender to the touch. Ulffa indulgently planned a hunt southward, and Rossa took the trail with the tribesmen.

He broke with the clan hunters when they turned aside at the beginning of the taboo land. Ross, his own mind submerged and taken over by his Beaker cover, hesitated too. Yet he could not give up, and the others left him there, his eyes on the forbidden heights, unhappy and tormented by more than the headaches which still came and went with painful regularity. In the mountains lay what he sought—a hidden something within his brain told him that over and over—but the mountains were taboo, and he should not venture into them.

How long he might have hesitated there if he had not come upon the trail, Ross did not know. But on the day after the hunters of Ulffa's clan left, a glint of sunlight striking between two trees pointed out a woodsman's blaze on a third tree trunk. The two halves of Ross's memory clicked together for an instant as he examined that cut. He knew that it marked a trace and he pushed on, hunting a second cut and then a third. Convinced that these would lead him into the unknown territory, Ross's desire to explore overcame the grafted superstitions of his briefing.

There were other signs that this was an often-traveled route: a spring cleared of leaves and walled with stone, a couple of steps cut in the turf on a steep slope. Ross moved warily, alert to any sound. He might not be an expert woodsman, but he was learning fast, perhaps the faster because his false memories now supplanted the real ones.

That night he built no fire, crawling instead into the heart of a rotted log to sleep, awakening once to the call of a wolf and another time at the distant crash of a dead tree yielding to wind.

In the morning he was about to climb back to the trail he had prudently left the night before when he saw five bearded, fur-clad men looking much the same as Ulffa's people. Ross hugged the earth and watched them pass out of sight before he followed.

All that day he wove an up-and-down trail behind the small band, sometimes catching sight of them as they topped a rise well ahead or stopped to eat. It was late afternoon when he crept cautiously to the top of a ridge and gazed down into a valley.

There was a town in that valley, sturdy houses of logs behind a stockade. He had seen towns vaguely like it before, yet it had a dreamlike quality as if it were not as real as it appeared.

Ross rested his chin on his arms and watched that town and the people moving in it. Some were fur-clad hunters, but others dressed quite differently. He started up with a little cry at the sight of one of the men who had walked so swiftly from one house to the next; surely he was a Beaker trader!

His unease grew stronger with every moment he watched, but it was the oddness he sensed in that town which bothered him and not any warning that he, himself, was in danger. He had gotten to his knees to see better when out of nowhere a rope sang through the air, settling about his chest with a vicious jerk which not only drove the air from his lungs but pinioned his arms tight to his body.

CHAPTER 10

Having been cuffed and battered into submission more quickly than would have been possible three weeks earlier, Murdock now stood sullenly surveying the man who, though he dressed like a Beaker trader, persisted in using a language Ross did not know.

"We do not play as children here." At last the man spoke words Ross could understand. "You will answer me or else others shall ask the questions, and less gently. I say to you now—who are you and from where do you come?"

For a moment Ross glowered across the table at him, his inbred antagonism to authority aroused by that contemptuous demand, but then common sense cautioned. His initial introduction to this village had left him bruised and with one of his headaches. There was no reason to let them beat him until he was in no shape to make a break for freedom when and if there was an opportunity.

"I am Rossa of the traders," he returned, eying the man with a carefully measured stare. "I came into this land in search of my kinsmen who were taken by raiders in the night."

The man, who sat on a stool by the table, smiled slowly. Again he spoke in the strange tongue, and Ross merely stared stolidly back. His words were short and explosive sounding, and the man's smile faded; his annoyance grew as he continued to speak.

One of Ross's two guards ventured to interrupt, using the Beaker language. "From where did you come?" He was a quiet-faced, slender man, not like his companion, who had roped Murdock from behind and was of the bully breed, able to subdue Ross's wildcat resistance in a very short struggle.

"I came to this land from the south," Ross answered, "after the manner of my people. This is a new land with furs and the golden tears of the sun to be gathered and bartered. The traders move in peace, and their hands are raised against no man. Yet in the darkness there came those who would slay without profit, for what reason I have no knowing."

The quiet man continued the questioning and Ross answered fully with details of the past of one Rossa, a Beaker merchant. Yes, he was from the south. His father was Gurdi, who had a trading post in the warm lands along the big river. This was Rossa's first trip to open new territory. He had come with his father's blood brother, Assha, who was a noted far voyager, and it was an honor to be chosen as donkey-leader for such a one as Assha. With Assha had been Macna, one who was also a far trader, though not as noted as Assha.

Of a certainty, Assha was of his own race! Ross blinked at that question. One need only to look upon him to know that he was of trader blood and no uncivilized woodsrunner. How long had he known Assha? Ross shrugged. Assha had come to his father's post the winter before and had stayed with them through the cold season. Gurdi and Assha had mingled blood after he pulled Gurdi free from the river in flood. Assha had lost his boat and trade goods in that rescue, so Gurdi had made good his loss this year. Detail by detail he gave the story. In spite of the fact that he provided these details glibly, sure that they were true, Ross continued to be haunted by an odd feeling that he was indeed reciting a tale of adventure which had happened long ago and to someone else. Perhaps that pain in his head made him think of these events as very colorless and far away.

"It would seem"—the quiet man turned to the one behind the table—"that this is indeed one Rossa, a Beaker trader."

But the man looked impatient, angry. He made a sign to the other guard, who turned Ross around roughly and sent him toward the door with a shove. Once again the leader gave an order in his own language, adding a few words more with a stinging snap that might have been a threat or a warning.

Ross was thrust into a small room with a hard floor and not even a skin rug to serve as a bed. Since the quiet man had ordered the removal of the ropes from Ross's arms, he leaned against the wall, rubbing the pain of returning circulation away from his wrists and trying to understand what had happened to him and where he was. Having spied upon it from the heights, he knew it wasn't an ordinary trading station, and he wanted to know what they did here. Also, somewhere in this village he hoped to find Assha and Macna.

At the end of the day his captors opened the door only long enough to push inside a bowl and a small jug. He felt for those in the dusk, dipping his fingers into a lukewarm mush of meal and drinking the water from the jug avidly. His headache dulled, and from experience Ross knew that this bout was almost over. If he slept, he would waken with a clearer mind and no pain. Knowing he was very tired, he took the precaution of curling up directly in front of the door so that no one could enter without arousing him.

It was still dark when he awoke with a curious urgency remaining from a dream he could not remember. Ross sat up, flexing his arms and shoulders to combat the stiffness which had come with his cramped sleep. He could not rid himself of a feeling that there was something to be done and that time was his enemy.

Assha! Gratefully he seized on that. He must find Assha and Macna, for the three of them could surely discover a way to get out of this village. That was what was so important!

He had been handled none too gently, and they were holding him a prisoner. But Ross believed that this was not the worst which could happen to him here, and he must be free before the worst did come. The question was, How could he escape? His bow and dagger were gone, and he did not even have his long cloak pin for a weapon, since he had given that to Frigga.

Running his hands over his body, Ross inventoried what remained of his clothing and possessions. He unfastened the bronze chain-belt still buckled in his kilt tunic, swinging the length speculatively in one hand. A masterpiece of craftsmanship, it consisted of patterned plates linked together with a series of five finely wrought chains and a front buckle in the form of a lion's head, its protruding tongue serving as a hook to support a dagger sheath. Its weight promised a weapon of sorts, which when added to the element of surprise might free him.

By rights they would be expecting him to produce some opposition, however. It was well known that only the best fighters, the shrewdest minds, followed the traders' roads. It was a proud thing to be a trader in the wilderness, a thought that warmed Ross now as he waited in the dark for what luck and Ba-Bal of the Bright Horns would send. Were he ever to return to Gurdi's post, Ba-Bal, whose boat rode across the sky from dawn to dusk, would have a fine ox, jars of the first brewing, and sweet-smelling amber laid upon his altar.

Ross had patience which he had learned from the mixed heritage of his two pasts, the real and the false graft. He could wait as he had waited many times before—quiet, and with outward ease—for the right moment to come. It came now with footsteps ringing sharply, halting before his cell door.

With the noiseless speed of a hunting cat, Ross flung himself from behind the door to a wall, where he would be hidden from the newcomer for that necessary instant or two. If his attack was to be successful, it must occur inside the room. He heard the sound of a bar being slid out of its brackets, and he poised himself, the belt rippling from his right hand.

The door was opening inward, and a man stood silhouetted against the outer light. He muttered, looking toward the corner where Ross had thrown his single garment in a roll which might just resemble, for the needed second or two, a man curled in slumber. The man in the doorway took the bait, coming forward far enough for Ross to send the door slamming shut as he himself sprang with the belt aimed for the other's head.

There was a startled cry, cut off in the middle as the belt plates met flesh and bone in a crushing force. Luck was with him! Ross caught up his kilt and belted it around him after he had made a hurried examination of the body now lying at his feet. He was not sure that the man was dead, but at any rate he was completely unconscious. Ross stripped off the man's cloak, located his dagger, freed it from the belt hook, and snapped it on his own.

Then inch by inch Ross edged open the door, peering through the crack. As far as he could see, the hall was empty, so he jerked the portal open, and dagger in hand, sprang out, ready for attack. He closed the door, slipping the bar back into its brackets. If the man inside revived and pounded for attention, his own friends might think it was Ross and delay investigating.

But the escape from the cell was the easiest part of what he planned to do, as Ross well knew. To find Assha and Macna in this maze of rooms occupied by the enemy was far more difficult. Although he had no idea in which of the village buildings they might be confined, this one was the largest and seemed to be the headquarters of the chief men, which meant it could also serve as their prison.

Light came from a torch in a bracket halfway down the hall. The wood burned smokily, giving off a resinous odor, and to Ross the glow was sufficient illumination. He slipped along as close to the wall as he could, ready to freeze at the slightest sound. But this portion of the building might well have been deserted, for he saw or heard no one. He tried the only two doors opening out of the hall, but they were secured on the other side.

Then he came to a bend in the corridor, and stopped short, hearing a murmur of low voices.

If he had used a hunter's tricks of silent tread and vigilant wariness before, Ross was doubly on guard now as he wriggled to a point from which he could see beyond that turn. Mere luck prevented him from giving himself away a moment later.

Assha! Assha, alive, well, apparently under no restraint, was just turning away from the same quiet man who had had a part in Ross's interrogation. That was surely Assha's brown hair, his slender wiry body draped with a Beaker's kilt. A familiar tilt of the head convinced Ross, though he could not see the man's face. The quiet man went down the hall, leaving Assha before a door. As he passed through it Ross sped forward and followed him inside.

Assha had crossed the bare room and was standing on a glowing plate in the floor. Ross, aroused to desperate action by some fear he did not understand, leaped after him. His left hand fell upon Assha's shoulder, turning the man half around as Ross, too, stepped upon the patch of luminescence.

Murdock had only an instant to realize that he was staring into the face of an astonished stranger. His hand flashed up in an edgewise blow which caught the other on the side of the throat, and then the world came apart about them. There was a churning, whirling sickness which griped and bent Ross almost double across the crumpled body of his victim. He held his head lest it be torn from his shoulders by the spinning thing which seemed based behind his eyes.

The sickness endured only for a moment, and some buried part of Ross's mind accepted it as a phenomenon he had experienced before. He came out of it gasping, to focus his attention once more on the man at his feet.

The stranger was still breathing. Ross stooped to drag him from the plate and began binding and gagging him with lengths torn from his kilt. Only when his captive was secure did he begin looking about him curiously.

The room was bare of any furnishings and now, as he glanced at the floor, Ross saw that the plate had lost its glow. The Beaker trader Rossa rubbed sweating palms on his kilt and thought fleetingly of forest ghosts and other mysteries. Not that the traders bowed to those ghosts which were the plague of lesser men and tribes, but anything which suddenly appeared and then disappeared without any logical explanation, needed thinking on.

Murdock pulled the prisoner, who was now reviving, to the far end of the room and then went back to the plate with the persistence of a man who refused to treat with ghosts and wanted something concrete to explain the unexplainable. Though he rubbed his hands across the smooth surface of the plate, it did not light up again.

His captive having writhed himself half out of the corner of the room, Ross debated the wisdom of another silencing—say a tap on the skull with the heavy hilt of his dagger. Deciding against it because he might need a guide, he freed the victim's ankle bonds and pulled him to his feet, holding the dagger ready where the man could see it. Were there any more surprises to be encountered in this place, Assha's double would test them first.

The door did not lead to the same corridor, or even the same kind of corridor Ross had passed through moments earlier. Instead they entered a short passage with walls of some smooth stuff which had almost the sheen of polished metal and were sleek and cold to the touch. In fact, the whole place was chill, chill as river water in the spring.

Still herding the prisoner before him, Ross came to the nearest door and looked within, to be faced by incomprehensible frames of metal rods and boxes. Rossa of the traders marveled and stared, but again, he realized that what he saw was not altogether strange. Part of one wall was a board on which small lights flashed and died, to flash again in winks of bright color. A mysterious object made of wire and disks hung across the back of a chair standing near-by.

The bound man lurched for the chair and fell, rolling toward the wall. Ross pushed him on until he was hidden behind one of the metal boxes. Then he made the rounds of the room, touching nothing, but studying what he could not understand. Puffs of warm air came in through grills near the floor, but the room had the same general chill as the hall outside.

Meanwhile the lights on the board had become more active, flashing on and off in complex patterns. Ross now heard a buzzing, as if a swarm of angry insects were gathered for an attack. Crouching beside his captive, Ross watched the lights, trying to discover the source of the sound.

The buzz grew shriller, almost demanding. Ross heard the tramp of heavy footgear in the corridor, and a man entered the room, crossing purposefully to the chair. He sat down and drew the wire-and-disk frame over his head. His hands moved under the lights, but Ross could not guess what he was doing.

The captive at Murdock's side tried to stir, but Ross's hand pinned him quiet. The shrill noise which had originally summoned the man at the lights was interrupted by a sharp pattern of long-and-short sounds, and his hands flew even more quickly while Ross took in every detail of the other's clothing and equipment. He was neither a shaggy tribesman nor a trader. He wore a dull-green outer garment cut in one piece to cover his arms and legs as well as his body, and his hair was so short that his round skull might have been shaven. Ross rubbed the back of his wrist across his eyes, experiencing again that dim other memory. Odd as this man looked, Murdock had seen his like before somewhere, yet the background had not been Gurdi's post on the southern river. Where and when had he, Rossa, ever been with such strange beings? And why could he not remember it all more clearly?

Boots sounded once more in the hall, and another figure strode in. This one wore furs, but he, too, was no woods hunter, Ross realized as he studied the newcomer in detail. The loose overshirt of thick fur with its hood thrown back, the high boots, and all the rest were not of any primitive fashioning. And the man had four eyes! One pair were placed normally on either side of his nose, and the other two, black-rimmed and murky, were set above on his forehead.

The fur-clad man tapped the one seated at the board. He freed his head partially from the wire cage so that they could talk together in a strange language while lights continued to flash and the buzzing died away. Ross's captive wriggled with renewed vigor and at last thrashed free a foot to kick at one of the metal installations. The resulting clang brought both men around. The one at the board tore his head cage off as he jumped to his feet, while the other brought out a gun.

Gun? One little fraction of Ross's mind wondered at his recognition of that black thing and of the danger it promised, even as he prepared for battle. He pushed his captive across the path of the man in fur and threw himself in the other direction. There was a blast to make a torment in his head as he hurled toward the door.

So intent was Ross upon escape that he did not glance behind but skidded out on his hands and knees, thus fortunately presenting a poor target to the third man coming down the hall. Ross's shoulder hit the newcomer at thigh level, and they tangled in a struggling mass which saved Ross's life as the others burst out behind them.

Ross fought grimly, his hands and feet moving in blows he was not conscious of planning. His opponent was no easy match and at last Ross was flattened, in spite of his desperate efforts. He was whirled over, his arms jerked behind him, and cold metal rings snapped about his wrists. Then he was rolled back, to lie blinking up at his enemies.

All three men gathered over him, barking questions which he could not understand. One of them disappeared and returned with Ross's former captive, his mouth a straight line and a light in his eyes Ross understood far better than words.

"You are the trader prisoner?" The man who looked like Assha leaned over Murdock, patches of red on his tanned skin where the gag and wrist bonds had been.

"I am Rossa, son of Gurdi, of the traders," Ross returned, meeting what he read in the other's expression with a ready defiance. "I was a prisoner, yes. But you did not keep me one for long then, nor shall you now."

The man's thin upper lip lifted. "You have done yourself ill, my young friend. We have a better prison here for you, one from which you shall not escape."

He spoke to the other men, and there was the ring of an order in his voice. They pulled Ross to his feet, pushing him ahead of them. During the short march Ross used his eyes, noticing things he could not identify in the rooms through which they passed. Men called questions and at last they paused long enough, Ross firmly in the hold of the fur-clad guard, for the other two to put on similar garments.

Ross had lost his cloak in the fight, but no fur shirt was given him. He shivered more and more as the chill which clung to that warren of rooms and halls bit into his half-clad body. He was certain of only one thing about this place; he could not possibly be in the crude buildings of the valley village. However, he was unable to guess where he was and how he had come there.

Finally, they went down a narrow room filled with bulky metal objects of bright scarlet or violet that gleamed weirdly and were equipped with rods along which all the colors of the rainbow ringed. Here was a round door, and when one of the guards used both hands to tug it open, the cold that swept in at them was a frigid breath that burned as it touched bare skin.

CHAPTER 11

It took Ross a while to learn that the dirty-white walls of this tunnel which were almost entirely opaque, with dark objects showing dimly through them here and there, were of solid ice. A black wire was hooked overhead and at regular intervals hung with lights which did nothing to break the sensation of glacial cold about them.

Ross shuddered. Every breath he drew stung in his lungs; his bare shoulders and arms and the exposed section of thigh between kilt and boot were numb. He could only move on stiffly, pushed ahead by his guards when he faltered. He guessed that were he to lose his footing here and surrender to the cold, he would forfeit the battle entirely and with it his life.

He had no way of measuring the length of the boring through the solid ice, but they were at last fronted by another opening, a ragged one which might have been hacked with an ax. They emerged from it into the wildest scene Ross had ever seen. Of course, he was familiar with ice and snow, but here was a world surrendered completely to the brutal force of winter in a strange, abnormal way. It was a still, dead white-gray world in which nothing moved save the wind which curled the drifts.

His guards covered their eyes with the murky lenses they had worn pushed up on their foreheads within the shelter, for above them sunlight dazzled on the ice crest. Ross, his eyes smarting, kept his gaze centered on his feet. He was given no time to look about. A rope was produced, a loop of it flipped in a noose about his throat, and he was towed along like a leashed dog. Before them was a path worn in the snow, not only by the passing of booted feet, but with more deeply scored marks as if heavy objects had been sledded there. Ross slipped and stumbled in the ruts, fearing to fall lest he be dragged. The numbness of his body reached into his head. He was dizzy, the world about him misting over now and again with a haze which arose from the long stretches of unbroken snow fields.

Tripping in a rut, he went down upon one knee, his flesh too numbed now to feel the additional cold of the snow, snow so hard that its crust delivered a knife's cut. Unemotionally, he watched a thin line of red trickle in a sluggish drop or two down the blue skin of his leg. The rope jerked him forward, and Ross scrambled awkwardly until one of his captors hooked a fur mitten in his belt and heaved him to his feet once more.

The purpose of that trek through the snow was obscure to Ross. In fact, he no longer cared, save that a hard rebel core deep inside him would not let him give up as long as his legs could move and he had a scrap of conscious will left in him. It was more difficult to walk now. He skidded and went down twice more. Then, the last time he slipped, he sledded past the man who led him, sliding down the slope of a glass-slick slope. He lay at the foot, unable to get up. Through the haze and deadening blanket of the cold he knew that he was being pulled about, shaken, generally mishandled; but this time he could not respond. Someone snapped open the rings about his wrists.

There was a call, echoing eerily across the ice. The fumbling about his body changed to a tugging and once more he was sent rolling down the slope. But the rope was now gone from his throat, and his arms were free. This time when he brought up hard against an obstruction he was not followed.

Ross's conscious mind—that portion of him that was Rossa, the trader—was content to lie there, to yield to the lethargy born of the frigid world about him. But the subconscious Ross Murdock of the Project prodded at him. He had always had a certain cold hatred which could crystalize and become a spur. Once it had been hatred of circumstances and authority; now it became hatred for those who had led him into this wilderness with the purpose, as he knew now, of leaving him to freeze and die.

Ross pulled his hands under him. Though there was no feeling in them, they obeyed his will clumsily. He levered himself up and looked around. He lay in a narrow crevicelike cut, partly walled in by earth so frozen as to resemble steel. Crusted over it in long streaks from above were tongues of ice. To remain here was to serve his captors' purpose.

Ross inched his way to his feet. This opening, which was intended as his grave, was not so deep as the men had thought it in their hurry to be rid of him. He believed that he could climb out if he could make his body answer to his determination.

Somehow Ross made that supreme effort and came again to the rutted path from which they had tumbled him. Even if he could, there was no sense in going along that rutted trail, for it led back to the ice-encased building from which he had been brought. They had thrust him out to die; they would not take him in.

But a road so well marked must have some goal, and in hopes that he might find shelter at the other end, Ross turned to the left. The trace continued down the slope. Now the towering walls of ice and snow were broken by rocky teeth as if they had bitten deep upon this land, only to be gnawed in return. Rounding one of those rock fangs, Ross looked at a stretch of level ground. Snow lay here, but the beaten-down trail led straight through it to the rounded side of a huge globe half buried in the ground, a globe of dark material which could only be man-made.

Ross was past caution. He must get to warmth and shelter or he was done for, and he knew it. Wavering and weaving, he went on, his attention fixed on the door ahead—a closed oval door. With a sob of exhausted effort, Ross threw himself against it. The barrier gave, letting him fall forward into a queer glimmering radiance of bluish light.

The light rousing him because it promised more, he crawled on past another door which was flattened back against the inner wall. It was like making one's way down a tube. Ross paused, pressing his lifeless hands against his bare chest under the edge of his tunic, suddenly realizing that there was warmth here. His breath did not puff out in frosty streamers before him, nor did the air sear his lungs when he ventured to draw in more than shallow gulps.

With that realization a measure of animal caution returned to him. To remain where he was, just inside the entrance, was to court disaster. He must find a hiding place before he collapsed, for he sensed he was very near the end of his ability to struggle. Hope had given him a flash of false strength, the impetus to move, and he must make the most of that gift.

His path ended at a wide ladder, coiling in slow curves into gloom below and shadows above. He sensed that he was in a building of some size. He was afraid to go down, for even looking in that direction almost finished his sense of balance, so he climbed up.

Step by step, Ross made that painful journey, passing levels from which three or four hallways ran out like the radii of a spider's web. He was close to the end of his endurance when he heard a sound, echoed, magnified, from below. It was someone moving. He dragged his body into the fourth level where the light was very faint, hoping to crawl far enough into one of the passages to remain unseen from the stair. But he had gone only part-way down his chosen road when he collapsed, panting, and fell back against the wall. His hands pawed vainly against that sleek surface. He was falling through it!

Ross had a second, perhaps two, of stupefied wonder. Lying on a soft surface, he was enfolded by a warmth which eased his bruised and frozen body. There was a sharp prick in his thigh, another in his arm, and the world was a hazy dream until he finally slept in the depths of exhaustion.

There were dreams, detailed ones, and Ross stirred uneasily as his sleep thinned to waking. He lay with his eyes closed, fitting together odd bits of—dreams? No, he was certain that they were memories. Rossa of the Beaker traders and Ross Murdock of the project were again fused into one and the same person. How it had happened he did not know, but it was true.

Opening his eyes, he noticed a curved ceiling of soft blue which misted at the edges into gray. The restful color acted on his troubled, waking mind like a soothing word. For the first time since he had been struck down in the night his headache was gone. He raised his hand to explore that old hurt near his hairline that had been so tender only yesterday that it could not bear pressure. There remained only a thin, rough line like a long-healed scar, that was all.

Ross lifted his head to look about him. His body lay supported in a cradlelike arrangement of metal, almost entirely immersed in a red gelatinous substance with a clean, aromatic odor. Just as he was no longer cold, neither was he hungry. He felt as fit as he ever had in his life. Sitting up in the cradle, he stroked the jelly away from his shoulders and chest. It fell from him cleanly, leaving no trace of grease or dampness on his skin.

There were other fixtures in the small cylinderlike chamber besides that odd bed in which he had lain. Two bucket-shaped seats were placed at the narrow fore part of the room and before those seats was a system of controls he could not comprehend.

As Ross swung his feet to the floor there was a click from the side which brought him around, ready for trouble. But the noise had been caused by the opening of a door into a small cupboard. Inside the cupboard lay a fat package. Obviously this was an invitation to investigate the offering.

The package contained a much folded article of fabric, compressed and sealed in a transparent bag which he fumbled twice before he succeeded in releasing its fastening. Ross shook out a garment of material such as he had never seen before. Its sheen and satin-smooth surface suggested metal, but its stuff was as supple as fine silk. Color rippled across it with every twist and turn he gave to the length—dark blue fading to pale violet, accented with wavering streaks of vivid and startling green.

Ross experimented with a row of small, brilliant-green studs which made a transverse line from the right shoulder to the left hip, and they came apart. As he climbed into the suit the stuff modeled to his body in a tight but perfect fit. Across the shoulders were bands of green to match the studs, and the stockinglike tights were soled with a thick substance which formed a cushion for his feet.

He pressed the studs together, felt them lock, and then stood smoothing that strange, beautiful fabric, unable to account for either it or his surroundings. His head was clear; he could remember every detail of his flight up to the time he had fallen through the wall. And he was certain that he had passed through not only one, but two, of the Red time posts. Could this be the third? If so, was he still a captive? Why would they leave him to freeze in the open country one moment and then treat him this way later?

He could not connect the ice-encased building from which the Reds had taken him with this one. At the sound of another soft noise Ross glanced over his shoulder just in time to see the cradle of jelly, from which he had emerged, close in upon itself until its bulk was a third of its former size. Compact as a box, it folded up against the wall.

Ross, his cushioned feet making no sound, advanced to the bucket-chairs. But lowering his body into one of them for a better look at what vaguely resembled the control of a helicopter—like the one in which he had taken the first stage of his fantastic journey across space and time—he did not find it comfortable. He realized that it had not been constructed to accommodate a body shaped precisely like his own.

A body like his own.... That jelly bath or bed or whatever it was.... The clothing which adapted so skillfully to his measurements....

Ross leaned forward to study the devices on the control board, confirming his suspicions. He had made the final jump of them all! He was now in some building of that alien race upon whose existence Millaird and Kelgarries had staked the entire project. This was the source, or one of the sources, from which the Reds were getting the knowledge which fitted no modern pattern.

A world encased in ice and a building with strange machinery. This thing—a cylinder with a pilot's seat and a set of controls. Was it an alien place? But the jelly bath—and the rest of it.... Had his presence activated that cupboard to supply him with clothing? And what had become of the tunic he was wearing when he entered?

Ross got up to search the chamber. The bed-bath was folded against the wall, but there was no sign of his Beaker clothing, his belt, the hide boots. He could not understand his own state of well being, the lack of hunger and thirst.

There were two possible explanations for it all. One was that the aliens still lived here and for some reason had come to his aid. The other was that he stood in a place where robot machinery worked, though those who had set it up were no longer there. It was difficult to separate his memory of the half-buried globe he had seen from his sickness of that moment. Yet he knew that he had climbed and crawled through emptiness, neither seeing nor hearing any other life. Now Ross restlessly paced up and down, seeking the door through which he must have come, but there was not even a line to betray such an opening.

"I want out," he said aloud, standing in the center of the cramped room, his fists planted on his hips, his eyes still searching for the vanished door. He had tapped, he had pushed, he had tried every possible way to find it. If he could only remember how he had come in! But all he could recall was leaning against a wall which moved inward and allowed him to fall. But where had he fallen? Into that jelly bath?

Ross, stung by a sudden idea, glanced at the ceiling. It was low enough so that by standing on tiptoes he could drum his fingers on its surface. Now he moved to the place directly above where the cradle had swung before it had folded itself away.

Rapping and poking, his efforts were rewarded at last. The blue curve gave under his assault. He pushed now, rising on his toes, though in that position he could exert little pressure. Then as if some faulty catch had been released, the ceiling swung up so that he lost his footing and would have fallen had he not caught the back of one of the bucket-seats.

He jumped and by hooking his hands over the edge of the opening, was able to work his way up and out, to face a small line of light. His fingers worked at that, and he opened a second door, entering a familiar corridor.

Holding the door open, Ross looked back, his eyes widening at what he saw. For it was plain now that he had just climbed out of a machine with the unmistakable outline of a snub-nosed rocket. The small flyer—or a jet, or whatever it was—had been fitted into a pocket in the side of the big structure as a ship into a berth, and it must have been set there to shoot from that enclosing chamber as a bullet is shot from a rifle barrel. But why?

Ross's imagination jumped from fact to theory. The torpedo craft could be an atomic jet. All right, he had been in bad shape when he fell into it by chance and the bed machine had caught him as if it had been created for just such a duty. What kind of a small plane would be equipped with a restorative apparatus? Only one intended to handle emergencies, to transport badly injured living things who had to leave the building in a hurry.

In other words, a lifeboat!

But why would a building need a lifeboat? That would be rather standard equipment for a ship. Ross stepped into the corridor and stared about him with open and incredulous wonder. Could this be some form of ship, grounded here, deserted and derelict, and now being plundered by the Reds? The facts fitted! They fitted so well with all he had been able to discover that Ross was sure it was true. But he determined to prove it beyond all doubt.

He closed the door leading to the lifeboat berth, but not so securely that he could not open it again. That was too good a hiding place. On his cushioned feet he padded back to the stairway, and he stood there listening. Far below were sounds, a rasp of metal against metal, a low murmur of muted voices. But from above there was nothing, so he would explore above before he ventured into that other danger zone.

Ross climbed, passing two more levels, to come out into a vast room with a curving roof which must fill the whole crown of the globe. Here was such a wealth of machines, controls, things he could not understand that he stood bewildered, content for the moment merely to look. There were—he counted slowly—five control boards like those he had seen in the small escape ship. Each of these was faced by two or three of the bucket-seats, only these swung in webbing. He put his hand on one, and it bobbed elastically.

The control boards were so complicated that the one in the lifeboat might have been a child's toy in comparison. The air in the ship had been good; in the lifeboat it had held the pleasant odor of the jelly; but here Ross sniffed a faint but persistent hint of corruption, of an old malodor.

He left the vantage point by the stairs and paced between the control boards and their empty swinging seats. This was the main control room, of that he was certain. From this point all the vast bulk beneath him had been set in motion, sailed here and there. Had it been on the sea, or through the air? The globe shape suggested an air-borne craft. But a civilization so advanced as this would surely have left some remains. Ross was willing to believe that he could be much farther back in time than 2000 B.C., but he was still sure that traces of those who could build a thing like this would have existed in the twentieth century A.D.

Maybe that was how the Reds had found this. Something they had turned up within their country—say, in Siberia, or some of the forgotten corners of Asia—had been a clue.

Having had little schooling other than the intensive cramming at the base and his own informal education, the idea of the race who had created this ship overawed Ross more than he would admit. If the project could find this, turn loose on it the guys who knew about such things.... But that was just what they were striving for, and he was the only project man to have found the prize. Somehow, someway, he had to get back—out of this half-buried ship and its icebound world—back to where he could find his own people. Perhaps the job was impossible, but he had to try. His survival was considered impossible by the men who had thrown him into the crevice, but here he was. Thanks to the men who had built this ship, he was alive and well.

Ross sat down in one of the uncomfortable seats to think and thus avoided immediate disaster, for he was hidden from the stairs on which sounded the tap of boots. A climber, maybe two, were on their way up, and there was no other exit from the control cabin.

CHAPTER 12

Ross dropped from the web-slung chair to the floor and made himself as small as possible under the platform at the front of the cabin. Here, where there was a smaller control board and two seats placed closely together, the odd, unpleasant odor clung and became stronger to Ross's senses as he waited tensely for the climbers to appear. Though he had searched, there was nothing in sight even faintly resembling a weapon. In a last desperate bid for freedom he crept back to the stairwell.

He had been taught a blow during his training period, one which required a precise delivery and, he had been warned, was often fatal. He would use it now. The climber was very close. A cropped head arose through the floor opening, and Ross struck, knowing as his hand chopped against the folds of a fur hood that he had failed.

But the impetus of that unexpected blow saved him after all. With a choked cry the man disappeared, crashing down upon the one following him. A scream and shouts were heard from below, and a shot ripped up the well as Ross scrambled away from it. He might have delayed the final battle, but they had him cornered. He faced that fact bleakly. They need only sit below and let nature take its course. His session in the lifeboat had restored his strength, but a man could not live forever without food and water.

However, he had bought himself perhaps a yard of time which must be put to work. Turning to examine the seats, Ross discovered that they could be unhooked from their webbing swings. Freeing all of them, he dragged their weight to the stairwell and jammed them together to make a barricade. It could not hold long against any determined push from below, but, he hoped, it would deflect bullets if some sharpshooter tried to wing him by ricochet. Every so often there was the crash of a shot and some shouting, but Ross was not going to be drawn out of cover by that.

He paced around the control cabin, still hunting for a weapon. The symbols on the levers and buttons were meaningless to him. They made him feel frustrated because he imagined that among that countless array were some that might help him out of the trap if he could only guess their use.

Once more he stood by the platform thinking. This was the point from which the ship had been sailed—in the air or on some now frozen sea. These control boards must have given the ship's master the means not only of propelling the vast bulk, but of unloading and loading cargo, lighting, heating, ventilation, and perhaps defense! Of course, every control might be dead now, but he remembered that in the lifeboat the machines had worked successfully, fulfilled expertly the duty for which they had been constructed.

The only step remaining was to try his luck. Having made his decision, Ross simply shut his eyes as he had in a very short and almost forgotten childhood, turned around three times, and pointed. Then he looked to see where luck had directed him.

His finger indicated a board before which there had been three seats, and he crossed to it slowly, with a sense that once he touched the controls he might inaugurate a chain of events he could not stop. The crash of a shot underlined the fact that he had no other recourse.

Since the symbols meant nothing, Ross concentrated on the shapes of the various devices and chose one which vaguely resembled the type of light switch he had always known. Since it was up, he pressed it down, counting to twenty slowly as he waited for a reaction. Below the switch was an oval button marked with two wiggles and a double dot in red. Ross snapped it level with the panel, and when it did not snap back, he felt somehow encouraged. When the two levers flanking that button did not push in or move up and down, Ross pulled them out without even waiting to count off.

This time he had results! A crackling of noise with a singsong rhythm, the volume of which, low at first, arose to a drone filled the cabin. Ross, deafened by the din, twisted first one lever and then the other until he had brought the sound to a less piercing howl. But he needed action, not just noise; he moved from behind the first chair to the next one. Here were five oval buttons, marked in the same vivid green as that which trimmed his clothing—two wiggles, a dot, a double bar, a pair of entwined circles, and a crosshatch.

Why make a choice? Recklessness bubbled to the surface, and Ross pushed all the buttons in rapid succession. The results were, in a measure, spectacular. Out of the top of the control board rose a triangle of screen which steadied and stood firm while across it played a rippling wave of color. Meanwhile the singsong became an angry squawking as if in protest.

Well, he had something, even if he didn't know what it was! And he had also proved that the ship was alive. However, Ross wanted more than a squawk of exasperation, which was exactly what the noise had become. It almost sounded, Ross decided as he listened, as if he were being expertly chewed out in another language. Yes, he wanted more than a series of squawks and a fanciful display of light waves on a screen.

At the section of board before the third and last seat there was less choice—only two switches. As Ross flicked up the first the pattern on the screen dwindled into a brown color shot with cream in which there was a suggestion of a picture. Suppose one didn't put the switch all the way up? Ross examined the slot in which the bar moved and now noted a series of tiny point marks along it. Selective? It would not do any harm to see. First he hurried back to the cork of chairs he had jammed into the stairwell. The squawks were now coming only at intervals, and Ross could hear nothing to suggest that his barrier was being forced.

He returned to the lever and moved it back two notches, standing open-mouthed at the immediate result. The cream-and-brown streaks were making a picture! Moving another notch down caused the picture to skitter back and forth on the screen. With memories of TV tuning to guide him, Ross brought the other lever down to a matching position, and the dim and shadowy images leaped into clear and complete focus. But the color was still brown, not the black and white he had expected.

Only, he was also looking into a face! Ross swallowed, his hand grasping one of the strings of chair webbing for support. Perhaps because in some ways it did resemble his own, that face was more preposterously nonhuman. The visage on the screen was sharply triangular with a small, sharply pointed chin and a jaw line running at an angle from a broad upper face. The skin was dark, covered largely with a soft and silky down, out of which hooked a curved and shining nose set between two large round eyes. On top of that astonishing head the down rose to a peak not unlike a cockatoo's crest. Yet there was no mistaking the intelligence in those eyes, nor the other's amazement at sight of Ross. They might have been staring at each other through a window.

Squawk ... squeek ... squawk.... The creature in the mirror—on the vision plate—or outside the window—moved its absurdly small mouth in time to those sounds. Ross swallowed again and automatically made answer.

"Hello." His voice was a weak whistle, and perhaps it did not reach the furry-faced one, for he continued his questions if questions they were. Meanwhile Ross, over his first stupefaction, tried to see something of the creature's background. Though the objects were slightly out of focus, he was sure he recognized fittings similar to those about him. He must be in communication with another ship of the same type and one which was not deserted!

Furry-face had turned his head away to squawk rapidly over his shoulder, a shoulder which was crossed by a belt or sash with an elaborate pattern. Then he got up from his seat and stood aside to make room for the one he had summoned.

If Furry-face had been a startling surprise, Ross was now to have another. The man who now faced him on the screen was totally different. His skin registered as pale—cream-colored—and his face was far more human in shape, though it was hairless as was the smooth dome of his skull. When one became accustomed to that egg slickness, the stranger was not bad-looking, and he was wearing a suit which matched the one Ross had taken from the lifeboat.

This one did not attempt to say anything. Instead, he stared at Ross long and measuringly, his eyes growing colder and less friendly with every second of that examination. Ross had resented Kelgarries back at the project, but the major could not match Baldy for the sheer weight of unpleasant warning he could pack into a look. Ross might have been startled by Furry-face, but now his stubborn streak arose to meet this implied challenge. He found himself breathing hard and glaring back with an intensity which he hoped would get across and prove to Baldy that he would not have everything his own way if he proposed to tangle with Ross.

His preoccupation with the stranger on the screen betrayed Ross into the hands of those from below. He heard their attack on the barricade too late. By the time he turned around, the cork of seats was heaved up and a gun was pointing at his middle. His hands went up in small reluctant jerks as that threat held him where he was. Two of the fur-clad Reds climbed into the control chamber.

Ross recognized the leader as Ashe's double, the man he had followed across time. He blinked for just an instant as he faced Ross and then shouted an order at his companion. The other spun Murdock around, bringing his hands down behind him to clamp his wrists together. Once again Ross fronted the screen and saw Baldy watching the whole scene with an expression suggesting that he had been shocked out of his complacent superiority.

"Ah...." Ross's captors were staring at the screen and the unearthly man there. Then one flung himself at the control panel and his hands whipped back and forth, restoring to utter silence both screen and room.

"What are you?" The man who might have been Ashe spoke slowly in the Beaker tongue, drilling Ross with his stare as if by the force of his will alone he could pull the truth out of his prisoner.

"What do you think I am?" Ross countered. He was wearing the uniform of Baldy, and he had clearly established contact with the time owners of this ship. Let that worry the Red!

But they did not try to answer him. At a signal he was led to the stair. To descend that ladder with his hands behind him was almost impossible, and they had to pause at the next level to unclasp the handcuffs and let him go free. Keeping a gun on him carefully, they hurried along, trying to push the pace while Ross delayed all he could. He realized that in his recognition of the power of the gun back in the control chamber, his surrender to its threat, he had betrayed his real origin. So he must continue to confuse the trail to the project in every possible way left to him. He was sure that this time they would not leave him in the first convenient crevice.

He knew he was right when they covered him with a fur parka at the entrance to the ship, once more manacling his hands and dropping a noose leash on him.

So, they were taking him back to their post here. Well, in the post was the time transporter which could return him to his own kind. It would be, it must be possible to get to that! He gave his captors no more trouble but trudged, outwardly dispirited, along the rutted way through the snow up the slope and out of the valley.

He did manage to catch a good look at the globe-ship. More than half of it, he judged, was below the surface of the ground. To be so buried it must either have lain there a long time or, if it were an air vessel, crashed hard enough to dig itself that partial grave. Yet Ross had established contact with another ship like it, and neither of the creatures he had seen were human, at least not human in any way he knew.

Ross chewed on that as he walked. He believed that those with him were looting the ship of its cargo, and by its size, that cargo must be a large one. But cargo from where? Made by what hands, what *kind* of hands? Enroute to what port? And how had the Reds located the ship in the first place?

There were plenty of questions and very few answers. Ross clung to the hope that somehow he had endangered the Reds' job here by activating the communication system of the derelict and calling the attention of its probable owners to its fate.

He also believed that the owners might take steps to regain their property. Baldy had impressed him deeply during those few moments of silent appraisal, and he knew he would not like to be on the receiving end of any retaliation from the other. Well, now he had only one chance, to keep the Reds guessing as long as he could and hope for some turn of fate which would allow him to try for the time transport. How the plate operated he did not know, but he had been transferred here from the Beaker age and if he could return to that time, escape might be possible. He had only to reach the river and follow it down to the sea where the sub was to make rendezvous at intervals. The odds were overwhelmingly against him, and Ross knew it. But there was no reason, he decided, to lie down and roll over dead to please the Reds.

As they approached the post Ross realized how much skill had gone into its construction. It looked as if they were merely coming up to the outer edge of a glacier tongue. Had it not been for the track in the snow, there would have been no reason to suspect that the ice covered anything but a thick core of its own substance. Ross was shoved through the white-walled tunnel to the building beyond.

He was hurried through the chain of rooms to a door and thrust through, his hands still fastened. It was dark in the cubby and colder than it had been outside. Ross stood still, waiting for his eyes to adjust to the gloom. It was several moments after the door had slammed shut that he caught a faint thud, a dull and hollow sound.

"Who is here?" he used the Beaker speech, determining to keep to the rags of his cover, which probably was a cover no longer. There was no reply, but after a pause that distant beat began again. Ross stepped cautiously forward, and by the simple method of running fullface into the walls, discovered that he was in a bare cell. He also discovered that the noise lay behind the left-hand wall, and he stood with his ear flat against it, listening. The sound did not have the regular rhythm of a machine in use—there were odd pauses between some blows, others came in a quick rain. It was as if someone were digging!

Were the Reds engaged in enlarging their icebound headquarters? Having listened for a considerable time, Ross doubted that, for the sound was too irregular. It seemed almost as if the longer pauses were used to check up on the result of labor—was it the extent of the excavation or the continued preservation of secrecy?

Ross slipped down along the wall, his shoulders still resting against it, and rested with his head twisted so he could hear the tapping. Meanwhile he flexed his wrists inside the hoops which confined them, and folding his hands as small as possible, tried to slip them through the rings. The only result was that he chafed his skin raw to no advantage. They had not taken off his parka, and in spite of the chill about him, he was too warm. Only that part of his body covered by the suit he had taken from the ship was comfortable; he could almost believe that it possessed some built-in conditioning device.

With no hope of relief Ross rubbed his hands back and forth against the wall, scraping the hoops on his wrists. The distant pounding had ceased, and this time the pause lengthened into so long a period that Ross fell asleep, his head falling forward on his chest, his raw wrists still pushed against the surface behind him.

He was hungry when he awoke, and with that hunger his rebellion sparked into flame. Awkwardly he got to his feet and lurched along to the door through which he had been thrown, where he proceeded to kick at the barrier. The cushiony stuff forming the soles of his tights muffled most of the force of those blows, but some noise was heard outside, for the door opened and Ross faced one of the guards.

"Food! I want to eat!" He put into the Beaker language all the resentment boiling in him.

The fellow ignoring him, reached in a long arm, and nearly tossing the prisoner off balance, dragged him out of the cell. Ross was marched into another room to face what appeared to be a tribunal. Two of the men there he knew—Ashe's double and the quiet man who had questioned him back in the other time station. The third, clearly one of greater authority, regarded Ross bleakly.

"Who are you?" the quiet man asked.

"Rossa, son of Gurdi. And I would eat before I make talk with you. I have not done any wrong that you should treat me as a barbarian who has stolen salt from the trading post—"

"You are an agent," the leader corrected him dispassionately, "of whom you will tell us in due time. But first you shall speak of the ship, of what you found there, and why you meddled with the controls.... Wait a moment before you refuse, my young friend." He raised his hand from his lap, and once again Ross faced an automatic. "Ah, I see that you know what I hold—odd knowledge for an innocent Bronze Age trader. And please have no doubts about my hesitation to use this. I shall not kill you, naturally," the man continued, "but there are certain wounds which supply a maximum of pain and little serious damage. Remove his parka, Kirschov."

Once more Ross was unmanacled, the fur stripped from him. His questioner carefully studied the suit he wore under it. "Now you will tell us exactly what we wish to hear."

There was a confidence in that statement which chilled Ross; Major Kelgarries had displayed its like. Ashe had it in another degree, and certainly it had been present in Baldy. There was no doubt that the speaker meant exactly what he said. He had at his command methods which would wring from his captive the full sum of what he wanted, and there would be no consideration for that captive during the process.

His implied threat struck as cold as the glacial air, and Ross tried to meet it with an outward show of uncracked defenses. He decided to pick and choose from his information, feeding them scraps to stave off the inevitable. Hope dies very hard, and Ross having been pushed into corners long before his work at the project, had had considerable training in verbal fencing with hostile authority. He would volunteer nothing.... Let it be pulled from him reluctant word by word! He would spin it out as long as he could and hope that time might fight for him.

"You are an agent...."

Ross accepted this statement as one he would neither affirm nor deny.

"You came to spy under the cover of a barbarian trader," smoothly, without pause, the man changed language in mid-sentence, slipping from the Beaker speech into English.

But long experience in meeting the dangerous with an expression of complete lack of comprehension was Ross's weapon now. He stared somewhat stupidly at his interrogator with that bewildered, boyish look he had so long cultivated to bemuse enemies in his past.

Whether he could have held out long against the other's skill—for Ross possessed no illusions concerning the type of examiner he now faced—he was never to know. Perhaps the drastic interruption that occurred the next moment saved for Ross a measure of self-esteem.

There was a distant boom, hollow and thunderous. Underneath and around them the floor, walls, and ceiling of the room moved as if they had been pried from their setting of ice and were being rolled about by the exploring thumb and forefinger of some impatient giant.

CHAPTER 13

Ross swayed against a guard, was fended off, and bounced against the wall as the man shouted words Ross could not understand. A determined roar from the leader brought a semblance of order, but it was plain that they had not been expecting this. Ross was hustled out of the room back to his cell. His guards were opening the cell door when a second shock was felt and he was thrust into safekeeping with no ceremony.

He half crouched against the questionable security of the wall, waiting through two more twisting earth waves, both of which were accompanied or preceded by dull sounds. Bombing! That last wrench was really bad. Ross found himself lying on the floor, feeling tremors rippling along the earth. His stomach knotted convulsively with a fear unlike any he had known before. It was as if the very security of the world had been jerked from under him.

But that last explosion—if it was an explosion—appeared to be the end. Ross sat up gingerly after several long moments during which no more shocks moved the floor and walls. A line of light marked the door, showing cracks where none had previously existed. Ross, not yet ready to try standing erect, was heading toward it on his hands and knees when a sharp noise behind him brought him to a stop.

There was no light to see by, but he was certain that the scrape of metal against metal sounded from the far side of the wall. He crawled back and put his ear to the surface. Now he heard not only that scraping, but an undercurrent of clicks, chippings....

Under his exploring hands the surface remained as smooth as ever, however. Then suddenly, perhaps a foot from his head, there sounded a rip of metal. The wall was being holed from the other side! Ross caught a flicker of very weak light, and moving in it was the point of a tool pulling at the smooth surface of the wall. It broke away with a brittle sound, and a hand holding a light reached through the aperture.

Ross wondered if he should catch that wrist, but the hope that the digger might just possibly be an ally kept him motionless. After the hand with the light whipped back beyond the wall, a wide section gave away and a hunched figure crawled through, followed by a second. In the limited glow he saw the first tunneler clearly enough.

"Assha!"

Ross was unprepared for what followed his cry. The lean brown man moved with a panther's striking speed, and Ross was forced back. A hand like a steel ring on his throat shut the breath away from his bursting lungs; the other's muscular body held him flat in spite of his struggles. The light of the small flash glowed inches beyond his eyes as he fought to fill his lungs. Then the hand on his throat was gone and he gasped, a little dizzy.

"Murdock! What are you doing—?" Ashe's clipped voice was muffled by another sudden explosion. This time the earth tremors not only hurled them from their feet, but seemed to run along the walls and across the ceiling. Ross, burying his face in the crook of his arm, could not rid himself of the fear that the building was being slowly twisted into scrap. When the shock was over he raised his head.

"What's going on?" He heard McNeil ask.

"Attack." That was Ashe. "But why, and by whom—don't ask me! You are a prisoner, I suppose, Murdock?"

"Yes, sir." Ross was glad that his voice sounded normal enough.

He heard someone sigh and guessed it was McNeil. "Another digging party." There was tired disgust in that.

"I don't understand," Ross appealed to that section of the dark where Ashe had been. "Have you been here all the time? Are you trying to dig your way out? I don't see how you can cut out of this glacier that we're parked under—"

"Glacier!" Ashe's exclamation was as explosive as the tremors. "So we're inside a glacier! That explains it. Yes, we've been here—"

"On ice!" McNeil commented and then laughed. "Glacier—ice—that's right, isn't it?"

"We're collaborating," Ashe continued. "Supplying our dear friends with a lot of information they already have and some flights of fancy they never dreamed about. However, they didn't know we had a few surprise packets of our own strewn about. It's amazing what the boys back at the project can pack away in a belt, or between layers of hide in a boot. So we've been engaged in some research of our own—"

"But I didn't have any escape gadgets." Ross was struck by the unfairness of that.

"No," Ashe agreed, his voice even and cold, "they are not entrusted to first-run men. You might slip up and use them at the wrong moment. However, you appear to have done fairly well...."

The heat of Ross's rising anger was chilled by the noise which cracked over their heads, ground to them through the walls, flattened and threatened them. He had thought those first shocks the end of this ice burrow and the world; he knew that this one was.

And the silence that followed was as threatening in its way as the clamor had been. Then there was a shout, a shriek. The space of light near the cell door was widening as that barrier, broken from its lock, swung open slowly. The fear of being trapped sent the men in that direction.

"Out!"

Ross was ready enough to respond to that order, but they were stopped by a crackle of sound that could be only one thing—rapid-fire guns. Somewhere in this warren a fight was in progress. Ross, remembering the arrogant face of the bald ship's officer, wondered if this was not an attack in force—the aliens against the looting Reds. If so, would the ship people distinguish between those found here. He feared not.

The room outside was clear, but not for long. As they lay watching, two men backed in, then whirled to stare at each other. A voice roared from beyond as if ordering them back to some post. One of them took a step forward in reluctant obedience, but the other grabbed his arm and pulled him away. They turned to run, and an automatic cracked.

The man nearest Ross gave a queer little cough and folded forward to his knees, sprawling on his face. His companion stared at him wildly for an instant, and then skidded into the passage beyond, escaping by inches a shot which clipped the door as he lunged through it.

No one followed, for outside there was a crescendo of noise—shouting, cries of pain, an unidentifiable hissing. Ashe darted into the room, taking cover by the body. Then he came back, the fellow's gun in his hand, and with a jerk of his head summoned the other two. He motioned them on in a direction away from the sounds of battle.

"I don't get all this," McNeil commented as they reached the next passage. "What's going on? Mutiny? Or have our boys gotten through?"

"It must be the ship people," Ross answered.

"What ship?" Ashe caught him up swiftly.

"The big one the Reds have been looting—"

"Ship?" echoed McNeil. "And *where* did you get that rig?" In the bright light it was easy to see Ross's alien dress. McNeil fingered the elastic material wonderingly.

"From the ship," Ross returned impatiently. "But if the ship people are attacking, I don't think they will notice any difference between us and the Reds...."

There was a burst of ear-splitting sound. For the third time Ross was thrown from his feet. This time the burrow lights flickered, dimmed, and went out.

"Oh, fine," commented McNeil bitterly out of the dark. "I never did care for blindman's buff."

"The transfer plate—" Ross clung to his own plan of escape—"if we can reach that—"

The light which had served Ashe and McNeil in their tunneling clicked on. Since the earth shocks appeared to be over for a while, they moved on, with Ashe in the lead and McNeil bringing up the rear. Ross hoped Ashe knew the way. The sound of fighting had died out, so one side or the other must have gained the victory. They might have only a few moments left to pass undetected.

Ross's sense of direction was fairly acute, but he could not have gone so unerringly to what he sought as Ashe did. Only he did not lead them to the room with the glowing plate, and Ross stifled a protest as they came instead to a small record room.

On a table were three spools of tape which Ashe caught up avidly, thrusting two in the front of his baggy tunic, passing the third to McNeil. Then he sped about trying the cupboards on the walls, but all were locked. His hand falling from the last latch, Ashe came back to the door where Ross waited.

"To the plate!" Ross urged.

Ashe surveyed the cupboards once more regretfully. "If we could have just ten minutes here—"

McNeil snorted. "Listen, you may yearn to be the filling in an ice sandwich, but I don't! Another shock and we'll be buried so deep even a drill couldn't find us. Let's get out now. The kid is right about that—if we still can."

Once more Ashe took the lead and they wove through ghostly rooms to what must have been the heart of the post—the transfer point. To Ross's unvoiced relief the plate was glowing. He had been nagged by the fear that when the lights blew out the transfer plate might also have been affected. He jumped for the plate.

Neither Ashe nor McNeil wasted time in joining him there. As they clung together there was a cry from behind them, underlined by a shot. Ross, feeling Ashe sag against him, caught him in his arms. By the reflected glow of the plate he saw the Red leader of the post and behind him, his hairless face hanging oddly bodiless in the gloom, was the alien. Were those two now allies? Before Ross could be sure that he had really seen them, the wracking of space time caught him and the rest of the room faded away.

"... free. Get a move on!"

Ross glanced across Ashe's bowed shoulders to McNeil's excited face. The other was pulling at Ashe, who was only half-conscious. A stream of blood from a hole in his bare shoulder soaked the upper edge of his Beaker tunic, but as they steadied him between them, he gained some measure of awareness and moved his feet as they pulled him off the plate.

Well, they were free if only for a few seconds, and there was no reception committee waiting for them. Ross gave thanks silently for those two small favors. But if they were now returned to the Bronze Age village, they were still in enemy territory. With Ashe wounded, the odds against them were so high it was almost hopeless.

Working hurriedly with strips torn from McNeil's kilt, they managed to stop the flow of blood from Ashe's wound. Although he was still groggy, he was fighting, driven by the fear which whipped them all—time was one of their foremost enemies. Ross, Ashe's gun in hand, kept watch on the transfer plate, ready to shoot at anything appearing there.

"That will have to do!" Ashe pulled free from McNeil. "We must move." He hesitated, and then pulling the spools of tape from his bloodstained tunic, passed them to McNeil. "You'd better carry these."

"All right," the other answered almost absently.

"Move!" The force of that order from Ashe sent them into the corridor beyond. "The plate...."

But the plate remained clear. And Ross noted that they must have returned to the proper time, for the walls about them were the logs and stone of the village he remembered.

"Someone coming through?"

"Should be—soon."

They fled, the hide boots of the other two making only the faintest whisper of sound, Ross's foam-soled feet none at all. He could not have found the door to the outer world, but again Ashe guided them, and only once did they have to seek cover. At last they faced a barred door. Ashe leaned against the wall, McNeil supporting him, as Ross pulled free the locking beam. They let themselves out into the night.

"Which way?" McNeil asked.

To Ross's surprise Ashe did not turn to the gate in the outer stockade. Instead he gestured at the mountain wall in the opposite direction. "They'll expect us to try for the valley pass. So we had better go up the slope there."

"That has the look of a tough climb," ventured McNeil.

Ashe stirred. "When it becomes too tough for me"—his voice was dry—"I shall say so, never fear."

He started out with some of his old ease of movement, but his companions closed in on either side, ready to offer aid. Ross often wondered later if they could have won free of the village on their own efforts that night. He was sure their resolution would have been equal to the attempt, but their escape would have depended upon a fabulous run of luck such as men seldom encounter.

As it was, they had just reached a pool of shadow beside a small hut some two buildings away from the one they had fled, when the fireworks began. As if on signal the three fugitives threw themselves flat. From the roof of the building at the center of the village a pencil of brilliant-green light pointed straight up into the sky, and around that spear of radiance the roof sprouted tongues of more natural red-and-yellow flames. Figures shot from doors as the fire lapped down the peak of the roof.

"Now!" In spite of the rising clamor, Ashe's voice carried to his two companions.

The three sprinted for the palisade, mingling with bewildered men who ran out of the other cabins. The waves of fire washed on, providing light, too much light. Ashe and McNeil could pass as part of the crowd, but Ross's unusual clothing might be easily marked.

Others were running for the wall. Ross and McNeil boosted Ashe to the top, saw him over in safety. McNeil followed. Ross was just reaching to draw himself up when he was enveloped in a beam of light.

A high, screeching call, unlike any shout he had heard, split the clamor. Frantically Ross tried for a hold, knowing that he was presenting a perfect target for those behind. He gained the top of the stockade, looked down into a black block of shadow, not knowing whether Ashe and McNeil were waiting for him or had gone ahead. Hearing that strange cry again, Ross leaped blindly out into the darkness.

He landed badly, hitting hard enough to bruise, but thanks to the skill he had learned for parachuting, he broke no bones. He got to his feet and blundered on in the general direction of the mountain Ashe had picked as their goal. There were others coming over the wall of the village and moving through the shadows, so he dared not call out for fear of alerting the enemy.

The village had been set in the widest part of the valley. Behind its stockade the open ground narrowed swiftly, like the point of a funnel, and all fugitives from the settlement had to pass through that channel to escape. Ross's worst fear was that he had lost contact with Ashe and McNeil, and that he would never be able to pick up their trail in the wilderness ahead.

Thankful for the dark suit he wore which was protective covering in the night, he twice ducked into the brush to allow parties of refugees to pass him. Hearing them speak the guttural clicking speech he had learned from Ulffa's people, Ross deduced that they were innocent of the village's real purpose. These people were convinced they had been attacked by night demons. Perhaps there had only been a handful of Reds in that hidden retreat.

Ross pulled himself up a hard climb, and pausing to catch his breath, looked back. He was not overly surprised to see figures moving leisurely about the village examining the cabins, perhaps in search of the inhabitants. Each of those searchers was clad in a form-fitting suit that matched his own, and their bulbous hairless heads gleamed white in the firelight. Ross was astonished to see that they passed straight through walls of flame, apparently unconcerned and unsinged by the heat.

The human beings trapped in the town wailed and ran, or lay and beat their heads and hands on the ground, supine before the invaders. Each captive was dragged back to a knot of aliens near the main building. Some were hurled out again into the dark, unharmed; a few others were retained. A sorting of prisoners was plainly in progress. There was no question that the ship people had followed through into this time, and that they had their own arrangements for the Reds.

Ross had no desire to learn the particulars. He started climbing again, finding the pass at last. Beyond, the ground fell away again, and Ross went forward into the full darkness of the night with a vast surge of thankfulness.

Finally, he stopped simply because he was too weary, too hungry, to keep on his feet without stumbling, and a fall in the dark on these heights could be costly. Ross discovered a small hollow behind a stunted tree and crept into it as best he could, his heart laboring against his ribs, a hot stab of pain cutting into his side with every breath he drew.

He awoke all at once with the snap of a fighting man who is alert to ever present danger. A hand lay warm and hard over his mouth, and above it his eyes met McNeil's. When he saw that Ross was awake McNeil withdrew his hand. The morning sunlight was warm about them. Moving clumsily because of his stiff, bruised body, Ross crawled out of the hollow. He looked around, but McNeil stood there alone. "Ashe?" Ross questioned him.

McNeil, showing a haggard face covered with several days' growth of rusty-brown beard, nodded his head toward the slope. Fumbling inside his kilt, he brought out something clenched in his fist and offered it to Ross. The latter held out his palm and McNeil covered it with a handful of coarse-ground grain. Just to look at the stuff made Ross long for a drink, but he mouthed it and chewed, getting up to follow McNeil down into the tree-grown lower slopes.

"It's not good." McNeil spoke jerkily, using Beaker speech. "Ashe is out of his head some of the time. That hole in his shoulder is worse than we thought it was, and there's always the threat of infection. This whole wood is full of people flushed out of that blasted village! Most of them—all I've seen—are natives. But they have it firmly planted in their minds now that there are devils after them. If they see you wearing that suit—"

"I know, and I'd strip if I could," Ross agreed. "But I'll have to get other clothing first; I can't run bare in this cold."

"That might be safer," McNeil growled. "I don't know just what happened back there, but it certainly must have been plenty!"

Ross swallowed a very dry mouthful of grain and then stooped to scoop up some leftover snow in the shadow of a tree root. It was not as refreshing as a real drink, but it helped. "You said Ashe is out of his head. What do we do for him, and what are your plans?"

"We have to reach the river, somehow. It drains to the sea, and at its mouth we are supposed to make contact with the sub."

The proposal sounded impossible to Ross, but so many impossible things had happened lately he was willing to go along with the idea—as long as he could. Gathering up more snow, he stuffed it into his mouth before he followed the already disappearing McNeil.

CHAPTER 14

"... that's my half of it. The rest of it you know." Ross held his hands close to the small fire sheltered in the pit he had helped dig and flexed his cold-numbed fingers in the warmth.

From across the handful of flames Ashe's eyes, too bright in a fever-flushed face, watched him demandingly. The fugitives had taken cover in an angle where the massed remains of an old avalanche provided a cave-pocket. McNeil was off scouting in the gray drizzle of the day, and their escape from the village was now some forty-eight hours behind them.

"So the crackpots were right, after all. They only had their times mixed." Ashe shifted on the bed of brush and leaves they had raked together for his comfort.

"I don't understand—"

"Flying saucers," Ashe returned with an odd little laugh. "It was a wild possibility, but it was on the books from the start. This certainly will make Kelgarries turn red—"

"Flying saucers?"

Ashe must be out of his head from the fever, Ross supposed. He wondered what he should do if Ashe tried to get up and walk away. He could not tackle a man with a bad hole in his shoulder, nor was he certain he could wrestle Ashe down in a real fight.

"That globe-ship was never built on this world. Use your head, Murdock. Think about your furry-faced friend and the baldy with him. Did either look like normal Terrans to you?"

"But—a spaceship!" It was something that had so long been laughed to scorn. When men had failed to break into space after the initial excitement of the satellite launchings, space flight had become a matter for jeers. On the other hand, there was the evidence collected by his own eyes and ears, his own experience. The services of the lifeboat had been techniques outside of his experience.

"This was insinuated once"—Ashe was lying flat now, gazing speculatively up at the projection of logs and earth which made them a partial roof—"along with a lot of other bright ideas, by a gentleman named Charles Fort, who took a lot of pleasure in pricking what he considered to be vastly over-inflated scientific pomposity. He gathered together four book loads of reported incidents of unexplainable happenings which he dared the scientists of his day to explain. And one of his bright suggestions was that such phenomena as the vast artificial earthworks found in Ohio and Indiana were originally thrown up by space castaways to serve as S O S signals. An intriguing idea, and now perhaps we may prove it true."

"But if such spaceships were wrecked on this world, I still don't see why we didn't find traces of them in our own time."

"Because that wreck you explored was bedded in a glacial era. Do you have any idea how long ago that was, counting from our own time? There were at least three glacial periods—and we don't know in which one the Reds went visiting. That age began about a million years before we were born, and the last of the ice ebbed out of New York State some thirty-eight thousand years ago, boy. That was the early Stone Age, reckoning it by the scale of human development, with an extremely thin population of the first real types of man clinging to a few warmer fringes of wilderness.

"Climatic changes, geographical changes, all altered the face of our continents. There was a sea in Kansas; England was part of Europe. So, even though as many as fifty such ships were lost here, they could all have been ground to bits by the ice flow, buried miles deep in quakes, or rusted away generations before the first really intelligent man arrived to wonder at them. Certainly there couldn't be too many such wrecks to be found. What do you think this planet was, a flypaper to attract them?"

"But if ships crashed here once, why didn't they later when men were better able to understand them?" Ross countered.

"For several reasons—all of them possible and able to be fitted into the fabric of history as we know it on this world. Civilizations rise, exist, and fall, each taking with it into the limbo of forgotten things some of the discoveries which made it great. How did the Indian civilizations of the New World learn to harden gold into a useable point for a cutting weapon? What was the secret of building possessed by the ancient Egyptians? Today you will find plenty of men to argue these problems and half a hundred others.

"The Egyptians once had a well-traveled trade route to India. Bronze Age traders opened up roads down into Africa. The Romans knew China. Then came an end to each of these empires, and those trade routes were forgotten. To our European ancestors of the Middle Ages, China was almost a legend, and the fact that the Egyptians had successfully sailed around the Cape of Good Hope was unknown. Suppose our space voyagers represented some star-born confederacy or empire which lived, rose to its highest point, and fell again into planet-bound barbarism all before the first of our species painted pictures on a cave wall?

"Or take it that this world was an unlucky reef on which too many ships and cargoes were lost, so that our whole solar system was posted, and skippers of star ships thereafter avoided it? Or they might even have had some rule that when a planet developed a primitive race of its own, it was to be left strictly alone until it discovered space flight for itself."

"Yes." Every one of Ashe's suppositions made good sense, and Ross was able to believe them. It was easier to think that both Furry-face and Baldy were inhabitants of another world than to think their kind existed on this planet before his own species was born. "But how did the Reds locate that ship?"

"Unless that information is on the tapes we were able to bring along, we shall probably never know," Ashe said drowsily. "I might make one guess—the Reds have been making an all-out effort for the past hundred years to open up Siberia. In some sections of that huge country there have been great climatic changes almost overnight in the far past. Mammoths have been discovered frozen in the ice with half-digested tropical plants in their stomach. It's as if the beasts were given some deep-freeze treatment instantaneously. If in their excavations the Reds came across the remains of a spaceship, remains well enough preserved for them to realize what they had discovered, they might start questing back in time to find a better one intact at an earlier date. That theory fits everything we know now."

"But why would the aliens attack the Reds now?"

"No ship's officers ever thought gently of pirates." Ashe's eyes closed.

There were questions, a flood of them, that Ross wanted to ask. He smoothed the fabric on his arm, that stuff which clung so tightly to his skin yet kept him warm without any need for more covering. If Ashe were right, on what world, what kind of world, had that material been woven, and how far had it been brought that he could wear it now?

Suddenly McNeil slid into their shelter and dropped two hares at the edge of the fire.

"How goes it?" he said, as Ross began to clean them.

"Reasonably well," Ashe, his eyes still closed, replied to that before Ross could. "How far are we from the river? And do we have company?"

"About five miles—if we had wings." McNeil answered in a dry tone. "And we have company all right, lots of it!"

That brought Ashe up, leaning forward on his good elbow. "What kind?"

"Not from the village." McNeil frowned at the fire which he fed with economic handfuls of sticks. "Something's happening on this side of the mountains. It looks as if there's a mass migration in progress. I counted five family clans on their way west—all in just this one morning."

"The village refugees' stories about devils might send them packing," Ashe mused.

"Maybe." But McNeil did not sound convinced. "The sooner we head downstream, the better. And I hope the boys will have that sub waiting where they promised. We do possess one thing in our favor—the spring floods are subsiding."

"And the high water should have plenty of raft material." Ashe lay back again. "We'll make those five miles tomorrow."

McNeil stirred uneasily and Ross, having cleaned and spitted the hares, swung them over the flames to broil. "Five miles in this country," the younger man observed, "is a pretty good day's march"—he did not add as he wanted to—"for a well man."

"I will make it," Ashe promised, and both listeners knew that as long as his body would obey him he meant to keep that promise. They also knew the futility of argument.

Ashe proved to be a prophet to be honored on two counts. They did make the trek to the river the next day, and there was a wealth of raft material marking the high-water level of the spring flood. The migrations McNeil had reported were still in progress, and the three men hid twice to watch the passing of small family clans. Once a respectably sized tribe, including wounded men, marched across their route, seeking a ford at the river.

"They've been badly mauled," McNeil whispered as they watched the people huddled along the water's edge while scouts cast upstream and down, searching for a ford. When they returned with the news that there was no ford to be found, the tribesmen then sullenly went to work with flint axes and knives to make rafts.

"Pressure—they are on the run." Ashe rested his chin on his good forearm and studied the busy scene. "These are not from the village. Notice the dress and the red paint on their faces. They're not like Ulffa's kin either. I wouldn't say they were local at all."

"Reminds me of something I saw once—animals running before a forest fire. They can't all be looking for new hunting territory," McNeil returned.

"Reds sweeping them out," Ross suggested. "Or could the ship people—?"

Ashe started to shake his head and then winced. "I wonder...." The crease between his level brows deepened. "The ax people!" His voice was still a whisper, but it carried a note of triumph as if he had fitted some stubborn jigsaw piece into its proper place.

"Ax people?"

"Invasion of another people from the east. They turned up in prehistory about this period. Remember, Webb spoke of them. They used axes for weapons and tamed horses."

"Tartars"—McNeil was puzzled—"This far west?"

"Not Tartars, no. You needn't expect those to come boiling out of middle Asia for some thousands of years yet. We don't know too much about the ax people, save that they moved west from the interior plains. Eventually they crossed to Britain; perhaps they were the ancestors of the Celts who loved horses too. But in their time they were a tidal wave."

"The sooner we head downstream, the better." McNeil stirred restlessly, but they knew that they must keep to cover until the tribesmen below were gone. So they lay in hiding another night, witnessing on the next morning the arrival of a smaller party of the red-painted men, again with wounded among them. At the coming of this rear guard the activity on the river bank rose close to frenzy.

The three men out of time were doubly uneasy. It was not for them to merely cross the river. They had to build a raft which would be water-worthy enough to take them downstream—to the sea if they were lucky. And to build such a sturdy raft would take time, time they did not have now.

In fact, McNeil waited only until the last tribal raft was out of bow shot before he plunged down to the shore, Ross at his heels. Since they lacked even the stone tools of the tribesmen, they were at a disadvantage, and Ross found he was hands and feet for Ashe, working under the other's close direction. Before night closed in they had a good beginning and two sets of blistered hands, as well as aching backs.

When it was too dark to work any longer, Ashe pointed back over the track they had followed. Marking the mountain pass was a light. It looked like fire, and if it was, it must be a big one for them to be able to sight it across this distance.

"Camp?" McNeil wondered.

"Must be," Ashe agreed. "Those who built that blaze are in such numbers that they don't have to take precautions."

"Will they be here by tomorrow?"

"Their scouts might, but this is early spring, and forage can't have been too good on the march. If I were the chief of that tribe, I'd turn aside into the meadow land we skirted yesterday and let the herds graze for a day, maybe more. On the other hand, if they need water—"

"They will come straight ahead!" McNeil finished grimly. "And we can't be here when they arrive."

Ross stretched, grimacing at the twinge of pain in his shoulders. His hands smarted and throbbed, and this was just the beginning of their task. If Ashe had been fit, they might have trusted to logs for support and swum downstream to hunt a safer place for their shipbuilding project. But he knew that Ashe could not stand such an effort.

Ross slept that night mainly because his body was too exhausted to let him lie awake and worry. Roused in the earliest dawn by McNeil, they both crawled down to the water's edge and struggled to bind stubbornly resisting saplings together with cords twisted from bark. They reinforced them at crucial points with some strings torn from their kilts, and strips of rabbit hide saved from their kills of the past few days. They worked with hunger gnawing at them, having no time now to hunt. When the sun was well westward they had a clumsy craft which floated sluggishly. Whether it would answer to either pole or improvised paddle, they could not know until they tried it.

Ashe, his face flushed and his skin hot to the touch, crawled on board and lay in the middle, on the thin heap of bedding they had put there for him. He eagerly drank the water they carried to him in cupped hands and gave a little sigh of relief as Ross wiped his face with wet grass, muttering something about Kelgarries which neither of his companions understood.

McNeil shoved off and the bobbing craft spun around dizzily as the current pulled it free from the shore. They made a brave start, but luck deserted them before they had gotten out of sight of the spot where they embarked.

Striving to keep them in mid-current, McNeil poled furiously, but there were too many rocks and snagged trees projecting from the banks. Sharing that sweep of water with them, and coming up fast, was a full-sized tree. Twice its mat of branches caught on some snag, holding it back, and Ross breathed a little more freely, but it soon tore free again and rolled on, as menacing as a battering ram.

"Get closer to shore!" Ross shouted the warning. Those great, twisted roots seemed aimed straight at the raft, and he was sure if that mass struck them fairly, they would not have a chance. He dug in with his own pole, but his hasty push did not meet bottom; the stake in his hands plunged into some pothole in the hidden river bed. He heard McNeil cry out as he toppled into the water, gasping as the murky liquid flooded his mouth, choking him.

Half dazed by the shock, Ross struck out instinctively. The training at the base had included swimming, but to fight water in a pool under controlled conditions was far different from fighting death in a river of icy water when one had already swallowed a sizable quantity of that flood.

Ross had a half glimpse of a dark shadow. Was it the edge of the raft? He caught at it desperately, skinning his hands on rough bark, dragged on by it. The tree! He blinked his eyes to clear them of water, to try to see. But he could not pull his exhausted body high enough out of the water to see past the screen of roots; he could only cling to the small safety he had won and hope that he could rejoin the raft somewhere downstream.

After what seemed like a very long time he wedged one arm between two water-washed roots, sure that the support would hold his head above the surface. The chill of the stream struck at his hands and head, but the protection of the alien clothing was still effective, and the rest of his body was not cold. He was simply too tired to wrest himself free and trust again to the haphazard chance of making shore through the gathering dusk.

Suddenly a shock jarred his body and strained the arm he had thrust among the roots, wringing a cry out of him. He swung around and brushed footing under the water; the tree had caught on a shore snag. Pulling loose from the roots, he floundered on his hands and knees, falling afoul of a mass of reeds whose roots were covered with stale-smelling mud. Like a wounded animal he dragged himself through the ooze to higher land, coming out upon an open meadow flooded with moonlight.

For a while he lay there, his cold, sore hands under him, plastered with mud and too tired to move. The sound of a sharp barking aroused him—an imperative, summoning bark, neither belonging to a wolf nor a hunting fox. He listened to it dully and then, through the ground upon which he lay, Ross felt as well as heard the pounding of hoofs.

Hoofs—horses! Horses from over the mountains—horses which might mean danger. His mind seemed as dull and numb as his hands, and it took quite a long time for him to fully realize the menace horses might bring.

Getting up, Ross noticed a winged shape sweeping across the disk of the moon like a silent dart. There was a single despairing squeak out of the grass about a hundred feet away, and the winged shape arose again with its prey. Then the barking sound once more—eager, excited barking.

Ross crouched back on his heels and saw a smoky brand of light moving along the edge of the meadow where the band of trees began. Could it be a herd guard? Ross knew he had to head back toward the river, but he had to force himself on the path, for he did not know whether he dared enter the stream again. But what would happen if they hunted him with the dog? Confused memories of how water spoiled scent spurred him on.

Having reached the rising bank he had climbed so laboriously before, Ross miscalculated and tumbled back, rolling down into the mud of the reed bed. Mechanically he wiped the slime from his face. The tree was still anchored there; by some freak the current had rammed its rooted end up on a sand spit.

Above in the meadow the barking sounded very close, and now it was answered by a second canine belling. Ross wormed his way back through the reeds to the patch of water between the tree and the bank. His few poor efforts at escape were almost half-consciously taken; he was too tired to really care now.

Soon he saw a four-footed shape running along the top of the bank, giving tongue. It was then joined by a larger and even more vocal companion. The dogs drew even with Ross, who wondered dully if the animals could sight him in the shadows below, or whether they only scented his presence. Had he been able, he would have climbed over the log and taken his chances in the open water, but now he could only lie where he was—the tangle of roots between him and the bank serving as a screen, which would be little enough protection when men came with torches.

Ross was mistaken, however, for his worm's progress across the reed bed had liberally besmeared his dark clothing and masked the skin of his face and hands, giving him better cover than any he could have wittingly devised. Though he felt naked and defenseless, the men who trailed the hounds to the river bank, thrusting out the torch over the edge to light the sand spit, saw nothing but the trunk of the tree wedged against a mound of mud.

Ross heard a confused murmur of voices broken by the clamor of the dogs. Then the torch was raised out of line of his dazzled eyes. He saw one of the indistinct figures above cuff away a dog and move off, calling the hounds after it. Reluctantly, still barking, the animals went. Ross, with a little sob, subsided limply in the uncomfortable net of roots, still undiscovered.

CHAPTER 15

It was such a small thing, a tag of ragged stuff looped about a length of splintered sapling. Ross climbed stiffly over the welter of drift caught on the sand spit and pulled it loose, recognizing the string even before he touched it. That square knot was of McNeil's tying, and as Murdock sat down weakly in the sand and mud, nervously fingering the twisted cord, staring vacantly at the river, his last small hope died. The raft must have broken up, and neither Ashe nor McNeil could have survived the ultimate disaster.

Ross Murdock was alone, marooned in a time which was not his own, with little promise of escape. That one thought blanked out his mind with its own darkness. What was the use of getting up again, of trying to find food for his empty stomach, or warmth and shelter?

He had always prided himself on being able to go it alone, had thought himself secure in that calculated loneliness. Now that belief had been washed away in the river along with most of the will power which had kept him going these past days. Before, there had always been some goal, no matter how remote. Now, he had nothing. Even if he managed to reach the mouth of the river, he had no idea of where or how to summon the sub from the overseas post. All three of the time travelers might already have been written off the rolls, since they had not reported in.

Ross pulled the rag free from the sapling and wreathed it in a tight bracelet about his grimed wrist for some unexplainable reason. Worn and tired, he tried to think ahead. There was no chance of again contacting Ulffa's tribe. Along with all the other woodland hunters they must have fled before the advance of the horsemen. No, there was no reason to go back, and why make the effort to advance?

The sun was hot. This was one of those spring days which foretell the ripeness of summer. Insects buzzed in the reed banks where a green sheen showed. Birds wheeled and circled in the sky, some flock disturbed, their cries reaching Ross in hoarse calls of warning.

He was still plastered with patches of dried mud and slime, the reek of it thick in his nostrils. Now Ross brushed at a splotch on his knee, picking loose flakes to expose the alien cloth of his suit underneath, seemingly unbefouled. All at once it became necessary to be clean again at least.

Ross waded into the stream, stooping to splash the brown water over his body and then rubbing away the resulting mud. In the sunlight the fabric had a brilliant glow, as if it not only drew the light but reflected it. Wading farther out into the water, he began to swim, not with any goal in view, but because it was easier than crawling back to land once more.

Using the downstream current to supplement his skill, he watched both banks. He could not really hope to see either the raft or indications that its passengers had won to shore, but somewhere deep inside him he had not yet accepted the probable.

The effort of swimming broke through that fog of inertia which had held him since he had awakened that morning. It was with a somewhat healthier interest in life that Ross came ashore again on an arm of what was a bay or inlet angling back into the land. Here the banks of the river were well above his head, and believing that he was well sheltered, he stripped, hanging his suit in the sunlight and letting the unusual heat of the day soothe his body.

A raw fish, cornered in the shallows and scooped out, furnished one of the best meals he had ever tasted. He had reached for the suit draped over a willow limb when the first and only warning that his fortunes had once again changed came, swiftly, silently, and with deadly promise.

One moment the willows had moved gently in the breeze, and then a spear suddenly set them all quivering. Ross, clutching the suit to him with a frantic grab, skated about in the sand, going to one knee in his haste.

He found himself completely at the mercy of the two men standing on the bank well above him. Unlike Ulffa's people or the Beaker traders, they were very tall, with heavy braids of light or sun-bleached hair swinging forward on their wide chests. Their leather tunics hung to mid-thigh above leggings which were bound to their limbs with painted straps. Cuff bracelets of copper ringed their forearms, and necklaces of animal teeth and beads displayed their personal wealth. Ross could not remember having seen their like on any of the briefing tapes at the base.

One spear had been a warning, but a second was held ready, so Ross made the age-old signal of surrender, reluctantly dropping his suit and raising his hands palm out and shoulder high.

"Friend?" Ross asked in the Beaker tongue. The traders ranged far, and perhaps there was a chance they had had contact with this tribe.

The spear twirled, and the younger stranger effortlessly leaped down the bank, paddling over to Ross to pick up the suit he had dropped, holding it up while he made some comment to his companion. He seemed fascinated by the fabric, pulling and smoothing it between his hands, and Ross wondered if there was a chance of trading it for his own freedom.

Both men were armed, not only with the long-bladed daggers favored by the Beaker folk, but also with axes. When Ross made a slight effort to lower his hands the man before him reached to his belt ax, growling what was plainly a warning. Ross blinked, realizing that they might well knock him out and leave him behind, taking the suit with them.

Finally, they decided in favor of including him in their loot. Throwing the suit over one arm, the stranger caught Ross by the shoulder and pushed him forward roughly. The pebbled beach was painful to Ross's feet, and the breeze which whipped about him as he reached the top of the bank reminded him only too forcibly of his ordeal in the glacial world.

Murdock was tempted to make a sudden dash out on the point of the bank and dive into the river, but it was already too late. The man who was holding the spear had moved behind him, and Ross's wrist, held in a vise grip at the small of his back, kept him prisoner as he was pushed on into the meadow. There three shaggy horses grazed, their nose ropes gathered into the hands of a third man.

A sharp stone half buried in the ground changed the pattern of the day. Ross's heel scraped against it, and the resulting pain triggered his rebellion into explosion. He threw himself backward, his bruised heel sliding between the feet of his captor, bringing them both to the ground with himself on top. The other expelled air from his lungs in a grunt of surprise, and Ross whipped over, one hand grasping the hilt of the tribesman's dagger while the other, free of that prisoning wrist-lock, chopped at the fellow's throat.

Dagger out and ready, Ross faced the men in a half crouch as he had been drilled. They stared at him in open-mouthed amazement, then too late the spears went up. Ross placed the point of his looted weapon at the throat of the now quiet man by whom he knelt, and he spoke the language he had learned from Ulffa's people.

"You strike—this one dies."

They must have read the determined purpose in his eyes, for slowly, reluctantly, the spears went down. Having gained so much of a victory, Ross dared more. "Take—" he motioned to the waiting horses—"take and go!"

For a moment he thought that this time they would meet his challenge, but he continued to hold the dagger above the brown throat of the man who was now moaning faintly. His threat continued to register, for the other man shrugged the suit from his arm, left it lying on the ground, and retreated. Holding the nose rope of his horse, he mounted, waved the herder up also, and both of them rode slowly away.

The prisoner was slowly coming around, so Ross only had time to pull on the suit; he had not even fastened the breast studs before those blue eyes opened. A sunburned hand flashed to a belt, but the dagger and ax which had once hung there were now in Ross's possession. He watched the tribesman carefully as he finished dressing.

"What you do?" The words were in the speech of the forest people, distorted by a new accent.

"You go—" Ross pointed to the third horse the others had left behind—"I go—" he indicated the river—"I take these"—he patted the dagger and the ax. The other scowled.

"Not good...."

Ross laughed, a little hysterically. "Not good you," he agreed, "good—me!"

To his surprise the tribesman's stiff face relaxed, and the fellow gave a bark of laughter. He sat up, rubbing at his throat, a big grin pulling at the corners of his mouth.

"You—hunter?" The man pointed northeast to the woodlands fringing the mountains.

Ross shook his head. "Trader, me."

"Trader," the other repeated. Then he tapped one of the wide metal cuffs at his wrist. "Trade—this?"

"That. More things."

"Where?"

Ross pointed downstream. "By bitter water—trade there."

The man appeared puzzled. "Why you here?"

"Ride river water, like you ride," he said, pointing to the horse. "Ride on trees—many trees tied together. Trees break apart—I come here."

The conception of a raft voyage apparently got across, for the tribesman was nodding. Getting to his feet, he walked across to take up the nose rope of the waiting horse. "You come camp—Foscar. Foscar chief. He like you show trick how you take Tulka, make him sleep—hold his ax, knife."

Ross hesitated. This Tulka seemed friendly now, but would that friendliness last? He shook his head. "I go to bitter water. My chief there."

Tulka was scowling again. "You speak crooked words—your chief there!" He pointed eastward with a dramatic stretch of the arm. "Your chief speak Foscar. Say he give much these—" he touched his copper cuffs—"good knives, axes—get you back."

Ross stared at him without understanding. Ashe? Ashe in this Foscar's camp offering a reward for him? But how could that be?

"How you know my chief?"

Tulka laughed, this time derisively. "You wear shining skin—your chief wear shiny skin. He say find other shiny skin—give many good things to man who bring you back."

Shiny skin! The suit from the alien ship! Was it the ship people? Ross remembered the light on him as he climbed out of the Red village. He must have been sighted by one of the spacemen. But why were they searching for him, alerting the natives in an effort to scoop him up? What made Ross Murdock so important that they must have him? He only knew that he was not going to be taken if he could help it, that he had no desire to meet this "chief" who had offered treasure for his capture.

"You will come!" Tulka went into action, his mount flashing forward almost in a running leap at Ross, who stumbled back when horse and rider loomed over him. He swung up the ax, but it was a weapon with which he had had no training, too heavy for him.

As his blow met only thin air the shoulder of the mount hit him, and Ross went down, avoiding by less than a finger's breadth the thud of an unshod hoof against his skull. Then the rider landed on him, crushing him flat. A fist connected with his jaw, and for Ross the sun went out.

He found himself hanging across a support which moved with a rocking gait, whose pounding hurt his head, keeping him half dazed. Ross tried to move, but he realized that his arms were behind his back, fastened wrist to wrist, and a warm weight centered in the small of his spine to hold him face down on a horse. He could do nothing except endure the discomfort as best he could and hope for a speedy end to the gallop.

Over his head passed the cackle of speech. He caught short glimpses of another horse matching pace to the one that carried him. Then they swept into a noisy place where the shouting of many men made a din. The horse stopped and Ross was pulled from its back and dropped to the trodden dust, to lie blinking up dizzily, trying to focus on the scene about him.

They had arrived at the camp of the horsemen, whose hide tents served as a backdrop for the fair long-haired giants and the tall women hovering about to view the captive. The circle about him then broke, and men stood aside for a newcomer. Ross had believed that his original captors were physically imposing, but this one was their master. Lying on the ground at the chieftain's feet, Ross felt like a small and helpless child.

Foscar, if Foscar this was, could not yet have entered middle age, and the muscles which moved along his arms and across his shoulders as he leaned over to study Tulka's prize made him bear-strong. Ross glared up at him, that same hot rage which had led to his attack on Tulka now urging him to the only defiance he had left—words.

"Look well, Foscar. Free me, and I would do more than *look* at you," he said in the speech of the woods hunters.

Foscar's blue eyes widened and he lowered a fist which could have swallowed in its grasp both of Ross's hands, linking those great fingers in the stuff of the suit and drawing the captive to his feet, with no sign that his act had required any effort. Even standing, Ross was a good eight inches shorter than the chieftain. Yet he put up his chin and eyed the other squarely, without giving ground.

"So—yet still my hands are tied." He put into that all the taunting inflection he could summon. His reception by Tulka had given him one faint clue to the character of these people; they might be brought to acknowledge the worth of one who stood up to them.

"Child—" The fist shifted from its grip on the fabric covering Ross's chest to his shoulder, and now under its compulsion Ross swayed back and forth.

"Child?" From somewhere Ross raised that short laugh. "Ask Tulka. I be no child, Foscar. Tulka's ax, Tulka's knife—they were in my hand. A horse Tulka had to use to bring me down."

Foscar regarded him intently and then grinned. "Sharp tongue," he commented. "Tulka lost knife—ax? So! Ennar," he called over his shoulder, and one of the men stepped out a pace beyond his fellows.

He was shorter and much younger than his chief, with a boy's rangy slimness and an open, good-looking face, his eyes bright on Foscar with a kind of eager excitement. Like the other tribesmen he was armed with belt dagger and ax, and since he wore two necklaces and both cuff bracelets and upper armlets as did Foscar, Ross thought he must be a relative of the older man.

"Child!" Foscar clapped his hand on Ross's shoulder and then withdrew the hold. "Child!" He indicated Ennar, who reddened. "You take from Ennar ax, knife," Foscar ordered, "as you took from Tulka." He made a sign, and someone cut the thongs about Ross's wrists.

Ross rubbed one numbed hand against the other, setting his jaw. Foscar had stung his young follower with that contemptuous "child," so the boy would be eager to match all his skill against the prisoner. This would not be as easy as his taking Tulka by surprise. But if he refused, Foscar might well order him killed out of hand. He had chosen to be defiant; he would have to do his best.

"Take—ax, knife—" Foscar stepped back, waving at his men to open out a ring encircling the two young men.

Ross felt a little sick as he watched Ennar's hand go to the haft of the ax. Nothing had been said about Ennar's not using his weapons in defense, but Ross discovered that there was some sense of sportmanship in the tribesmen, after all. It was Tulka who pushed to the chief's side and said something which made Foscar roar bull-voiced at his youthful champion.

Ennar's hand came away from the ax hilt as if that polished wood were white-hot, and he transferred his discomfiture to Ross as the other understood. Ennar had to win now for his own pride's sake, and Ross felt *he* had to win for his life. They circled warily, Ross watching his opponent's eyes rather than those half-closed hands held at waist level.

Back at the base he had been matched with Ashe, and before Ashe with the tough-bodied, skilled, and merciless trainers in unarmed combat. He had had beaten into his bruised flesh knowledge of holds and blows intended to save his skin in just such an encounter. But then he had been well-fed, alert, prepared. He had not been knocked silly and then transported for miles slung across a horse after days of exposure and hard usage. It remained to be learned—was Ross Murdock as tough as he always thought himself to be? Tough or not, he was in this until he won—or dropped.

Comments from the crowd aroused Ennar to the first definite action. He charged, stooping low in a wrestler's stance, but Ross squatted even lower. One hand flicked to the churned dust of the ground and snapped up again, sending a cloud of grit into the tribesman's face. Then their bodies met with a shock, and Ennar sailed over Ross's shoulder to skid along the earth.

Had Ross been fresh, the contest would have ended there and then in his favor. But when he tried to whirl and throw himself on his opponent he was too slow. Ennar was not waiting to be pinned flat, and it was Ross's turn to be caught at a disadvantage.

A hand shot out to catch his leg just above the ankle, and once again Ross obeyed his teaching, falling easily at that pull, to land across his opponent. Ennar, disconcerted by the too-quick success of his attack, was unprepared for this. Ross rolled, trying to escape steel-fingered hands, his own chopping out in edgewise blows, striving to serve Ennar as he had Tulka.

He had to take a lot of punishment, though he managed to elude the powerful bear's hug in which he knew the other was laboring to engulf him, a hold which would speedily crush him into submission. Clinging to the methods he had been taught, he fought on, only now he knew, with a growing panic, that his best was not good enough. He was too spent to make an end. Unless he had some piece of great good luck, he could only delay his own defeat.

Fingers clawed viciously at his eyes, and Ross did what he had never thought to do in any fight—he snapped wolfishly, his teeth closing on flesh as he brought up his knee and drove it home into the body wriggling on his. There was a gasp of hot breath in his face as Ross called upon the last few rags of his strength, tearing loose from the other's slackened hold. He scrambled to one knee. Ennar was also on his knees, crouching like a four-legged beast ready to spring. Ross risked everything on a last gamble. Clasping his hands together, he raised them as high as he could and brought them down on the nape of the other's neck. Ennar sprawled forward face-down in the dust where seconds later Ross joined him.

CHAPTER 16

Murdock lay on his back, gazing up at the laced hides which stretched to make the tent roofing. Having been battered just enough to feel all one aching bruise, Ross had lost interest in the future. Only the present mattered, and it was a dark one. He might have fought Ennar to a standstill, but in the eyes of the horsemen he had also been beaten, and he had not impressed them as he had hoped. That he still lived was a minor wonder, but he deduced that he continued to breathe only because they wanted to exchange him for the reward offered by the aliens from out of time, an unpleasant prospect to contemplate.

His wrists were lashed over his head to a peg driven deeply into the ground; his ankles were bound to another. He could turn his head from side to side, but any further movement was impossible. He ate only bits of food dropped into his mouth by a dirty-fingered slave, a cowed hunter captured from a tribe overwhelmed in the migration of the horsemen.

"Ho—taker of axes!" A toe jarred into his ribs, and Ross bit back the grunt of pain which answered that rude bid for his attention. He saw in the dim light Ennar's face and was savagely glad to note the discolorations about the right eye and along the jaw line, the signatures left by his own skinned knuckles.

"Ho—warrior!" Ross returned hoarsely, trying to lade that title with all the scorn he could summon.

Ennar's hand, holding a knife, swung into his limited range of vision. "To clip a sharp tongue is a good thing!" The young tribesman grinned as he knelt down beside the helpless prisoner.

Ross knew a thrill of fear worse than any pain. Ennar might be about to do just what he hinted! Instead, the knife swung up and Ross felt the sawing at the cords about his wrists, enduring the pain in the raw gouges they had cut in his flesh with gratitude that it was not mutilation which had brought Ennar to him. He knew that his arms were free, but to draw them down from over his head was almost more than he could do, and he lay quiet as Ennar loosed his feet.

"Up!"

Without Ennar's hands pulling at him, Ross could not have reached his feet. Nor did he stay erect once he had been raised, crashing forward on his face as the other let him go, hot anger eating at him because of his own helplessness.

In the end, Ennar summoned two slaves who dragged Ross into the open where a council assembled about a fire. A debate was in progress, sometimes so heated that the speakers fingered their knife or ax hilts when they shouted their arguments. Ross could not understand their language, but he was certain that he was the subject under discussion and that Foscar had the deciding vote and had not yet given the nod to either side.

Ross sat where the slaves had dumped him, rubbing his smarting wrists, so deathly weary in mind and beaten in body that he was not really interested in the fate they were planning for him. He was content merely to be free of his bonds, a small favor, but one he savored dully.

He did not know how long the debate lasted, but at length Ennar came to stand over him with a message. "Your chief—he give many good things for you. Foscar take you to him."

"My chief is not here," Ross repeated wearily, making a protest he knew they would not heed. "My chief sits by the bitter water and waits. He will be angry if I do not come. Let Foscar fear his anger—"

Ennar laughed. "You run from your chief. He will be happy with Foscar when you lie again under his hand. You will not like that—I think it so!"

"I think so, too," Ross agreed silently.

He spent the rest of that night lying between the watchful Ennar and another guard, though they had the humanity not to bind him again. In the morning he was allowed to feed himself, and he fished chunks of venison out of a stew with his unwashed fingers. But in spite of the messiness, it was the best food he had eaten in days.

The trip, however, was not to be a comfortable one. He was mounted on one of the shaggy horses, a rope run under the animal's belly to loop one foot to the other. Fortunately, his hands were bound so he was able to grasp the coarse, wiry mane and keep his seat after a fashion. The nose rope of his mount was passed to Tulka, and Ennar rode beside him with only half an eye for the path of his own horse and the balance of his attention for the prisoner.

They headed northeast, with the mountains as a sharp green-and-white goal against the morning sky. Though Ross's sense of direction was not too acute, he was certain that they were making for the general vicinity of the hidden village, which he believed the ship people had destroyed. He tried to discover something of the nature of the contact which had been made between the aliens and the horsemen.

"How find other chief?" he asked Ennar.

The young man tossed one of his braids back across his shoulder and turned his head to face Ross squarely. "Your chief come our camp. Talk with Foscar—two—four sleeps ago."

"How talk with Foscar? With hunter talk?"

For the first time Ennar did not appear altogether certain. He scowled and then snapped, "He talk—Foscar, us. We hear right words—not woods creeper talk. He speak to us good."

Ross was puzzled. How could the alien out of time speak the proper language of a primitive tribe some thousands of years removed from his own era? Were the ship people also familiar with time travel? Did they have their own stations of transfer? Yet their fury with the Reds had been hot. This was a complete mystery.

"This chief—he look like me?"

Again Ennar appeared at a loss. "He wear covering like you."

"But was he like me?" persisted Ross. He didn't know what he was trying to learn, only that it seemed important at that moment to press home to at least one of the tribesmen that he *was* different from the man who had put a price on his head and to whom he was to be sold.

"Not like!" Tulka spoke over his shoulder. "You look like hunter people—hair, eyes—Strange chief no hair on head, eyes not like—"

"You saw him too?" Ross demanded eagerly.

"I saw. I ride to camp—they come so. Stand on rock, call to Foscar. Make magic with fire—it jump up!" He pointed his arm stiffly at a bush before them on the trail. "They point little, little spear—fire come out of the ground and burn. They say burn our camp if we do not give them man. We say—not have man. Then they say many good things for us if we find and bring man—"

"But they are not my people," Ross cut in. "You see, I have hair, I am not like them. They are bad—"

"You may be taken in war by them—chief's slave." Ennar had a reply to that which was logical according to the customs of his own tribe. "They want slave back—it is so."

"My people strong too, much magic," Ross pushed. "Take me to bitter water and they pay much—more than stranger chief!"

Both tribesmen were amused. "Where bitter water?" asked Tulka.

Ross jerked his head to the west. "Some sleeps away—"

"Some sleeps!" repeated Ennar jeeringly. "We ride some sleeps, maybe many sleeps where we know not the trails—maybe no people there, maybe no bitter water—all things you say with split tongue so that we not give you back to master. We go this way not even one sleep—find chief, get good things. Why we do hard thing when we can do easy?"

What argument could Ross offer in rebuttal to the simple logic of his captors? For a moment he raged inwardly at his own helplessness. But long ago he had learned that giving away to hot fury was no good unless one did it deliberately to impress, and then only when one had the upper hand. Now Ross had no hand at all.

For the most part they kept to the open, whereas Ross and the other two agents had skulked in wooded areas on their flight through this same territory. So they approached the mountains from a different angle, and though he tried, Ross could pick out no familiar landmarks. If by some miracle he was able to free himself from his captors, he could only head due west and hope to strike the river.

At midday their party made camp in a grove of trees by a spring. The weather was as unseasonably warm as it had been the day before, and flies, brought out of cold-weather hiding, attacked the stamping horses and crawled over Ross. He tried to keep them off with swings of his bound hands, for their bites drew blood.

Having been tumbled from his mount, he remained fastened to a tree with a noose about his neck while the horsemen built a fire and broiled strips of deer meat.

It would seem that Foscar was in no hurry to get on, since after they had eaten, the men continued to lounge at ease, some even dropping off to sleep. When Ross counted faces he learned that Tulka and another had both disappeared, possibly to contact and warn the aliens they were coming.

It was midafternoon before the scouts reappeared, as unobtrusively as they had gone. They went before Foscar with a report which brought the chief over to Ross. "We go. Your chief waits—"

Ross raised his swollen, bitten face and made his usual protest. "Not my chief!"

Foscar shrugged. "He say so. He give good things to get you back under his hand. So—he your chief!"

Once again Ross was boosted on his mount, and bound. But this time the party split into two groups as they rode off. He was with Ennar again, just behind Foscar, with two other guards bringing up the rear. The rest of the men, leading their mounts, melted into the trees. Ross watched that quiet withdrawal speculatively. It argued that Foscar did not trust those he was about to do business with, that he was taking certain precautions of his own. Only Ross could not see how that distrust, which might be only ordinary prudence on Foscar's part, could in any way be an advantage for him.

They rode at a pace hardly above a walk into a small open meadow narrowing at the east. Then for the first time Ross was able to place himself. They were at the entrance to the valley of the village, about a mile away from the narrow throat above which Ross had lain to spy and had been captured, for he had come from the north over the spurs of rising ridges.

Ross's horse was pulled up as Foscar drove his heel into the ribs of his own mount, sending it at a brisker pace toward the neck of the valley. There was a blot of blue there—more than one of the aliens were waiting. Ross caught his lip between his teeth and bit down on it hard. He had stood up to the Reds, to Foscar's tribesmen, but he shrank from meeting those strangers with an odd fear that the worst the men of his own species could do would be but a pale shadow to the treatment he might meet at their hands.

Foscar was now a toy man astride a toy horse. He halted his galloping mount to sit facing the handful of strangers. Ross counted four of them. They seemed to be talking, though there was still a good distance separating the mounted man and the blue suits.

Minutes passed before Foscar's arm raised in a wave to summon the party guarding Ross. Ennar kicked his horse to a trot, towing Ross's mount behind, the other two men thudding along more discreetly. Ross noted that they were both armed with spears which they carried to the fore as they rode.

They were perhaps three quarters of the way to join Foscar, and Ross could see plainly the bald heads of the aliens as their faces turned in his direction. Then the strangers struck. One of them raised a weapon shaped similarly to the automatic Ross knew, except that it was longer in the barrel.

Ross did not know why he cried out, except that Foscar had only an ax and dagger which were both still sheathed at his belt. The chief sat very still, and then his horse gave a swift sidewise swerve as if in fright. Foscar collapsed, limp, bonelessly, to the trodden turf, to lie unmoving face down.

Ennar whooped, a cry combining defiance and despair in one. He reined up with violence enough to set his horse rearing. Then, dropping his hold on the leading rope of Ross's mount, he whirled and set off in a wild dash for the trees to the left. A spear lanced across Ross's shoulder, ripping at the blue fabric, but his horse whirled to follow the other, taking him out of danger of a second thrust. Having lost his opportunity, the man who had wielded the spear dashed by at Ennar's back.

Ross clung to the mane with both hands. His greatest fear was that he might slip from the saddle pad and since he was tied by his feet, lie unprotected and helpless under those dashing hoofs. Somehow he managed to cling to the horse's neck, his face lashed by the rough mane while the animal pounded on. Had Ross been able to grasp the dangling nose rope, he might have had a faint chance of controlling that run, but as it was he could only hold fast and hope.

He had only broken glimpses of what lay ahead. Then a brilliant fire, as vivid as the flames which had eaten up the Red village, burst from the ground a few yards ahead, sending the horse wild. There was more fire and the horse changed course through the rising smoke. Ross realized that the aliens were trying to cut him off from the thin safety of the woodlands. Why they didn't just shoot him as they had Foscar he could not understand.

The smoke of the burning grass was thick, cutting between him and the woods. Might it also provide a curtain behind which he could hope to escape both parties? The fire was sending the horse back toward the waiting ship people. Ross could hear a confused shouting in the smoke. Then his mount made a miscalculation, and a tongue of red licked too close. The animal screamed, dashing on blindly straight between two of the blazes and away from the blue-clad men.

Ross coughed, almost choking, his eyes watering as the stench of singed hair thickened the smoke. But he had been carried out of the fire circle and was shooting back into the meadowland. Mount and unwilling rider were well away from the upper end of that cleared space when another horse cut in from the left, matching speed to the uncontrolled animal to which Ross clung. It was one of the tribesmen riding easily.

The trick worked, for the wild race slowed to a gallop and the other rider, in a feat of horsemanship at which Ross marveled, leaned from his seat to catch the dangling nose rope, bringing the runaway against his own steady steed. Ross shaken, still coughing from the smoke and unable to sit upright, held to the mane. The gallop slowed to a rocking pace and finally came to a halt, both horses blowing, white-foam patches on their chests and their riders' legs.

Having made his capture, the tribesman seemed indifferent to Ross, looking back instead at the wide curtain of grass smoke, frowning as he studied the swift spread of the fire. Muttering to himself, he pulled the lead rope and brought Ross's horse to follow in the direction from which Ennar had brought the captive less than a half hour earlier.

Ross tried to think. The unexpected death of their chief might well mean his own, should the tribe's desire for vengeance now be aroused. On the other hand, there was a faint chance that he could now better impress them with the thought that he was indeed of another clan and that to aid him would be to work against a common enemy.

But it was hard to plan clearly, though wits alone could save him now. The parley which had ended with Foscar's murder had brought Ross a small measure of time. He was still a captive, even though of the tribesmen and not the unearthly strangers. Perhaps to the ship people these primitives were hardly higher in scale than the forest animals.

Ross did not try to talk to his present guard, who towed him into the western sun of late afternoon. They halted at last in that same small grove where they had rested at noon. The tribesman fastened the mounts and then walked around to inspect the animal Ross had ridden. With a grunt he loosened the prisoner and spilled him unceremoniously on the ground while he examined the horse. Ross levered himself up to sight the mark of the burn across that roan hide where the fire had blistered the skin.

Thick handfuls of mud from the side of the spring were brought and plastered over the seared strip. Then, having rubbed down both animals with twists of grass, the man came over to Ross, pushed him back to the ground, and studied his left leg.

Ross understood. By rights, his thigh should also have been scorched where the flame had hit, yet he had felt no pain. Now as the tribesman examined him for a burn, he could not see even the faintest discoloration of the strange fabric. He remembered how the aliens had strolled unconcerned through the burning village. As the suit had insulated him against the cold of the ice, so it would seem that it had also protected him against the fire, for which he was duly thankful. His escape from injury was a puzzle to the tribesman, who, failing to find any trace of burn on him, left Ross alone and went to sit well away from his prisoner as if he feared him.

They did not have long to wait. One by one, those who had ridden in Foscar's company gathered at the grove. The very last to come were Ennar and Tulka, carrying the body of their chief. The faces of both men were smeared with dust and when the others sighted the body they, too, rubbed dust into their cheeks, reciting a string of words and going one by one to touch the dead chieftain's right hand.

Ennar, resigning his burden to the others, slid from his tired horse and stood for a long moment, his head bowed. Then he gazed straight at Ross and came across the tiny clearing to stand over the man of a later time. The boyishness which had been a part of him when he had fought at Foscar's command was gone. His eyes were merciless as he leaned down to speak, shaping each word with slow care so that Ross could understand the promise—that frightful promise:

"Woods rat, Foscar goes to his burial fire. And he shall take a slave with him to serve him beyond the sky—a slave to run at his voice, to shake when he thunders. Slave-dog, you shall run for Foscar beyond the sky, and he shall have you forever to walk upon as a man walks upon the earth. I, Ennar, swear that Foscar shall be sent to the chiefs in the sky in all honor. And that you, dog-one, shall lie at his feet in that going!"

He did not touch Ross, but there was no doubt in Ross's mind that he meant every word he spoke.

CHAPTER 17

The preparations for Foscar's funeral went on through the night. A wooden structure, made up of tied fagots dragged in from the woodland, grew taller beyond the big tribal camp. The constant crooning wail of the women in the tents produced a minor murmur of sound, enough to drive a man to the edge of madness. Ross had been left under guard where he could watch it all, a refinement of torture which he would earlier have believed too subtle for Ennar. Though the older men carried minor commands among the horsemen, because Ennar was the closest of blood kin among the adult males, he was in charge of the coming ceremony.

The pick of the horse herd, a roan stallion, was brought in to be picketed near Ross as sacrifice number two, and two of the hounds were in turn leashed close by. Foscar, his best weapons to hand and a red cloak lapped about him, lay waiting on a bier. Near-by squatted the tribal wizard, shaking his thunder rattle and chanting in a voice which approached a shriek. This wild activity might have been a scene lifted directly from some tape stored at the project base. It was very difficult for Ross to remember that this was reality, that he was to be one of the main actors in the coming event, with no timely aid from Operation Retrograde to snatch him to safety.

Sometime during that nightmare he slept, his weariness of body overcoming him. He awoke, dazed, to find a hand clutching his mop of hair, pulling his head up.

"You sleep—you do not fear, Foscar's dog-one?"

Groggily Ross blinked up. Fear? Sure, he was afraid. Fear, he realized with a clear thrust of consciousness such as he had seldom experienced before, had always stalked beside him, slept in his bed. But he had never surrendered to it, and he would not now if he could help it.

"I do not fear!" He threw that creed into Ennar's face in one hot boast. He *would* not fear!

"We shall see if you speak so loudly when the fire bites you!" The other spat, yet in that oath there was a reluctant recognition of Ross's courage.

"When the fire bites...." That sang in Ross's head. There was something else—if he could only remember! Up to that moment he had kept a poor little shadow of hope. It is always impossible—he was conscious again with that strange clarity of mind—for a man to face his own death honestly. A man always continues to believe to the last moment of his life that something will intervene to save him.

The men led the horse to the mound of fagots which was now crowned with Foscar's bier. The stallion went quietly, until a tall tribesman struck true with an ax, and the animal fell. The hounds were also killed and laid at their dead master's feet.

But Ross was not to fare so easily. The wizard danced about him, a hideous figure in a beast mask, a curled fringe of dried snakeskins swaying from his belt. Shaking his rattle, he squawked like an angry cat as they pulled Ross to the stacked wood.

Fire—there was something about fire—if he could only remember! Ross stumbled and nearly fell across one leg of the dead horse they were propping into place. Then he remembered that tongue of flame in the meadow grass which had burned the horse but not the rider. His hands and his head would have no protection, but the rest of his body was covered with the flame-resistant fabric of the alien suit. Could he do it? There was such a slight chance, and they were already pushing him onto that mound, his hands tied. Ennar stooped, and bound his ankles, securing him to the brush.

So fastened, they left him. The tribe ringed around the pyre at a safe distance, Ennar and five other men approaching from different directions, torches aflame. Ross watched those blazing knots thrust into the brush and heard the crackle of the fire. His eyes, hard and measuring, studied the flash of flame from dried brush to seasoned wood.

A tongue of yellow-red flame licked up at him. Ross hardly dared to breathe as it wreathed about his foot, his hide fetters smoldering. The insulation of the suit did not cut all the heat, but it allowed him to stay put for the few seconds he needed to make his escape spectacular.

The flame had eaten through his foot bonds, and yet the burning sensation on his feet and legs was no greater than it would have been from the direct rays of a bright summer sun. Ross moistened his lips with his tongue. The impact of heat on his hands and his face was different. He leaned down, held his wrists to the flame, taking in stoical silence the burns which freed him.

Then, as the fire curled up so that he seemed to stand in a frame of writhing red banners, Ross leaped through that curtain, protecting his bowed head with his arms as best he could. But to the onlookers it seemed he passed unhurt through the heart of a roaring fire.

He kept his footing and stood facing that part of the tribal ring directly before him. He heard a cry, perhaps of fear, and a blazing torch flew through the air and struck his hip. Although he felt the force of the blow, the burning bits of the head merely slid down his thigh and leg, leaving no mark on the smooth blue fabric.

"Ahhhhhhh!"

Now the wizard capered before him, shaking his rattle to make a deafening din. Ross struck out, slapping the sorcerer out of his path, and stooped to pick up the smoldering brand which had been thrown at him. Whirling it about his head, though every movement was torture to his scorched hands, he set it flaming once more. Holding it in front of him as a weapon, he stalked directly at the men and women before him.

The torch was a poor enough defense against spears and axes, but Ross did not care—he put into this last gamble all the determination he could summon. Nor did he realize what a figure he presented to the tribesmen. A man who had crossed a curtain of fire without apparent hurt, who appeared to wash in tongues of flame without harm, and who now called upon fire in turn as a weapon, was no man but a demon!

The wall of people wavered and broke. Women screamed and ran; men shouted. But no one threw a spear or struck with an ax. Ross walked on, a man possessed, looking neither to the right or left. He was in the camp now, stalking toward the fire burning before Foscar's tent. He did not turn aside for that either, but holding the torch high, strode through the heart of the flames, risking further burns for the sake of insuring his ultimate safety.

The tribesmen melted away as he approached the last line of tents, with the open land beyond. The horses of the herd, which had been driven to this side to avoid the funeral pyre, were shifting nervously, the scent of burning making them uneasy.

Once more Ross whirled the dying torch about his head. Recalling how the aliens had sent his horse mad, he tossed it behind him into the grass between the tents and the herd. The tinder-dry stuff caught immediately. Now if the men tried to ride after him, they would have trouble.

Without hindrance he walked across the meadow at the same even pace, never turning to look behind. His hands were two separate worlds of smarting pain; his hair and eyebrows were singed, and a finger of burn ran along the angle of his jaw. But he was free, and he did not believe that Foscar's men would be in any haste to pursue him. Somewhere before him lay the river, the river which ran to the sea. Ross walked on in the sunny morning while behind him black smoke raised a dark beacon to the sky.

Afterward he guessed that he must have been lightheaded for several days, remembering little save the pain in his hands and the fact that it was necessary to keep moving. Once he fell to his knees and buried both hands in the cool, moist earth where a thread of stream trickled from a pool. The muck seemed to draw out a little of the agony while he drank with a fever thirst.

Ross seemed to move through a haze which lifted at intervals during which he noted his surroundings, was able to recall a little of what lay behind him, and to keep to the correct route. However, the gaps of time in between were forever lost to him. He stumbled along the banks of a river and fronted a bear fishing. The massive beast rose on its hind legs, growled, and Ross walked by it uncaring, unmenaced by the puzzled animal.

Sometimes he slept through the dark periods which marked the nights, or he stumbled along under the moon, nursing his hands against his breast, whimpering a little when his foot slipped and the jar of that mishap ran through his body. Once he heard singing, only to realize that it was himself who sang hoarsely a melody which would be popular thousands of years later in the world through which he wavered. But always Ross knew that he must go on, using that thick stream of running water as a guide to his final goal, the sea.

After a long while those spaces of mental clarity grew longer, appearing closer together. He dug small shelled things from under stones along the river and ate them avidly. Once he clubbed a rabbit and feasted. He sucked birds' eggs from a nest hidden among some reeds—just enough to keep his gaunt body going, though his gray eyes were now set in what was almost a death's-head.

Ross did not know just when he realized that he was again being hunted. It started with an uneasiness which differed from his previous fever-bred hallucinations. This was an inner pulling, a growing compulsion to turn and retrace his way back toward the mountains to meet something, or someone, waiting for him on the backward path.

But Ross kept on, fearing sleep now and fighting it. For once he had lain down to rest and had wakened on his feet, heading back as if that compulsion had the power to take over his body when his waking will was off guard.

So he rested, but he dared not sleep, the desire constantly tearing at his will, striving to take over his weakened body and draw it back. Perhaps against all reason he believed that it was the aliens who were trying to control him. Ross did not even venture to guess why they were so determined to get him. If there were tribesmen on his trail as well, he did not know, but he was sure that this was now purely a war of wills.

As the banks of the river were giving way to marshes, he had to wade through mud and water, detouring the boggy sections. Great clouds of birds whirled and shrieked their protests at his coming, and sleek water animals paddled and poked curious heads out of the water as this two-legged thing walked mechanically through their green land. Always that pull was with him, until Ross was more aware of fighting it than of traveling.

Why did they want him to return? Why did they not follow him? Or were they afraid to venture too far from where they had come through the transfer? Yet the unseen rope which was tugging at him did not grow less tenuous as he put more distance between himself and the mountain valley. Ross could understand neither their motives nor their methods, but he could continue to fight.

The bog was endless. He found an island and lashed himself with his suit belt to the single willow which grew there, knowing that he must have sleep, or he could not hope to last through the next day. Then he slept, only to waken cold, shaking, and afraid. Shoulder deep in a pool, he was aware that in his sleep he must have opened the belt buckle and freed himself, and only the mishap of falling into the water had brought him around to sanity.

Somehow he got back to the tree, rehooked the buckle and twisted the belt around the branches so that he was sure he could not work it free until daybreak. He lapsed into a deepening doze, and awoke, still safely anchored, with the morning cries of the birds. Ross considered the suit as he untangled the belt. Could the strange clothing be the tie by which the aliens held to him? If he were to strip, leaving the garment behind, would he be safe?

He tried to force open the studs across his chest, but they would not yield to the slight pressure which was all his seared fingers could exert, and when he pulled at the fabric, he was unable to tear it. So, still wearing the livery of the off-world men, Ross continued on his way, hardly caring where he went or how. The mud plastered on him by his frequent falls was some protection against the swarm of insect life his passing stirred into attack. However, he was able to endure a swollen face and slitted eyes, being far more conscious of the wrenching feeling within him than the misery of his body.

The character of the marsh began to change once more. The river was splitting into a dozen smaller streams, shaping out fanlike. Looking down at this from one of the marsh hillocks, Ross knew a faint surge of relief. Such a place had been on the map Ashe had made them memorize. He was close to the sea at last, and for the moment that was enough.

A salt-sharpened wind cut at him with the force of a fist in the face. In the absence of sunlight the leaden clouds overhead set a winterlike gloom across the countryside. To the constant sound of birdcalls Ross tramped heavily through small pools, beating a path through tangles of marsh grass. He stole eggs from nests, sucking his nourishment eagerly with no dislike for the fishy flavor, and drinking from stagnant, brackish ponds.

Suddenly Ross halted, at first thinking that the continuous roll of sound he heard was thunder. Yet the clouds overhead were massed no more than before and there was no sign of lightning. Continuing on, he realized that the mysterious sound was the pounding of surf—he was near the sea!

Willing his body to run, he weaved forward at a reeling trot, pitting all his energy against the incessant pull from behind. His feet skidded out of marsh mud into sand. Ahead of him were dark rocks surrounded by the white lace of spray.

Ross headed straight toward that spray until he stood knee-deep in the curling, foam-edged water and felt its tug on his body almost as strong as that other tug upon his mind. He knelt, letting the salt water sting to life every cut, every burn, sputtering as it filled his mouth and nostrils, washing from him the slime of the bog lands. It was cold and bitter, but it was the sea! He had made it!

Ross Murdock staggered back and sat down suddenly in the sand. Glancing about, he saw that his refuge was a rough triangle between two of the small river arms, littered with the debris of the spring floods which had grounded here after rejection by the sea. Although there was plenty of material for a fire, he had no means of kindling a flame, having lost the flint all Beaker traders carried for such a purpose.

This was the sea, and against all odds he had reached it. He lay back, his self-confidence restored to the point where he dared once more to consider the future. He watched the swooping flight of gulls drawing patterns under the clouds above. For the moment he wanted nothing more than to lie here and rest.

But he did not surrender to this first demand of his over-driven body for long. Hungry and cold, sure that a storm was coming, he knew he had to build a fire—a fire on shore could provide him with the means of signaling the sub. Hardly knowing why—because one part of the coastline was as good as another—Ross began to walk again, threading a path in and out among the rocky outcrops.

So he found it, a hollow between two such windbreaks within which was a blackened circle of small stones holding charred wood, with some empty shells piled near-by. Here was unmistakable evidence of a camp! Ross plunged forward, thrusting a hand impetuously into the black mass of the dead fire. To his astonishment, he touched warmth!

Hardly daring to disturb those precious bits of charcoal, he dug around them, then carefully blew into what appeared to be dead ashes. There was an answering glow! He could not have just imagined it.

From a pile of wood that had been left behind, Ross snatched a small twig, poking it at the coal after he had rubbed it into a brush on the rough rock. He watched, all one ache of hope. The twig caught!

With his stiff fingers so clumsy, he had to be very careful, but Ross had learned patience in a hard school. Bit by bit he fed that tiny blaze until he had a real fire. Then, leaning back against the rock, he watched it.

It was now obvious that the placement of the original fire had been chosen with care, for the outcrops gave it wind shelter. They also provided a dark backdrop, partially hiding the flames on the landward side but undoubtedly making them more visible from the sea. The site seemed just right for a signal fire—but to what?

Ross's hands shook slightly as he fed the blaze. It was only too clear why anyone would make a signal on this shore. McNeil—or perhaps both he and Ashe—had survived the breakup of the raft, after all. They had reached this point—abandoned no earlier than this morning, judging by the life remaining in the coals—and put up the signal. Then, just as arranged, they had been collected by the sub, by now on its way back to the hidden North American post. There was no hope of any pickup for him now. Just as he had believed them dead after he had found that rag on the sapling, so they must have thought him finished after his fall in the river. He was just a few hours too late!

Ross folded his arms across his hunched knees and rested his head on them. There was no possible way he could ever reach the post or his own kind—ever again. Thousands of miles lay between him and the temporary installation in this time.

He was so sunk in his own complete despair that he was long unaware of finally being free of the pressure to turn back which had so long haunted him. But as he roused to feed the fire he got to wondering. Had those who hunted him given up the chase? Since he had lost his own race with time, he did not really care. What did it matter?

The pile of wood was getting low, but he decided that did not matter either. Even so, Ross got to his feet, moving over to the drifts of storm wrack to gather more. Why should he stay here by a useless beacon? But somehow he could not force himself to move on, as futile as his vigil seemed.

Dragging the sun-dried, bleached limbs of long-dead trees to his half shelter, he piled them up, working until he laughed at the barricade he had built. "A siege!" For the first time in days he spoke aloud. "I might be ready for a siege...." He pulled over another branch, added it to his pile, and kneeled down once more by the flames.

There were fisherfolk to be found along this coast, and tomorrow when he was rested he would strike south and try to find one of their primitive villages. Traders would be coming into this territory now that the Red-inspired raiders were gone. If he could contact them....

But that spark of interest in the future died almost as soon as it was born. To be a Beaker trader as an agent for the project was one thing, to live the role for the rest of his life was something else.

Ross stood by his fire, staring out to sea for a sign he knew he would never see again as long as he lived. Then, as if a spear had struck between his shoulder blades, he was attacked.

The blow was not physical, but came instead as a tearing, red pain in his head, a pressure so terrible he could not move. He knew instantly that behind him now lurked the ultimate danger.

CHAPTER 18

Ross fought to break that hold, to turn his head, to face the peril which crept upon him now. Unlike anything he had ever met before in his short lifetime, it could only have come from some alien source. This strange encounter was a battle of will against will! The same rebellion against authority which had ruled his boyhood, which had pushed him into the orbit of the project, stiffened him to meet this attack.

He was going to turn his head; he was going to see who stood there. He *was*! Inch by inch, Ross's head came around, though sweat stung his seared and bitten flesh, and every breath was an effort. He caught a half glimpse of the beach behind the rocks, and the stretch of sand was empty. Overhead the birds were gone—as if they had never existed. Or, as if they had been swept away by some impatient fighter, who wanted no distractions from the purpose at hand.

Having successfully turned his head, Ross decided to turn his body. His left hand went out, slowly, as if it moved some great weight. His palm gritted painfully on the rock and he savored that pain, for it pierced through the dead blanket of compulsion that was being used against him. Deliberately he ground his blistered skin against the stone, concentrating on the sharp torment in his hand as the agony shot up his arm. While he focused his attention on the physical pain, he could feel the pressure against him weaken. Summoning all his strength, Ross swung around in a movement which was only a shadow of his former feline grace.

The beach was still empty, except for the piles of driftwood, the rocks, and the other things he had originally found there. Yet he knew that something was waiting to pounce. Having discovered that for him pain was a defense weapon, he had that one resource. If they took him, it would be after besting him in a fight.

Even as he made this decision, Ross was conscious of a curious weakening of the force bent upon him. It was as if his opponents had been surprised, either at his simple actions of the past few seconds or at his determination. Ross leaped upon that surprise, adding it to his stock of unseen weapons.

He leaned forward, still grinding his torn hand against the rock as a steadying influence, took up a length of dried wood, and thrust its end into the fire. Having once used fire to save himself, he was ready and willing to do it again, although at the same time, another part of him shrank from what he intended.

Holding his improvised torch breast-high, Ross stared across it, searching the land for the faintest sign of his enemies. In spite of the fire and the light he held before him, the dusk prevented him from seeing too far. Behind him the crash of the surf could have covered the noise of a marching army.

"Come and get me!"

He whirled his brand into bursting life and then hurled it straight into the drift among the dunes. He was grabbing for a second brand almost before the blazing head of the first had fallen into the twisted, bleached roots of a dead tree.

He stood tense, a second torch now kindled in his hand. The sharp vise of another's will which had nipped him so tightly a moment ago was easing, slowly disappearing as water might trickle away. Yet he could not believe that this small act of defiance had so daunted his unseen opponent as to make him give up the struggle this easily. It was more likely the pause of a wrestler seeking for a deadlier grip.

The brand in his hand—Ross's second line of defense—was a weapon he was loath to use, but would use if he were forced to it. He kept his hand mercilessly flat against the rock as a reminder and a spur.

Fire twisted and crackled among the driftwood where the first torch had lodged, providing a flickering light yards from where he stood. He was grateful for it in the gloom of the gathering storm. If they would only come to open war before the rain struck....

Ross sheltered his torch with his body as spray, driven inward from the sea, spattered his shoulders and his back. If it rained, he would lose what small advantage the fire gave him, but then he would find some other way to meet them. They would neither break him nor take him, even if he had to wade into the sea and swim out into the lash of the cold northern waves until he could not move his tired limbs any longer.

Once again that steel-edge will struck at Ross, probing his stubbornness, assaulting his mind. He whirled the torch, brought the scorching breath of the flame across the hand resting on the rock. Unable to control his own cry of protest, he was not sure he had the fortitude to repeat such an act.

He had won again! The pressure had fallen away in a flick, almost as if some current had been snapped off. Through the red curtain of his torment

Ross sensed a surprise and disbelief. He was unaware that in this queer duel he was using both a power of will and a depth of perception he had never known he possessed. Because of his daring, he had shaken his opponents as no physical attack could have affected them.

"Come and get me!" He shouted again at the barren shoreline where the fire ate at the drift and nothing stirred, yet something very much alive and conscious lay hidden. This time there was more than simple challenge in Ross's demand—there was a note of triumph.

The spray whipped by him, striking at his fire, at the brand he held. Let the sea water put both out! He would find another way of fighting. He was certain of that, and he sensed that those out there knew it too and were troubled.

The fire was being driven by the wind along the crisscross lines of bone-white wood left high on the beach, forming a wall of flame between him and the interior, not, however, an insurmountable barrier to whatever lurked there.

Again Ross leaned against the rock, studying the length of beach. Had he been wrong in thinking that they were within the range of his voice? The power they had used might carry over a greater distance.

"Yahhhh—" Instead of a demand, he now voiced a taunting cry, screaming his defiance. Some wild madness had been transmitted to him by the winds, the roaring sea, his own pain. Ready to face the worst they could send against him, he tried to hurl that thought back at them as they had struck with their united will at him. No answer came to his challenge, no rise to counter-attack.

Moving away from the rock, Ross began to walk forward toward the burning drift, his torch ready in his hand. "I am here!" he shouted into the wind. "Come out—face me!"

It was then that he saw those who had tracked him. Two tall thin figures, wearing dark clothes, were standing quietly watching him, their eyes dark holes in the white ovals of their faces.

Ross halted. Though they were separated by yards of sand and rock and a burning barrier, he could feel the force they wielded. The nature of that force had changed, however. Once it had struck with a vigorous spear point; now it formed a shield of protection. Ross could not break through that shield, and they dared not drop it. A stalemate existed between them in this strange battle, the like of which Ross's world had not known before.

He watched those expressionless white faces, trying to find some reply to the deadlock. There flashed into his mind the certainty that while he lived and moved, and they lived and moved, this struggle, this unending pursuit, would continue. For some mysterious reason they wanted to have him under their control, but that was never going to happen if they all had to remain here on this strip of water-washed sand until they starved to death! Ross tried to drive that thought across to them.

"Murrrrdock!" That croaking cry borne out of the sea by the wind might almost have come from the bill of a sea bird.

"Murrrrdock!"

Ross spun around. Visibility had been drastically curtailed by the lowering clouds and the dashing spray, but he could see a round dark thing bobbing on the waves. The sub? A raft?

Sensing a movement behind him, Ross wheeled about as one of the alien figures leaped the blazing drift, heedless of the flames, and ran light-footedly toward him in what could only be an all-out attempt at capture. The man had ready a weapon like the one that had felled Foscar. Ross threw himself at his opponent in a reckless dive, falling on him with a smashing impact.

In Ross's grasp the alien's body was fragile, but he moved fluidly as Murdock fought to break his grip on the hand weapon and pin him to the sand. Ross was too intent upon his own part of the struggle to heed the sounds of a shot over his head and a thin, wailing cry. He slammed his opponent's hand against a stone, and the white face, inches away from his own, twisted silently with pain.

Fumbling for a better hold, Ross was sent rolling. He came down on his left hand with a force which brought tears to his eyes and stopped him just long enough for the other to regain his feet.

The blue-suited man sprinted back to the body of his fellow where it lay by the drift. He slung his unconscious comrade over the barrier with more ease than Ross would have believed possible and vaulted the barrier after him. Ross, half crouched on the sand, felt unusually light and empty. The strange tie which had drawn and held him to the strangers had been broken.

"Murdock!"

A rubber raft rode in on the waves, two men aboard it. Ross got up, pulling at the studs of his suit with his right hand. He could believe in what he saw now—the sub had not left, after all. The two men running toward him through the dusk were of his own kind.

"Murdock!"

It did not seem at all strange that Kelgarries reached him first. Ross, caught up in this dream, appealed to the major for aid with the studs. If the strangers from the ship did trace him by the suit, they were not going to follow the sub back to the post and serve the project as they had the Reds.

"Got—to—get—this—off—" He pulled the words out one by one, tugging frantically at the stubborn studs. "They can trace this and follow us—"

Kelgarries needed no better explanation. Ripping loose the fastenings, he pulled the clinging fabric from Ross, sending him reeling with pain as he pulled the left sleeve down the younger man's arm.

The wind and spray were ice on his body as they dragged him down to the raft, bundling him aboard. He did not at all remember their arrival on board the sub. He was lying in the vibrating heart of the undersea ship when he opened his eyes to see Kelgarries regarding him intently. Ashe, a coat of bandage about his shoulder and chest, lay on a neighboring bunk. McNeil stood watching a medical corpsman lay out supplies.

"He needs a shot," the medic was saying as Ross blinked at the major.

"You left the suit—back there?" Ross demanded.

"We did. What's this about them tracing you by it? Who was tracing you?"

"Men from the space ship. That's the only way they could have trailed me down the river." He was finding it difficult to talk, and the protesting medic kept waving a needle in his direction, but somehow in bursts of half-finished sentences Ross got out his story—Foscar's death, his own escape from the chief's funeral pyre, and the weird duel of wills back on the beach. Even as he poured it out he thought how unlikely most of it must sound. Yet Kelgarries appeared to accept every word, and there was no expression of disbelief on Ashe's face.

"So that's how you got those burns," said the major slowly when Ross had finished his story. "Deliberately searing your hand in the fire to break their hold—" He crashed his fist against the wall of the tiny cabin and then, when Ross winced at the jar, he hurriedly uncurled those fingers to press Ross's shoulder with a surprisingly warm and gentle touch. "Put him to sleep," he ordered the medic. "He deserves about a month of it, I should judge. I think he has brought us a bigger slice of the future than we had hoped for...."

Ross felt the prick of the needle and then nothing more. Even when he was carried ashore at the post and later when he was transported into his proper time, he did not awaken. He only approached a strange dreamy state in which he ate and drowsed, not caring for the world beyond his own bunk.

But there came a day when he did care, sitting up to demand food with a great deal of his old self-assertion. The doctor looked him over, permitting him to get out of bed and try out his legs. They were exceedingly uncooperative at first, and Ross was glad he had tried to move only from his bunk to a waiting chair.

"Visitors welcome?"

Ross looked up eagerly and then smiled, somewhat hesitatingly, at Ashe. The older man wore his arm in a sling but otherwise seemed his usual imperturbable self.

"Ashe, tell me what happened. Are we back at the main base? What about the Reds? We weren't traced by the ship people, were we?"

Ashe laughed. "Did Doc just wind you up to let you spin, Ross? Yes, this is home, sweet home. As for the rest—well, it is a long story, and we are still picking up pieces of it here and there."

Ross pointed to the bunk in invitation. "Can you tell me what is known?" He was still somewhat at a loss, his old secret awe of Ashe tempering his outward show of eagerness. Ross still feared one of those snubs the other so well knew how to deliver to the bumptious. But Ashe did come in and sit down, none of his old formality now in evidence.

"You have been a surprise package, Murdock." His observation had some of the ring of the old Ashe, but there was no withdrawal behind the words. "Rather a busy lad, weren't you, after you were bumped off into that river?"

Ross's reply was a grimace. "You heard all about that!" He had no time for his own adventures, already receding into a past which made them both dim and unimportant. "What happened to you—and to the project—and—"

"One thing at a time, and don't rush your fences." Ashe was surveying him with an odd intentness which Ross could not understand. He continued to explain in his "instructor" voice. "We made it down the river—how, don't ask me. That was something of a 'project' in itself," he laughed. "The raft came apart piece by piece, and we waded most of the last couple of miles, I think. I'm none too clear on the details; you'll have to get those out of McNeil, who was still among those present then. Other than that, we cannot compete with your adventures. We built a signal fire and sat by it toasting our shins for a few days, until the sub came to collect us—"

"And took you off." Ross experienced a fleeting return of that hollow feeling he had known on the shore when the still-warm coals of the signal fire had told him the story of his too-late arrival.

"And took us off. But Kelgarries agreed to spin out our waiting period for another twenty-four hours, in case you did manage to survive that toss you took into the river. Then we sighted your spectacular display of fireworks on the beach, and the rest was easy."

"The ship people didn't trace us back to post?"

"Not that we know of. Anyway, we've closed down the post on that time level. You might be interested in a very peculiar tale our modern agents have picked up, floating over and under the iron curtain. A blast went off in the Baltic region of this time, wiping some installation clean off the map. The Reds have kept quiet as to the nature of the explosion and the exact place where it occurred."

"The aliens followed *them* all the way up to this time!"—Ross half rose from the chair—"But why? And why did they trail me?"

"That we can only guess. But I don't believe that they were moved by any private vengeance for the looting of their derelict. There is some more imperative reason why they don't want us to find or use anything from one of their cargoes—"

"But they were in power thousands of years ago. Maybe they and their worlds are gone now. Why should things we do today matter to them?"

"Well, it does matter, and in some very important way. And we have to learn that reason."

"How?" Ross looked down at his left hand, encased in a mitten of bandage under which he very gingerly tried to stretch a finger. Maybe he should have been eager to welcome another meeting with the ship people, but if he were truly honest, he had to admit that he did not. He glanced up, sure that Ashe had read all that hesitation and scorned him for it. But there was no sign that his discomfiture had been noticed.

"By doing some looting of our own," Ashe answered. "Those tapes we brought back are going to be a big help. More than one derelict was located. We were right in our surmise that the Reds first discovered the remains of one in Siberia, but it was in no condition to be explored. They already had the basic idea of the time traveler, so they applied it to the hunting down of other ships, with several way stops to throw people like us off the scent. So they found an intact ship, and also several others. At least three are on *this* side of the Atlantic where they couldn't get at them very well. Those we can deal with now—"

"Won't the aliens be waiting for us to try that?"

"As far as we can discover they don't know where any of these ships crashed. Either there were no survivors, or passengers and crew took off in lifeboats while they were still in space. They might never have known of the Reds' activities if you hadn't triggered that communicator on the derelict."

Ross was reduced to a small boy who badly needed an alibi for some piece of juvenile mischief. "I didn't mean to." That excuse sounded so feeble that he was surprised into a laugh, only to see Ashe grinning back at him.

"Seeing as how your action also put a very effective spike in the opposition's wheel, you are freely forgiven. Anyway, you have also provided us with a pretty good idea of what we may be up against with the aliens, and we'll be prepared for that next time."

"Then there will be a next time?"

"We are calling in all time agents, concentrating our forces in the right period. Yes, there will be a next time. We have to learn just what they are trying so hard to protect."

"What do you think it is?"

"Space!" Ashe spoke the word softly as if he relished the promise it held.

"Space?"

"That ship you explored was a derelict from a galactic fleet, but it was a ship and it used the principle of space flight. Do you understand now? In these lost ships lies the secret which will make us free of all the stars! We must claim it."

"Can we—?"

"Can *we*?" Ashe was laughing at Ross again with his eyes, though his face remained sober. "Then *you* still want to be counted in on this game?"

Ross looked down again at his bandaged hand and remembered swiftly so many things—the coast of Britain on a misty morning, the excitement of prowling the alien ship, the fight with Ennar, even the long nightmare of his flight down the river, and lastly, the exultation he had tasted when he had faced the alien and had locked wills—to hold steady. He knew that he could not, would not, give up what he had found here in the service of the project as long as it was in his power to cling to it.

"Yes." It was a very simple answer, but when his eyes met Ashe's, Ross knew that it would serve better than any solemn oath.

THE DEFIANT AGENTS

CONTENTS

1

No windows broke any of the four plain walls of the office; there was no focus of outer-world sunlight on the desk there. Yet the five disks set out on its surface appeared to glow—perhaps the heat of the mischief they could cause ... had caused ... blazed in them.

But fanciful imaginings did not cushion or veil cold, hard fact. Dr. Gordon Ashe, one of the four men peering unhappily at the display, shook his head slightly as if to free his mind of such cobwebs.

His neighbor to the right, Colonel Kelgarries, leaned forward to ask harshly: "No chance of a mistake?"

"You saw the detector." The thin gray string of a man behind the desk answered with chill precision. "No, no possible mistake. These five have definitely been snooped."

"And two choices among them," Ashe murmured. That was the important point now.

"I thought these were under maximum security," Kelgarries challenged the gray man.

Florian Waldour's remote expression did not change. "Every possible precaution was in force. There was a sleeper—a hidden agent—planted—"

"Who?" Kelgarries demanded.

Ashe glanced around at his three companions—Kelgarries, colonel in command of one sector of Project Star, Florian Waldour, the security head on the station, Dr. James Ruthven....

"Camdon!" he said, hardly able to believe this answer to which logic had led him.

Waldour nodded.

For the first time since he had known and worked with Kelgarries Ashe saw him display open astonishment.

"Camdon? But he was sent us by—" The colonel's eyes narrowed. "He must have been sent.... There were too many cross checks to fake that!"

"Oh, he was sent, all right." For the first time there was a note of emotion in Waldour's voice. "He was a sleeper, a very deep sleeper. They must have planted him a full twenty-five or thirty years ago. He's been just what he claimed to be as long as that."

"Well, he certainly was worth their time and trouble, wasn't he?" James Ruthven's voice was a growling rumble. He sucked in thick lips, continuing to stare at the disks. "How long ago were these snooped?"

Ashe's thoughts turned swiftly from the enormity of the betrayal to that important point. The time element—that was the primary concern now that the damage was done, and they knew it.

"That's one thing we don't know." Waldour's reply came slowly as if he hated the admission.

"We'll be safer, then, if we presume the very earliest period." Ruthven's statement was as ruthless in its implications as the shock they had had when Waldour announced the disaster.

"Eighteen months ago?" Ashe protested.

But Ruthven was nodding. "Camdon was in on this from the very first. We've had the tapes in and out for study all that time, and the new detector against snooping was not put in service until two weeks ago. This case came up on the first checking round, didn't it?" he asked Waldour.

"First check," the security man agreed. "Camdon left the base six days ago. But he has been in and out on his liaison duties from the first."

"He had to go through those search points every time," Kelgarries protested. "Thought nothing could get through those." The colonel brightened. "Maybe he got his snooper films and then couldn't take them off base. Have his quarters been turned out?"

Waldour's lips lifted in a grimace of exasperation. "Please, Colonel," he said wearily, "this is not a kindergarten exercise. In confirmation of his success, listen...." He touched a button on his desk and out of the air came the emotionless chant of a newscaster.

"Fears for the safety of Lassiter Camdon, space expediter for the Western Conference Space Council, have been confirmed by the discovery of burned wreckage in the mountains. Mr. Camdon was returning from a mission to the Star Laboratory when his plane lost contact with Ragnor Field. Reports of a storm in that vicinity immediately raised concern—" Waldour snapped off the voice.

"True—or a cover for his escape?" Kelgarries wondered aloud.

"Could be either. They may have deliberately written him off when they had all they wanted," Waldour acknowledged. "But to get back to our troubles—Dr. Ruthven is right to assume the worst. I believe we can only insure the recovery of our project by thinking that these tapes were snooped anywhere from eighteen months ago to last week. And we must work accordingly!"

There was silence in the room as they all considered that. Ashe slipped down in his chair, his thoughts enmeshed in memories. First there had been Operation Retrograde, when specially trained "time agents" had shuttled back and forth in history, striving to locate and track down the mysterious source of alien knowledge which the eastern Communistic nations had suddenly begun to use.

Ashe himself and a younger partner, Ross Murdock, had been part of the final action which had solved the mystery, having traced that source of knowledge not to an earlier and forgotten Terran civilization but to wrecked spaceships from an eon-old galactic empire—an empire which had flourished when glacial ice covered most of Europe and northern America and Terrans were cave-dwelling primitives. Murdock, trapped by the Reds in one of those wrecked ships, had inadvertently summoned its original owners, who had descended to trace—through the Russian time stations—the looters of their wrecks, destroying the whole Red time-travel system.

But the aliens had not chanced on the parallel western system. And a year later that had been put into Project Folsom One. Again Ashe, Murdock, and a newcomer, the Apache Travis Fox, had gone back into time to the Arizona of the Folsom hunters, discovering what they wanted—two ships, one wrecked, the other intact. And when the full efforts of the project had been centered on bringing the intact ship back into the present, chance had triggered controls set by the dead alien commander. A party of four, Ashe, Murdock, Fox, and a technician, had then made an involuntary voyage into space, touching three worlds on which the galactic civilization of the far past was now marked only by ruins.

Voyage tape fed into the controls of the ship had taken the men, and, when rewound, had—by a miracle—returned them to Terra with a cargo of similar tapes found in a building on a world which might have been the central capital for a government comprised not of countries or of worlds but of solar systems. Tapes—each one the key to another planet.

And that ancient galactic knowledge was treasure such as the Terrans had never dreamed of possessing, though there were the attendant fears that such discoveries could be weapons in enemy hands. There had been an enforced sharing with other nations of tapes chosen at random at a great drawing. And each nation secretly remained convinced that, in spite of the untold riches it might hold as a result of chance, its rivals had done better. Right at this moment, Ashe did not in the least doubt, there were agents of his own party intent on accomplishing at the Red project just what Camdon had done there. However, that did not help in solving their present dilemma concerning Operation Cochise, one part of their project, but perhaps the most important now.

Some of the tapes were duds, either too damaged to be useful, or set for worlds hostile to Terrans lacking the equipment the earlier star-traveling race had had at its command. Of the five tapes they now knew had been snooped, three would be useless to the enemy.

But one of the remaining two.... Ashe frowned. One was the goal toward which they had been working feverishly for a full twelve months. To plant a colony across the gulf of space—a successful colony—later to be used as a steppingstone to other worlds....

"So we have to move faster." Ruthven's comment reached Ashe through his stream of memories.

"I thought you required at least three more months to conclude personnel training," Waldour observed.

Ruthven lifted a fat hand, running the nail of a broad thumb back and forth across his lower lip in a habitual gesture Ashe had learned to mistrust. As the latter stiffened, bracing for a battle of wills, he saw Kelgarries come alert too. At least the colonel more often than not was ready to counter Ruthven's demands.

"We test and we test," said the fat man. "Always we test. We move like turtles when it would be better to race like greyhounds. There is such a thing as overcaution, as I have said from the first. One would think"—his accusing glance included Ashe and Kelgarries—"that there had never been any improvising in this project, that all had always been done by the book. I say that this is the time we must take the big gamble, or else we may find we have been outbid for space entirely. Let those others discover even one alien installation they can master and—" his thumb shifted from his lip, grinding down on the desk top as if it were crushing some venturesome but entirely unimportant insect—"and we are finished before we really begin."

There were a number of men in the project who would agree with that, Ashe knew. And a greater number in the country and conference at large. The public was used to reckless gambles which paid off, and there had been enough of those in the past to give an impressive argument for that point of view. But Ashe, himself, could not agree to a speed-up. He had been out among the stars, shaved disaster too closely because the proper training had not been given.

"I shall report that I advise a take-off within a week," Ruthven was continuing. "To the council I shall say that—"

"And I do not agree!" Ashe cut in. He glanced at Kelgarries for the quick backing he expected, but instead there was a lengthening moment of silence. Then the colonel spread out his hands and said sullenly:

"I don't agree either, but I don't have the final say-so. Ashe, what would be needed to speed up any take-off?"

It was Ruthven who replied. "We can use the Redax, as I have said from the start."

Ashe straightened, his mouth tight, his eyes hard and angry.

"And I'll protest that ... to the council! Man, we're dealing with human beings—selected volunteers, men who trust us—not with laboratory animals!"

Ruthven's thick lips pouted into what was close to a smile of derision. "Always the sentimentalists, you experts in the past! Tell me, Dr. Ashe, were you always so thoughtful of your men when you sent agents back into time? And certainly a voyage into space is less a risk than time travel. These volunteers know what they have signed for. They will be ready—"

"Then you propose telling them about the use of Redax—what it does to a man's mind?" countered Ashe.

"Certainly. They will receive all necessary instructions."

Ashe was not satisfied and he would have spoken again, but Kelgarries interrupted:

"If it comes to that, none of us here has any right to make final decisions. Waldour has already sent in his report about the snoop. We'll have to await orders from the council."

Ruthven levered himself out of his chair, his solid bulk stretching his uniform coveralls. "That is correct, Colonel. In the meantime I would suggest we all check to see what can be done to speed up each one's portion of labor." Without another word, he tramped to the door.

Waldour eyed the other two with mounting impatience. It was plain he had work to do and wanted them to leave. But Ashe was reluctant. He had a feeling that matters were slipping out of his control, that he was about to face a crisis which was somehow worse than just a major security leak.

Was the enemy always on the other side of the world? Or could he wear the same uniform, even share the same goals?

In the outer corridor he still hesitated, and Kelgarries, a step or so in advance, looked back over his shoulder impatiently.

"There's no use fighting—our hands are tied." His words were slurred, almost as if he wanted to disown them.

"Then you'll agree to use the Redax?" For the second time within the hour Ashe felt as if he had taken a step only to have firm earth turn into slippery, shifting sand underfoot.

"It isn't a matter of my agreeing. It may be a matter of getting through or not getting through—now. If they've had eighteen months, or even twelve...!" The colonel's fingers balled into a fist. "And *they* won't be delayed by any humanitarian reasoning—"

"Then you believe Ruthven will win the council's approval?"

"When you are dealing with frightened men, you're talking to ears closed to anything but what they want to hear. After all, we can't prove that the Redax will be harmful."

"But we've only used it under rigidly controlled conditions. To speed up the process would mean a total disregard of those controls. Snapping a party of men and women back into their racial past and holding them there for too long a period...." Ashe shook his head.

"You have been in Operation Retrograde from the start, and we've been remarkably successful—"

"Operating in a different way, educating picked men to return to certain points in history where their particular temperaments and characteristics fitted the roles they were selected to play, yes. And even then we had our percentage of failures. But to try this—returning people not physically into time, but *mentally and emotionally* into prototypes of their ancestors—that's something else again. The Apaches have volunteered, and they've been passed by the psychologists and the testers. But they're Americans of today, not tribal nomads of two or three hundred years ago. If you break down some barriers, you might just end up breaking them all."

Kelgarries was scowling. "You mean—they might revert utterly, have no contact with the present at all?"

"That's just what I do mean. Education and training, yes, but full awakening of racial memories, no. The two branches of conditioning should go slowly and hand in hand, otherwise—real trouble!"

"Only we no longer have the time to go slow. I'm certain Ruthven will be able to push this through—with Waldour's report to back him."

"Then we'll have to warn Fox and the rest. They must be given a choice in the matter."

"Ruthven said that would be done." The colonel did not sound convinced of that.

Ashe snorted. "If I hear him telling them, I'll believe it!"

"I wonder whether we can...."

Ashe half turned and frowned at the colonel. "What do you mean?"

"You said yourself that we had our failures in time travel. We expected those, accepted them, even when they hurt. When we asked for volunteers for this project we had to make them understand that there was a heavy element of risk involved. Three teams of recruits—the Eskimos from Point Barren, the Apaches, and the Islanders—all picked because their people had a high survival rating in the past, to be colonists on widely different types of planets. Well, the Eskimos and the Islanders aren't matched to any of the worlds on those snooped tapes, but Topaz is waiting for the Apaches. And we may have to move them in there in a hurry. It's a rotten gamble any way you see it!"

"I'll appeal directly to the council."

Kelgarries shrugged. "All right. You have my backing."

"But you believe such an effort hopeless?"

"You know the red-tape merchants. You'll have to move fast if you want to beat Ruthven. He's probably on a straight line now to Stanton, Reese, and Margate. This is what he has been waiting for!"

"There are the news syndicates; public opinion would back us—"

"You don't mean that, of course." Kelgarries was suddenly coldly remote.

Ashe flushed under the heavy brown which overlay his regular features. To threaten a silence break was near blasphemy here. He ran both hands down the fabric covering his thighs as if to rub away some soil on his palms.

"No," he replied heavily, his voice dull. "I guess I don't. I'll contact Hough and hope for the best."

"Meanwhile," Kelgarries spoke briskly, "we'll do what we can to speed up the program as it now stands. I suggest you take off for New York within the hour—"

"Me? Why?" Ashe asked with a trace of suspicion.

"Because I can't leave without acting directly against orders, and that would put us wrong immediately. You see Hough and talk to him personally—put it to him straight. He'll have to have all the facts if he's going to counter any move from Stanton before the council. You know every argument we can use and all the proof on our side, and you're authority enough to make it count."

"If I can do all that, I will." Ashe was alert and eager. The colonel, seeing his change of expression, felt easier.

But Kelgarries stood a moment watching Ashe as he hurried down a side corridor, before he moved on slowly to his own box of office. Once inside he sat for a long unhappy time staring at the wall and seeing nothing but the pictures produced by his thoughts. Then he pressed a button and read off the symbols which flashed on a small visa-screen set in his desk. Another button pushed, and he picked up a hand mike to relay an order which might postpone trouble for a while. Ashe was far too valuable a man to lose, and his emotions could boil him straight into disaster over this.

"Bidwell—reschedule Team A. They are to go to the Hypno-Lab instead of the reserve in ten minutes."

Releasing the mike, he again stared at the wall. No one dared interrupt a hypno-training period, and this one would last three hours. Ashe could not possibly see the trainees before he left for New York. And that would remove one temptation from his path—he would not talk at the wrong time.

Kelgarries' mouth twisted sourly. He had no pride in what he was doing. And he was perfectly certain that Ruthven would win and that Ashe's fears of Redax were well founded. It all came back to the old basic tenet of the service: the end justified the means. They must use every method and man under their control to make sure that Topaz would remain a western possession, even though that strange planet now swung far beyond the sky which covered both the western and eastern alliances on Terra. Time had run out too fast; they were being forced to play what cards they held, even though those might be very low ones. Ashe would be back, but not, Kelgarries hoped, until this had been decided one way or another. Not until this was finished.

Finished! Kelgarries blinked at the wall. Perhaps *they* were finished, too. No one would know until the transport ship landed on that other world which appeared on the direction tape symbolized by a jewellike disk of gold-brown which had given it the code name of Topaz.

2

There were an even dozen of the air-borne guardians, each following the swing of its own orbital path just within the atmospheric envelope of the planet which glowed as a great bronze-golden gem in the four-world system of a yellow star. The globes had been launched to form a web of protection around Topaz six months earlier, and the highest skill had gone into their production. Just as contact mines sown in a harbor could close that landfall to ships not knowing the secret channel, so was this world supposedly closed to any spaceship not equipped with the signal to ward off the sphere missiles.

That was the theory of the new off-world settlers whose protection they were to be, already tested as well as possible, but as yet not put to the ultimate proof. The small bright globes spun undisturbed across a two-mooned sky at night and made reassuring blips on an installation screen by day.

Then a thirteenth object winked into being, began the encircling, closing spiral of descent. A sphere resembling the warden-globes, it was a hundred times their size, and its orbit was purposefully controlled by instruments under the eye and hand of a human pilot.

Four men were strapped down on cushioned sling-seats in the control cabin of the Western Alliance ship, two hanging where their fingers might reach buttons and levers, the others merely passengers, their own labor waiting for the time when they would set down on the alien soil of Topaz. The planet hung there in their visa-screen, richly beautiful in its amber gold, growing larger, nearer, so that they could pick out features of seas, continents, mountain ranges, which had been studied on tape until they were familiar, yet now were strangely unfamiliar too.

One of the warden-globes alerted, oscillated in its set path, whirled faster as its delicate interior mechanisms responded to the awakening spark which would send it on its mission of destruction. A relay clicked, but for the smallest fraction of a millimeter failed to set the proper course. On the instrument, far below, which checked the globe's new course the mistake was not noted.

The screen of the ship spiraling toward Topaz registered a path which would bring it into violent contact with the globe. They were still some hundreds of miles apart when the alarm rang. The pilot's hand clawed out at the bank of controls; under the almost intolerable pressure of their descent, there was so little he could do. His crooked fingers fell back powerlessly from the buttons and levers; his mouth was a twisted grimace of bleak acceptance as the beat of the signal increased.

One of the passengers forced his head around on the padded rest, fought to form words, to speak to his companion. The other was staring ahead at the screen, his thick lips wide and flat against his teeth in a snarl of rage.

"They ... are ... here...."

Ruthven paid no attention to the obvious as stated by his fellow scientist. His fury was a red, pulsing thing inside him, fed by his own helplessness. To be pinned here so near his goal, fastened up as a target for an inanimate but cunningly fashioned weapon, ate into him like a stream of deadly acid. His big gamble would puff out in a blast of fire to light up Topaz's sky, with nothing left—nothing. On the armrest of his sling-seat his nails scratched deep.

The four men in the control cabin could only sit and watch, waiting for the rendezvous which would blot them out. Ruthven's flaming anger was a futile blaze. His companion in the passenger seat had closed his eyes, his lips moving soundlessly in an expression of his own scattered thoughts. The pilot and his assistant divided their attention between the screen, with its appalling message, and the controls they could not effectively use, feverishly seeking a way out in these last moments.

Below them in the bowl of the ship were those who would not know the end consciously—save in one compartment. In a padded cage a prick-eared head stirred where it rested on forepaws, slitted eyes blinked, aware not only of familiar surroundings, but also of the tension and fear generated by human minds and emotions levels above. A pointed nose raised, and there was a growling deep in a throat covered with thick buff-gray hair.

The growl aroused another similar captive. Knowing yellow eyes met yellow eyes. An intelligence, which was certainly not that of the animal body which contained it, fought down instinct raging to send both those bodies hurtling at the fastenings of the twin cages. Curiosity and the ability to adapt had been bred into both from time immemorial. Then something else had been added to sly and cunning brains. A step up had been taken—to weld intelligence to cunning, connect thought to instinct.

More than a generation earlier mankind had chosen barren desert—the "white sands" of New Mexico—as a testing ground for atomic experiments.

Humankind could be barred, warded out of the radiation limits; the natural desert dwellers, four-footed and winged, could not be so controlled.

For thousands of years, since the first southward roving Amerindian tribes had met with their kind, there had been a hunter of the open country, a smaller cousin of the wolf, whose natural abilities had made an undeniable impression on the human mind. He was in countless Indian legends as the Shaper or the Trickster, sometimes friend, sometimes enemy. Godling for some tribes, father of all evil for others. In the wealth of tales the coyote, above all other animals, had a firm place.

Driven by the press of civilization into the badlands and deserts, fought with poison, gun, and trap, the coyote had survived, adapting to new ways with all his legendary cunning. Those who had reviled him as vermin had unwillingly added to the folklore which surrounded him, telling their own tales of robbed traps, skillful escapes. He continued to be a trickster, laughing on moonlit nights from the tops of ridges at those who would hunt him down.

Then, close to the end of the twentieth century, when myths were scoffed at, the stories of the coyote's slyness began once more on a fantastic scale. And finally scientists were sufficiently intrigued to seek out this creature that seemed to display in truth all the abilities credited to his immortal namesake by pre-Columbian tribes.

What they discovered was indeed shattering to certain closed minds. For the coyote had not only adapted to the country of the white sands; he had evolved into something which could not be dismissed as an animal, clever and cunning, but limited to beast range. Six cubs had been brought back on the first expedition, coyote in body, their developing minds different. The grandchildren of those cubs were now in the ship's cages, their mutated senses alert, ready for the slightest chance of escape. Sent to Topaz as eyes and ears for less keenly endowed humans, they were not completely under the domination of man. The range of their mental powers was still uncomprehended by those who had bred, trained, and worked with them from the days their eyes had opened and they had taken their first wobbly steps away from their dams.

The male growled again, his lips wrinkling back in a snarl as the emanations of fear from the men he could not see reached panic peak. He still crouched, belly flat, on the protecting pads of his cage; but he strove now to wriggle closer to the door, just as his mate made the same effort.

Between the animals and those in the control cabin lay the others—forty of them. Their bodies were cushioned and protected with every ingenious device known to those who had placed them there so many weeks earlier. Their minds were free of the ship, roving into places where men had not trod before, a territory potentially more dangerous than any solid earth could ever be.

Operation Retrograde had returned men bodily into the past, sending agents to hunt mammoths, follow the roads of the Bronze Age traders, ride with Attila and Genghis Khan, pull bows among the archers of ancient Egypt. But Redax returned men in mind to the paths of their ancestors, or this was the theory. And those who slept here and now in their narrow boxes, lay under its government, while the men who had arbitrarily set them so could only assume they were actually reliving the lives of Apache nomads in the wide southwestern wastes of the late eighteenth and early nineteenth centuries.

Above, the pilot's hand pushed out again, fighting the pressure to reach one particular button. That, too, had been a last-minute addition, an experiment which had only had partial testing. To use it was the final move he could make, and he was already half convinced of its uselessness.

With no faith and only a very wan hope, he sent that round of metal flush with the board. What followed no one ever lived to explain.

On the planet the installation which tracked the missiles flashed on a screen bright enough to blind momentarily the duty man on watch, and its tracker was shaken off course. When it jiggled back into line it was no longer the efficient eye-in-the-sky it had been, though its tenders were not to realize that for an important minute or two.

While the ship, now out of control, sped in dizzy whirls toward Topaz, engines fought blindly to stabilize, to re-establish their functions. Some succeeded, some wobbled in and out of the danger zone, two failed. And in the control cabin three dead men spun in prisoning seats.

Dr. James Ruthven, blood bubbling from his lips with every shallow breath he could draw, fought the stealthy tide of blackness which crept up his brain, his stubborn will holding to rags of consciousness, refusing to acknowledge the pain of his fatally injured body.

The orbiting ship was on an erratic path. Slowly the machines were correcting, relays clicking, striving to bring it to a landing under auto-pilot.

All the ingenuity built into a mechanical brain was now centered in landing the globe.

It was not a good landing, in fact a very bad one, for the sphere touched a mountain side, scraped down rocks, shearing away a portion of its outer bulk. But the mountain barrier was now between it and the base from which the missiles had been launched, and the crash had not been recorded on that tracking instrument. So far as the watchers several hundred miles away knew, the warden in the sky had performed as promised. Their first line of defense had proven satisfactory, and there had been no unauthorized landing on Topaz.

In the wreckage of the control cabin Ruthven pawed at the fastenings of his sling-chair. He no longer tried to suppress the moans every effort tore out of him. Time held the whip, drove him. He rolled from his seat to the floor, lay there gasping, as again he fought doggedly to remain above the waves—those frightening, fast-coming waves of dark faintness.

Somehow he was crawling, crawling along a tilted surface until he gained the well where the ladder to the lower section hung, now at an acute angle. It was that angle which helped him to the next level.

He was too dazed to realize the meaning of the crumpled bulkheads. There was a spur of bare rock under his hands as he edged over and around twisted metal. The moans were now a gobbling, burbling, almost continuous cry as he reached his goal—a small cabin still intact.

For long moments of anguish he paused by the chair there, afraid that he could not make the last effort, raise his almost inert bulk up to the point where he could reach the Redax release. For a second of unusual clarity he wondered if there was any reason for this supreme ordeal, whether any of the sleepers could be aroused. This might now be a ship of the dead.

His right hand, his arm, and finally his bulk over the seat, he braced himself and brought his left hand up. He could not use any of the fingers; it was like lifting numb, heavy weights. But he lurched forward, swept the unfeeling lump of cold flesh down against the release in a gesture which he knew must be his final move. And, as he fell back to the floor, Dr. Ruthven could not be certain whether he had succeeded or failed. He tried to screw his head around, to focus his eyes upward at that switch. Was it down or still stubbornly up, locking the sleepers into confinement? But there was a fog between; he could not see it—or anything.

The light in the cabin flickered, was gone as another circuit in the broken ship failed. It was dark, too, in the small cubby below which housed the two cages. Chance, which had snuffed out nineteen lives in the space globe, had missed ripping open that cabin on the mountain side. Five yards down the corridor the outside fabric of the ship was split wide open, the crisp air native to Topaz entering, sending a message to two keen noses through the combination of odors now pervading the wreckage.

And the male coyote went into action. Days ago he had managed to work loose the lower end of the mesh which fronted his cage, but his mind had told him that a sortie inside the ship was valueless. The odd rapport he'd had with the human brains, unknown to them, had operated to keep him to the old role of cunning deception, which in the past had saved countless of his species from sudden and violent death. Now with teeth and paws he went diligently to work, urged on by the whines of his mate, that tantalizing smell of an outside world tickling their nostrils—a wild world, lacking the taint of man-places.

He slipped under the loosened mesh and stood up to paw at the front of the female's cage. One forepaw caught in the latch and pressed it down, and the weight of the door swung against him. Together they were free now to reach the corridor and see ahead the subdued light of a strange moon beckoning them on into the open.

The female, always more cautious than her mate, lingered behind as he trotted forward, his ears a-prick with curiosity. Their training had been the same since cubhood—to range and explore, but always in the company and at the order of man. This was not according to the pattern she knew, and she was suspicious. But to her sensitive nose the smell of the ship was an offense, and the puffs of breeze from without enticing. Her mate had already slipped through the break; now he barked with excitement and wonder, and she trotted on to join him.

Above, the Redax, which had never been intended to stand rough usage, proved to be a better survivor of the crash than most of the other installations. Power purred along a network of lines, activated beams, turned off and on a series of fixtures in those coffin-beds. For five of the sleepers—nothing. The cabin which had held them was a flattened smear against the mountain side. Three more half aroused, choked, fought for life and breath in a darkness which was a mercifully short nightmare, and succumbed.

But in the cabin nearest the rent through which the coyotes had escaped, a young man sat up abruptly, looking into the dark with wide-open, terror-haunted eyes. He clawed for purchase against the smooth edge of the box in which he had lain, somehow got to his knees, weaving weakly back and forth, and half fell, half pushed to the floor where he could stand only by keeping his hold on the box.

Dazed, sick, weak, he swayed there, aware only of himself and his own sensations. There were small sounds in the dark, a stilled moan, a gasping sigh. But that meant nothing. Within him grew a compulsion to be out of this place, his terror making him lurch forward.

His flailing hand rapped painfully against an upright surface which his questing fingers identified hazily as an exit. Unconsciously he fumbled along the surface of the door until it gave under that weak pressure. Then he was out, his head swimming, drawn by the light behind the wall rent.

He progressed toward that in a scrambling crawl, making his way over the splintered skin of the globe. Then he dropped with a jarring thud onto the mound of earth the ship had pushed before it during its downward slide. Limply he tumbled on in a small cascade of clods and sand, hitting against a less movable rock with force enough to roll him over on his back and stun him again.

The second and smaller moon of Topaz swung brightly through the sky, its weird green rays making the blood-streaked face of the explorer an alien mask. It had passed well on to the horizon, and its large yellow companion had risen when a yapping broke the small sounds of the night.

As the *yipp, yipp, yipp* arose in a crescendo, the man stirred, putting one hand to his head. His eyes opened, he looked vaguely about him and sat up. Behind him was the torn and ripped ship, but he did not look back at it.

Instead, he got to his feet and staggered out into the direct path of the moonlight. Inside his brain there was a whirl of thoughts, memories, emotions. Perhaps Ruthven or one of his assistants could have explained that chaotic mixture for what it was. But for all practical purposes Travis Fox—Amerindian Time Agent, member of Team A, Operation Cochise—was far less of a thinking animal now than the two coyotes paying their ritual addresses to a moon which was not the one of their vanished homeland.

Travis wavered on, drawn somehow by that howling. It was familiar, a thread of something real through all the broken clutter in his head. He stumbled, fell, crawled up again, but he kept on.

Above, the female coyote lowered her head, drew a test sniff of a new scent. She recognized that as part of the proper way of life. She yapped once at her mate, but he was absorbed in his night song, his muzzle pointed moonward as he voiced a fine wailing.

Travis tripped, pitched forward on his hands and knees, and felt the jar of such a landing shoot up his stiffened forearms. He tried to get up, but his body only twisted, so he landed on his back and lay looking up at the moon.

A strong, familiar odor ... then a shadow looming above him. Hot breath against his cheek, and the swift sweep of an animal tongue on his face. He flung up his hand, gripped thick fur, and held on as if he had found one anchor of sanity in a world gone completely mad.

3

Travis, one knee braced against the red earth, blinked as he parted a screen of tall rust-brown grass with cautious fingers to look out into a valley where golden mist clouded most of the landscape. His head ached with dull persistence, the pain fostered in some way by his own bewilderment. To study the land ahead was like trying to see through one picture interposed over another and far different one. He knew what ought to be there, but what was before him was very dissimilar.

A buff-gray shape flitted through the tall cover grass, and Travis tensed. *Mba'a*—coyote? Or were these companions of his actually *ga-n*, spirits who could choose their shape at will and had, oddly, this time assumed the bodies of man's tricky enemy? Were they *ndendai*—enemies—or *dalaanbiyat'i*, allies? In this mad world he did not know.

Ei'dik'e? His mind formed a word he did not speak: Friend?

Yellow eyes met his directly. Dimly he had been aware, ever since awaking in this strange wilderness with the coming of morning light, that the four-footed ones trotting with him as he walked aimlessly had unbeastlike traits. Not only did they face him eye-to-eye, but in some ways they appeared able to read his thoughts.

He had longed for water to ease the burning in his throat, the ever-present pain in his head, and the creatures had nudged him in another direction, bringing him to a pool where he had mouthed liquid with a strange sweet, but not unpleasant taste.

Now he had given them names, names which had come out of the welter of dreams which shadowed his stumbling journey across this weird country.

Nalik'ideyu (Maiden-Who-Walks-Ridges) was the female who continued to shepherd him along, never venturing too far from his side. Naginlta (He-Who-Scouts-Ahead) was the male who did just that, disappearing at long intervals and then returning to face the man and his mate as if conveying some report necessary to their journey.

It was Nalik'ideyu who sought out Travis now, her red tongue lolling from her mouth as she panted. Not from exertion, he was certain of that. No, she was excited and eager ... on the hunt! That was it—a hunt!

Travis' own tongue ran across his lips as an impression hit him with feral force. There was meat—rich, fresh—just ahead. Meat that lived, waiting to be killed. Inside him his own avid hunger roused, shaking him farther out of the crusting dream.

His hands went to his waist, but the groping fingers did not find what vague memory told him should be there—a belt, heavy with knife in sheath.

He examined his own body with attention to find he was adequately covered by breeches of a smooth, dull brown material which blended well with the vegetation about him. He wore a loose shirt, belted in at the narrow waist by a folded strip of cloth, the ends of which fluttered free. On his feet were tall moccasins, the leg pieces extending some distance up his calves, the toes turned up in rounded points.

Some of this he found familiar, but these were fragments of memory; again his mind fitted one picture above another. One thing he did know for sure—he had no weapons. And that realization struck home with a thrust of real and terrible fear which tore away more of the bewilderment cloaking his mind.

Nalik'ideyu was impatient. Having advanced a step or two, she now looked back at him over her shoulder, yellow eyes slitted, her demand on him as instant and real as if she had voiced understandable words. Meat was waiting, and she was hungry. Also she expected Travis to aid in the hunt—at once.

Though he could not match her fluid grace in moving through the grass, Travis followed her, keeping to cover. He shook his head vigorously, in spite of the stab of pain the motion cost him, and paid more attention to his surroundings. It was apparent that the earth under him, the grass around, the valley of the golden haze, were all real, not part of a dream. Therefore that other countryside which he kept seeing in a ghostly fashion was a hallucination.

Even the air which he drew into his lungs and expelled again, had a strange smell, or was it taste? He could not be sure which. He knew that hypno-training could produce queer side effects, but ... this....

Travis paused, staring unseeingly before him at the grass still waving from the coyote's passage. Hypno-training! What was that? Now three pictures fought to focus in his mind: the two landscapes which did not match and a shadowy third. He shook his head again, his hands to his temples. This—this only was real: the ground, the grass, the valley, the hunger in him, the hunt waiting....

He forced himself to concentrate on the immediate present and the portion of world he could see, feel, scent, which lay here and now about him.

The grass grew shorter as he proceeded in Nalik'ideyu's wake. But the haze was not thinning. It seemed to hang in patches, and when he ventured through the edge of a patch it was like creeping through a fog of golden, dancing motes with here and there a glittering speck whirling and darting like a living thing. Masked by the stuff, Travis reached a line of brush and sniffed.

It was a warm scent, a heavy odor he could not identify and yet one he associated with a living creature. Flat to earth, he pushed head and shoulders under the low limbs of the bush to look ahead.

Here was a space where the fog did not hold, a pocket of earth clear under the morning sun. And grazing there were three animals. Again shock cleared a portion of Travis' bemused brain.

They were about the size, he thought, of antelopes, and they had a general resemblance to those beasts in that they had four slender legs, a rounded body, and a head. But they had alien features, so alien as to hold him in open-mouthed amazement.

The bodies had bare spots here and there, and patches of creamy—fur? Or was it hair which hung in strips, as if the creatures had been partially plucked in a careless fashion? The necks were long and moved about in a serpentine motion, as though their spines were as limber as reptiles'. On the end of those long and twisting necks were heads which also appeared more suitable to another species—broad, rather flat, with a singular toadlike look—but furnished with horns set halfway down the nose, horns which began in a single root and then branched into two sharp points.

They were unearthly! Again Travis blinked, brought his hand up to his head as he continued to view the browsers. There were three of them: two larger and with horns, the other a smaller beast with less of the ragged fur and only the beginning button of a protuberance on the nose; it was probably a calf.

One of those mental alerts from the coyotes broke his absorption. Nalik'ideyu was not interested in the odd appearance of the grazing creatures; she was intent upon their usefulness in another way—as a full and satisfying meal—and she was again impatient with him for his dull response.

His examination took a more practical turn. An antelope's defense was speed, though it could be tricked into hunting range through its inordinate curiosity. The slender legs of these beasts suggested a like degree of speed, and Travis had no weapons at all.

Those nose horns had an ugly look; this thing might be a fighter rather than a runner. But the suggestion which had flashed from coyote to him had taken root. Travis was hungry, he was a hunter, and here was meat on the hoof, queer as it looked.

Again he received a message. Naginlta was on the opposite side of the clearing. If the creatures depended on speed, then Travis believed they could probably outrun not only him but the coyotes as well—which left cunning and some sort of plan.

Travis glanced at the cover where he knew Nalik'ideyu crouched and from which had come that flash of agreement. He shivered. These were truly no animals, but *ga-n*, *ga-n* of power! And as *ga-n* he must treat them, accede to their will. Spurred by that, the Apache gave only flicks of attention to the browsers while at the same time he studied the part of the landscape uncovered by mist.

Without weapons or speed, they must conceive a trap. Again Travis sensed that agreement which was *ga-n* magic, and with it the strong impression urging him to the right. He was making progress with skill he did not even recognize and which he had never been conscious of learning.

The bushes and small, droop-limbed trees, their branches not clothed with leaves from proper twigs but with a reddish bristly growth protruding directly from their surfaces, made a partial wall for the pocket-sized meadow. That screen reached a rocky cleft where the mist curled in a long tongue through a wall twice Travis' height. If the browsers could be maneuvered into taking the path through that cleft....

Travis searched about him, and his hands closed upon the oldest weapon of his species, a stone pulled from an earth pocket and balanced neatly in the palm of his hand. It was a long chance but his best one.

The Apache took the first step on a new and fearsome road. These *ga-n* had put their thoughts—or their desires—into his mind. Could he so contact them in return?

With the stone clenched in his fist, his shoulders back against the wall not too far from the cleft opening, Travis strove to think out, clearly and simply, this poor plan of his. He did not know that he was reacting the way scientists deep space away had hoped he might. Nor did Travis guess that at this point he had already traveled far beyond the expectations of the men who had bred and trained the two mutant coyotes. He only believed that this might be the one way he could obey the wishes of the two spirits he thought far more powerful than any man. So he pictured in his mind the cleft, the running creatures, and the part the *ga-n* could play if they so willed.

Assent—in its way as loud and clear as if shouted. The man fingered the stone, weighed it. There would probably be just one moment when he could use it to effect, and he must be ready.

From this point he could no longer see the small meadow where the grazers were. But Travis knew, as well as if he watched the scene, that the coyotes were creeping in, belly flat to earth, adding a feline stealth and patience to their own cunning.

There! Travis' head jerked, the alert had come, the drive was beginning. He tensed, gripping his stone.

A yapping bark was answered by a sound he could not describe, a noise which was neither cough nor grunt but a combination of both. Again a yap-yap....

A toad-head burst through the screen of brush, the double horn on its nose festooned with a length of grass torn up by the roots. Wide eyes—milky and seeming to be without pupils—fastened on Travis, but he could not be sure the thing saw him, for it kept on, picking up speed as it approached the cleft. Behind it ran the calf, and that guttural cry was bubbling from its broad flat lips.

The long neck of the adult writhed, the frog-head swung closer to the ground so that the twin points of the horn were at a slant—aimed now at Travis. He had been right in his guess at their deadliness, but he had only a fleeting chance to recognize that fact as the thing bore down, its whole attitude expressing the firm intention of goring him.

He hurled his stone and then flung his body to one side, stumbling and rolling into the brush where he fought madly to regain his feet, expecting at any moment to feel trampling hoofs and thrusting horns. There was a crash to his right, and the bushes and grass were wildly shaken.

On his hands and knees the Apache retreated, his head turned to watch behind him. He saw the flirt of a triangular flap-tail in the mouth of the cleft. The calf had escaped. And now the threshing in the bushes stilled.

Was the thing stalking him? He got to his feet, for the first time hearing clearly the continued yapping, as if a battle was in progress. Then the second of the adult beasts came into view, backing and turning, trying to keep lowered head with menacing double horn always pointed to the coyotes dancing a teasing, worrying circle about it.

One of the coyotes flung up its head, looked upslope, and barked. Then, as one, both rushed the fighting beast, but for the first time from the same side, leaving it a clear path to retreat. It made a rush before which they fled easily, and then it whirled with a speed and grace, which did not fit its ungainly, ill-proportioned body, and jumped toward the cleft, the coyotes making no effort to hinder its escape.

Travis came out of cover, approaching the brush which had concealed the crash of the other animal. The actions of the coyotes had convinced him that there was no danger now; they would never have allowed the escape of their prey had the first beast not been in difficulties.

His shot with the stone, the Apache decided as he stood moments later surveying the twitching crumpled body, must have hit the thing in the head, stunning it. Then the momentum of its charge had carried it full force against the rock to kill it. Blind luck—or the power of the *ga-n*? He pulled back as the coyotes came padding up shoulder to shoulder to inspect the kill. It was truly more theirs than his.

Their prey yielded not only food but a weapon for Travis. Instead of the belt knife he had remembered having, he was now equipped with two. The double horn had been easy to free from the shattered skull, and some careful work with stones had broken off one prong at just the angle he wanted. So now he had a short and a longer tool, defense. At least they were better than the stone with which he had entered the hunt.

Nalik'ideyu pushed past him to lap daintily at the water. Then she sat up on her haunches, watching Travis as he smoothed the horn with a stone.

"A knife," he said to her, "this will be a knife. And—" he glanced up, measuring the value of the wood represented by trees and bushes—"then a bow. With a bow we shall hunt better."

The coyote yawned, her yellow eyes half closed, her whole pose one of satisfaction and contentment.

"A knife," Travis repeated, "and a bow." He needed weapons; he had to have them!

Why? His hand stopped scraping. Why? The toad-faced double horn had been quick to attack, but Travis could have avoided it, and it had not hunted him first. Why was he ridden by this fear that he must not be unarmed?

He dipped his hand into the pool of the spring and lifted the water to cool his sweating face. The coyote moved, turned around in the grass, crushing down the growth into a nest in which she curled up, head on paws. But Travis sat back on his heels, his now idle hands hanging down between his knees, and forced himself to the task of sorting out jumbled memories.

This landscape was wrong—totally unlike what it should be—but it was real. He had helped kill this alien creature. He had eaten its meat, raw. Its horn lay within touch now. All that was real and unchangeable. Which meant that the rest of it, that other desert world in which he had wandered with his kind, ridden horses, raided invading men of another race, that was not real—or else far, far removed from where he now sat.

Yet there had been no dividing line between those two worlds. One moment he had been in the desert place, returning from a successful foray against the Mexicans. Mexicans! Travis caught at that identification, tried to use it as a thread to draw closer to the beginning of his mystery.

Mexicans.... And he was an Apache, one of the Eagle people, one who rode with Cochise. No!

Sweat again beaded his face where the water had cooled it. He was not of that past. He was Travis Fox, of the very late twentieth century, not a nomad of the middle nineteenth! He was of Team A of the project!

The Arizona desert and then this! From one to the other in an instant. He looked about him in rising fear. Wait! He had been in the dark when he got out of the desert, lying in a box. Getting out, he had crawled down a passage to reach moonlight, strange moonlight.

A box in which he had lain, a passage with smooth metallic walls, and an alien world at the end of it.

The coyote's ears twitched, her head came up, she was staring at the man's drawn face, at his eyes with their core of fear. She whined.

Travis caught up the two pieces of horn, thrust them into his sash belt, and got to his feet. Nalik'ideyu sat up, her head cocked a little to one side. As the man turned to seek his own back trail she padded along in his wake and whined for Naginlta. But Travis was more intent now on what he must prove to himself than he was on the actions of the two animals.

It was a wandering trail, and now he did not question his skill in being able to follow it so unerringly. The sun was hot. Winged things buzzed from the bushes, small scuttling things fled from him through the tall grass. Once Naginlta growled a warning which led them all to a detour, and Travis might not have picked up the proper trace again had not the coyote scout led him to it.

"Who are you?" he asked once, and then guessed it would have better been said, "What are you?" These were not animals, or rather they were more than the animals he had always known. And one part of him, the part which remembered the desert rancherias where Cochise had ruled, said they were spirits. Yet that other part of him.... Travis shook his head, accepting them now for what they were—welcome company in an alien place.

The day wore on close to sunset, and still Travis followed that wandering trail. The need which drove him kept him going through the rough country of hills and ravines. Now the mist lifted above towering walls of mountains very near him, yet not the mountains of his memory. These were dull brown, with a forbidding look, like sun-dried skulls baring teeth in warning against all comers.

With great difficulty, Travis topped a rise. Ahead against the skyline stood both coyotes. And, as the man joined them, first one and then the other flung back its head and sounded the sobbing, shattering cry which had been a part of that other life.

The Apache looked down. His puzzle was answered in part. The wreckage crumpled on the mountain side was identifiable—a spaceship! Cold fear gripped him and his own head went back; from between his tight lips came a cry as desolate and despairing as the one the animals had voiced.

4

Fire, mankind's oldest ally, weapon, tool, leaped high before the naked stone of the mountain side. Men sat cross-legged about it, fifteen of them. And behind, guarded by the flames and that somber circle, were the women. There was a uniformity in this gathering. The members were plainly all of the same racial stock, of medium height, stocky yet fined down to the peak of stamina and endurance, their skin brown, their shoulder-length hair black. And they were all young—none over thirty, some still in their late teens. Alike, too, was a certain drawn look in their faces, a tenseness of the eyes and mouth as they listened to Travis.

"So we must be on Topaz. Do any of you remember boarding the ship?"

"No. Only that we awoke within it." Across the fire one chin lifted; the eyes which caught Travis' held a deep, smoldering anger. "This is more trickery of the Pinda-lick-o-yi, the White Eyes. Between us there has never been fair dealing. They have broken their promise as a man breaks a rotten stick, for their words are as rotten. And it was you, Fox, who brought us to listen to them."

A stir about the circle, a murmur from the women.

"And do I not also sit here with you in this strange wilderness?" he countered.

"I do not understand," another of the men held out his hand, palm up, in a gesture of asking—"what has happened to us. We were in the old Apache world.... I, Jil-Lee, was riding with Cuchillo Negro as we went down to the taking of Ramos. And then I was here, in a broken ship and beside me a dead man who was once my brother. How did I come out of the past of our people into another world across the stars?"

"Pinda-lick-o-yi tricks!" The first speaker spat into the fire.

"It was the Redax, I think," Travis replied. "I heard Dr. Ashe discuss this. A new machine which could make a man remember not his own past, but the past of his ancestors. While we were on that ship we must have been under its influence, so we lived as our people lived a hundred years or more ago—"

"And the purpose of such a thing?" Jil-Lee asked.

"To make us more like our ancestors perhaps. It is part of what they told us at the project. To venture into these new worlds requires a different type of man than lives on Terra today. Traits we have forgotten are needed to face the dangers of wild places."

"You, Fox, have been beyond the stars before, and you found there were such dangers to face?"

"It is true. You have heard of the three worlds I saw when the ship from the old days took us off, unwilling, to the stars. Did you not all volunteer to pioneer in this manner so you could also see strange and new things?"

"But we did not agree to be returned to the past in medicine dreams and be sent unknowingly into space!"

Travis nodded. "Deklay is right. But I know no more than you why we were so sent, or why the ship crashed. We have found Dr. Ruthven's body in the cabin with that new installation. Only we have discovered nothing else which tells us why we were brought here. With the ship broken, we must stay."

They were silent now, men and women alike. Behind them lay several days of activity, nights of exhausted slumber. Against the cliff wall lay the packs of supplies they had salvaged from the wreck. By mutual consent they had left the vicinity of the broken globe, following their old custom of speedily withdrawing from a place of death.

"This is a world empty of men?" Jil-Lee wanted to know.

"So far we have found only animal signs, and the *ga-n* have not warned us of anything else—"

"Those devil ones!" Again Deklay spat into the fire. "I say we should have no dealings with them. The *mba'a* is no friend to the People."

Again a murmur which seemed one of agreement answered that outburst. Travis stiffened. Just how much influence had the Redax had over them? He knew from his own experience that sometimes he had an odd double reaction—two different feelings which almost sickened him when they struck simultaneously. And he was beginning to suspect that with some of the others the return to the past had been far more deep and lasting. Now Jil-Lee was actually to reason out what had happened. While Deklay had reverted to an ancestor who had ridden with Victorio or Magnus Colorado! Travis had a flash of premonition, a chill which made him half foresee a time when the past and the present might well split them apart—fatally.

"Devil or *ga-n*." A man with a quiet face, rather deeply sunken eyes, spoke for the first time. "We are in two minds because of this Redax, so let us not do anything in haste. Back in the desert world of the People I have seen the *mba'a*, and he was very clever. With the badger he went hunting, and when the badger had dug up the rat's nest, so did the *mba'a* wait on the other side of the thorny bush and catch those who would escape that way. Between him and the badger there was no war. These two who sit over yonder now—they are also hunters and they seem friendly to us. In a strange place a man needs all the help he can find. Let us not call names out of old tales, which may mean nothing in fact."

"Buck speaks straightly," Jil-Lee agreed. "We seek a camp which can be defended. For perhaps there are men here whose hunting territory we have invaded, though we have not yet seen them. We are a people small in number and alone. Let us walk softly on trails which are strange to our feet."

Inwardly Travis sighed in relief. Buck, Jil-Lee ... for the moment their sensible words appeared to swing the opinions of the party. If either of them could be established as *haldzil*, or clan leader, they would all be safer. He himself had no aspirations in that direction and dared not push too hard. It had been his initial urging which had brought them as volunteers into the project. Now he was doubly suspect, and especially by those who thought as Deklay, he was considered too alien to their old ways.

So far their protests had been fewer than he anticipated. Although brothers and sisters had followed each other into the team after the immemorial desire of Apaches to cling to family ties, they were not a true clan with solidity of that to back them, but representatives of half a dozen.

Basically, back on Terra, they had all been among the most progressive of their people—progressive, that is, in the white man's sense of the word. Travis had a fleeting recognition of his now oblique way of thinking. He, too, had been marked by the Redax. They had all been educated in the modern fashion and all possessed a spirit of adventure which marked them over their fellows. They had volunteered for the team and successfully passed the tests to weed out the temperamentally unfit or fainthearted. But all that was before Redax....

Why had they been submitted to that? And why this flight? What had pushed Dr. Ashe and Murdock and Colonel Kelgarries, time agents he knew and trusted, into dispatching them without warning to Topaz? Something had happened, something which had given Dr. Ruthven ascendancy over those others and had started them on this wild trip.

Travis was conscious of a stir about the firelit circle. The men were rising, moving back into the shadows, stretching out on the blankets they had found among other stores on the ship. They had discovered weapons there—knives, bows, quivers of arrows, all of which they had been trained to use in the intensive schooling of the project and which needed no more repair than they themselves could give. And the rations they carried were field supplies, few of them. Tomorrow they must begin hunting in earnest....

"Why has this thing been done to us?" Buck was beside Travis, those quiet eyes sliding past him to seek the fire once more. "I do not think you were told when the rest of us were not—"

Travis seized upon that. "There are those who say that I knew, agreed?"

"That is so. Once we stood at the same place in time—in our thoughts, our desires. Now we stand at many places, as if we climbed a stairway, each at his own speed—a stairway the Pinda-lick-o-yi has set us upon. Some here, some there, some yet farther above...." He sketched a series of step outlines in the air. "And in this there is trouble—"

"The truth," Travis agreed. "Yet it is also true that I knew nothing of this, that I climb with you on these stairs."

"So I believe. But there comes a time when it is best not to be a woman stirring a pot of boiling stew but rather one who stands quietly at a distance—"

"You mean?" Travis pressed.

"I say that alone among us you have crossed the stars before, therefore new things are not so hard to understand. And we need a scout. Also the coyotes run in your footsteps, and you do not fear them."

It made good sense. Let him scout ahead of the party, taking the coyotes with him. Stay away from the camp for a while and speak small—until the people on Buck's stairway were more closely united.

"I go in the morning," Travis agreed. He could slip away tonight, but just now he could not force himself away from the fire, from the companionship.

"You might take Tsoay with you," Buck continued.

Travis waited for him to enlarge on that suggestion. Tsoay was one of the youngest of their group, Buck's own cross-cousin and near-brother.

"It is well," Buck explained, "that we learn this land, and it has always been our custom that the younger walk in the footprints of the older. Also, not only should trails be learned, but also men."

Travis caught the thought behind that. Perhaps by taking the younger men as scouts, one after another, he could build up among them a following of sorts. Among the Apaches, leadership was wholly a matter of personality. Until the reservation days, chieftains had gained their position by force of character alone, though they might come successively from one family clan over several generations.

He did not want the chieftainship here. No, but neither did he want growing whispers working about him to cut him off from his people. To every Apache severance from the clan was a little death. He must have those who would back him if Deklay, or those who thought like Deklay, turned grumbling into open hostility.

"Tsoay is one quick to learn," Travis agreed. "We go at dawn—"

"Along the mountain range?" Buck inquired.

"If we seek a protected place for the rancheria, yes. The mountains have always provided good strongholds for the People."

"And you think there is need for a fort?"

Travis shrugged. "I have been one day's journey out into this world. I saw nothing but animals. But that is no promise that elsewhere there are no enemies. The planet was on the tapes we brought back from that other world, and so it was known to the others who once rode between star and star as we rode between ranch and town. If they had this world set on a journey tape, it was for a reason; that reason may still be in force."

"Yet it was long ago that these star people rode so...." Buck mused. "Would the reason last so long?"

Travis remembered two other worlds, one of weird desert inhabited by beast things—or had they once been human, human to the point of possessing intelligence?—that had come out of sand burrows at night to attack a spaceship. And the second world where the ruins of a giant city had stood choked with jungle vegetation, where he had made a blowgun from tubes of rustless metal as a weapon gift for small winged men—but were they men? Both had been remnants of that ancient galactic empire.

"Some things could so remain," he answered soberly. "If we find them, we must be careful. But first a good site for the rancheria."

"There is no return to home for us," Buck stated flatly.

"Why do you say that? There could be a rescue ship later—"

The other raised his eyes again to Travis. "When you slept under the Redax how did you ride?"

"As a warrior—raiding ... living...."

"And I—I was one with *go'ndi*," Buck returned simply.

"But—"

"But the white man has assured us that such power—the power of a chief—does not exist? Yes, the Pinda-lick-o-yi has told us so many things. He is busy, busy with his tools, his machines, always busy. And those who think in another fashion cannot be measured by his rules, so they are foolish dreamers. Not all white men think so. There was Dr. Ashe—he was beginning to understand a little.

"Perhaps I, too, am standing still, halfway up the stairway of the past. But of this I am very sure: For us, there will be no return to our own place. And the time will come when something new shall grow from the seed of the past. Also it is necessary that you be one of the tenders of that growth. So I urge you, take Tsoay, and the next time, Lupe. For the young who may be swayed this way and that by words—as the wind shakes a small tree—must be given firm roots."

In Travis education warred with instinct, just as the picture Redax had planted in his mind had warred with his awaking to this alien landscape. Yet now he believed he must be guided by what he felt. And he knew that no man of his race would claim *go'ndi*, the power of spirit known only to a great chief, unless he had actually felt it swell within him. It might have been fostered by hallucination in the past, but the aura of it carried into the here and now. And Travis had no doubts that Buck believed implicitly in what he said, and that belief carried credulity to others.

"This is wisdom, *Nantan*—"

Buck shook his head. "I am no *nantan*, no chief. But of some things I am sure. You also be sure of what lies within you, younger brother!"

On the third day, ranging eastward along the base of the mountain range, Travis found what he believed would be an acceptable camp site. There was a canyon with a good spring of water cut round by well-marked game trails. A series of ledges brought him up to a small plateau where scrub wood could be used to build the wickiups. Water and food lay within reach, and the ledge approach was easy to defend. Even Deklay and his fellow malcontents were forced to concede the value of the site.

His duty to the clan accomplished, Travis returned to his own concern, one which had haunted him for days. Topaz had been taped by men of the vanished star empire. Therefore, the planet was important, but why? As yet he had found no indication that anything above the intelligence level of the split horns was native to this world. But he was gnawed by the certainty that there *was* something here, waiting.... And the desire to learn what it was became an ever-burning ache.

Perhaps he was what Deklay had accused him of being, one who had come to follow the road of the Pinda-lick-o-yi too closely. For Travis was content to scout with only the coyotes for company, and he did not find the loneliness of the unknown planet as intimidating as most of the others.

He was checking his small trail pack on the fourth day after they had settled on the plateau when Buck and Jil-Lee hunkered down beside him.

"You go to hunt—?" Buck broke the silence first.

"Not for meat."

"What do you fear? That *ndendai*—enemy people—have marked this as their land?" Jil-Lee questioned.

"That may be true, but now I hunt for what this world was at one time, the reason why the ancient star men marked it as their own."

"And this knowledge may be of value to us?" Jil-Lee asked slowly. "Will it bring food to our mouths, shelter for our bodies—mean life for us?"

"All that is possible. It is the unknowing which is bad."

"True. Unknowing is always bad," Buck agreed. "But the bow which is fitted to one hand and strength of arm, may not be suited to another. Remember that, younger brother. Also, do you go alone?"

"With Naginlta and Nalik'ideyu I am not alone."

"Take Tsoay with you also. The four-footed ones are indeed *ga-n* for the service of those they like, but it is not good that man walks alone from his kind."

There it was again, the feeling of clan solidarity which Travis did not always share. On the other hand, Tsoay would not be a hindrance. On other scouts the boy had proved to have a keen eye for the country and a liking for experimentation which was not a universal attribute even among those of his own age.

"I would go to find a path through the mountains; it may be a long trail," Travis half protested.

"You believe what you seek may lie to the north?"

Travis shrugged. "I do not know. How can I? But it will be another way of seeking."

"Tsoay shall go. He keeps silent before older warriors as is proper for the untried, but his thoughts fly free as do yours," Buck replied. "It is in him also, this need to see new places."

"There is this," Jil-Lee got to his feet, "—do not go so far, brother, that you may not easily find a way to return. This is a wide land, and within it we are but a handful of men alone—"

"That, too, I know." Travis thought he could read more than one kind of warning in Jil-Lee's words.

    *   *   *   *   *

They were the second day away from the plateau camp, and climbing, when they chanced upon the pass Travis had hoped might exist. Before them lay an abrupt descent to what appeared to be open plains country cloaked in a dusky amber Travis now knew was the thick grass found in the southern valleys. Tsoay pointed with his chin.

"Wide land—good for horses, cattle, ranches...."

But all those lay far beyond the black space surrounding them. Travis wondered if there was any native animal which could serve man in place of the horse.

"Do we go down?" Tsoay asked.

From this point Travis could sight no break far out on the amber plain, no sign of any building or any disturbance of its smooth emptiness. Yet it drew him. "We go," he decided.

Close as it had looked from the pass, the plain was yet a day and a night, spent in careful watching by turns, ahead of them. It was midmorning of the second day that they left the foothill breaks, and the grass of the open country was waist high about them. Travis could see it rippling where the coyotes threaded ahead. Then he was conscious of a persistent buzzing, a noise which irritated faintly until he was compelled to trace it to its source.

The grass had been trampled flat for an irregular patch, with a trail of broken stalks out of the heart of the plain. At one side was a buzzing, seething mass of glitter-winged insects which Travis already knew as carrion eaters. They arose reluctantly from their feast as he approached.

He drew a short breath which was close to a grunt of astounded recognition. What lay there was so impossible that he could not believe the evidence of his eyes. Tsoay gave a sharp exclamation, went down on one knee for a closer examination, then looked at Travis over his shoulder, his eyes wide, more than a trace of excitement in his voice.

"Horse dung—and fresh!"

5

"There was one horse, unshod but ridden. It came here from the plains and it had been ridden hard, going lame. There was a rest here, maybe shortly after dawn." Travis sorted out what they had learned by a careful examination of the ground.

Nalik'ideyu and Naginlta, Tsoay, watched and listened as if the coyotes as well as the boy could understand every word.

"There is that also—" Tsoay indicated the one trace left by the unknown rider, an impression blurred as if some attempt had been made to conceal it.

"Small and light, the rider is both. Also in fear, I think—"

"We follow?" Tsoay asked.

"We follow," Travis assented. He looked to the coyotes, and as he had learned to do, thought out his message. This trail was the one to be followed. When the rider was sighted they were to report back if the Apaches had not yet caught up.

There was no visible agreement; the coyotes simply vanished through the wall of grass.

"Then there are others here," Tsoay said as he and Travis began their return to the foothills. "Perhaps there was a second ship—"

"That horse," Travis said, shaking his head. "There was no provision in the project for the shipping of horses."

"Perhaps they have always been here."

"Not so. To each world its own species of beasts. But we shall know the truth when we look upon that horse—and its rider."

It was warmer this side of the mountains, and the heat of the plains beat at them. Travis thought that the horse might well be seeking water if allowed his head. Where did he come from? And why had his rider gone in haste and fear?

This was rough, broken country and the tired, limping horse seemed to have picked the easiest way through it, without any hindrance from the man with him. Travis spotted a soft patch of ground with a deep-set impression. This time there had been no attempt at erasure; the boot track was plain. The rider had dismounted and was leading the horse—yet he was moving swiftly.

They followed the tracks around the bend of a shallow cut and found Nalik'ideyu waiting for them. Between her forefeet was a bundle still covered with smears of soft earth, and behind her were drag marks from a hole under the overhang of a bush. The coyote had plainly just disinterred her find. Travis squatted down to examine it, using his eyes before his hands.

It was a bag made of hide, probably the hide of one of the split horns by its color and the scraps of long hair which had been left in a simple decorative fringe along the bottom. The sides had been laced together neatly by someone used to working in leather, the closing flap lashed down tightly with braided thong loops.

As the Apache leaned closer to it he could smell a mixture of odors—the hide itself, horse, wood smoke, and other scents—strange to him. He undid the fastenings and pulled out the contents.

There was a shirt, with long full sleeves, of a gray wool undyed from the sheep. Then a very bulky short jacket which, after fingering it doubtfully, Travis decided was made of felt. It was elaborately decorated with highly colorful embroidery, and there was no mistaking the design—a heavy antlered Terran deer in mortal combat with what might be a puma. It was bordered with a geometric pattern of beautiful, oddly familiar work. Travis smoothed it flat over his knee and tried to remember where he had seen its like before ... a book! An illustration in a book! But which book, when? Not recently, and it was not a pattern known to his own people.

Twisted into the interior of the jacket was a silklike scarf, clear, light blue—the blue of Terra's cloudless skies on certain days, so different from the yellow shield now hanging above them. A small case of leather, with silhouetted designs cut from hide and affixed to it, designs as intricate and complex as the embroidery on the jacket—art of a high standard. In the case a knife and spoon, the bowl and blade of dull metal, the handles of horn carved with horse heads, the tiny wide-open eyes set with glittering stones.

Personal possessions dear to the owner, so that when they must be abandoned for flight they were hidden with some hope of recovery. Travis slowly repacked them, trying to fold the garments into their original creases. He was still puzzled by those designs.

"Who?" Tsoay touched the edge of the jacket with one finger, his admiration for it plain to read.

"I don't know. But it is of our own world."

"That is a deer, though the horns are wrong," Tsoay agreed. "And the puma is very well done. The one who made this knows animals well."

Travis pushed the jacket back into the bag and laced it shut. But he did not return it to the hiding place. Instead, he made it a part of his own pack. If they did not succeed in running down the fugitive, he wanted an opportunity for closer study, a chance to remember just where he had seen that picture before.

The narrow valley where they had discovered the bag sloped upward, and there were signs that their quarry found the ground harder to cover. The second discard lay in open sight—again a leather bag which Nalik'ideyu sniffed and then began to lick eagerly, thrusting her nose into its flaccid interior.

Travis picked it up, finding it damp to the touch. It had an odd smell, like that of sour milk. He ran a finger around inside, brought it out wet; yet this was neither water bag nor canteen. And he was completely mystified when he turned it inside out, for though the inner surface was wet, the bag was empty. He offered it to the coyote, and she took it promptly.

Holding it firmly to the earth with her forepaws, she licked the surface, though Travis could see no deposit which might attract her. It was clear that the bag had once held some sort of food.

"Here they rested," Tsoay said. "Not too far ahead now—"

But now they were in the kind of country where a man could hide in order to check on his back trail. Travis studied the terrain and then made his own plans. They would leave the plainly marked trace of the fugitive, strike out upslope to the east and try to parallel the other's route. In that maze of rock outcrops and wood copses there was tricky going.

Nalik'ideyu gave a last lick to the bag as Travis signaled her. She regarded him, then turned her head to survey the country before them. At last she trotted on, her buff coat melting into the vegetation. With Naginlta she would scout the quarry and keep watch, leaving the men to take the longer way around.

Travis pulled off his shirt, folding it into a packet and tucking it beneath the folds of his sash-belt, just as his ancestors had always done before a fight. Then he cached his pack and Tsoay's. As they began the stiff climb they carried only their bows, the quivers slung on their shoulders, and the long-bladed knives. But they flitted like shadows and, like the coyotes, their red-brown bodies became indistinguishable against the bronze of the land.

They should be, Travis judged, not more than an hour away from sundown. And they had to locate the stranger before the dark closed in. His respect for their quarry had grown. The unknown might have been driven by fear, but he held to a good pace and headed intelligently for just the kind of country which would serve him best. If Travis could only remember where he had seen the like of that embroidery! It had a meaning which might be important now....

Tsoay slipped behind a wind-gnarled tree and disappeared. Travis stooped under a line of bush limbs. Both were working their way south, using the peak ahead as an agreed landmark, pausing at intervals to examine the landscape for any hint of a man and horse.

Travis squirmed snake fashion into an opening between two rock pillars and lay there, the westering sun hot on his bare shoulders and back, his chin propped on his forearm. In the band holding back his hair he had inserted some concealing tufts of wiry mountain grass, the ends of which drooped over his rugged features.

Only seconds earlier he had caught that fragmentary warning from one of the coyotes. What they sought was very close, it was right down there. Both animals were in ambush, awaiting orders. And what they found was familiar, another confirmation that the fugitive was Terran, not native to Topaz.

With searching eyes, Travis examined the site indicated by the coyotes. His respect for the stranger was raised another notch. In time either he or Tsoay might have sighted that hideaway without the aid of the animal scouts; on the other hand, they might have failed. For the fugitive had truly gone to earth, using some pocket or crevice in the mountain wall.

There was no sign of the horse, but a branch here and there had been pulled out of place, the scars of their removal readable when one knew where to look. Odd, Travis began to puzzle over what he saw. It was almost as if whatever pursuit the stranger feared would come not at ground level but from above; the precautions the stranger had taken were to veil his retreat to the reaches of the mountain side.

Had he expected any trailer to make a flanking move from up that slope where the Apaches now lay? Travis' teeth nipped the weathered skin of his forearm. Could it be that at some time during the day's journeying the fugitive had doubled back, having seen his trackers? But there had been no traces of any such scouting, and the coyotes would surely have warned them. Human eyes and ears could be tricked, but Travis trusted the senses of Naginlta and Nalik'ideyu far above his own.

No, he did not believe that the rider expected the Apaches. But the man did expect someone or something which would come upon him from the heights. The heights.... Travis rolled his head slightly to look at the upper reaches of the hills about him—with suspicion.

In their own journey across the mountains and through the pass they had found nothing threatening. Dangerous animals might roam there. There had been some paw marks, one such trail the coyotes had warned against. But the type of precautions the stranger had taken were against intelligent, thinking beings, not against animals more likely to track by scent than by sight.

And if the stranger expected an attack from above, then Travis and Tsoay must be alert. Travis analyzed each feature of the hillside, setting in his mind a picture of every inch of ground they must cross. Just as he had wanted daylight as an ally before, so now was he willing to wait for the shadows of twilight.

He closed his eyes in a final check, able to recall the details of the hiding place, knowing that he could reach it when the conditions favored, without mistake. Then he edged back from his vantage point, and raising his fingers to his lips, made a small angry chittering, three times repeated. One of the species inhabiting these heights, as they had noted earlier, was a creature about as big as the palm of a man's hand, resembling nothing so much as a round ball of ruffled feathers, though its covering might actually have been a silky, fluffy fur. Its short legs could cover ground at an amazing speed, and it had the bold impudence of a creature with few natural enemies. This was its usual cry.

Tsoay's hand waved Travis on to where the younger man had taken position behind the bleached trunk of a fallen tree.

"He hides," Tsoay whispered.

"Against trouble from above." Travis added his own observation.

"But not us, I think."

So Tsoay had come to that conclusion too? Travis tried to gauge the nearness of twilight. There was a period after the passing of Topaz' sun when the dusky light played odd tricks with shadows. That would be the first time for their move. He said as much, and Tsoay nodded eagerly. They sat with their backs to a boulder, the tree trunk serving as a screen, and chewed methodically on ration tablets. There was energy and sustenance in the tasteless squares which would support men, even though their stomachs continued to demand the satisfaction of fresh meat.

Taking turns, they dozed a little. But the last banners of Topaz' sun were still in the sky when Travis judged the shadows cover enough. He had no way of knowing how the stranger was armed. Though he used a horse for transportation, he might well carry a rifle and the most modern Terran sidearms.

The Apaches' bows were little use for infighting, but they had their knives. However, Travis wanted to take the fugitive unharmed if he could. There was information he must have. So he did not even draw his knife as he started downhill.

When he reached a pool of violet dusk at the bottom of the small ravine Naginlta's eyes regarded him knowingly. Travis signaled with his hand and thought out what would be the coyotes' part in this surprise attack. The prick-eared silhouette vanished. Uphill the chitter of a fluff-fur sounded twice—Tsoay was in position.

A howl ... wailing ... sobbing ... was heard, one of the keening songs of the *mba'a*. Travis darted forward. He heard the nicker of a frightened horse, a clicking which could have marked the pawing of hoof on gravel, saw the brush hiding the stranger's hole tremble, a portion of it fall away.

Travis sped on, his moccasins making no sound on the ground. One of the coyotes gave tongue for the second time, the eerie wailing rising to a yapping which echoed from the rocks about them. Travis poised for a dive.

Another section of those artfully heaped branches had given way and a horse reared, its upflung head plainly marked against the sky. A blurred figure weaved back and forth before it, trying to control the mount. The stranger had his hands full, certainly no weapon drawn—this was it!

Travis leaped. His hands found their mark, the shoulders of the stranger. There was a shrill cry from the other as he tried to turn in the Apache's hold, to face his attacker. But Travis bore them both on, rolling almost under the feet of the horse, sliding downhill, the unknown's writhing body pinned down by the Apache's weight and his clasp, tight as an iron grip, about the other's chest and upper arms.

He felt his opponent go limp, but was suspicious enough not to release that hold, for the heavy breathing of the stranger was not that of an unconscious man. They lay so, the unknown still tight in Travis' hold but no longer fighting. The Apache could hear Tsoay soothing the horse with the purring words of a practiced horseman.

Still the stranger did not resume the struggle. They could not lie in this position all night, Travis thought with a wry twist of amusement. He shifted his hold, and got the lightning-quick response he had expected. But it was not quite quick enough, for Travis had the other's hands behind his back, cupping slender, almost delicate wrists together.

"Throw me a cord!" he called to Tsoay.

The younger man ran up with an extra bow cord, and in a moment they had bonds on the struggling captive. Travis rolled their catch over, reaching down for a fistful of hair to pull the head into a patch of clearer light.

In his grasp that hair came loose, a braid unwinding. He grunted as he looked down into the stranger's face. Dust marks were streaked now with tear runnels, but the gray eyes which turned fiercely on him said that their owner cried more in rage than fear.

His captive might be wearing long trousers tucked into curved, toed boots, and a loose overblouse, but she was certainly not only a woman, but a very young and attractive one. Also, at the present moment, an exceedingly angry one. And behind that anger was fear, the fear of one fighting hopelessly against insurmountable odds. But as she eyed Travis now her expression changed.

He felt she had expected another captor altogether and was astounded at the sight of him. Her tongue touched her lips, moistening them, and now the fear in her was another kind—the wary fear of one facing a totally new and perhaps dangerous thing.

"Who are you?" Travis spoke in English, for he had no doubts that she was Terran.

Now she sucked in her breath with a gasp of pure astonishment.

"Who are *you*?" she parroted his question in a marked accent. English was not her native tongue, he was sure.

Travis reached out, and again his hands closed on her shoulders. She started to twist and then realized he was merely pulling her up to a sitting position. Some of the fear had left her eyes, an intent interest taking its place.

"You are not Sons of the Blue Wolf," she stated in her heavily accented speech.

Travis smiled. "I am the Fox, not the Wolf," he returned. "And the Coyote is my brother." He snapped his fingers at the shadows, and the two animals came noiselessly into sight. Her gaze widened even more at Naginlta and Nalik'ideyu, and she deduced the bond which must exist between her captor and the beasts.

"This woman is also of our world." Tsoay spoke in Apache, looking over their prisoner with frank interest. "Only she is not of the People."

Sons of the Blue Wolf? Travis thought again of the embroidery designs on the jacket. Who had called themselves by that picturesque title—where—and when in time?

"What do you fear, Daughter of the Blue Wolf?" he asked.

And with that question he seemed to touch some button activating terror. She flung back her head so that she could see the darkening sky.

"The flyer!" Her voice was muted as if more than a whisper would carry to the stars just coming into brilliance above them. "They will come ... tracking. I did not reach the inner mountains in time."

There was a despairing note in that which cut through to Travis, who found that he, too, was searching the sky, not knowing what he looked for or what kind of menace it promised, only that it was real danger.

6

"The night comes," Tsoay spoke slowly in English. "Do these you fear hunt in the dark?"

She shook her head to free her forehead from a coil of braid, pulled loose in her struggle with Travis.

"They do not need eyes or such noses as those four-footed hunters of yours. They have a machine to track—"

"Then what purpose is this brush pile of yours?" Travis raised his chin at the disturbed hiding place.

"They do not constantly use the machine, and one can hope. But at night they can ride on its beam. We are not far enough into the hills to lose them. Bahatur went lame, and so I was slowed...."

"And what lies in these mountains that those you fear dare not invade them?" Travis continued.

"I do not know, save if one can climb far enough inside, one is safe from pursuit."

"I ask it again: Who are you?" The Apache leaned forward, his face in the fast-fading light now only inches away from hers. She did not shrink from his close scrutiny but met him eye to eye. This was a woman of proud independence, truly a chief's daughter, Travis decided.

"I am of the People of the Blue Wolf. We were brought across the star lanes to make this world safe for ... for ... the...." She hesitated, and now there was a shade of puzzlement on her face. "There is a reason—a dream. No, there is the dream and there is reality. I am Kaydessa of the Golden Horde, but sometimes I remember other things—like this speech of strange words I am mouthing now—"

"The Golden Horde!" Travis knew now. The embroidery, Sons of the Blue Wolf, all fitted into a special pattern. But what a pattern! Scythian art, the ornament that the warriors of Genghis Khan bore so proudly. Tatars, Mongols—the barbarians who had swept from the fastness of the steppes to change the course of history, not only in Asia but across the plains of middle Europe. The men of the Emperor Khans who had ridden behind the yak-tailed standards of Genghis Khan, Kublai Khan, Tamerlane—!

"The Golden Horde," Travis repeated once again. "That lies far back in the history of another world, Wolf Daughter."

She stared at him, a queer, lost expression on her dust-grimed face.

"I know." Her voice was so muted he could hardly distinguish the words. "My people live in two times, and many do not realize that."

Tsoay had crouched down beside them to listen. Now he put out his hand, touching Travis' shoulder.

"Redax?"

"Or its like." For Travis was sure of one point. The project, which had been training three teams for space colonization—one of Eskimos, one of Pacific Islanders, and one of his own Apaches—had no reason or chance to select Mongols from the wild past of the raiding Hordes. There was only one nation on Terra which could have picked such colonists.

"You are Russian." He studied her carefully, intent on noting the effect of his words.

But she did not lose that lost look. "Russian ... Russian ..." she repeated, as if the very word was strange.

Travis was alarmed. Any Russian colony planted here could well possess technicians with machines capable of tracking a fugitive, and if mountain heights were protection against such a hunt, he intended to gain them, even by night traveling. He said this to Tsoay, and the other emphatically agreed.

"The horse is too lame to go on," the younger man reported.

Travis hesitated for a long second. Since the time they had stolen their first mounts from the encroaching Spanish, horses had always been wealth to his people. To leave an animal which could well serve the clan was not right. But they dared not waste time with a lame beast.

"Leave it here, free," he ordered.

"And the woman?"

"She goes with us. We must learn all we can of these people and what they do here. Listen, Wolf Daughter," again Travis leaned close to make sure she was listening to him as he spoke with emphasis—"you will travel with us into these high places, and there will be no trouble from you." He drew his knife and held the blade warningly before her eyes.

"It was already in my mind to go to the mountains," she told him evenly. "Untie my hands, brave warrior, you have surely nothing to fear from a woman."

His hand made a swift sweep and plucked a knife as long and keen as his from the folds of the sash beneath her loose outer garment.

"Not now, Wolf Daughter, since I have drawn your fangs."

He helped her to her feet and slashed the cord about her wrists with her knife, which he then fastened to his own belt. Alerting the coyotes, he dispatched them ahead; and the three started on, the Mongol girl between the two Apaches. The abandoned horse nickered lonesomely and then began to graze on tufts of grass, moving slowly to favor his foot.

The two moons rode the sky as the hours advanced, their beams fighting the shadows. Travis felt reasonably safe from any attack at ground level, depending upon the coyotes for warning. But he held them all to a steady pace. And he did not question the girl again until all three of them hunkered down at a small mountain spring, to dash icy water over their faces and drink from cupped hands.

"Why do you flee your own people, Wolf Daughter?"

"My name is Kaydessa," she corrected him.

He chuckled with laughter at the prim tone of her voice. "And you see here Tsoay of the People—the Apaches—while I am Fox." He was giving her the English equivalent of his tribal name.

"Apaches." She tried to repeat the word with the same accent he had used. "And what are Apaches?"

"Indians—Amerindians," he explained. "But you have not answered my question, Kaydessa. Why do you run from your own people?"

"Not from my people," she said, shaking her head determinedly. "From those others. It is like this—Oh, how can I make you understand rightly?" She spread her wet hands out before her in the moonlight, the damp patches on her sleeves clinging to her arms. "There are my people of the Golden Horde, though once we were different and we can remember bits of that previous life. Then there are also the men who live in the sky ship and use the machine so that we think only the thoughts they would have us think. Now why," she looked at Travis intently—"do I wish to tell you all this? It is strange. You say you are Indian—American—are we then enemies? There is a part memory which says that we are ... were...."

"Let us rather say," he corrected her, "that the Apaches and the Horde are not enemies here and now, no matter what was before." That was the truth, Travis recognized. By all accounts his people had come out of Asia in the very dim beginnings of migrating peoples. For all her dark-red hair and gray eyes, this girl who had been arbitrarily returned to a past just as they had been by Redax, could well be a distant clan-cousin.

"You—" Kaydessa's fingers rested for a moment on his wrist—"you, too, were sent here from across the stars. Is this not so?"

"It is so."

"And there are those here who govern you now?"

"No. We are free."

"How did you become free?" she demanded fiercely.

Travis hesitated. He did not want to tell of the wrecked ship, the fact that his people possessed no real defenses against the Russian-controlled colony.

"We went to the mountains," he replied evasively.

"Your governing machine failed?" Kaydessa laughed. "Ah, they are so great, those men of the machines. But they are smaller and weaker when their machines cannot obey them."

"It is so with your camp?" Travis probed gently. He was not quite sure of her meaning, but he dared not ask more detailed questions without dangerously revealing his own ignorance.

"In some manner their control machine—it can only work upon those within a certain distance. They discovered that in the days of the first landing, when hunters went out freely and many of them did not return. After that when hunters were sent out to learn how lay this land, they went along in the flyer with a machine so that there would be no more escapes. But we knew!" Kaydessa's fingers curled into small fists. "Yes, we knew that if we could get beyond the machines, there was freedom for us. And we planned—many of us—planned. Then nine or ten sleeps ago those others were very excited. They gathered in their ship, watching their machines. And something happened. For a while all those machines went dead.

"Jagatai, Kuchar, my brother Hulagur, Menlik...." She was counting the names off on her fingers. "They raided the horse herd, rode out...."

"And you?"

"I, too, should have ridden. But there was Aljar, my sister—Kuchar's wife. She was very near her time and to ride thus, fleeing and fast, might kill her and the child. So I did not go. Her son was born that night, but the others had the machine at work once more. We might long to go here," she brought her fist up to her breast, and then raised it to her head—"but there was that *here* which kept us to the camp and their will.

We only knew that if we could reach the mountains, we might find our people who had already gained their freedom."

"But you are here. How did you escape?" Tsoay wanted to know.

"They knew that I would have gone had it not been for Aljar. So they said they would make her ride out with them unless I played guide to lead them to my brother and the others. Then I knew I must take up the sword of duty and hunt with them. But I prayed that the spirits of the upper air look with favor upon me, and they granted aid...." Her eyes held a look of wonder. "For when we were out on the plains and well away from the settlement, a grass devil attacked the leader of the searching party, and he dropped the mind control and so it was broken. Then I rode. Blue Sky Above knows how I rode. And those others are not with their horses as are the people of the Wolf."

"When did this happen?"

"Three suns ago."

Travis counted back in his mind. Her date for the failure of the machine in the Russian camp seemed to coincide with the crash landing of the American ship. Had one thing any connection with the other? It was very possible. The planeting spacer might have fought some kind of weird duel with the other colony before it plunged to earth on the other side of the mountain range.

"Do you know where in these mountains your people hide?"

Kaydessa shook her head. "Only that I must head south, and when I reach the highest peak make a signal fire on the north slope. But that I cannot do now, for those in the flyer may see it. I know they are on my trail, for twice I have seen it. Listen, Fox, I ask this of you—I, Kaydessa, who am eldest daughter to the Khan—for you are like unto us, a warrior and a brave man, that I believe. It may be that you cannot be governed by their machine, for you have not rested under their spell, nor are of our blood. Therefore, if they come close enough to send forth the call, the call I must obey as if I were a slave dragged upon a horse rope, then do you bind my hands and feet and hold me here, no matter how much I struggle to follow that command. For that which is truly me does not want to go. Will you swear this by the fires which expel demons?"

The utter sincerity of her tone convinced Travis that she was pleading for aid against a danger she firmly believed in. Whether she was right about his immunity to the Russian mental control was another matter, and one he would rather not put to the test.

"We do not swear by your fires, Blue Wolf Maiden, but by the Path of the Lightning." His fingers moved as if to curl about the sacred charred wood his people had once carried as "medicine." "So do I promise!"

She looked at him for a long moment and then nodded in satisfaction.

They left the pool and pushed on toward the mountain slopes, working their way back to the pass. A low growl out of the dark brought them to an instant halt. Naginlta's warning was sharp; there was danger ahead, acute danger.

The moonlight from the moons made a weird pattern of light and dark on the stretch ahead. Anything from a slinking four-footed hunter to a war party of intelligent beings might have been lying in wait there.

A flitting shadow out of shadows. Nalik'ideyu pressed against Travis' legs, making a barrier of her warm body, attracting his attention to a spot at the left perhaps a hundred yards on. There was a great splotch of dark there, large enough to hide a really formidable opponent; that wordless communication between animal and man told Travis that such an opponent was just what was lurking there.

Whatever lay in ambush beside the upper track was growing impatient as its destined prey ceased to advance, the coyotes reported.

"Your left—beyond that pointed rock—in the big shadow—"

"Do you see it?" Tsoay demanded.

"No. But the *mba'a* do."

The men had their bows ready, arrows set to the cords. But in this light such weapons were practically useless unless the enemy moved into the path of the moon.

"What is it?" Kaydessa asked in a half whisper.

"Something waits for us ahead."

Before he could stop her, she set her fingers to her lips and gave a piercing whistle.

There was answering movement in the shadow. Travis shot at that, his arrow followed instantly by one from Tsoay. There was a cry, scaling up in a throat-scalding scream which made Travis flinch. Not because of the sound, but because of the hint which lay behind it—could it have been a human cry?

The thing flopped out into a patch of moonlight. It was four-limbed, its body silvery—and it was large. But the worst was that it had been groveling on all fours when it fell, and now it was rising on its hind feet, one forepaw striking madly at the two arrows dancing head-deep in its upper shoulder. Man? No! But something sufficiently manlike to chill the three downtrail.

A whirling four-footed hunter dashed in, snapped at the creature's legs, and it squalled again, aiming a blow with a forepaw; but the attacking coyote was already gone. Together Naginlta and Nalik'ideyu were harassing the creature, just as they had fought the split horn, giving the hunters time to shoot. Travis, although he again felt that touch of horror and disgust he could not account for, shot again.

Between them the Apaches must have sent a dozen arrows into the raving beast before it went to its knees and Naginlta sprang for its throat. Even then the coyote yelped and flinched, a bleeding gash across its head from the raking talons of the dying thing. When it no longer moved, Travis approached to see more closely what they had brought down. That smell....

Just as the embroidery on Kaydessa's jacket had awakened memories from his Terran past, so did this stench remind him of something. Where—when—had he smelled it before? Travis connected it with dark, dark and danger. Then he gasped in a half exclamation.

Not on this world, no, but on two others: two worlds of that broken stellar empire where he had been an involuntary explorer two planet years ago! The beast things which had lived in the dark of the desert world the Terrans' wandering galactic derelict had landed upon. Yes, the beast things whose nature they had never been able to deduce. Were they the degenerate dregs of a once intelligent species? Or were they animals, akin to man, but still animals?

The ape-things had controlled the night of the desert world. And they had been met again—also in the dark—in the ruins of the city which had been the final goal of the ship's taped voyage. So they were a part of the vanished civilization. And Travis' own vague surmise concerning Topaz was proven correct. This had not been an empty world for the long-gone space people. This planet had a purpose and a use, or else this beast would not have been here.

"Devil!" Kaydessa made a face of disgust.

"You know it?" Tsoay asked Travis. "What is it?"

"That I do not know, but it is a thing left over from the star people's time. And I have seen it on two other of their worlds."

"A man?" Tsoay surveyed the body critically. "It wears no clothes, has no weapons, but it walks erect. It looks like an ape, a very big ape. It is not a good thing, I think."

"If it runs with a pack—as they do elsewhere—this could be a very bad thing." Travis, remembering how these creatures had attacked in force on the other worlds, looked about him apprehensively. Even with the coyotes on guard, they could not stand up to such a pack closing in through the dark. They had better hole up in some defendable place and wait out the rest of the night.

Naginlta brought them to a cliff overhang where they could set their backs to the hard rock of the mountain, face outward to a space they could cover with arrow flight if the need arose. And the coyotes, lying before them with their noses resting on paws, would, Travis knew, alert them long before the enemy could close in.

They huddled against the rock, Kaydessa between them, alert at first to every sound of the night, their hearts beating faster at a small scrape of gravel, the rustle of a bush. Slowly, they began to relax.

"It is well that two sleep while one guards," Travis observed. "By morning we must push on, out of this country."

So the two Apaches shared the watch in turn, the Tatar girl at first protesting, and then falling exhausted into a slumber which left her breathing heavily.

Travis, on the dawn watch, began to speculate about the ape-thing they had killed. The two previous times he had met this creature it had been in ruins of the old empire. Were there ruins somewhere here? He wanted to make sure about that. On the other hand, there was the problem of the Tatar-Mongol settlement controlled by the Reds. There was no doubt in his mind that, were the Reds to suspect the existence of the Apache camp, they would make every attempt to hunt down and kill or capture the survivors from the American ship. A warning must be carried to the rancheria as quickly as they could make the return trip.

Beside him the girl stirred, raising her head. Travis glanced at her and then watched with attention. She was looking straight ahead, her eyes as fixed as if she were in a trance. Now she inched forward from the mountain wall, wriggling out of its shelter.

"What—?" Tsoay had awakened again. But Travis was already moving. He pushed on, rushing up to stand beside her, shoulder to shoulder.

"What is it? Where do you go?" he asked.

She made no answer, did not even seem aware of his voice. He caught at her arm and she pulled to free herself. When he tightened his grip she did not fight him actively as during their first encounter, but merely pulled and twisted as if she were being compelled to go ahead.

Compulsion! He remembered her plea the night before, asking his help against recapture by the machine. Now he deliberately tripped her, twisted her hands behind her back. She swayed in his hold, trying to win to her feet, paying no attention to him save as a hindrance against her answering that demanding call he could not hear.

7

"What happened?" Tsoay took a swift stride, stood over the writhing girl whose strength was now such that Travis had to exert all his efforts to control her.

"I think that the machine she spoke about is holding her. She is being drawn to it out of hiding as one draws a calf on a rope."

Both coyotes had arisen and were watching the struggle with interest, but there was no warning from them. Whatever called Kaydessa into such mindless and will-less answer did not touch the animals. And neither Apache felt it. So perhaps only Kaydessa's people were subject to it, as she had thought. How far away was that machine? Not too near, for otherwise the coyotes would have traced the man or men operating it.

"We cannot move her," Tsoay brought the problem into the open—"unless we bind and carry her. She is one of their kind. Why not let her go to them, unless you fear she will talk." His hand went to the knife in his belt, and Travis knew what primitive impulse moved in the younger man.

In the old days a captive who was likely to give trouble was efficiently eliminated. In Tsoay that memory was awake now. Travis shook his head.

"She has said that others of her kin are in these hills. We must not set two wolf packs hunting us," Travis said, giving the more practical reason which might better appeal to that savage instinct for self-preservation. "But you are right, since she has tried to answer this summons, we cannot force her with us. Therefore, do you take the back trail. Tell Buck what we have discovered and have him make the necessary precautions against either these Mongol outlaws or a Red thrust over the mountains."

"And you?"

"I stay to discover where the outlaws hide and learn all I can of this settlement. We may have reason to need friends—"

"Friends!" Tsoay spat. "The People need no friends! If we have warning, we can hold our own country! As the Pinda-lick-o-yi have discovered before."

"Bows and arrows against guns and machines?" Travis inquired bitingly. "We must know more before we make any warrior boasts for the future. Tell Buck what we have discovered. Also say I will join you before," Travis calculated—"ten suns. If I do not, send no search party; the clan is too small to risk more lives for one."

"And if these Reds take you—?"

Travis grinned, not pleasantly. "They shall learn nothing! Can their machines sort out the thoughts of a dead man?" He did not intend his future to end as abruptly as that, but also he would not be easy meat for any Red hunting party.

Tsoay took a share of their rations and refused the company of the coyotes. Travis realized that for all his seeming ease with the animals, the younger scout had little more liking for them than Deklay and the others back at the rancheria. Tsoay went at dawn, aiming at the pass.

Travis sat down beside Kaydessa. They had bound her to a small tree, and she strove incessantly to free herself, turning her head at an acute and painful angle, only to face the same direction in which she had been tied. There was no breaking the spell which held her. And she would soon wear herself out with that struggling. Then he struck an expert blow.

The girl sagged limply, and he untied her. It all depended now on the range of the beam or broadcast of that diabolical machine. From the attitude of the coyotes, he assumed that those using the machine had not made any attempt to come close. They might not even know where their quarry was; they would simply sit and wait in the foothills for the caller to reel in a helpless captive.

Travis thought that if he moved Kaydessa farther away from that point, sooner or later they would be out of range and she would awake from the knockout, free again. Although she was not light, he could manage to carry her for a while. So burdened, Travis started on, with the coyotes scouting ahead.

He speedily discovered that he had set himself an ambitious task. The going was rough, and carrying the girl reduced his advance to a snail-paced crawl. But it gave him time to make careful plans.

As long as the Reds held the balance of power on this side of the mountain range, the rancheria was in danger. Bows and knives against modern armament was no contest at all. And it would only be a matter of time before exploration on the part of the northern settlement—or some tracking down of Tatar fugitives—would bring the enemy across the pass.

The Apaches could move farther south into the unknown continent below the wrecked ship, thus prolonging the time before they were discovered. But that would only postpone the inevitable showdown.

Whether Travis could make his clan believe that, was also a matter of concern.

On the other hand, if the Red overlords could be met in some practical way.... Travis' mind fastened on that more attractive idea, worrying it as Naginlta worried a prey, tearing out and devouring the more delicate portions. Every bit of sense and prudence argued against such an approach, whose success could rest only between improbability and impossibility; yet that was the direction in which he longed to move.

Across his shoulder Kaydessa stirred and moaned. The Apache doubled his efforts to reach the outcrop of rock he could see ahead, chiseled into high relief by the winds. In its lee they would have protection from any sighting from below. Panting, he made it, lowering the girl into the guarded cup of space, and waited.

She moaned again, lifted one hand to her head. Her eyes were half open, and still he could not be sure whether they focused on him and her surroundings intelligently or not.

"Kaydessa!"

Her heavy eyelids lifted, and he had no doubt she could see him. But there was no recognition of his identity in her gaze, only surprise and fear—the same expression she had worn during their first meeting in the foothills.

"Daughter of the Wolf," he spoke slowly. "Remember!" Travis made that an order, an emphatic appeal to the mind under the influence of the caller.

She frowned, the struggle she was making naked on her face. Then she answered:

"You—Fox—"

Travis grunted with relief, his alarm subsiding. Then she *could* remember. "Yes," he responded eagerly.

But she was gazing about, her puzzlement growing. "Where is this—?"

"We are higher in the mountains."

Now fear was pushing out bewilderment. "How did I come here?"

"I brought you." Swiftly he outlined what had happened at their night camp.

The hand which had been at her head was now pressed tight across her lips as if she were biting furiously into its flesh to still some panic of her own, and her gray eyes were round and haunted.

"You are free now," Travis said.

Kaydessa nodded, and then dropped her hand to speak. "You brought me away from the hunters. You did not have to obey them?"

"I heard nothing."

"You do not hear—you feel!" She shuddered. "Please." She clawed at the stone beside her, pulling up to her feet. "Let us go—let us go quickly! They will try again—move farther in—"

"Listen," Travis had to be sure of one thing—"have they any way of knowing that they had you under control and that you have again escaped?"

Kaydessa shook her head, some of the panic again shadowing her eyes.

"Then we'll just go on—" his chin lifted to the wastelands before them—"try to keep out of their reach."

And away from the pass to the south, he told himself silently. He dared not lead the enemy to that secret, so he must travel west or hole up somewhere in this unknown wilderness until they could be sure Kaydessa was no longer susceptible to that call, or that they were safely beyond its beamed radius. There was the chance of contacting her outlaw kin, just as there was the chance of stumbling into a pack of the ape-things. Before dark they must discover a protected camp site.

They needed water, food. He had a bare half dozen ration tablets. But the coyotes could locate water.

"Come!" Travis beckoned to Kaydessa, motioning her to climb ahead of him so that he could watch for any indication of her succumbing once again to the influence of the enemy. But his burdened early morning flight had told on Travis more than he thought, and he discovered he could not spur himself on to a pace better than a walk. Now and again one of the coyotes, usually Nalik'ideyu, would come into view, express impatience in both stance and mental signal, and then be gone again. The Apache was increasingly aware that the animals were disturbed, yet to his tentative gropings at contact they did not reply. Since they gave no warning of hostile animal or man, he could only be on constant guard, watching the countryside about him.

They had been following a ledge for several minutes before Travis was aware of some strange features of that path. Perhaps he had actually noted them with a trained eye before his archaeological studies of the recent past gave him a reason for the faint marks. This crack in the mountain's skin might have begun as a natural fault, but afterward it had been worked with tools, smoothed, widened to serve the purpose of some form of intelligence!

Travis caught at Kaydessa's shoulder to slow her pace. He could not have told why he did not want to speak aloud here, but he felt the need for silence. She glanced around, perplexed, more so when he went down on his knees and ran his fingers along one of those ancient tool marks. He was certain it was very old. Inside of him anticipation bubbled. A road made with such labor could only lead to something of importance. He was going to make the discovery, the dream which had first drawn him into these mountains.

"What is it?" Kaydessa knelt beside him, frowning at the ledge.

"This was cut by someone, a long time ago," Travis half whispered and then wondered why. There was no reason to believe the road makers could hear him when perhaps a thousand years or more lay between the chipping of that stone and this day.

The Tatar girl looked over her shoulder. Perhaps she too was troubled by the sense that here time was subtly telescoped, that past and present might be meeting. Or was that feeling with them both because of their enforced conditioning?

"Who?" Now her voice sank in turn.

"Listen—" he regarded her intently—"did your people or the Reds ever find any traces of the old civilization here—ruins?"

"No." She leaned forward, tracing with her own finger the same almost-obliterated marks which had intrigued Travis. "But I think they have looked. Before they discovered that we could be free, they sent out parties—to hunt, they said—but afterward they always asked many questions about the country. Only they never asked about ruins. Is that what they wished us to find? But why? Of what value are old stones piled on one another?"

"In themselves, little, save for the knowledge they may give us of the people who piled them. But for what the stones might contain—much value!"

"And how do you know what they might contain, Fox?"

"Because I have seen such treasure houses of the star men," he returned absently. To him the marks on the ledge were a pledge of greater discoveries to come. He must find where that carefully constructed road ran—to what it led. "Let us see where this will take us."

But first he gave the chittering signal in four sharp bursts. And the tawny-gray bodies came out of the tangled brush, bounding up to the ledge. Together the coyotes faced him, their attention all for his halting communication.

Ruins might lie ahead; he hoped that they did. But on another planet such ruins had twice proved to be deadly traps, and only good fortune had prevented their closing on Terran explorers. If the ape-things or any other dangerous form of life had taken up residence before them, he wanted good warning.

Together the coyotes turned and loped along the now level way of the ledge, disappearing around a curve fitted to the mountain side while Travis and Kaydessa followed.

They heard it before they saw its source—a waterfall. Probably not a large one, but high. Rounding the curve, they came into a fine mist of spray where sunlight made rainbows of color across a filmy veil of water.

For a long moment they stood entranced. Kaydessa then gave a little cry, held out her hands to the purling mist and brought them to her lips again to suck the gathered moisture.

Water slicked the surface of the ledge, and Travis pushed her back against the wall of the cliff. As far as he could discern, their road continued behind the out-flung curtain of water, and footing on the wet stone was treacherous. With their backs to the solid security of the wall, facing outward into the solid drape of water, they edged behind it and came out into rainbowed sunlight again.

Here either provident nature or ancient art had hollowed a pocket in the stone which was filled with water. They drank. Then Travis filled his canteen while Kaydessa washed her face, holding the cold freshness of the moisture to her cheeks with both palms.

She spoke, but he could not hear her through the roar. She leaned closer and raised her voice to a half shout:

"This is a place of spirits! Do you not also feel their power, Fox?"

Perhaps for a space out of time he did feel something. This was a watering place, perhaps a never-ceasing watering place—and to his desert-born-and-bred race all water was a spirit gift never to be taken for granted. The rainbow—the Spirit People's sacred sign—old beliefs stirred in Travis, moving him. "I feel," he said, nodding in emphasis to his agreement.

They followed the ledge road to a section where a landslide of an earlier season had choked it. Travis worked a careful way across the debris, Kaydessa obeying his guidance in turn. Then they were on a sloping downward way which led to a staircase—the treads weather-worn and crumbling, the angle so steep Travis wondered if it had ever been intended for beings with a physique approximating the Terrans'.

They came to a cleft where an arch of stone was chiseled out as a roofing. Travis thought he could make out a trace of carving on the capstone, so worn by years and weather that it was now only a faint shadow of design.

The cleft was a door into another valley. Here, too, golden mist swirled in tendrils to disguise and cloak what stood there. Travis had found his ruins. Only the structures were intact, not breached by time.

Mist flowed in lapping tongues back and forth, confusing outlines, now shuttering, now baring oval windows which were spaced in diamonds of four on round tower surfaces. There were no visible cracks, no cloaking of climbing vegetation, nothing to suggest age and long roots in the valley. Nor did the architecture he could view match any he had seen on those other worlds.

Travis strode away from the cleft doorway. Under his moccasins was a block pavement, yellow and green stone set in a simple pattern of checks. This, too, was level, unchipped and undisturbed, save for a drift or two of soil driven in by the wind. And nowhere could he see any vegetation.

The towers were of the same green stone as half the pavement blocks, a glassy green which made him think of jade—if jade could be mined in such quantities as these five-story towers demanded.

Nalik'ideyu padded to him, and he could hear the faint click of her claws on the pavement. There was a deep silence in this place, as if the air itself swallowed and digested all sound. The wind which had been with them all the day of their journeying was left beyond the cleft.

Yet there was life here. The coyote told him that in her own way. She had not made up her mind concerning that life—wariness and curiosity warred in her now as her pointed muzzle lifted toward the windows overhead.

The windows were all well above ground level, but there was no opening in the first stories as far as Travis could see. He debated moving into the range of those windows to investigate the far side of the towers for doorways. The mist and the message from Nalik'ideyu nourished his suspicions. Out in the open he would be too good a target for whatever or whoever might be standing within the deep-welled frames.

The silence was shattered by a boom. Travis jumped, slewed half around, knife in hand.

Boom-boom ... a second heavy beat-beat ... then a clangor with a swelling echo.

Kaydessa flung back her head and called, her voice rising up as if tunneled by the valley walls. She then whistled as she had done when they fronted the ape-thing and ran on to catch at Travis' sleeve, her face eager.

"My people! Come—it is my people!"

She tugged him on before breaking into a run, weaving fearlessly around the base of one of the towers. Travis ran after her, afraid he might lose her in the mist.

Three towers, another stretch of open pavement, and then the mist lifted to show them a second carved doorway not two hundred yards ahead. The boom-boom seemed to pull Kaydessa, and Travis could do nothing but trail her, the coyotes now trotting beside him.

8

They burst through a last wide band of mist into a wilderness of tall grass and shrubs. Travis heard the coyotes give tongue, but it was too late. Out of nowhere whirled a leather loop, settling about his chest, snapping his arms tight to his body, taking him off his feet with a jerk to be dragged helplessly along the ground behind a galloping horse.

A tawny fury sprang in the air to snap at the horse's head. Travis kicked fruitlessly, trying to regain his feet as the horse reared, and fought against the control of his shouting rider. All through the melee the Apache heard Kaydessa shrilly screaming words he did not understand.

Travis was on his knees, coughing in the dust, exerting the muscles in his chest and shoulders to loosen the lariat. On either side of him the coyotes wove a snarling pattern of defiance, dashing back and forth to present no target for the enemy, yet keeping the excited horses so stirred up that their riders could use neither ropes nor blades.

Then Kaydessa ran between two of the ringing horses to Travis and jerked at the loop about him. The tough, braided leather eased its hold, and he was able to gasp in full lungfuls of air. She was still shouting, but the tone had changed from one of recognition to a definite scolding.

Travis won to his feet just as the rider who had lassoed him finally got his horse under rein and dismounted. Holding the rope, the man walked hand over hand toward them, as Travis back on the Arizona range would have approached a nervous, unschooled pony.

The Mongol was an inch or so shorter than the Apache, and his face was young, though he had a drooping mustache bracketing his mouth with slender spear points of black hair. His breeches were tucked into high red boots, and he wore a loose felt jacket patterned with the same elaborate embroidery Travis had seen on Kaydessa's. On his head was a hat with a wide fur border—in spite of the heat—and that too bore touches of scarlet and gold design.

Still holding his lariat, the Mongol reached Kaydessa and stood for a moment, eying her up and down before he asked a question. She gave an impatient twitch to the rope. The coyotes snarled, but the Apache thought the animals no longer considered the danger immediate.

"This is my brother Hulagur." Kaydessa made the introduction over her shoulder. "He does not have your speech."

Hulagur not only did not understand, he was also impatient. He jerked at the rope with such sudden force that Travis was almost thrown. Then Kaydessa dragged as fiercely on the lariat in the other direction and burst into a soaring harangue which drew the rest of the men closer.

Travis flexed his upper arms, and the slack gained by Kaydessa's action made the lariat give again. He studied the Tatar outlaws. There were five of them beside Hulagur, lean men, hard-faced, narrow-eyed, the ragged clothing of three pieced out with scraps of hide. Besides the swords with the curved blades, they were armed with bows, two to each man, one long, one shorter. One of the riders carried a lance, long tassels of woolly hair streaming from below its head. Travis saw in them a formidable array of barbaric fighting men, but he thought that man for man the Apaches could not only take on the Mongols with confidence, but might well defeat them.

The Apache had never been a hot-headed, ride-for-glory fighter like the Cheyenne, the Sioux, and the Comanche of the open plains. He estimated the odds against him, used ambush, trick, and every feature of the countryside as weapon and defense. Fifteen Apache fighting men under Chief Geronimo had kept five thousand American and Mexican troops in the field for a year and had come off victorious for the moment.

Travis knew the tales of Genghis Khan and his formidable generals who swept over Asia into Europe, unbeaten and seemingly undefeatable. But they had been a wild wave, fed by a reservoir of manpower from the steppes of their homeland, utilizing driven walls of captives to protect their own men in city assaults and attacks. He doubted if even that endless sea of men could have won the Arizona desert defended by Apaches under Cochise, Victorio, or Magnus Colorado. The white man had done it—by superior arms and attrition; but bow against bow, knife against sword, craft and cunning against craft and cunning—he did not think so....

Hulagur dropped the end of the lariat, and Kaydessa swung around, loosening the loop so that the rope fell to Travis' feet. The Apache stepped free of it, turned and passed between two of the horsemen to gather up the bow he had dropped. The coyotes had gone with him and when he turned again to face the company of Tatars, both animals crowded past him to the entrance of the valley, plainly urging him to retire there.

The horsemen had faced about also, and the warrior with the lance balanced the shaft of the weapon in his hand as if considering the possibility of trying to spear Travis. But just then Kaydessa came up, towing Hulagur by a firm hold on his sash-belt.

"I have told this one," she reported to Travis, "how it is between us and that you also are enemy to those who hunt us. It is well that you sit together beside a fire and talk of these things."

Again that boom-boom broke her speech, coming from farther out in the open land.

"You will do this?" She made of it a half question, half statement.

Travis glanced about him. He could dodge back into the misty valley of the towers before the Tatars could ride him down. However, if he could patch up some kind of truce between his people and the outlaws, the Apaches would have only the Reds from the settlement to watch. Too many times in Terran past had war on two fronts been disastrous.

"I come—carrying this—and not pulled by your ropes." He held up his bow in an exaggerated gesture so that Hulagur could understand.

Coiling the lariat, the Mongol looked from the Apache bow to Travis. Slowly, and with obvious reluctance, he nodded agreement.

At Hulagur's call the lancer rode up to the waiting Apache, stretched out a booted foot in the heavy stirrup, and held down a hand to bring Travis up behind him riding double. Kaydessa mounted in the same fashion behind her brother.

Travis looked at the coyotes. Together the animals stood in the door to the tower valley, and neither made any move to follow as the horses trotted off. He beckoned with his hand and called to them.

Heads up, they continued to watch him go in company with the Mongols. Then without any reply to his coaxing, they melted back into the mists. For a moment Travis was tempted to slide down and run the risk of taking a lance point between the shoulders as he followed Naginlta and Nalik'ideyu into retreat. He was startled, jarred by the new awareness of how much he had come to depend on the animals. Ordinarily, Travis Fox was not one to be governed by the wishes of a *mba'a*, intelligent and un-animallike as it might be. This was an affair of men, and coyotes had no part in it!

Half an hour later Travis sat in the outlaw camp. There were fifteen Mongols in sight, a half dozen women and two children adding to the count. On a hillock near their yurts, the round brush-and-hide shelters—not too different from the wickiups of Travis' own people—was a crude drum, a hide stretched taut over a hollowed section of log. And next to that stood a man wearing a tall pointed cap, a red robe, and a girdle from which swung a fringe of small bones, tiny animal skulls, and polished bits of stone and carved wood.

It was this man's efforts which sent the boom-boom sounding at intervals over the landscape. Was this a signal—part of a ritual? Travis was not certain, though he guessed that the drummer was either medicine man or shaman, and so of some power in this company. Such men were credited with the ability to prophesy and also endowed with mediumship between man and spirit in the old days of the great Hordes.

The Apache evaluated the rest of the company. As was true of his own party, these men were much the same age—young and vigorous. And it was also apparent that Hulagur held a position of some importance among them—if he were not their chief.

After a last resounding roll on the drum, the shaman thrust the sticks into his girdle and came down to the fire at the center of the camp. He was taller than his fellows, pole thin under his robes, his face narrow, clean-shaven, with brows arched by nature to give him an unchanging expression of scepticism. He strode along, his tinkling collection of charms providing him with a not unmusical accompaniment, and came to stand directly before Travis, eying him carefully.

Travis copied his silence in what was close to a duel of wills. There was that in the shaman's narrowed green eyes which suggested that if Hulagur did in fact lead these fighting men, he had an advisor of determination and intelligence behind him.

"This is Menlik." Kaydessa did not push past the men to the fireside, but her voice carried.

Hulagur growled at his sister, but his admonition made no impression on her, and she replied in as hot a tone. The shaman's hand went up, silencing both of them.

"You are—who?" Like Kaydessa, Menlik spoke a heavily accented English.

"I am Travis Fox, of the Apaches."

"The Apaches," the shaman repeated. "You are of the West, the American West, then."

"You know much, man of spirit talk."

"One remembers. At times one remembers," Menlik answered almost absently. "How does an Apache find his way across the stars?"

"The same way Menlik and his people did," Travis returned. "You were sent to settle this planet, and so were we."

"There are many more of you?" countered Menlik swiftly.

"Are there not many of the Horde? Would one man, or three, or four, be sent to hold a world?" Travis fenced. "You hold the north, we the south of this land."

"But *they* are not governed by a machine!" Kaydessa cut in. "They are free!"

Menlik frowned at the girl. "Woman, this is a matter for warriors. Keep your tongue silent between your jaws!"

She stamped one foot, standing with her fists on her hips.

"I am a Daughter of the Blue Wolf. And we are all warriors—men and women alike—so shall we be as long as the Horde is not free to ride where we wish! These men have won their freedom; it is well that we learn how."

Menlik's expression did not change, but his lids drooped over his eyes as a murmur of what might be agreement came from the group. More than one of them must have understood enough English to translate for the others. Travis wondered about that. Had these men and women who had outwardly reverted to the life of their nomad ancestors once been well educated in the modern sense, educated enough to learn the basic language of the nation their rulers had set up as their principal enemy?

"So you ride the land south of the mountains?" the shaman continued.

"That is true."

"Then why did you come hither?"

Travis shrugged. "Why does anyone ride or travel into new lands? There is a desire to see what may lie beyond—"

"Or to scout before the march of warriors!" Menlik snapped. "There is no peace between your rulers and mine. Do you ride now to take the herds and pastures of the Horde—or to try to do so?"

Travis turned his head deliberately from side to side, allowing them all to witness his slow and openly contemptuous appraisal of their camp.

"*This* is your Horde, Shaman? Fifteen warriors? Much has changed since the days of Temujin, has it not?"

"What do you know of Temujin—you, who are a man of no ancestors, out of the West?"

"What do I know of Temujin? That he was a leader of warriors and became Genghis Khan, the great lord of the East. But the Apaches had their warlords also, rider of barren lands. And I am of those who raided over two nations when Victorio and Cochise scattered their enemies as a man scatters a handful of dust in the wind."

"You talk bold, Apache...." There was a hint of threat in that.

"I speak as any warrior, Shaman. Or are you so used to talking with spirits instead of men that you do not realize that?"

He might have been alienating the shaman by such a sharp reply, but Travis thought he judged the temper of these people. To face them boldly was the only way to impress them. They would not treat with an inferior, and he was already at a disadvantage coming on foot, without any backing in force, into a territory held by horsemen who were suspicious and jealous of their recently acquired freedom. His only chance was to establish himself as an equal and then try to convince them that Apache and Tatar-Mongol had a common cause against the Reds who controlled the settlement on the northern plains.

Menlik's right hand went to his sash-girdle and plucked out a carved stick which he waved between them, muttering phrases Travis could not understand. Had the shaman retreated so far along the road to his past that he now believed in his own supernatural powers? Or was this to impress his watching followers?

"You call upon your spirits for aid, Menlik? But the Apache has the companionship of the ga-n. Ask of Kaydessa: Who hunts with the Fox in the wilds?" Travis' sharp challenge stopped that wand in mid-air. Menlik's head swung to the girl.

"He hunts with wolves who think like men." She supplied the information the shaman would not openly ask for. "I have seen them act as his scouts. This is no spirit thing, but real and of this world!"

"Any man may train a dog to his bidding!" Menlik spat.

"Does a dog obey orders which are not said aloud? These brown wolves come and sit before him, look into his eyes. And then he knows what lies within their heads, and they know what he would have them do. This is not the way of a master of hounds with his pack!"

Again the murmur ran about the camp as one or two translated. Menlik frowned. Then he rammed his sorcerer's wand back into his sash.

"If you are a man of power—such powers," he said slowly, "then you may walk alone where those who talk with spirits go—into the mountains." He then spoke over his shoulder in his native tongue, and one of the women reached behind her into a hut, brought out a skin bag and a horn cup. Kaydessa took the cup from her and held it while the other woman poured a white liquid from the bag to fill it.

Kaydessa passed the cup to Menlik. He pivoted with it in his hand, dribbling expertly over its brim a few drops at each point of the compass, chanting as he moved. Then he sucked in a mouthful of the contents before presenting the vessel to Travis.

The Apache smelled the same sour scent that had clung to the emptied bag in the foothills. And another part of memory supplied him with the nature of the drink. This was kumiss, a fermented mare's milk which was the wine and water of the steppes.

He forced himself to swallow a draft, though it was alien to his taste, and passed the cup back to Menlik. The shaman emptied the horn and, with that, set aside ceremony. With an upraised hand he beckoned Travis to the fire again, indicating a pot set on the coals.

"Rest ... eat!" he bade abruptly.

Night was gathering in. Travis tried to calculate how far Tsoay must have backtracked to the rancheria. He thought that he could have already made the pass and be within a day and a half from the Apache camp if he pushed on, as he would. As to where the coyotes were, Travis had no idea. But it was plain that he himself must remain in this encampment for the night or risk rousing the Mongols' suspicion once more.

He ate of the stew, spearing chunks out of the pot with the point of his knife. And it was not until he sat back, his hunger appeased, that the shaman dropped down beside him.

"The Khatun Kaydessa says that when she was slave to the caller, you did not feel its chains," he began.

"Those who rule you are not my overlords. The bonds they set upon your minds do not touch me." Travis hoped that that was the truth and his escape that morning had not been just a fluke.

"This could be, for you and I are not of one blood," Menlik agreed. "Tell me—how did you escape your bonds?"

"The machine which held us so was broken," Travis replied with a portion of the truth, and Menlik sucked in his breath.

"The machines, always the machines!" he cried hoarsely. "A thing which can sit in a man's head and make him do what it will against his will; it is demon sent! There are other machines to be broken, Apache."

"Words will not break them," Travis pointed out.

"Only a fool rides to his death without hope of striking a single blow before he chokes on the blood in his throat," Menlik retorted. "We cannot use bow or tulwar against weapons which flame and kill quicker than any storm lightning! And always the mind machines can make a man drop his knife and stand helplessly waiting for the slave collar to be set on his neck!"

Travis asked a question of his own. "I know that they can bring a caller part way into this mountain, for this very day I saw its effect upon the maiden. But there are many places in the hills well set for ambushes, and those unaffected by the machine could be waiting there. Would there be many machines so that they could send out again and again?"

Menlik's bony hand played with his wand. Then a slow smile curved his lips into the guise of a hunting cat's noiseless snarl.

"There is meat in that pot, Apache, rich meat, good for the filling of a lean belly! So men whose minds the machine could not trouble—such men to be waiting in ambush for the taking of the men who use such a machine—yes. But here would have to be bait, very good bait for such a trap, Lord of Wiles. Never do those others come far into the mountains. Their flyer does not lift well here, and they do not trust traveling on horseback. They were greatly angered to come so far in to reach Kaydessa, though they could not have been too close, or you would not have escaped at all. Yes, strong bait."

"Such bait as perhaps the knowledge that there were strangers across the mountains?"

Menlik turned his wand about in his hands. He was no longer smiling, and his glance at Travis was sharp and swift.

"Do you sit as Khan in your tribe, Lord?"

"I sit as one they will listen to." Travis hoped that was so. Whether Buck and the moderates would hold clan leadership upon his return was a fact he could not count upon as certain.

"This is a thing which we must hold council over," Menlik continued. "But it is an idea of power. Yes, one to think about, Lord. And I shall think...."

He got up and moved away. Travis blinked at the fire. He was very tired, and he disliked sleeping in this camp. But he must not go without the rest his body needed to supply him with a clear head in the morning. And not showing uneasiness might be one way of winning Menlik's confidence.

Travis settled his back against the spire of rock and raised his right hand into the path of the sun, cradling in his palm a disk of glistening metal. Flash ... flash ... he made the signal pattern just as his ancestors a hundred years earlier and far across space had used trade mirrors to relay war alerts among the Chiricahua and White Mountain ranges. If Tsoay had returned safely, and if Buck had kept the agreed lookout on that peak a mile or so ahead, then the clan would know that he was coming and with what escort.

He waited now, rubbing the small metal mirror absently on the loose sleeve of his shirt, waiting for a reply. Mirrors were best, not smoke fires which would broadcast too far the presence of men in the hills. Tsoay must have returned....

"What is it that you do?"

Menlik, his shaman's robe pulled up so that his breeches and boots were dark against the golden rock, climbed up beside the Apache. Menlik, Hulagur, and Kaydessa were riding with Travis, offering him one of their small ponies to hurry the trip. He was still regarded warily by the Tatars, but he did not blame them for their cautious attitude.

"Ah—" A flicker of light from the point ahead. One ... two ... three flashes, a pause, then two more together. He had been read. Buck had dispatched scouts to meet them, and knowing his people's skill at the business, Travis was certain the Tatars would never suspect their flanking unless the Apaches purposefully revealed themselves. Also the Tatars were not to go to the rancheria, but would be met at a mid-point by a delegation of Apaches. This was no time for the Tatars to learn just how few the clan numbered.

Menlik watched Travis flash an acknowledgment to the sentry ahead. "In this way you speak to your men?"

"This way I speak."

"A thing good and to be remembered. We have the drum, but that is for the ears of all with hearing. This is for the eyes only of those on watch for it. Yes, a good thing. And your people—they will meet with us?"

"They wait ahead," Travis confirmed.

It was close to midday and the heat, gathered in the rocky ways, was like a heaviness in the air itself. The Tatars had shucked their heavy jackets and rolled the fur brims of their hats far up their heads away from their

sweat-beaded faces. And at every halt they passed from hand to hand the
skin bag of kumiss.

Now even the ponies shuffled on with drooping heads, picking a way in
a cut which deepened into a canyon. Travis kept a watch for the scouts.
And not for the first time he thought of the disappearance of the coyotes.
Somehow, back in the Tatar camp, he had counted confidently on the
animals' rejoining him once he had started his return over the mountains.

But he had seen nothing of either beast, nor had he felt that
unexplainable mental contact with them which had been present since his
first awakening on Topaz. Why they had left him so unceremoniously after
defending him from the Mongol attack, and why they were keeping
themselves aloof now, he did not know. But he was conscious of a thread
of alarm for their continued absence, and he hoped he would find they had
gone back to the rancheria.

The ponies thudded dispiritedly along a sandy wash which bottomed the
canyon. Here the heat became a leaden weight and the men were panting
like four-footed beasts running before hunters. Finally Travis sighted what
he had been seeking, a flicker of movement on the wall well above. He
flung up his hand, pulling his mount to a stand. Apaches stood in full
view, bows ready, arrows on cords. But they made no sound.

Kaydessa cried out, booted her mount to draw equal with Travis.

"A trap!" Her face, flushed with heat, was also stark with anger.

Travis smiled slowly. "Is there a rope about you, Wolf Daughter?" he
inquired softly. "Are you now dragged across this sand?"

Her mouth opened and then closed again. The quirt she had half raised
to slash at him, flopped across her pony's neck.

The Apache glanced back at the two men. Hulagur's hand was on his
sword hilt, his eyes darting from one of those silent watchers to the next.
But the utter hopelessness of the Tatar position was too plain. Only Menlik
made no move toward any weapon, even his spirit wand. Instead, he sat
quietly in the saddle, displaying no emotion toward the Apaches save his
usual self-confident detachment.

"We go on." Travis pointed ahead.

Just as suddenly as they had appeared from the heart of the golden cliffs,
so did the scouts vanish. Most of them were already on their way to the
point Buck had selected for the meeting place. There had been only six

men up there, but the Tatars had no way of knowing just how large a portion of the whole clan that number was.

Travis' pony lifted his head, nickered, and achieved a stumbling trot. Somewhere ahead was water, one of those oases of growth and life which pocked the whole mountain range—to the preservation of all animals and all men.

Menlik and Hulagur pushed on until their mounts were hard on the heels of the two ridden by the girl and Travis. Travis wondered if they still waited for some arrow to strike home, though he saw that both men rode with outward disregard for the patrolling scouts.

A grass-leaf bush beckoned them on and again the ponies quickened pace, coming out into a tributary canyon which housed a small pool and a good stand of grass and brush. To one side of the water Buck stood, his arms folded across his chest, armed only with his belt knife. Grouped behind him were Deklay, Tsoay, Nolan, Manulito—Travis tabulated hurriedly. Manulito and Deklay were to be classed together—or had been when he was last in the rancheria. On Buck's stairway from the past, both had halted more than halfway down. Nolan was a quiet man who seldom spoke, and whose opinion Travis could not foretell. Tsoay would back Buck.

Probably such a divided party was the best Travis could have hoped to gather. A delegation composed entirely of those who were ready to leave the past of the Redax—a collection of Bucks and Jil-Lees—was outside the bounds of possibility. But Travis was none too happy to have Deklay in on this.

Travis dismounted, letting the pony push forward by himself to dip nose into the pool.

"This is," Travis pointed politely with his chin—"Menlik, one who talks with spirits.... Hulagur, who is son to a chief ... and Kaydessa, who is daughter to a chief. They are of the horse people of the north." He made the introduction carefully in English.

Then he turned to the Tatars. "Buck, Deklay, Nolan, Manulito, Tsoay," he named them all, "these stand to listen, and to speak for the Apaches."

But sometime later when the two parties sat facing each other, he wondered whether a common decision could come from the clansmen on his side of that irregular circle. Deklay's expression was closed; he had even edged a short way back, as if he had no desire to approach the strangers.

And Travis read into every line of Deklay's body his distrust and antagonism.

He himself began to speak, retelling his adventures since they had followed Kaydessa's trail, sketching in the situation at the Tatar-Mongol settlement as he had learned it from her and from Menlik. He was careful to speak in English so that the Tatars could hear all he was reporting to his own kind. And the Apaches listened blank-faced, though Tsoay must already have reported much of this. When Travis was done it was Deklay who asked a question:

"What have we to do with these people?"

"There is this—" Travis chose his words carefully, thinking of what might move a warrior still conditioned to riding with the raiders of a hundred years earlier, "the Pinda-lick-o-yi (whom we call 'Reds,') are never willing to live side by side with any who are not of their mind. And they have weapons such as make our bow cords bits of rotten string, our knives slivers of rust. They do not kill; they enslave. And when they discover that we live, then they will come against us—"

Deklay's lips moved in a wolf grin. "This is a large land, and we know how to use it. The Pinda-lick-o-yi will not find us—"

"With their eyes maybe not," Travis replied. "With their machines—that is another matter."

"Machines!" Deklay spat. "Always these machines.... Is that all you can talk about? It would seem that you are bewitched by these machines, which we have not seen—none of us!"

"It was a machine which brought you here," Buck observed. "Go you back and look upon the spaceship and remember, Deklay. The knowledge of the Pinda-lick-o-yi is greater than ours when it deals with metal and wire and things which can be made with both. Machines brought us along the road of the stars, and there is no tracker in the clan who could hope to do the same. But now I have this to ask: Does our brother have a plan?"

"Those who are Reds," Travis answered slowly, "they do not number many. But more may later come from our own world. Have you heard of such arriving?" he asked Menlik.

"Not so, but we are not told much. We live apart and no one of us goes to the ship unless he is summoned. For they have weapons to guard them, or long since they would have been dead. It is not proper for a man to eat from the pot, ride in the wind, sleep easy under the same sky with him who has slain his brother."

"They have then killed among your people?"

"They have killed," Menlik returned briefly.

Kaydessa stirred and muttered a word or two to her brother. Hulagur's head came up, and he exploded into violent speech.

"What does he say?" Deklay demanded.

The girl replied: "He speaks of our father who aided in the escape of three and so afterward was slain by the leader as a lesson to us—since he was our 'white beard,' the Khan."

"We have taken the oath in blood—under the Wolf Head Standard—that they will also die," Menlik added. "But first we must shake them out of their ship-shell."

"That is the problem," Travis elaborated for the benefit of his clansmen. "We must get these Reds away from their protected camp—out into the open. When they now go they are covered by this 'caller' which keeps the Tatars under their control, but it has no effect on us."

"So, again I say: What is all this to us?" Deklay got to his feet. "This machine does not hunt us, and we can make our camps in this land where no Pinda-lick-o-yi can find them—"

"We are not *dobe-gusndhe-he*—invulnerable. Nor do we know the full range of machines they can use. It does no one well to say '*doxa-da*'—this is not so—when he does not know all that lies in an enemy's wickiup."

To Travis' relief he saw agreement mirrored on Buck's face, Tsoay's, Nolan's. From the beginning he had had little hope of swaying Deklay; he could only trust that the verdict of the majority would be the accepted one. It went back to the old, old Apache institution of prestige. A *nantan*-chief had the *go'ndi*, the high power, as a gift from birth. Common men could possess horse power or cattle power; they might have the gift of acquiring wealth so they could make generous gifts—be *ikadntl'izi*, the wealthy ones who spoke for their family groups within the loose network of the tribe. But there was no hereditary chieftainship or even an undivided rule within a rancheria. The *nagunlka-dnat'an*, or war chief, often led only on the warpath and had no voice in clan matters save those dealing with a raid.

And to have a split now would fatally weaken their small clan. Deklay and those of a like mind might elect to withdraw and not one of the rest could deny him that right.

"We shall think on this," Buck said. "Here is food, water, pasturage for horses, a camp for our visitors. They will wait here." He looked at Travis. "You will wait with them, Fox, since you know their ways."

Travis' immediate reaction was objection, but then he realized Buck's wisdom. To offer the proposition of alliance to the Apaches needed an impartial spokesman. And if he himself did it, Deklay might automatically oppose the idea. Let Buck talk and it would be a statement of fact.

"It is well," Travis agreed.

Buck looked about, as if judging time from the lie of sun and shadow on the ground. "We shall return in the morning when the shadow lies here." With the toe of his high moccasin he made an impression in the soft earth. Then, without any formal farewell, he strode off, the others fast on his heels.

"He is your chief, that one?" Kaydessa asked, pointing after Buck.

"He is one having a large voice in council," Travis replied. He set about building up the cooking fire, bringing out the body of a split-horn calf which had been left them. Menlik sat on his heels by the pool, dipping up drinking water with his hand. Now he squinted his eyes against the probe of the sun.

"It will require much talking to win over the short one," he observed. "That one does not like us or your plan. Just as there will be those among the Horde who will not like it either." He flipped water drops from his fingers. "But this I do know, man who calls himself Fox, if we do not make a common cause, then we have no hope of going against the Reds. It will be for them as a man crushing fleas." He brought his hand down on his knee in emphatic slaps. "So ... and so ... and so!"

"This do I think also," Travis admitted.

"So let us both hope that all men will be as wise as we," Menlik said, smiling. "And since we can take a hand in that decision, this remains a time for rest."

The shaman might be content to sleep the afternoon away, but after he had eaten, Hulagur wandered up and down the valley, making a lengthy business of rubbing down their horses with twists of last season's grass. Now and then he paused beside Kaydessa and spoke, his uneasiness plain to Travis although he could not understand the words.

Travis had settled down in the shade, half dozing, yet alert to every movement of the three Tatars. He tried not to think of what might be happening in the rancheria by switching his mind to that misty valley of the towers. Did any of those three alien structures contain such a grab bag of the past as he, Ashe, and Murdock had found on that other world where the winged people had gathered together for them the artifacts of an older civilization? At that time he had created for their hosts a new weapon of defense, turning metal tubes into blow-guns. It had been there, too, where he had chanced upon the library of tapes, one of which had eventually landed Travis and his people here on Topaz.

Even if he did find racks of such tapes in one of those towers, there would be no way of using them—with the ship wrecked on the mountain side. Only—Travis' fingers itched where they lay quiet on his knees—there might be other things waiting. If he were only free to explore!

He reached out to touch Menlik's shoulder. The shaman half turned, opening his eyes with the languid effort of a sleepy cat. But the spark of intelligence awoke in them quickly.

"What is it?"

For a moment Travis hesitated, already regretting his impulse. He did not know how much Menlik remembered of the present. Remember of the present—one part of the Apache's mind was wryly amused at that snarled estimate of their situation. Men who had been dropped into their racial and ancestral pasts until the present time was less real than the dreams conditioning them had a difficult job evaluating any situation. But since Menlik had clung to his knowledge of English, he must be less far down that stairway.

"When we met you, Kaydessa and I, it was outside that valley." Travis was still of two minds about this questioning, but the Tatar camp had been close to the towers and there was a good chance the Mongols had explored them. "And inside were buildings ... very old...."

Menlik was fully alert now. He took his wand, played with it as he spoke:

"That is, or was, a place of much power, Fox. Oh, I know that you question my kinship with the spirits and the powers they give. But one learns not to dispute what one feels here—and here—" His long, somewhat grimy fingers went to his forehead and then to the bare brown chest where his shirt fell open. "I have walked the stone path in that valley, and there have been the whispers—"

"Whispers?"

Menlik twirled the wand. "Whispers which are too low for many ears to distinguish. You can hear them as one hears the buzzing of an insect, but never the words—no, never the words! But that is a place of great power!"

"A place to explore!"

But Menlik watched only his wand. "That I wonder, Fox, truly do I wonder. This is not our world. And here there may be that which does not welcome us."

Tricks-in-trade of a shaman? Or was it true recognition of something beyond human description? Travis could not be sure, but he knew that he must return to the valley and see for himself.

"Listen," Menlik said, leaning closer, "I have heard your tale, that you were on that first ship, the one which brought you unwilling along the old star paths. Have you ever seen such a thing as this?"

He smoothed a space of soft earth and with the narrow tip of his wand began to draw. Whatever role Menlik had played in the present before he had been reconditioned into a shaman of the Horde, he had had the ability of an artist, for with a minimum of lines he created a figure in that sketch.

It was a man or at least a figure with general human outlines. But the round, slightly oversized skull was bare, the clothing skintight to reveal unnaturally thin limbs. There were large eyes, small nose and mouth, rather crowded into the lower third of the head, giving an impression of an over-expanded brain case above. And it was familiar.

Not the flying men of the other world, certainly not the nocturnal ape-things. Yet for all its alien quality Travis was sure he had seen its like before. He closed his eyes and tried to visualize it apart from lines in the soil.

Such a head, white, almost like the bone of a skull laid bare, such a head lying face down on a bone-thin arm clad in a blue-purple skintight sleeve. Where had he seen it?

The Apache gave a sharp exclamation as he remembered fully. The derelict spaceship as he had first found it—the dead alien officer had still been seated at its controls! The alien who had set the tape which took them out into that forgotten empire—he was the subject of Menlik's drawing!

"Where? When did you see such a one?" The Apache bent down over the Tatar.

Menlik looked troubled. "He came into my mind when I walked the valley. I thought I could almost see such a face in one of the tower windows, but of that I am not sure. Who is it?"

"Someone from the old days—those who once ruled the stars," Travis answered. But were they still here then, the remnant of a civilization which had flourished ten thousand years ago? Were the Baldies, who centuries ago had hunted down so ruthlessly the Russians who had dared to loot their wrecked ships, still on Topaz?

He remembered the story of Ross Murdock's escape from those aliens in the far past of Europe, and he shivered. Murdock was tough, steel tough, yet his own description of that epic chase and the final meeting had carried with it his terror. What could a handful of primitively armed and almost primitively minded Terrans do now if they had to dispute Topaz with the Baldies?

10

"Beyond this—" Menlik worked his way to the very lip of a drop, raising a finger cautiously—"beyond this we do not go."

"But you say that the camp of your people lies well out in the plains—" Jil-Lee was up on one knee, using the field glasses they had brought from the stores of the wrecked ship. He passed them along to Travis. There was nothing to be sighted but the rippling amber waves of the tall grasses, save for an occasional break of a copse of trees near the foothills.

They had reached this point in the early morning, threading through the pass, making their way across the section known to the outlaws. From here they could survey the debatable land where their temporary allies insisted the Reds were in full control.

The result of the conference in the south had been this uneasy alliance. From the start Travis realized that he could not hope to commit the clan to any set plan, that even to get this scouting party to come against the stubborn resistance of Deklay and his reactionaries was a major achievement. There was now an opening wedge of six Apaches in the north.

"Beyond this," Menlik repeated, "they keep watch and can control us with the caller."

"What do you think?" Travis passed the glasses to Nolan.

If they were ever to develop a war chief, this lean man, tall for an Apache and slow to speak, might fill that role. He adjusted the lenses and began a detailed study-sweep of the open territory. Then he stiffened; his mouth, below the masking of the glasses, was tight.

"What is it?" Jil-Lee asked.

"Riders—two ... four ... five.... Also something else—in the air."

Menlik jerked back and grabbed at Nolan's arm, dragging him down by the weight of his body.

"The flyer! Come back—back!" He was still pulling at Nolan, prodding at Travis with one foot, and the Apaches stared at him with amazement.

The shaman sputtered in his own language, and then, visibly regaining command of himself, spoke English once more.

"Those are hunters, and they carry a caller. Either some others have escaped or they are determined to find our mountain camp."

Jil-Lee looked at Travis. "You did not feel anything when the woman was under that spell?"

Travis shook his head. Jil-Lee nodded and then said to the shaman: "We shall stay here and watch. But since it is bad for you—do you go. And we shall meet you near this place of the towers. Agreed?"

For a moment Menlik's face held a shadowy expression Travis tried to read. Was it resentment—resentment that he was forced to retreat when the others could stand their ground? Did the Tatar believe that he lost face this way? But the shaman gave a grunt of what they took as assent and slipped over the edge of the lookout point. A moment later they heard him speaking the Mongol tongue, warning Hulagur and Lotchu, his companions on the scout. Then came the clatter of pony hoofs as they rode their mounts away.

The Apaches settled back in the cup, which gave them a wide view over the plains. Soon it was not necessary to use the glasses in order to sight the advancing party of hunters—five riders, four wearing Tatar dress. The fifth had such an odd outline that Travis was reminded of Menlik's sketch of the alien. Under the sharper vision of the glasses he saw that the rider was equipped with a pack strapped between his shoulders and a bulbous helmet covering most of his head. Highly specialized equipment for communication, Travis guessed.

"That is a 'copter up above," Nolan said. "Different shape from ours."

They had been familiar with helicopters back on Terra. Ranchers used them for range inspection, and all of the Apache volunteers had flown in them. But Nolan was correct; this one possessed several unfamiliar features.

"The Tatars say they don't bring those very far into the mountains," Jil-Lee mused. "That could explain their man on horseback; he gets in where they don't fly."

Nolan fingered his bow. "If these Reds depend upon their machine to control what they seek, then they may be taken by surprise—"

"But not yet!" Travis spoke sharply. Nolan frowned at him.

Jil-Lee chuckled. "The way is not so dark for us, younger brother, that we need your torch held for our feet!"

Travis swallowed back any retort, accepting the fairness of that rebuke. He had no right to believe that he alone knew the best way of handling the enemy. Biting on the sourness of that realization, he lay quietly with the others, watching the riders enter the foothills perhaps a quarter of a mile to the west.

The helicopter was circling now over the men riding into a cut between two rises. When they were lost to view, the pilot made wider casts, and Travis thought the flyer's crew were probably in communication with the helmeted one of the quintet on the ground.

He stirred. "They are heading for the Tatar camp, just as if they know exactly where it is—"

"That also may be true," Nolan replied. "What do we know of these Tatars? They have freely said that the Reds can hold them in mind ropes when they wish. Already they may be so bound. I say—let us go back to our own country." He added to the decisiveness of that by handing Jil-Lee the glasses and sliding down from their perch.

Travis looked at the other. In a way he could understand the wisdom of Nolan's suggestion. But he was sure that withdrawal now would only postpone trouble. Sooner or later the Apaches would have to stand against the Reds, and if they could do it now while the enemy was occupied with trouble from the Tatars, so much the better.

Jil-Lee was following Nolan. But something in Travis rebelled. He watched the circling helicopter. If it was overhanging the action area of the horsemen, they had either reined in or were searching a relatively small section of the foothills.

Reluctantly Travis descended to the hollow where Jil-Lee stood with Nolan. Tsoay and Lupe and Rope were a little to one side as if the final orders would come from their seniors.

"It would be well," Jil-Lee said slowly, "if we saw what weapons they have. I want a closer look at the equipment of that one in the helmet. Also," he smiled straight at Nolan—"I do not think that they can detect the presence of warriors of the People unless we will it so."

Nolan ran a finger along the curve of his bow, shot a measuring glance right and left at the general contours of the country.

"There is wisdom in what you say, elder brother. Only this is a trail we shall take alone, not allowing the men with fur hats to know where we walk." He looked pointedly in Travis' direction.

"That is wisdom, *Ba'is'a*," Travis promptly replied, giving Nolan the old title accorded the leader of a war party. Travis was grateful for that much of a concession.

They swung into action, heading southeast at an angle which should bring them across the track of the enemy hunting party. The path was theirs at last, only moments after the passing of their quarry. None of the five riders was taking any precautions to cover his trail. Each moved with the confidence of one not having to fear any attack.

From cover the Apaches looked aloft. They could hear the faint hum of the helicopter. It was still circling, Tsoay reported from a higher check point, but those circles remained close over the plains area—the riders had already passed beyond the limits of that aerial sentry.

Three to a side, the Apaches advanced with the trail between them. They were carefully hidden when they caught up with the hunters. The four Tatars were grouped together; the fifth man, heavily burdened by his pack, had climbed from the saddle and was sitting on the ground, his hands busy with a flat plate which covered him from upper chest to belt.

Now that he had a chance to see them closely, Travis noted the lack of expression on the broad Tatar faces. The four men were blank of eye, astride their mounts with no apparent awareness of their present surroundings. Then as one, their heads swung around to the helmeted leader before they dismounted and stood motionless for a long moment in a way which reminded Travis of the coyotes' attitude when they endeavored to pass some message to him. But these men even lacked the signs of thinking intelligence the animals had.

The helmeted man's hand moved across his chest plate, and instantly his followers came into a measure of life. One put his hand to his forehead with an odd, half-dazed gesture. Another half crouched, his lips wrinkling back in a snarl. And the leader, watching him, laughed. Then he snapped an order, his hand poised over his control plate.

One of the four took the horse reins, made the mounts fast to near-by bushes. Then as one they began to walk forward, the Red bringing up the rear several paces behind the nearest Tatar. They were going upslope to the crest of a small ridge.

The Tatar who first reached the crest put his hands to cup his mouth, sent a ringing cry southward, and the faint "hu-hu-hu" echoed on and on through the hills.

Either Menlik had reached the camp in time, or his people were not to be so easily enticed. For though the hunters waited for a long time, there was no answer to that hail. At last the helmeted man called his captives, bringing them sullenly down to mount and ride again—a move which suited the Apaches.

They could not tell how close was the communication between the rider and the helicopter. And they were still too near the plains to attack unless it was necessary for their own protection. Travis dropped back to join Nolan.

"He controls them by that plate on his chest," he said. "If we would take them, we must get at that—"

"These Tatars use lariats in fighting. Did they not rope you as a calf is roped for branding? Then why do they not so take this Red, binding his arms to his sides?" The suspicion in Nolan's voice was plain.

"Perhaps in them is some conditioned control making it so that they cannot attack their rulers—"

"I do not like this matter of machines which can play this way and that with minds and bodies!" flared Nolan. "A man should only *use* a weapon, not be one!"

Travis could agree to that. Had they by the wreck of their own ship and the death of Ruthven, escaped just such an existence as these Tatars now endured? If so, why? He and all the Apaches were volunteers, eager and willing to form new world colonies. What had happened back on Terra that they had been so ruthlessly sent out without warning and under Redax? Another small piece of that puzzle, or maybe the heart of the whole picture snapped into place. Had the project learned in some way of the Tatar settlement on Topaz and so been forced to speed up that translation from late twentieth-century Americans to primitives? That would explain a lot!

Travis returned abruptly to the matter now at hand as he saw a peak ahead. The party they were trailing was heading directly for the outlaw hide-out. Travis hoped Menlik had warned them in time. There—that wall of cliff to his left must shelter the valley of the towers, though it was still miles ahead. Travis did not believe the hunters would be able to reach their goal unless they traveled at night. They might not know of the ape-things which could menace the dark.

But the enemy, whether he knew of such dangers or not, did not intend to press on. As the sun pulled away, leaving crevices and crannies shadow dark, the hunters stopped to make camp. The Apaches, after their custom on the war trail, gathered on the heights above.

"This Red seems to think that he shall find those he seeks sitting waiting for him, as if their feet were nipped tight in a trap," Tsoay remarked.

"It is the habit of the Pinda-lick-o-yi," Lupe added, "to believe they are greater than all others. Yet this one is a stupid fool walking into the arms of a she-bear with a cub." He chuckled.

"A man with a rifle does not fear a man armed only with a stick," Travis cut in quickly. "This one is armed with a weapon which he has good reason to believe makes him invulnerable to attack. If he rests tonight, he probably leaves his machine on guard."

"At least we are sure of one thing," Nolan said in half agreement. "This one does not suspect that there are any in these hills save those he can master. And his machine does not work against us. Thus at dawn—" He made a swift gesture, and they smiled in concert.

At dawn—the old time of attack. An Apache does not attack at night. Travis was not sure that any of them could break that old taboo and creep down upon the camp before the coming of new light.

But tomorrow morning they would take over this confident Red, strip him of his enslaving machine.

Travis' head jerked. It had come as suddenly as a blow between his eyes—to half stun him. What ... what was it? Not any physical impact—no, something which was dazing but still immaterial. He braced his whole body, awaiting its return, trying frantically to understand what had happened in that instant of vertigo and seeming disembodiment. Never had he experienced anything like it—or had he? Two years or more ago when he had gone through the time transfer to enter the Arizona of the Folsom Men some ten thousand years earlier—that moment of transfer had been something like this, a sensation of being awry in space and time with no stable footing to be found.

Yet he was lying here on very tangible rock and soil, and nothing about him in the shadow-hung landscape of Topaz had changed in the slightest. But that blow had left behind it a quivering residue of panic buried far inside him, a tender spot like an open wound.

Travis drew a deep breath which was almost a sob, levered himself up on one elbow to stare intently down into the enemy camp. Was this some attack from the other's unknown weapon? Suddenly he was not at all sure what might happen when the Apaches made that dawn rush.

Jil-Lee was in station on his right. Travis must compare notes with him to be sure that this was not indeed a trap. Better to retreat now than to be taken like fish in a net. He crept out of his place, gave the chittering signal call of the fluff-ball, and heard Jil-Lee's answer in a cleverly mimicked trill of a night insect.

"Did you feel something just now—in your head?" Travis found it difficult to put that sensation into words.

"Not so. But you did?"

He had—of course, he had! The remains of it were still in him, that point of panic. "Yes."

"The machine?"

"I don't know." Travis' confusion grew. It might be that he alone of the party had been struck. If so, he could be a danger to his own kind.

"This is not good. I think we had better hold council, away from here." Jil-Lee's whisper was the merest ghost of sound. He chirped again to be answered from Tsoay upslope, who passed on the signal.

The first moon was high in the sky as the Apaches gathered together. Again Travis asked his question: Had any of the others felt that odd blow? He was met by negatives.

But Nolan had the final word: "This is not good," he echoed Jil-Lee's comment. "If it was the Red machine at work, then we may all be swept into his net along with those he seeks. Perhaps the longer one remains close to that thing, the more influence it gains over him. We shall stay here until dawn. If the enemy would reach the place they seek, then they must pass below us, for that is the easiest road. Burdened with his machine, that Red has ever taken the easiest way. So, we shall see if he also has a defense against these when they come without warning." He touched the arrows in his quiver.

To kill from ambush meant that they might never learn the secret of the machine, but after his experience Travis was willing to admit that Nolan's caution was the wise way. Travis wanted no part of a second attack like that which had shaken him so. And Nolan had not ordered a general retreat. It must be in the war chief's thoughts as it was in Travis' that if the machine could have an influence over Apaches, it must cease to function.

They set their ambush with the age-old skill the Redax had grafted into their memories. Then there was nothing to do but wait.

It was an hour after dawn when Tsoay signaled that the enemy was coming, and shortly after, they heard the thud of ponies' hoofs. The first Tatar plodded into view, and by the stance of his body in the saddle, Travis knew the Red had him under full control. Two, then three Tatars passed between the teeth of the Apache trap. The fourth one had allowed a wider gap to open between himself and his fellows.

Then the Red leader came. His face below the bulge of the helmet was not happy. Travis believed the man was not a horseman by inclination. The Apache set arrow to bow cord, and at the chirp from Nolan, fired in concert with his clansmen.

Only one of those arrows found a target. The Red's pony gave a shrill scream of pain and terror, reared, pawing at the air, toppled back, pinning its shouting rider under it.

The Red had had a defense right enough, one which had somehow deflected the arrows. But he neither had protection against his own awkward seat in the saddle nor the arrow which had seriously wounded the now threshing pony.

Ahead the Tatars twisted and writhed, mouthed tortured cries, then dropped out of their saddles to lie limply on the ground as if the arrows aimed at the master had instead struck each to the heart.

11

Either the Red was lucky, or his reactions were quick. He had somehow rolled clear of the struggling horse as Lupe leaped from behind a boulder, knife out and ready. To the eyes of the Apaches the helmeted man lay easy prey to Lupe's attack. Nor did he raise an arm to defend himself, though one hand lay free across the plate on his chest.

But the young Apache stumbled, rebounding back as if he had run into an unseen wall—when his knife was still six inches away from the other. Lupe cried out, shook under a second impact as the Red fired an automatic with his other hand.

Travis dropped his bow, returned to the most primitive weapon of all. His hand closed around a stone and he hurled the fist-sized oval straight at the helmet so clearly outlined against the rocks below.

But even as Lupe's knife had never touched flesh, so was the rock deflected; the Red was covered by some protective field. This was certainly nothing the Apaches had seen before. Nolan's whistle summoned them to draw back.

The Red fired again, the sharp bark of the hand gun harsh and loud. He did not have any real target, for with the exception of Lupe the Apaches had gone to earth. Between the rocks the Red was struggling to his feet, but he moved slowly, favoring his side and one leg; he had not come totally unharmed from his tumble with the pony.

An armed enemy who could not be touched—one who knew there were more than outlaws in this region. The Red leader was far more of a threat to the Apaches now than he had ever been. He must not be allowed to escape.

He was holstering his gun, moving along with one hand against the rocks to steady himself, trying to reach one of the ponies that stood with trailing reins beside the inert Tatars.

But when the enemy reached the far side of that rock he would have to sacrifice either his steadying hold, or his touch on the chest plate where his other hand rested. Would he, then, for an instant be vulnerable?

The pony!

Travis put an arrow on bow cord and shot. Not at the Red, who had released his hold of the rock, preferring to totter instead of lose control of the chest plate—but into the air straight before the nose of the mount.

The pony neighed wildly, tried to turn, and its shoulder caught the free, groping hand of the Red and spun the man around and back, so that he flung up both hands in an effort to ward himself off the rocks. Then the pony stampeded down the break, its companions catching the same fever, trailing in a mad dash which kept the Red hard against the boulders.

He continued to stand there until the horses, save for the wounded one still kicking fruitlessly, were gone. Travis felt a sense of reprieve. They might not be able to get at the Red, but he was hurt and afoot, two strikes which might yet reduce him to a condition the Apaches could handle.

Apparently the other was also aware of that, for now he pushed out from the rocks and stumbled along after the ponies. But he went only a step or two. Then, settling back once more against a convenient boulder, he began to work at the plate on his chest.

Nolan appeared noiselessly beside Travis. "What does he do?" His lips were very close to the younger man's ear, his voice hardly more than a breath.

Travis shook his head slightly. The Red's actions were a complete mystery. Unless, now disabled and afoot, he was trying to summon aid. Though there was no landing place for a helicopter here.

Now was the time to try and reach Lupe. Travis had seen a slight movement in the fallen Apache's hand, the first indication that the enemy's shot had not been as fatal as it had looked. He touched Nolan's arm, pointed to Lupe; and then, discarding his bow and quiver beside the war leader, he stripped for action. There was cover down to the wounded Apache which would aid him. He must pass one of the Tatars on the way, but none of the tribesmen had shown any signs of life since they had fallen from their saddles at the first attack.

With infinite care, Travis lowered himself into a narrow passage, took a lizard's way between brush and boulder, pausing only when he reached the Tatar for a quick check on the potential enemy.

The lean brown face was half turned, one cheek in the sand, but the slack mouth, the closed eyes were those, Travis believed, of a dead man. By some action of his diabolic machine the Red must have snuffed out his four captives—perhaps in the belief that they were part of the Apache attack.

Travis reached the rock where Lupe lay. He knew that Nolan was watching the Red and would give him warning if he suddenly showed an interest in anything but his machine. The Apache reached out, his hands closing on Lupe's ankles. Beneath his touch, flesh and muscle tensed. Lupe's eyes were open, focused now on Travis. There was a bleeding furrow above his right ear. The Red had tried a difficult head shot, failing in his aim by a mere fraction of an inch.

Lupe made a swift move for which Travis was ready. His grip on the other's body helped to tumble them both around a rock which lay between them and the Red. There was the crack of another shot and dust spurted from the side of the boulder. But they lay together, safe for the present, as Travis was sure the enemy would not risk an open attack on their small fortress.

With Travis' aid Lupe struggled back up to the site where Nolan waited. Jil-Lee was there to make competent examination of the boy's wound.

"Creased," he reported. "A sore head, but no great damage. Perhaps a scar later, warrior!" He gave Lupe an encouraging thump on the shoulder, before plastering an aid pack over the cut.

"Now we go!" Nolan spoke with emphatic decision.

"He saw enough of us to know we are not Tatars."

Nolan's eyes were cold, his mouth grim as he faced Travis.

"And how can we fight him—?"

"There is a wall—a wall you cannot see—about him," Lupe broke in. "When I would strike at him, I could not!"

"A man with invisible protection and a gun," Jil-Lee took up the argument. "How would you deal with him, younger brother?"

"I don't know," Travis admitted. Yet he also believed that if they withdrew, left the Red here to be found by his own people, the enemy would immediately begin an investigation of the southern country. Perhaps, pushed by their need for learning more about the Apaches, they would bring the helicopter in over the mountains. The answer to all Apache dangers, for now, lay in the immediate future of this one man.

"He is hurt, he cannot go far on foot. And even if he calls the 'copter, there is no landing place. He will have to move elsewhere to be picked up." Travis thought aloud, citing the thin handful of points in their favor.

Tsoay nodded toward the rim of the ravine. "Rocks up there and rocks can roll. Start an earthslide...."

Something within Travis balked at that. From the first he had been willing enough to slug it out with the Red, weapon to weapon, man to man. Also, he had wanted to take a captive, not stand over a body. But to use the nature of the country against the enemy, that was the oldest Apache trick of all and one they would have to be forced to employ.

Nolan had already nodded in assent, and Tsoay and Jil-Lee started off. Even if the Red did possess a protective wall device, could it operate in full against a landslide? They all doubted that.

The Apaches reached the cliff rim without exposing themselves to the enemy's fire. The Red still sat there calmly, his back against the rock, his hands busy with his equipment as if he had all the time in the world.

Then suddenly came a scream from more than one throat.

"*Dar-u-gar!*" The ancient war cry of the Mongol Hordes.

Then over the lip of the other slope rose a wave of men—their curved swords out, a glazed set to their eyes—heading for the Amerindians with utter disregard for any personal safety. Menlik in the lead, his shaman's robe flapping wide below his belt like the wings of some oversized predatory bird. Hulagur ... Jagatai ... men from the outlaws' camp. And they were not striving to destroy their disabled overlord in the vale below, but to wipe out the Apaches!

Only the fact that the Apaches were already sheltered behind the rocks they were laboring to dislodge gave them a precious few moments of grace. There was no time to use their bows. They could only use knives to meet the swords of the Tatars, knives and the fact that they could fight with unclouded minds.

"He has them under control!" Travis pawed at Jil-Lee's shoulder. "Get him—they'll stop!"

He did not wait to see if the other Apache understood. Instead, he threw the full force of his own body against the rock they had made the center stone of their slide. It gave, rolled, carrying with it and before it the rest of the piled rubble. Travis stumbled, fell flat, and then a body thudded down upon him, and he was fighting for his life to keep a blade from his throat. Around him were the shouts and cries of embroiled warriors; then all was silenced by a roar from below.

Glazed eyes in a face only a foot from his own, the twisted, panting mouth sending gusts of breath into his nostrils. Suddenly there was reason back in those eyes, a bewilderment, which became fear ... panic.... The Tatar's body twisted in Travis' hold, striving now not to attack, but to win free. As the Apache loosened his grip the other jerked away, so that for a moment or two they lay gasping, side by side.

Men sat up to look at men. There was a spreading stain down Jil-Lee's side and one of the Tatars sprawled near him, both his hands on his chest, coughing violently.

Menlik clawed at the trunk of a wind-twisted mountain tree, pulled himself to his feet, and stood swaying as might a man long ill and recovering from severe exertion.

Insensibly both sides drew apart, leaving a space between Tatar and Apache. The faces of the Amerindians were grim, those of the Mongols bewildered and then harsh as they eyed their late opponents with dawning reason. What had begun in compulsion for the Tatars might well flare now into rational combat—and from that to a campaign of extermination.

Travis was on his feet. He looked over the lip of the drop. The Red was still in his place down there, a pile of rubble about him. His protection must have failed, for his head was back at an unnatural angle and the dent in his helmet could be easily seen.

"That one is dead—or helpless!" Travis cried out. "Do you still wish to fight for him, Shaman?"

Menlik came away from the tree and walked to the edge of the drop. The others, too, were moving forward. After the shaman looked down he stooped, picked up a small stone, and flung it at the motionless Red. There was a crack of sound. They all saw the tiny spurt of flame, a curl of smoke from the plate on the Red's chest. Not only the man, but his control was finished now.

A wolfish growl and two of the Tatars swung over, started down to the Red. Menlik shouted and they slackened pace.

"We want that," he cried in English. "Perhaps so we can learn—"

"The learning is yours," Jil-Lee replied. "Just as this land is yours, Shaman. But I warn you, from this day do not ride south!"

Menlik turned, the charms on his belt clicking. "So that is the way it is to be, Apache?"

"That is the way it shall be, Tatar! We do not ride to war with allies who may turn their knives against our backs because they are slaves to a machine the enemy controls."

The Tatar's long, slender-fingered hands opened and closed. "You are a wise man, Apache, but sometimes more than wisdom alone is needed—"

"We are wise men, Shaman, let it rest there," Jil-Lee replied somberly.

Already the Apaches were on their way, putting two cliff ridges behind them before they halted to examine and cover their wounds.

"We go." Nolan's chin lifted, indicating the southern route. "Here we do not come again; there is too much witchcraft in this place."

Travis stirred, saw that Jil-Lee was frowning at him.

"Go—?" he repeated.

"Yes, younger brother? You would continue to run with these who are governed by a machine?"

"No. Only, eyes are needed on this side of the mountains."

"Why?" This time Jil-Lee was plainly on the side of the conservatives. "We have now seen this machine at work. It is fortunate that the Red is dead. He will carry no tales of us back to his people as you feared. Thus, if we remain south from now on, we are safe. And this fight between Tatar and Red is none of ours. What do you seek here?"

"I must go again to the place of the towers," Travis answered with the truth. But his friends were facing him with heavy disapproval—now a full row of Deklays.

"Did you not tell us that you felt this strange thing during the night we waited about the camp? What if you become one with these Tatars and are also controlled by the machine? Then you, too, can be made into a weapon against us—your clansmen!" Jil-Lee was almost openly hostile.

Sense was on his side. But in Travis was this other desire of which he was becoming more conscious by the minute. There was a reason for those towers, perhaps a reason important enough for him to discover and run the risk of angering his own people.

"There may be this—" Nolan's voice was remote and cold, "you may already be a piece of this thing, bound to the machines. If so, we do not want you among us."

There it was—an open hostility with more power behind it than Deklay's motiveless disapproval had carried. Travis was troubled. The family, the clan—they were important. If he took the wrong step now and was outlawed from that tight fortress, then as an Apache he would indeed be a lost man. In the past of his people there had been renegades from the tribe—men such as the infamous Apache Kid who had killed and killed again, not only white men but his own people. Wolf men living wolves' lives in the hills. Travis was threatened with that. Yet—up the ladder of civilization, down the ladder—why did this feverish curiosity ride him so cruelly now?

"Listen," Jil-Lee, his side padded with bandages, stepped closer—"and tell me, younger brother, what is it that you seek in these towers?"

"On another world there were secrets of the old ones to be found in such ancient buildings. Here that might also be true."

"And among the secrets of those old ones," Nolan's voice was still harsh—"were those which brought us to this world, is that not so?"

"Did any man drive you, Nolan, or you, Tsoay, or you, Jil-Lee, or any of us, to promise to go beyond the stars? You were told what might be done, and you were eager to try it. You were all volunteers!"

"Save for this voyage when we were told nothing," Jil-Lee answered, cutting straight to the heart of the matter. "Yet, Nolan, I do not believe that it is for more voyage tapes that our younger brother now searches, nor would those do us any good—as our ship will not rise again from here. What is it that you do seek?"

"Knowledge—weapons, maybe. Can we stand against these machines of the Reds? Yet many of the devices they now use are taken from the star ships they have looted through time. To every weapon there is a defense."

Nolan blinked and for the first time a hint of interest touched the mask of his face. "To the bow, the rifle," he said softly, "to the rifle, the machine gun, to the cannon, the big bomb. The defense can be far worse than the first weapon. So you think that in these towers there may be things which shall be to the Reds' machines as the bomb is to the cannon of the Horse Soldiers?"

Travis had an inspiration. "Did not our people lay aside the bow for the rifle when we went up against the Bluecoats?"

"We do not so go up against these Reds!" protested Lupe.

"Not now. But what if they come across the mountains, perhaps driving the Tatars before them to do their fighting—?"

"And you believe that if you find weapons in these towers, you will know how to use them?" Jil-Lee asked. "What will give you that knowledge, younger brother?"

"I do not claim such knowledge," Travis countered. "But this much I do have: Once I studied to be an archaeologist and I have seen other storehouses of these star people. Who else among us can say as much as that?"

"That is the truth," Jil-Lee acknowledged. "Also there is good sense in this seeking out of the tower things. Let the Reds find such first—if they exist at all—and then we may truly be caught in a box canyon with only death at our heels."

"And you would go to these towers now?" Nolan demanded.

"I can cut across country and then rejoin you on the other side of the pass!" The feeling of urgency which had been mounting in Travis was now so demanding that he wanted to race ahead through the wilderness. He was surprised when Jil-Lee put out his palm up as if to warn the younger man.

"Take care, younger brother! This is not a lucky business. And remember, if one goes too far down a wrong trail, there is sometimes no returning—"

"We shall wait on the other side of the pass for one day," Nolan added. "Then—" he shrugged—"where you go will be your own affair."

Travis did not understand that promise of trouble. He was already two steps down his chosen path.

12

Travis had taken a direct cross route through the heights, but not swiftly enough to reach his objective before nightfall. And he had no wish to enter the tower valley by moonlight. In him two emotions now warred. There was the urge to invade the towers, to discover their secret, and flaring higher and higher the beginnings of a new fear. Was he now a battlefield for the superstitions of his race reborn by the Redax and his modern education in the Pinda-lick-o-yi world—half Apache brave of the past, half modern archaeologist with a thirst for knowledge? Or was the fear rooted more deeply and for another reason?

Travis crouched in a hollow, trying to understand what he felt. Why was it suddenly so overwhelmingly important for him to investigate the towers? If he only had the coyotes with him.... Why and where had they gone?

He was alive to every noise out of the night, every scent the wind carried to him. The night had its own life, just as the daylight hours held theirs. Only a few of those sounds could he identify, even less did he see. There was one wide-winged, huge flying thing which passed across the green-gold plate of the nearer moon. It was so large that for an instant Travis believed the helicopter had come. Then the wings flapped, breaking the glide, and the creature merged in the shadows of the night—a hunter large enough to be a serious threat, and one he had never seen before.

Relying on his own small defense, the strewing of brittle sticks along the only approach to the hollow, Travis dozed at intervals, his head down on his forearm across his bent knees. But the cold cramped him and he was glad to see the graying sky of pre-dawn. He swallowed two ration tablets and a couple of mouthfuls of water from his canteen and started on.

By sunup he had reached the ledge of the waterfall, and he hurried along the ancient road at a pace which increased to a run the closer he drew to the valley. Deliberately he slowed, his native caution now in control, so that he was walking as he passed through the gateway into the swirling mists which alternately exposed and veiled the towers.

There was no change in the scene from the time he had come there with Kaydessa. But now, rising from a comfortable sprawl on the yellow-and-green pavement, was a welcoming committee—Nalik'ideyu and Naginlta showing no more excitement at his coming than if they had parted only moments before.

Travis went down on one knee, holding out his hand to the female, who had always been the more friendly. She advanced a step or two, touched a cold nose to his knuckles, and whined.

"Why?" He voiced that one word, but behind it was a long list of questions. Why had they left him? Why were they here where there was no hunting? Why did they meet him now as if they had calmly expected his return?

Travis glanced from the animals to the towers, those windows set in diamond pattern. And again he was visited by the impression that he was under observation. With the mist floating across those openings, it would be easy for a lurker to watch him unseen.

He walked slowly on into the valley, his moccasins making no sound on the pavement, but he could hear the faint click of the coyotes' claws as they paced beside him, on each hand. The sun did not penetrate here, making merely a gilt fog of the mist. As he approached within touching distance of the first tower, it seemed to Travis that the mist was curling about him; he could no longer see the archway through which he had entered the valley.

"Naye'nezyani—Slayer of Monsters—give strength to the bow arm, to the knife wrist!" Out of what long-buried memory did that ancient plea come? Travis was hardly aware of the sense of the words until he spoke them aloud. "You who wait—*shi inday to-dah ishan*—an Apache is not food for you! I am Fox of the Itcatcudnde'yu—the Eagle People; and beside me walk *ga'ns* of power...."

Travis blinked and shook his head as one waking. Why had he spoken so, using words and phrases which were not part of any modern speech?

He moved on, around the base of the first tower, to find no door, no break in its surface below the second-story windows—to the next structure and the next, until he had encircled all three. If he were to enter any, he must find a way of reaching the lowest windows.

On he went to the other opening of the valley, the one which gave upon the territory of the Tatar camp. But he did not sight any of the Mongols as he hacked down a sapling, trimmed, and smoothed it into a blunt-pointed lance. His sash-belt, torn into even strips and knotted together, gave him a rope which he judged would be barely long enough for his purpose.

Then Travis made a chancy cast for the lower window of the nearest tower. On the second try the lance slipped in, and he gave a quick jerk, jamming the lance as a bar across the opening. It was a frail ladder but the best he could improvise. He climbed until the sill of the window was within reach and he could pull himself up and over.

The sill was a wide one, at least a twenty-four-inch span between the inner and outer surface of the tower. Travis sat there for a minute, reluctant to enter. Near the end of his dangling scarf-rope the two coyotes lay on the pavement, their heads up, their tongues lolling from their mouths, their expressions ones of detached interest.

Perhaps it was the width of the outer wall that subdued the amount of light in the room. The chamber was circular, and directly opposite him was a second window, the lowest of the matching diamond pattern. He took the four-foot drop from the sill to the floor but lingered in the light as he surveyed every inch of the room. There were no furnishings at all, but in the very center sank a well of darkness. A smooth pillar, glowing faintly, rose from its core. Travis' adjusting eyes noted how the light came in small ripples—green and purple, over a foundation shade of dark blue.

The pillar seemed rooted below and it extended up through a similar opening in the ceiling, providing the only possible exit up or down, save for climbing from window to window outside. Travis moved slowly to the well. Underfoot was a smooth surface overlaid with a velvet carpet of dust which arose in languid puffs as he walked. Here and there he sighted prints in the dust, strange triangular wedges which he thought might possibly have been made by the claws of birds. But there were no other footprints. This tower had been undisturbed for a long, long time.

He came to the well and looked down. There was dark there, dark in which the pulsations of light from the pillar shown the stronger. But that glow did not extend beyond the edge of the well through which the thick rod threaded. Even by close examination he could detect no break in the smooth surface of the pillar, nothing remotely resembling hand- or footholds. If it did serve the purpose of a staircase, there were no treads.

At last Travis put out his hand to touch the surface of the pillar. And then he jerked back—to no effect. There was no breaking contact between his fingers and an unknown material which had the sleekness of polished metal but—and the thought made him slightly queasy—the warmth and very slight give of flesh!

He summoned all his strength to pull free and could not. Not only did that hold grip him, but his other hand and arm were being drawn to join the first! Inside Travis primitive fears awoke full force, and he threw back his head, voicing a cry of panic as wild as that of a hunting beast.

An instant later, his left palm was as tight a prisoner as his right. And with both hands so held, his whole body was suddenly snapped forward, off the safe foundation of the floor, tight to the pillar.

In this position he was sucked down into the well. And while unable to free himself from the pillar, he did slip along its length easily enough. Travis shut his eyes in an involuntary protest against this weird form of capture, and a shiver ran through his body as he continued to descend.

After the first shock had subsided the Apache realized that he was not truly falling at all. Had the pillar been horizontal instead of vertical, he would have gauged its speed that of a walk. He passed through two more room enclosures; he must already be below the level of the valley floor outside. And he was still a prisoner of the pillar, now in total darkness.

His feet came down against a level surface, and he guessed he must have reached the end. Again he pulled back, arching his shoulders in a final desperate attempt at escape, and stumbled away as he was released.

He came up sideways against a wall and stood there panting. The light, which might have come from the pillar but which seemed more a part of the very air, was bright enough to reveal that he was in a corridor running into greater dark both right and left.

Travis took two strides back to the pillar, fitted his palms once again to its surface, with no result. This time his flesh did not adhere and there was no possible way for him to climb that slick pole. He could only hope that at some point the corridor would give him access to the surface. But which way to go—?

At last he chose the right-hand path and started along it, pausing every few steps to listen. But there was no sound except the soft pad of his own feet. The air was fresh enough, and he thought he could detect a faint current coming toward him from some point ahead—perhaps an exit.

Instead, he came into a room and a small gasp of astonishment was wrung out of him. The walls were blank, covered with the same ripples of blue-purple-green light which colored the pillar. Just before him was a table and behind it a bench, both carved from the native yellow-red mountain rock. And there was no exit except the doorway in which he now stood.

Travis walked to the bench. Immovable, it was placed so that whoever sat there must face the opposite wall of the chamber with the table before him. And on the table was an object Travis recognized immediately from his voyage in the alien star ship, one of the reader-viewers through which the involuntary explorers had learned what little they knew of the older galactic civilization.

A reader—and beside it a box of tapes. Travis touched the edge of that box gingerly, half expecting it to crumble into nothingness. This was a place long deserted. Stone table, bench, the towers could survive through centuries of abandonment, but these other objects....

The substance of the reader was firm under the film of dust; there was less dust here than had been in the upper tower chamber. Hardly knowing why, Travis threw one leg over the bench and sat down behind the table, the reader before him, the box of tapes just beyond his hand.

He surveyed the walls and then looked away hurriedly. The rippling colors caught at his eyes. He had a feeling that if he watched that ebb and flow too long, he would be captured in some subtle web of enchantment just as the Reds' machine had caught and held the Tatars. He turned his attention to the reader. It was, he believed, much like the one they had used on the ship.

This room, table, bench, had all been designed with a set purpose. And that purpose—Travis' fingers rested on the box of tapes he could not yet bring himself to open—that purpose was to use the reader, he would swear to that. Tapes so left must have had a great importance for those who left them. It was as if the whole valley was a trap to channel a stranger into this underground chamber.

Travis snapped open the box, fed the first disk into the reader, and applied his eyes to the vision tube at its apex.

The rippling walls looked just the same when he looked up once more, but the cramp in his muscles told Travis that time had passed—perhaps hours instead of minutes—since he had taken out the first disk. He cupped his hands over his eyes and tried to think clearly. There had been sheets of meaningless symbol writing, but also there had been many clear, three-dimensional pictures, accompanied by a singsong commentary in an alien tongue, seemingly voiced out of thin air. He had been stuffed with ragged bits and patches of information, to be connected only by guesses, and some wild guesses, too. But this much he did know—these towers had been built by the bald spacemen, and they were highly important to that vanished stellar civilization. The information in this room, as disjointed as it had been for him, led to a treasure trove on Topaz greater than he had dreamed.

Travis swayed on the bench. To know so much and yet so little! If Ashe were only here, or some other of the project technicians! A treasure such as Pandora's box had been, peril for one who opened it and did not understand. The Apache studied the three walls of blue-purple-green in turn and with new attention. There were ways through those walls; he was fairly sure he could unlock at least one of them. But not now—certainly not now!

And there was another thing he knew: The Reds must *not* find this. Such a discovery on their part would not only mean the end of his own people on Topaz, but the end of Terra as well. This could be a new and alien Black Death spread to destroy whole nations at a time!

If he could—much as his archaeologist's training would argue against it—he would blot out this whole valley above and below ground. But while the Reds might possess a means of such destruction, the Apaches did not. No, he and his people must prevent its discovery by the enemy by doing what he had seen as necessary from the first—wiping out the Red leaders! And that must be done before they chanced upon the towers!

Travis arose stiffly. His eyes ached, his head felt stuffed with pictures, hints, speculations. He wanted to get out, back into the open air where perhaps the clean winds of the heights would blow some of this frightening half knowledge from his benumbed mind. He lurched down the corridor, puzzled now by the problem of getting back to the window level.

Here, before him, was the pillar. Without hope, but still obeying some buried instinct, Travis again set his hands to its surface. There was a tug at his cramped arms; once more his body was sucked to the pillar. This time he was rising!

He held his breath past the first level and then relaxed. The principle of this weird form of transportation was entirely beyond his understanding, but as long as it worked in reverse he didn't care to find out. He reached the windowed chamber, but the sunlight had left it; instead, the clean cut of moon sweep lay on the dusty floor. He must have been hours in that underground place.

Travis pulled away from the embrace of the pillar. The bar of his wooden lance was still across the window and he ran for it. To catch the scouting party at the pass he must hurry. The report they would make to the clan now had to be changed radically in the face of his new discoveries. The Apaches dared not retreat southward and withdraw from the fight, leaving the Reds to use what treasure lay here.

As he hit the pavement below he looked about for the coyotes. Then he tried the mind call. But as mysteriously as they had met him in the valley, so now were they gone again. And Travis had no time to hunt for them. With a sigh, he began his race to the pass.

In the old days, Travis remembered, Apache warriors had been able to cover forty-five or fifty miles a day on foot and over rough territory. But perhaps his modern breeding had slowed him. He had been so sure he could catch up before the others were through the pass. But he stood now in the hollow where they had camped, read the sign of overturned stone and bent twig left for him, and knew they would reach the rancheria and report the decision Deklay and the others wanted before he could head them off.

Travis slogged on. He was so tired now that only the drug from the sustenance tablets he mouthed at intervals kept him going at a dogged pace, hardly more than a swift walk. And always his mind was haunted by fragments of pictures, pictures he had seen in the reader. The big bomb had been the nightmare of his own world for so long, and what was that against the forces the bald star rovers had been able to command?

He fell beside a stream and slept. There was sunshine about him as he arose to stagger on. What day was this? How long had he sat in the tower chamber? He was not sure of time any more. He only knew that he must reach the rancheria, tell his story, somehow win over Deklay and the other reactionaries to prove the necessity for invading the north in force.

A rocky point which was a familiar landmark came into focus. He padded on, his chest heaving, his breath whistling through parched, sun-cracked lips. He did not know that his face was now a mask of driven resolution.

"Hahhhhhh—"

The cry reached his dulled ears. Travis lifted his head, saw the men before him and tried to think what that show of weapons turned toward him could mean.

A stone thudded to earth only inches before his feet, to be followed by another. He wavered to a stop.

"Ni'ilgac—!"

Witch? Where was a witch? Travis shook his head. There was no witch.

"Do ne'ilka da'!"

The old death threat, but why—for whom?

Another stone, this one hitting him in the ribs with force enough to send him reeling back and down. He tried to get up again, saw Deklay grin widely and take aim—and at last Travis realized what was happening.

Then there was a bursting pain in his head and he was falling—falling into a well of black, this time with no pillar of blue to guide him.

13

The rasp of something wet and rough, persistent against his cheek; Travis tried to turn his head to avoid the contact and was answered by a burst of pain which trailed off into a giddiness, making him fear another move, no matter how minor. He opened his eyes and saw the pointed ears, the outline of a coyote head between him and a dull gray sky, was able to recognize Nalik'ideyu.

A wetness other than that from the coyote's tongue slid down his forehead now. The dull clouds overhead had released the first heavy rain Travis had experienced since their landing on Topaz. He shivered as the chill damp of his clothes made him aware that he must have been lying out in the full force of the downpour for some time.

It was a struggle to get to his knees, but Nalik'ideyu mouthed a hold on his shirt, tugging and pulling so that somehow he crept into a hollow beneath the branches of a tree where the spouting water was lessened to a few pattering drops.

There the Apache's strength deserted him again and he could only hunch over, his bent knees against his chest, trying to endure the throbbing misery in his head, the awful floating sensation which followed any movement. Fighting against that, he tried to remember just what had happened.

The meeting with Deklay and at least four or five others ... then the Apache accusation of witchcraft, a serious thing in the old days. Old days! To Deklay and his fellows, these *were* the old days! And the threat that Deklay or some other had shouted at him—"*Do ne'ilka da'*"—meant literally: "It won't dawn for you—death!"

Stones, the last thing Travis remembered were the stones. Slowly his hands went out to explore his body. There was more than one bruised area on his shoulders and ribs, even on his thighs. He must still have been a target after he had fallen under the stone which had knocked him unconscious. Stoned ... outlawed! But why? Surely Deklay's hostility could not have swept Buck, Jil-Lee, Tsoay, even Nolan, into agreeing to that? Now he could not think straight.

Travis became aware of warmth, not only of warmth and the soft touch of a furred body by his side, but a comforting communication of mind, a feeling he had no words to describe adequately. Nalik'ideyu was sitting crowded against him, her nose thrust up to rest on his shoulder. She breathed in soft puffs which stirred the loose locks of his rain-damp hair. And now he flung one arm about her, a gesture which brought a whisper of answering whine.

He was past wondering about the actions of the coyotes, only supremely thankful for Nalik'ideyu's present companionship. And a moment later when her mate squeezed under the low loop of a branch and joined them in this natural wickiup, Travis held out his other hand, drew it lovingly across Naginlta's wet hide.

"Now what?" he asked aloud. Deklay could only have taken such a drastic action with the majority of the clan solidly behind him. It could well be that this reactionary was the new chief, this act of Travis' expulsion merely adding to Deklay's growing prestige.

The shivering which had begun when Travis recovered consciousness, still shook him at intervals. Back on Terra, like all the others in the team, he had had every inoculation known to the space physicians, including several experimental ones. But the cold virus could still practically immobilize a man, and this was no time to give body room to chills and fever.

Catching his breath as his movements touched to life the pain in one bruise after another, Travis peeled off his soaked clothing, rubbed his body dry with handfuls of last year's leaves culled from the thick carpet under him, knowing there was nothing he could do until the whirling in his head disappeared. So he burrowed into the leaves until only his head was uncovered, and tried to sleep, the coyotes curling up one on either side of his nest.

He dreamed but later could not remember any incident from those dreams, save a certain frustration and fear. When he awoke, again to the sound of steady rain, it was dark. He reached out—both coyotes were gone. His head was clearer and suddenly he knew what must be done. As soon as his body was strong enough, he, too, would return to instincts and customs of the past. This situation was desperate enough for him to challenge Deklay.

In the dark Travis frowned. He was slightly taller, and three or four years younger than his enemy. But Deklay had the advantage in a stouter build and longer reach. However, Travis was sure that in his present life Deklay had never fought a duel—Apache fashion. And an Apache duel was not a meeting anyone entered into lightly. Travis had the right to enter the rancheria and deliver such a challenge. Then Deklay must meet him or admit himself in the wrong. That part of it was simple.

But in the past such duels had just one end, a fatal one for at least one of the fighters. If Travis took this trail, he must be prepared to go the limit. And he didn't want to kill Deklay! There were too few of them here on Topaz to make any loss less than a real catastrophe. While he had no liking for Deklay, neither did he nurse any hatred. However, he must challenge the other or remain a tribal outcast; and Travis had no right to gamble with time and the future, not after what he had learned in the tower. It might be his life and skill, or Deklay's, against the blotting out of them all—and their home world into the bargain.

First, he must locate the present camp of the clan. If Nolan's arguments had counted, they would be heading south away from the pass. And to follow would draw him farther from the tower valley. Travis' battered face ached as he grinned bitterly. This was another time when a man could wish he were two people, a scout on sentry duty at the valley, the fighter heading in the opposite direction to have it out with Deklay. But since he was merely one man he would have to gamble on time, one of the trickiest risks of all.

Before dawn Nalik'ideyu returned, carrying with her a bird—or at least birds must have been somewhere in the creature's ancestry, but the present representative of its kind had only vestigial remnants of wings, its trailing feet and legs well developed and far more powerful.

Travis skinned the corpse, automatically putting aside some spine quills to feather future arrows. Then he ate slivers of dusky meat raw, throwing the bones to Nalik'ideyu.

Though he was still stiff and sore, Travis was determined to be on his way. He tried mind contact with the coyote, picturing the Apaches, notably Deklay, as sharply as he could by mental image. And her assent was clear in return. She and her mate were willing to lead him to the tribe. He gave a light sigh of relief.

As he slogged on through the depressing drizzle, the Apache wondered again why the coyotes had left him before and waited in the tower valley. What link was there between the animals of Terra and the remains of the long-ago empire of the stars? For he was certain it was not by chance that Nalik'ideyu and Naginlta had lingered in that misty place. He longed to communicate with them directly, to ask questions and be answered.

Without their aid, Travis would never have been able to track the clan. The drizzle alternated with slashing bursts of rain, torrential enough to drive the trackers to the nearest cover. Overhead the sky was either dull bronze or night black. Even the coyotes paced nose to ground, often making wide casts for the trail while Travis waited.

The rain lasted for three days and nights, filling watercourses with rapidly rising streams. Travis could only hope that the others were having the same difficulty traveling that he was, perhaps the more so since they were burdened with packs. The fact that they kept on meant that they were determined to get as far from the northern mountains as they could.

On the fourth morning the bronze of the clouds slowly thinned into the usual gold, and the sun struck across hills where mist curled like steam from a hundred bubbling pots. Travis relaxed in the welcome warmth, feeling his shirt dry on his shoulders. It was still a waterlogged terrain ahead which should continue to slow the clan. He had high expectations of catching up with them soon, and now the worst of his bruises had faded. His muscles were limber, and he had worked out his plan as best he could.

Two hours later he sat in ambush, waiting for the scout who was walking into his hands. Under the direction of the coyotes, Travis had circled the line of march, come in ahead of the clan. Now he needed an emissary to state his challenge, and the fact that the scout he was about to jump was Manulito, one of Deklay's supporters, suited Travis' purpose perfectly. He gathered his feet under him as the other came opposite, and sprang.

The rush carried Manulito off his feet and face down on the sod while Travis made the best of his advantage and pinned the wildly fighting man under him. Had it been one of the older braves he might not have been so successful, but Manulito was still a boy by Apache standards.

"Lie still!" Travis ordered. "Listen well—so you can say to Deklay the words of the Fox!"

The frenzied struggles ceased. Manulito managed to wrench his head to the left so he could see his captor. Travis loosened his grip, got to his feet. Manulito sat up, his face darkly sullen, but he did not reach for his knife.

"You will say this to Deklay: The Fox says he is a man of little sense and less courage, preferring to throw stones rather than meet knife to knife as does a warrior. If he thinks as a warrior, let him prove it—his strength against my strength—after the ways of the People!"

Some of the sullenness left Manulito's expression. He was eager, excited.

"You would duel with Deklay after the old custom?"

"I would. Say this to Deklay, openly so that all men may hear. Then Deklay must also give answer openly."

Manulito flushed at that implication concerning his leader's courage, and Travis knew that he would deliver the challenge openly. To keep his hold on the clan the latter must accept it, and there would be an audience of his people to witness the success or defeat of their new chief and his policies.

As Manulito disappeared Travis summoned the coyotes, putting full effort into getting across one message. Any tribe led by Deklay would be hostile to the mutant animals. They must go into hiding, run free in the wilderness if the gamble failed Travis. Now they withdrew into the bushes but not out of reach of his mind.

He did not have too long to wait. First came Jil-Lee, Buck, Nolan, Tsoay, Lupe—those who had been with him on the northern scout. Then the others, the warriors first, the women making a half circle behind, leaving a free space in which Deklay walked.

"I am the Fox," Travis stated. "And this one has named me witch and *natdahe*, outlaw of the mountains. Therefore do I come to name names in my turn. Hear me, People: This Deklay—he would walk among you as *'izesnantan*, a great chief—but he does not have the *go'ndi*, the holy power of a chief. For this Deklay is a fool, with a head filled by nothing but his own wishes, not caring for his clan brothers. He says he leads you into safety; I say he leads you into the worst danger any living man can imagine—even in peyote dreams! He is one twisted in his thoughts, and he would make you twisted also—"

Buck cut in sharply, hushing the murmur of the massed clan.

"These are bold words, Fox. Will you back them?"

Travis' hands were already peeling off his shirt. "I will back them," he stated between set teeth. He had known since his awakening after the stoning that this next move was the only one left for him to make. But now that the testing of his action came, he could not be certain of the outcome, of anything save that the final decision of this battle might affect more than the fate of two men. He stripped, noting that Deklay was doing the same.

Having stepped into the center of the glade, Nolan was using the point of his knife to score a deep-ridged circle there. Naked except for his moccasins, with only his knife in his hand, Travis took the two strides which put him in the circle facing Deklay. He surveyed his opponent's finely muscled body, realizing that his earlier estimate of Deklay's probable advantages were close to the mark. In sheer strength the other outmatched him. Whether Deklay was skillful with his knife was another question, one which Travis would soon be able to answer.

They circled, eyes intent upon each move, striving to weigh and measure each other's strengths and weaknesses. Knife dueling among the Pinda-lick-o-yi, Travis remembered, had once been an art close to finished swordplay, with two evenly matched fighters able to engage for a long time without seriously marking each other. But this was a far rougher and more deadly game, with none of the niceties of such a meeting.

He evaded a vicious thrust from Deklay.

"The bull charges," he laughed. "And the Fox snaps!" By some incredible stroke of good fortune, the point of his weapon actually grazed Deklay's arm, drawing a thin, red inch-long line across the skin.

"Charge again, bull. Feel once more the Fox's teeth!"

He strove to goad Deklay into a crippling loss of temper, knowing how the other could explode into violent rage. It was dangerous, that rage, but it could also make a man blindly careless.

There was an inarticulate sound from Deklay, a dusky swelling in the man's face. He spat, as might an enraged puma, and rushed at Travis who did not quite manage to avoid the lunge, falling back with a smarting slash across the ribs.

"The bull gores!" Deklay bellowed. "Horns toss the Fox!"

He rushed again, elated by the sight of the trickling wound on Travis' side. But the slighter man slipped away.

Travis knew he must be careful in such evasions. One foot across the ridged circle and he was finished as much as if Deklay's blade had found its mark. Travis tried a thrust of his own, and his foot came down hard on a sharp pebble. Through the sole of his moccasin pain shot upward, caused him to stumble. Again the scarlet flame of a wound, down his shoulder and forearm this time.

Well, there was one trick, he knew. Travis tossed the knife into the air, caught it with his left hand. Deklay was now facing a left-handed fighter and must adjust to that.

"Paw, bull, rattle your horns!" Travis cried. "The Fox still shows his teeth!"

Deklay recovered from his instant of surprise. With a cry which was indeed like the bellow of an old range bull, he rushed into grapple, sure of his superior strength against a younger and already wounded man.

Travis ducked, one knee thumping the ground. He groped out with his right hand, caught up a handful of earth, and flung it into the dusky brown face. Again it seemed that luck was on his side. That handful could not be as blinding as sand, but some bit of the shower landed in Deklay's eye.

For a space of seconds Deklay was wide open—open for a blow which would rip him up the middle, the blow Travis could not and would not deliver.

Instead, he took the offensive recklessly, springing straight for his opponent. As the earth-grimed fingers of one hand clawed into Deklay's face, he struck with the other, not with the point of the knife but with its shaft. But Deklay, already only half conscious from the blow, had his own chance. He fell to the ground, leaving his knife behind, two inches of steel between Travis' ribs.

Somehow—he didn't know from where he drew that strength—Travis kept his feet and took one step and then another, out of the circle until the comforting brace of a tree trunk was against his bare back. Was he finished—?

He fought to nurse his rags of consciousness. Had he summoned Buck with his eyes? Or had the urgency of what he had to say reached somehow from mind to mind? The other was at his side, but Travis put out a hand to ward him off.

"Towers—" He struggled to keep his wits through the pain and billowing weakness beginning to creep through him. "Reds mustn't get to the towers! Worse than the bomb ... end us all!"

He had a hazy glimpse of Nolan and Jil-Lee closing in about him. The desire to cough tore at him, but they had to know, to believe....

"Reds get to the towers—everything finished. Not only here ... maybe back home too...."

Did he read comprehension on Buck's face? Would Nolan and Jil-Lee and the rest believe him? Travis could not suppress the cough any longer, and the ripping pain which followed was the worst he had ever experienced. But still he kept his feet, tried to make them understand.

"Don't let them get to the towers. Find that storehouse!"

Travis stood away from the tree, reached out to Buck his earth and bloodstained hand. "I swear ... truth ... this must be done!"

He was going down, and he had a queer thought that once he reached the ground everything would end, not only for him but also for his mission. Trying to see the faces of the men about him was like attempting to identify the people in a dream.

"Towers!" He had meant to shout it, but he could not even hear for himself that last word as he fell.

14

Travis' back was braced against blanketed packs as he steadied a piece of light-yellow bark against one bent knee scowling at the lines drawn on it in faint green.

"We are here then ... and the ship there—" His thumb was set on one point of the crude map, forefinger on the other. Buck nodded.

"That is so. Tsoay, Eskelta, Kawaykle, they watch the trails. There is the pass, two other ways men can come on foot. But who can watch the air?"

"The Tatars say the Reds dare not bring the 'copter into the mountains. After they first landed they lost a flyer in a tricky air-current flow up there. They have only one left and won't risk it. If only they aren't reinforced before we can move!" There it was again, that constant gnawing fear of time, time shortening into a rope to strangle them all.

"You think that the knowledge of our ship will bring them into the open?"

"That—or information about the towers would be the only things important enough to pull out their experts. They could send a controlled Tatar party to explore the ship, sure. But that wouldn't give them the technical reports they need. No, I think if they knew a wrecked Western Confederation ship was here, it would bring them—or enough of them to lessen the odds. We have to catch them in the open. Otherwise, they can hole up forever in that ship-fort of theirs."

"And just how do we let them know our ship is here? Send out another scouting party and let them be trailed back?"

"That's our last resource." Travis continued to frown at the map. Yes, it would be possible to let the Reds sight and trail an Apache party. But there was none in the clan who were expendable. Surely there was some other way of laying the trap with the wrecked ship for bait. Capture one of the Reds, let him escape again, having seen what they wanted him to see? Again a time-wasting business. And how long would they have to wait and what risks would they take to pick up a Red prisoner?

"If the Tatars were dependable...." Buck was thinking aloud.

But that "if" was far too big. They could not trust the Tatars. No matter how much the Mongols wanted to aid in pulling down the Reds, as long as they could be controlled by the caller they were useless. Or were they?

"Thought of something?" Buck must have caught Travis' change of expression.

"Suppose a Tatar saw our ship and then was picked up by a Red hunting patrol and they got the information out of him?"

"Do you think any outlaw would volunteer to let himself be picked up again? And if he did, wouldn't the Reds also be able to learn that he had been set up for the trap?"

"An escaped prisoner?" Travis suggested.

Now Buck was plainly considering the possibilities of such a scheme. And Travis' own spirits rose a little. The idea was full of holes, but it could be worked out. Suppose they capture, say, Menlik, bring him here as a prisoner, let him think they were about to kill him because of that attack back in the foothills. Then let him escape, pursue him northward to a point where he could be driven into the hands of the Reds? Very chancy, but it just might work. Travis was favoring a gamble now, since his desperate one with the duel had paid off.

The risk he had accepted then had cost him two deep wounds, one of which might have been serious if Jil-Lee's project-sponsored medical training had not been to hand. But it had also made Travis one of the clan again, with his people willing to listen to his warning concerning the tower treasury.

"The girl—the Tatar girl!"

At first Travis did not understand Buck's ejaculation.

"We get the girl," the other elaborated, "let her escape, then hunt her to where they'll pick her up. Might even imprison her in the ship to begin with."

Kaydessa? Though something within him rebelled at that selection for the leading role in their drama, Travis could see the advantage of Buck's choice. Woman-stealing was an ancient pastime among primitive cultures. The Tatars themselves had found wives that way in the past, just as the Apache raiders of old had taken captive women into their wickiups. Yes, for raiders to steal a woman would be a natural act, accepted as such by the Reds. For the same woman to endeavor to escape and be hunted by her captors also was reasonable. And for such a woman, cut off from her outlaw kin, to eventually head back toward the Red settlement as the only hope of evading her enemies—logical all the way!

"She would have to be well frightened," Travis observed with reluctance.

"That can be done for us—"

Travis glanced at Buck with sharp annoyance. He would not allow certain games out of their common past to be played with Kaydessa. But Buck had something very different from old-time brutality in mind.

"Three days ago, while you were still flat on your back, Deklay and I went back to the ship—"

"Deklay?"

"You beat him openly, so he must restore his honor in his own sight. And the council has forbidden another duel or challenge," Buck replied. "Therefore he will continue to push for recognition in another way. And now that he has heard your story and knows we must face the Reds, not run from them, he is eager to take the war trail—too eager. So we returned to the ship to make another search for weapons—"

"There were none there before except those we had...."

"Nor now either. But we discovered something else." Buck paused and Travis was shaken out of his absorption with the problem at hand by a note in the other's voice. It was as if Buck had come upon something he could not summon the right words to describe.

"First," Buck continued, "there was this dead thing there, near where we found Dr. Ruthven. It was something like a man ... but all silvery hair—"

"The ape-things! The ape-things from the other worlds! What else did you see?" Travis had dropped the map. His side gave him a painful twinge as he caught at Buck's sleeve. The bald space rovers—did they still exist here somewhere? Had they come to explore the ship built on the pattern of their own but manned by Terrans?

"Nothing except tracks, a lot of them, in every open cabin and hole. I think there must have been a sizable pack of the things."

"What killed the dead one?"

Buck wet his lips. "I think—fear...." His voice dropped a little, almost apologetically, and Travis stared.

"The ship is changed. Inside, there is something wrong. When you walk the corridors your skin crawls, you think there is something behind you. You hear things, see things from the corners of your eyes.... When you turn, there's nothing, nothing at all! And the higher you climb into the ship, the worse it is. I tell you, Travis, never have I felt anything like it before!"

"It was a ship of many dead," Travis reminded him. Had the age-old Apache fear of the dead been activated by the Redax into an acute phobia—to strike down such a level-headed man as Buck?

"No, at first that, too, was my thought. Then I discovered that it was worst not near that chamber where we lay our dead, but higher, in the Redax cabin. I think perhaps the machine is still running, but running in a wrong way—so that it does not awaken old memories of our ancestors now, but brings into being all the fears which have ever haunted us through the dark of the ages. I tell you, Travis, when I came out of that place Deklay was leading me by the hand as if I were a child. And he was shivering as a man who will never be warm again. There is an evil there beyond our understanding. I think that this Tatar girl, were she only to stay there a very short time, would be well frightened—so frightened that any trained scientist examining her later would know there was a mystery to be explored."

"The ape-things—could they have tried to run the Redax?" Travis wondered. To associate machines with the creatures was outwardly pure folly. But they had been discovered on two of the planets of the old civilization, and Ashe had thought that they might represent the degenerate remnants of a once intelligent species.

"That is possible. If so, they raised a storm which drove them out and killed one of them. The ship is a haunted place now."

"But for us to use the girl...." Travis had seen the logic in Buck's first suggestion, but now he differed. If the atmosphere of the ship was as terrifying as Buck said, to imprison Kaydessa there, even temporarily, was still wrong.

"She need not remain long. Suppose we should do this: We shall enter with her and then allow the disturbance we would feel to overcome us. We could run, leave her alone. When she left the ship, we could then take up the chase, shepherding her back to the country she knows. Within the ship we would be with her and could see she did not remain too long."

Travis could see a good prospect in that plan. There was one thing he would insist on—if Kaydessa was to be in that ship, he himself would be one of the "captors." He said as much, and Buck accepted his determination as final.

They dispatched a scouting party to infiltrate the territory to the north, to watch and wait their chance of capture. Travis strove to regain his feet, to be ready to move when the moment came.

Five days later he was able to reach the ridge beyond which lay the wrecked ship. With him were Jil-Lee, Lupe, and Manulito. They satisfied themselves that the globe had had no visitors since Buck and Deklay; there was no sign that the ape-things had returned.

"From here," Travis said, "the ship doesn't look too bad, almost as if it might be able to take off again."

"It might lift," Jil-Lee gestured to the mountaintop behind the curve of the globe—"about that far. The tubes on this side are intact."

"What would happen were the Reds to get inside and try to fly again?" Manulito wondered aloud.

Travis was struck by a sudden idea, one perhaps just as wild as the other inspirations he had had since landing on Topaz, but one to be studied and explored—not dismissed without consideration. Suppose enough power remained to lift the ship partially and then blow it up? With the Red technicians on board at the time.... But he was no engineer, he had no idea whether any part of the globe might or might not work again.

"They are not fools; a close look would tell them it is a wreck," Jil-Lee countered.

Travis walked on. Not too far ahead a yellow-brown shape moved out of the brush, stood stiff-legged in his path, facing the ship and growling in a harsh rumble of sound. Whatever moved or operated in that wreck was picked up by the acute sense of the coyote, even at this distance.

"On!" Travis edged around the snarling animal. With one halting step and then another, it followed him. There was a sharp warning yelp from the brush, and a second coyote head appeared. Naginlta followed Travis, but Nalik'ideyu refused to approach the grounded globe.

Travis surveyed the ship closely, trying to remember the layout of its interior. To turn the whole sphere into a trap—was it possible? How had Ashe said the Redax worked? Something about high-frequency waves stimulating certain brain and nerve centers.

What if one were shielded from those rays? That tear in the side—he himself must have climbed through that the night they crashed. And the break was not too far from the space lock. Near the lock was a storage compartment. And if it had not been jammed, or its contents crushed, they might have something. He beckoned to Jil-Lee.

"Give me a hand—up there."

"Why?"

"I want to see if the space suits are intact."

Jil-Lee regarded Travis with open bewilderment, but Manulito pushed forward. "We do not need those suits to walk here, Travis. This air we can breathe—"

"Not for the air, and not in the open." Travis advanced at a deliberate pace. "Those suits may be insulated in more ways than one—"

"Against a mixed-up Redax broadcast, you mean!" Jil-Lee exclaimed. "Yes, but you stay here, younger brother. This is a risky climb, and you are not yet strong."

Travis was forced to accede to that, waiting as Manulito and Lupe climbed up to the tear and entered. At least Buck and Deklay's experience had forewarned them and they would be prepared for the weird ghosts haunting the interior.

But when they returned, pulling between them the limp space suit, both men were pale, the shiny sheen of sweat on their foreheads, their hands shaking. Lupe sat down on the ground before Travis.

"Evil spirits," he said, giving to this modern phenomenon the old name. "Truly ghosts and witches walk in there."

Manulito had spread the suit on the ground and was examining it with a care which spoke of familiarity.

"This is unharmed," he reported. "Ready to wear."

The suits were all tailored for size, Travis knew. And this fitted a slender, medium-sized man. It would fit him, Travis Fox. But Manulito was already unbuckling the fastenings with practiced ease.

"I shall try it out," he announced. And Travis, seeing the awkward climb to the entrance of the ship, had to agree that the first test should be carried out by someone more agile at the moment.

Sealed into the suit, with the bubble helmet locked in place, the Apache climbed back into the globe. The only form of communication with him was the rope he had tied about him, and if he went above the first level, he would have to leave that behind.

In the first few moments they saw no twitch of alarm running along the rope. After counting fifty slowly, Travis gave it a tentative jerk, to find it firmly fastened within. So Manulito had tied it there and was climbing to the control cabin.

They continued to wait with what patience they could muster. Naginlta, pacing up and down a good distance from the ship, whined at intervals, the warning echoed each time by his mate upslope.

"I don't like it—" Travis broke off when the helmeted figure appeared again at the break. Moving slowly in his cumbersome clothing, Manulito reached the ground, fumbled with the catch of his head covering and then stood, taking deep, lung-filling gulps of air.

"Well?" Travis demanded.

"I see no ghosts," Manulito said, grinning. "This is ghost-proof!" He slapped his gloved hand against the covering over his chest. "There is also this—from what I know of these ships—some of the relays still work. I think this could be made into a trap. We could entice the Reds in and then...." His hand moved in a quick upward flip.

"But we don't know anything about the engines," Travis replied.

"No? Listen—you, Fox, are not the only one to remember useful knowledge." Manulito had lost his cheerful grin. "Do you think we are just the savages those big brains back at the project wished us to be? They have played a trick on us with their Redax. So, we can play a few tricks, too. Me—? I went to M.I.T., or is that one of the things you no longer remember, Fox?"

Travis swallowed hastily. He really had forgotten that fact until this very minute. From the beginning, the Apache team had been carefully selected and screened, not only for survival potential, which was their basic value to the project, but also for certain individual skills. Just as Travis' grounding in archaeology had been one advantage, so had Manulito's technical training made a valuable, though different, contribution. If at first the Redax, used without warning, had smothered that training, perhaps the effects were now fading.

"You can do something, then?" he asked eagerly.

"I can try. There is a chance to booby trap the control cabin at least. And that is where they would poke and pry. Working in this suit will be tough. How about my trying to smash up the Redax first?"

"Not until after we use it on our captive," Jil-Lee decided. "Then there would be some time before the Reds come—"

"You talk as if they *will* come," cut in Lupe. "How can you be sure?"

"We can't," Travis agreed. "But we can count on this much, judging from the past. Once they know that there is a wrecked ship here, they will be forced to explore it. They cannot afford an enemy settlement on this side of the mountains. That would be, according to their way of thinking, an eternal threat."

Jil-Lee nodded. "That is true. This is a complicated plan, yes, and one in which many things may go wrong. But it is also one which covers all the loopholes we know of."

With Lupe's aid Manulito crawled out of the suit. As he leaned it carefully against a supporting rock he said:

"I have been thinking of this treasure house in the towers. Suppose we could find new weapons there...."

Travis hesitated. He still shrank from the thought of opening the secret places behind those glowing walls, to loose a new peril.

"If we took weapons from there and lost the fight...." He advanced his first objection and was glad to see the expression of comprehension on Jil-Lee's face.

"It would be putting the weapons straight into Red hands," the other agreed.

"We may have to chance it before we're through," Manulito warned. "Suppose we do get some of their technicians into this trap. That isn't going to open up their main defense for us. We may need a bigger nutcracker than we've ever seen."

With a return of that queasy feeling he had known in the tower, Travis knew Manulito was speaking sense. They might have to open Pandora's box before the end of this campaign.

15

They camped another two days near the wrecked ship while Manulito prowled the haunted corridors and cabins in his space suit, planning his booby trap. At night he drew diagrams on pieces of bark and discussed the possibility of this or that device, sometimes lapsing into technicalities his companions could not follow. But Travis was well satisfied that Manulito knew what he was doing.

On the morning of the third day Nolan slipped into their midst. He was dust-grimed, his face gaunt, the signs of hard travel plain to read. Travis handed him the nearest canteen, and they watched him drink sparingly in small sips before he spoke.

"They come ... with the girl—"

"You had trouble?" asked Jil-Lee.

"The Tatars had moved their camp, which was only wise, since the Reds must have had a line on the other one. And they are now farther to the west. But—" he wiped his lips with the back of his hand—"also we saw your towers, Fox. And that is a place of power!"

"No sign that the Reds are prowling there?"

Nolan shook his head. "To my mind the mists there conceal the towers from aerial view. Only one coming on foot could tell them from the natural crags of the hills."

Travis relaxed. Time still granted them a margin of grace. He glanced up to see Nolan smiling faintly.

"This maiden, she is a kin to the puma of the mountains," he announced. "She has marked Tsoay with her claws until he looks like the ear-clipped yearling fresh from the branding chute—"

"She is not hurt?" Travis demanded.

This time Nolan chuckled openly. "Hurt? No, we had much to do to keep her from hurting us, younger brother. That one is truly as she claims, a daughter of wolves. And she is also keen-witted, marking a return trail all the way, though she does not know that is as we wish. Did we not pick the easiest way back for just that reason? Yes, she plans to escape."

Travis stood up. "Let us finish this quickly!" His voice came out on a rough note. This plan had never had his full approval. Now he found it less and less easy to think about taking Kaydessa into the ship, allowing the emotional torment lurking there to work upon her. Yet he knew that the girl would not be hurt, and he had made sure he would be beside her within the globe, sharing with her the horror of the unseen.

A rattling of gravel down the narrow valley opening gave warning to those by the campfire. Manulito had already stowed the space suit in hiding. To Kaydessa they must have seemed reverted entirely to savagery.

Tsoay came first, an angry raking of four parallel scratches down his left cheek. And behind him Buck and Eskelta shoved the prisoner, urging her on with a show of roughness which did not descend to actual brutality. Her long braids had shaken loose, and a sleeve was torn, leaving one slender arm bare. But none of the fighting spirit had left her.

They thrust her out into the circle of waiting men and she planted her feet firmly apart, glaring at them all indiscriminately until she sighted Travis. Then her anger became hotter and more deadly.

"Pig! Rooter in the dirt! Diseased camel—" she shouted at him in English and then reverted to her own tongue, her voice riding up and down the scale. Her hands were tied behind her back, but there were no bonds on her tongue.

"This is one who can speak thunders, and shoot lightnings from her mouth," Buck commented in Apache. "Put her well away from the wood, lest she set it aflame."

Tsoay held his hands over his ears. "She can deafen a man when she cannot set her mark on him otherwise. Let us speedily get rid of her."

Yet for all their jeering comments, their eyes held respect. Often in the past a defiant captive who stood up boldly to his captors had received more consideration than usual from Apache warriors; courage was a quality they prized. A Pinda-lick-o-yi such as Tom Jeffords, who rode into Cochise's camp and sat in the midst of his sworn enemies for a parley, won the friendship of the very chief he had been fighting. Kaydessa had more influence with her captors than she could dream of holding.

Now it was time for Travis to play his part. He caught the girl's shoulder and pushed her before him toward the wreck.

Some of the spirit seemed to have left her thin, tense body, and she went without any more fight. Only when they came into full view of the ship did she falter. Travis heard her breathe a gasp of surprise.

As they had planned, four of the Apaches—Jil-Lee, Tsoay, Nolan, and Buck—fanned out toward the heights about the ship. Manulito had already gone to cover, to don the space suit and prepare for any accident.

Resolutely Travis continued to propel Kaydessa ahead. At the moment he did not know which was worse, to enter the ship expecting the fear to strike, or to meet it unprepared. He was ready to refuse to enter, not to allow the girl, sullenly plodding on under his compulsion, to face that unseen but potent danger.

Only the memory of the towers and the threat of the Reds finding and exploiting the treasure there kept him going. Eskelta went first, climbing to the tear. Travis cut the ropes binding Kaydessa's wrists and gave her a slight slap between the shoulders.

"Climb, woman!" His anxiety made that a harsh order and she climbed.

Eskelta was inside now, heading for the cabin which might reasonably be selected as a prison. They planned to get the girl as far as that point and then stage their act of being overcome by fear, allowing her to escape.

Stage an act? Travis was not two feet along that corridor before he knew that there would be little acting needed on his part. The thing which pervaded the ship did not attack sharply, rather it seeped into his mind and body as if he drew in poison with every breath, sent it racing along his veins with every beat of a laboring heart. Yet he could not put any name to his feelings, except an awful, weakening fear which weighted him heavier with every step he took.

Kaydessa screamed. Not this time in rage, but with such fervor that Travis lost his hold, staggered back to the wall. She whirled about, her face contorted, and sprang at him.

It was indeed like trying to fight a wildcat and after the first second or two he was hard put to protect his eyes, his face, his side, without injuring her in return. She scrambled over him, running for the break in the wall, and disappeared. Travis gasped, and started to crawl for the break. Eskelta loomed over him, pulled him up in haste.

They reached the opening but did not climb through. Travis was uncertain as to whether he could make that descent yet, and Eskelta was obeying orders in not venturing out too soon.

Below, the ground was bare. There was no sign of the Apaches, though they were in hiding there—and none of Kaydessa. Travis was amazed that she had vanished so quickly.

Still uneasy from the emanation within, they perched within the shadow of the break until Travis thought that the fugitive had a good five-minute start. Then he nodded a signal to Eskelta.

By the time they reached ground level Travis felt a warm wetness spreading under his shielding palm and he knew the wound had opened. He spoke a word or two in hot protest against that mishap, knowing it would keep him from the trail. Kaydessa must be covered all the way back across the pass, not only to be shepherded away from her people and toward the plains where she could be picked up by a Red patrol, but also to keep her from danger. And he had planned from the first to be one of those shepherds.

Now he was about as much use as a trail-lame pony. However, he could send deputies. He thought out his call, and Nalik'ideyu's head appeared in a frame of bush.

"Go, both of you and run with her! Guard—!" He said the words in a whisper, thought them with a fierce intensity as he centered his gaze on the yellow eyes in the pointed coyote face. There was a feeling of assent, and then the animal was gone. Travis sighed.

The Apache scouts were subtle and alert, but the coyotes could far outdo any man. With Nalik'ideyu and Naginlta flanking her flight, Kaydessa would be well guarded. She would probably never see her guards or know that they were running protection for her.

"That was a good move," Jil-Lee said, coming out of concealment. "But what have you done to yourself?" He stepped closer, pulling Travis' hand away from his side. By the time Lupe came to report, Travis was again wound in a strapping bandage pulled tightly about his lower ribs, and reconciled to the fact that any trailing he would do must be well to the rear of the first party.

"The towers," he said to Jil-Lee. "If our plan works, we can catch part of the Reds here. But we still have their ship to take, and for that we need help which we may find at the towers. Or at least we can be on guard there if they return with Kaydessa on that path."

Lupe dropped down lightly from an upper ledge. He was grinning.

"That woman is one who thinks. She runs from the ship first as a rabbit with a wolf at her heels. Then she begins to think. She climbs—" He lifted one finger to the slope behind them. "She goes behind a rock to watch under cover. When Fox comes from the ship with Eskelta, again she climbs. Buck lets himself be seen, so she moves east, as we wish—"

"And now?" questioned Travis.

"She is keeping to the high ways; almost she thinks like one of the People on the war trail. Nolan believes she will hole up for the night somewhere above. He will make sure."

Travis licked his lips. "She has no food or water."

Jil-Lee's lips shaped a smile. "They will see that she comes upon both as if by chance. We have planned all of this, as you know, younger brother."

That was true. Travis knew that Kaydessa would be guided without her knowledge by the "accidental" appearance now and then of some pursuer—just enough to push her along.

"Then, too, she is now armed," Jil-Lee added.

"How?" demanded Travis.

"Look to your own belt, younger brother. Where is your knife?"

Startled, Travis glanced down. His sheath was empty, and he had not needed that blade since he had drawn it to cut meat at the morning meal. Lupe laughed.

"She had steel in her hand when she came out of that ghost ship."

"Took it from me while we struggled!" Travis was openly surprised. He had considered the frenzy displayed by the Tatar girl as an outburst of almost mindless terror. Yet Kaydessa had had wit enough to take his knife! Could this be another case where one race was less affected by a mind machine than the other? Just as the Apaches had not been governed by the Red caller, so the Tatars might not be as sensitive to the Redax.

"She is a strong one, that woman—one worth many ponies." Eskelta reverted to the old measure of a wife's value.

"That is true!" Travis agreed emphatically and then was annoyed at the broadening of Jil-Lee's smile. Abruptly he changed the subject.

"Manulito is setting the booby trap in the ship."

"That is well. He and Eskelta will remain here, and you with them."

"Not so! We must go to the towers—" Travis protested.

"I thought," Jil-Lee cut in, "that you believed the weapons of the old ones too dangerous for us to use."

"Maybe they will be forced into our hands. But we must be sure the towers are not entered by the Reds on their way here."

"That is reasonable. But for you, younger brother, no trailing today, perhaps not tomorrow. If that wound opens again, you might have much bad trouble."

Travis was forced to accept that, in spite of his worry and impatience. And the next day when he did move on he had only the report that Kaydessa had sheltered beside a pool for the night and was doggedly moving back across the mountains.

Three days later Travis, Jil-Lee, and Buck came into the tower valley. Kaydessa was in the northern foothills, twice turned back from the west and the freedom of the outlaws by the Apache scouts. And only half an hour before, Tsoay had reported by mirror what should have been welcome news: the Red helicopter was cruising as it had on the day they watched the hunters enter the uplands. There was an excellent chance of the fugitive's being sighted and picked up soon.

Tsoay had also spotted a party of three Tatars watching the helicopter. But after one wide sweep of the flyer they had taken to their ponies and ridden away at the fastest pace their mounts could manage in this rough territory.

On a stretch of smooth earth Buck scratched a trail, and they studied it. The Reds would have to follow this route to seek the wrecked ship—a route covered by Apache sentinels. And following the chain of communication the result of the trap would be reported to the party at the towers.

The waiting was the most difficult; too many imponderables did not allow for unemotional thinking. Travis was down to the last shred of patience when word came on the second morning at the hidden valley that Kaydessa had been picked up by a Red patrol—drawn out to meet them by the caller.

"Now—the tower weapons!" Buck answered the report with an imperative order to Travis. And the other knew he could no longer postpone the inevitable. And only by action could he blot out the haunting mental picture of Kaydessa once more drawn into the bondage she so hated.

Flanked by Jil-Lee and Buck, he climbed back through the tower window and faced the glowing pillar.

He crossed the room, put out both hands to the sleek pole, uncertain if the weird transport would work again. He heard the sharp gasp from the others as his body was sucked against the pillar and carried downward through the well. Buck followed him, and Jil-Lee came last. Then Travis led the way along the underground corridor to the room with the table and the reader.

He sat down on the bench, fumbled with the pile of tape disks, knowing that the other two were watching him with almost hostile intentness. He snapped a disk into the reader, hoping he could correctly interpret the directions it gave.

He looked up at the wall before him. Three ... four steps, the correct move—and then an unlocking....

"You know?" Buck demanded.

"I can guess—"

"Well?" Jil-Lee moved to the table. "What do we do?"

"This—" Travis came from behind the table, walked to the wall. He put out both hands, flattened his palms against the green-blue-purple surface and slid them slowly along. Under his touch, the material of the wall was cool and hard, unlike the live feel the pillar had. Cool until—

One palm, held at arm's length had found the right spot. He slid the other hand along in the opposite direction until his arms were level with his shoulders. His fingers were able now to press on those points of warmth. Travis tensed and pushed hard with all ten fingers.

At first, as one second and then two passed and there was no response to the pressure, Travis thought he had mistaken the reading of the tape. Then, directly before his eyes, a dark line cut vertically down the wall. He applied more pressure until his fingers were half numb with effort. The line widened slowly. Finally he faced a slit some eight feet in height, a little more than two in width, and there the opening remained.

Light beyond, a cold, gray gleam—like that of a cloudy winter day on Terra—and with it the chill of air out of some arctic wasteland. Favoring his still bandaged side, Travis scraped through the door ahead of the others, and came into the place of gray cold.

"Wauggh!" Travis heard that exclamation from Jil-Lee, could have echoed it himself except that he was too astounded by what he had seen to say anything at all.

The light came from a grid of bars set far above their heads into the native rock which roofed this storehouse, for storehouse it was. There were orderly lines of boxes, some large enough to contain a tank, others no bigger than a man's fist. Symbols in the same blue-green-purple lights of the outer wall shone from their sides.

"What—?" Buck began one question and then changed it to another: "Where do we begin to look?"

"Toward the far end." Travis started down the center aisle between rows of the massed spoils of another time and world—or worlds. The same tape which had given him the clue to the unlocking of the door, emphasized the importance of something stored at the far end, an object or objects which must be used first. He had wondered about that tape. A sensation of urgency, almost of despair, had come through the gabble of alien words, the quick sequence of diagrams and pictures. The message might have been taped under a threat of some great peril.

There was no dust on the rows of boxes or on the floor underfoot. A current of cold, fresh air blew at intervals down the length of the huge chamber. They could not see the next aisle across the barriers of stored goods, but the only noise was a whisper and the faint sounds of their own feet. They came out into an open space backed by the wall, and Travis saw what had been so important.

"No!" His protest was involuntary, but his denial loud enough to echo.

Six—six of them—tall, narrow cases set upright against the wall; and from their depths, five pairs of dark eyes staring back at him in cold measurement. These were the men of the ships—the men Menlik had dreamed of—their bald white heads, their thin bodies with the skintight covering of the familiar blue-green-purple. Five of them were here, alive—watching ... waiting....

Five men—and six boxes. That small fact broke the spell in which those eyes held Travis. He looked again at the sixth box to his right. Expecting to meet another pair of eyes this time, he was disconcerted to face only emptiness. Then, as his gaze traveled downward, he saw what lay on the floor there—a skull, a tangle of bones, tattered material cobwebbed into dusty rags by time. Whatever had preserved five of the star men intact, had failed the sixth of their company.

"They are alive!" Jil-Lee whispered.

"I do not think so," Buck answered. Travis took another step, reached out to touch the transparent front of the nearest coffin case. There was no change in the eyes of the alien who stood within, no indication that if the Apaches could see him, he would be able to return their interest. The five stares which had bemused the visitors at first, did not break to follow their movements.

But Travis knew! Whether it was some message on the tape which the sight of the sleepers made clear, or whether some residue of the driving purpose which had set them there now reached his mind, was immaterial. He knew the purpose of this room and its contents, why it had been made and the reason its six guardians had been left as prisoners—and what they wanted from anyone coming after them.

"They sleep," he said softly.

"Sleep?" Buck caught him up.

"They sleep in something like deep freeze."

"Do you mean they can be brought to life again!" Jil-Lee cried.

"Maybe not now—it must be too long—but they were meant to wait out a period and be restored."

"How do you know that?" Buck asked.

"I don't know for certain, but I think I understand a little. Something happened a long time ago. Maybe it was a war, a war between whole star systems, bigger and worse than anything we can imagine. I think this planet was an outpost, and when the supply ships didn't come any more, when they knew they might be cut off for some length of time, they closed down. Stacked their supplies and machines here and then went to sleep to wait for their rescuers...."

"For rescuers who never came," Jil-Lee said softly. "And there is a chance they could be revived even now?"

Travis shivered. "Not one I would want to take."

"No," Buck's tone was somber, "that I agree to, younger brother. These are not men as we know them, and I do not think they would be good *dalaanbiyat'i*—allies. They had *go'ndi* in plenty, these star men, but it is not the power of the People. No one but a madman or a fool would try to disturb this sleep of theirs."

"The truth you speak," Jil-Lee agreed. "But where in this," he turned his shoulder to the sleeping star men and looked back at the filled chamber—"do we find anything which will serve us here and now?"

Again Travis had only the scrappiest information to draw upon. "Spread out," he told them. "Look for the marking of a circle surrounding four dots set in a diamond pattern."

They went, but Travis lingered for a moment to look once more into the bleak and bitter eyes of the star men. How many planet years ago had they sealed themselves into those boxes? A thousand, ten thousand? Their empire was long gone, yet here was an outpost still waiting to be revived to carry on its mysterious duties. It was as if in Saxon-invaded Britain long ago a Roman garrison had been frozen to await the return of the legions. Buck was right; there was no common ground today between Terran man and these unknowns. They must continue to sleep undisturbed.

Yet when Travis also turned away and went back down the aisle, he was still aware of a persistent pull on him to return. It was as though those eyes had set locking cords to will him back to release the sleepers. He was glad to turn a corner, to know that they could no longer watch him plunder their treasury.

"Here!" That was Buck's voice, but it echoed so oddly across the big chamber that Travis had difficulty in deciding what part of the warehouse it was coming from. And Buck had to call several times before Travis and Jil-Lee joined him.

There was the circle-dot-diamond symbol shining on the side of a case. They worked it out of the pile, setting it in the open. Travis knelt to run his hands along the top. The container was an unknown alloy, tough, unmarked by the years—perhaps indestructible.

Again his fingers located what his eyes could not detect—the impressions on the edge, oddly shaped impressions into which his finger tips did not fit too comfortably. He pressed, bearing down with the full strength of his arms and shoulders, and then lifted up the lid.

The Apaches looked into a set of compartments, each holding an object with a barrel, a hand grip, a general resemblance to the sidearms of their own world and time, but sufficiently different to point up the essential strangeness. With infinite care Travis worked one out of the vise-support which held it. The weapon was light in weight, lighter than any automatic he had ever held. Its barrel was long, a good eighteen inches—the grip alien in shape so that it didn't fit comfortably into his hand, the trigger nonexistent, but in its place a button on the lower part of the barrel which could be covered by an outstretched finger.

"What does it do?" asked Buck practically.

"I'm not sure. But it is important enough to have a special mention on the tape." Travis passed the weapon along to Buck and worked another loose from its holder.

"No way of loading I can see," Buck said, examining the weapon with care and caution.

"I don't think it fires a solid projectile," Travis replied. "We'll have to test them outside to find out just what we do have."

The Apaches took only three of the weapons, closing the box before they left. And as they wriggled back through the crack door, Travis was visited again by that odd flash of compelling, almost possessive power he had experienced when they had lain in ambush for the Red hunting party. He took a step or two forward until he was able to catch the edge of the reading table and steady himself against it.

"What is the matter?" Both Buck and Jil-Lee were watching him; apparently neither had felt that sensation. Travis did not reply for a second. He was free of it now. But he was sure of its source; it had not been any backlash of the Red caller! It was rooted here—a compulsion triggered to make the original intentions of the outpost obeyed, a last drag from the sleepers. This place had been set up with a single purpose: to protect and preserve the ancient rulers of Topaz. And perhaps the very presence here of the intruding Terrans had released a force, started an unseen installation.

Now Travis answered simply: "They want out...."

Jil-Lee glanced back at the slit door, but Buck still watched Travis.

"They call?" he asked.

"In a way," Travis admitted. But the compulsion had already ebbed; he was free. "It is gone now."

"This is not a good place," Buck observed somberly. "We touch that which should not be held by men of our earth." He held out the weapon.

"Did not the People take up the rifles of the Pinda-lick-o-yi for their defense when it was necessary?" Jil-Lee demanded. "We do what we must. After seeing that," his chin indicated the slit and what lay behind it—"do you wish the Reds to forage here?"

"Still," Buck's words came slowly, "this is a choice between two evils, rather than between an evil and a good—"

"Then let us see how powerful this evil is!" Jil-Lee headed for the corridor leading to the pillar.

*   *   *   *   *

It was late afternoon when they made their way through the swirling mists of the valley under the archway giving on the former site of the outlaw Tatar camp. Travis sighted the long barrel of the weapon at a small bush backed by a boulder, and he pressed the firing button. There was no way of knowing whether the weapon was loaded except to try it.

The result of his action was quick—quick and terrifying. There was no sound, no sign of any projectile ... ray-gas ... or whatever might have issued in answer to his finger movement. But the bush—the bush was no more!

A black smear made a ragged outline of the extinguished branches and leaves on the rock which had stood behind. The earth might still enclose roots under a thin coating of ash, but the bush was gone!

"The breath of Naye'nezyani—powerful beyond belief!" Buck broke their horrified silence first. "In truth evil is here!"

Jil-Lee raised his gun—if gun it could be called—aimed at the rock with the bush silhouette plain to see and fired.

This time they were able to witness disintegration in progress, the crumble of the stone as if its substance was no more than sand lapped by river water. A pile of blackened rubble remained—nothing more.

"To use this on a living thing?" Buck protested, horror basing the doubt in his voice.

"We do not use it against living things," Travis promised, "but against the ship of the Reds—to cut that to pieces. This will open the shell of the turtle and let us at its meat."

Jil-Lee nodded. "Those are true words. But now I agree with your fears of this place, Travis. This is a devil thing and must not be allowed to fall into the hands of those who—"

"Will use it more freely than we plan to?" Buck wanted to know. "We reserve to ourselves that right because we hold our motives higher? To think that way is also a crooked trail. We will use this means because we must, but afterward...."

Afterward that warehouse must be closed, the tapes giving the entrance clue destroyed. One part of Travis fought that decision, right though he knew it to be. The towers were the menace he had believed. And what was more discouraging than the risk they now ran, was the belief that the treasure was a poison which could not be destroyed but which might spread from Topaz to Terra.

Suppose the Western Conference had discovered that storehouse and explored its riches, would they have been any less eager to exploit them? As Buck had pointed out, one's own ideals could well supply reasons for violence. In the past Terra had been racked by wars of religion, one fanatically held opinion opposed to another. There was no righteousness in such struggles, only fatal ends. The Reds had no right to this new knowledge—but neither did they. It must be locked against the meddling of fools and zealots.

"Taboo—" Buck spoke that word with an emphasis they could appreciate. "Knowledge must be set behind the invisible barriers of taboo, and that could work."

"These three—no more—we found no other weapons!" Jil-Lee added a warning suggestion.

"No others," Buck agreed and Travis echoed, adding:

"We found tombs of the space people, and these were left with them. Because of our great need we borrowed them, but they must be returned to the dead or trouble will follow. And they may only be used against the fortress of the Reds by us, who first found them and have taken unto ourselves the wrath of disturbed spirits."

"Well thought! That is an answer to give the People. The towers are the tombs of dead ones. When we return these they shall be taboo. We are agreed?" Buck asked.

"We are agreed!"

Buck tried his weapon on a sapling, saw it vanish into nothingness. None of the Apaches wanted to carry the strange guns against their bodies; the power made them objects of fear, rather than arms to delight a warrior. And when they returned to their temporary camp, they laid all three on a blanket and covered them up. But they could not cover up the memories of what had happened to bush, rock, and tree.

"If such are their small weapons," Buck observed that evening, "then what kind of things did they have to balance our heavy armament? Perhaps they were able to burn up worlds!"

"That may be what happened elsewhere," Travis replied. "We do not know what put an end to their empire. The capital-planet we found on the first voyage had not been destroyed, but it had been evacuated in haste. One building had not even been stripped of its furnishings." He remembered the battle he had fought there, he and Ross Murdock and the winged native, standing up to an attack of the ape-things while the winged warrior had used his physical advantage to fly above and bomb the enemies with boxes snatched from the piles....

"And here they went to sleep in order to wait out some danger—time or disaster—they did not believe would be permanent," Buck mused.

Travis thought he would flee from the eyes of the sleepers throughout his dreams that night, but on the contrary he slept heavily, finding it hard to rouse when Jil-Lee awakened him for his watch. But he was alert when he saw a four-footed shape flit out of the shadows, drink water from the stream, and shake itself vigorously in a spray of drops.

"Naginlta!" he greeted the coyote. Trouble? He could have shouted that question, but he put a tight rein on his impatience and strove to communicate in the only method possible.

No, what the coyote had come to report was not trouble but the fact that the one he had been set to guard was headed back into the mountains, though others came with her—four others. Nalik'ideyu still watched their camp. Her mate had come for further orders.

Travis squatted before the animal, cupped the coyote's jowls between his palms. Naginlta suffered his touch with only a small whine of uneasiness.

With all his power of mental suggestion, Travis strove to reach the keen brain he knew was served by the yellow eyes looking into his.

The others with Kaydessa were to be led on, taken to the ship. But Kaydessa must not suffer harm. When they reached a spot near-by—Travis thought of a certain rock beyond the pass—then one of the coyotes was to go ahead to the ship. Let the Apaches there know....

Manulito and Eskelta should also be warned by the sentry along the peaks, but additional alerting would not go amiss. Those four with Kaydessa—they must reach the trap!

"What was that?" Buck rolled out of his blanket.

"Naginlta—" The coyote sped back into the dark again. "The Reds have taken the bait, a party of at least four with Kaydessa are moving into the foothills, heading south."

But the enemy party was not the only one on the move. In the light of day a sentry's mirror from a point in the peaks sent another warning down to their camp.

Out in their mountain meadows the Tatar outlaws were on horseback, moving toward the entrance of the tower valley. Buck knelt by the blanket covering the alien weapons.

"Now what?"

"We'll have to stop them," Travis replied, but he had no idea of just how they would halt those determined Mongol horsemen.

17

There were ten of them riding on small, wiry steppe ponies—men and women both, and well armed. Travis recalled it was the custom of the Horde that the women fought as warriors when necessary. Menlik—there was no mistaking the flapping robe of their leader. And they were singing! The rider behind the shaman thumped with violent energy a drum fastened beside his saddle horn, its heavy boom, boom the same call the Apache had heard before. The Mongols were working themselves into the mood for some desperate effort, Travis deduced. And if they were too deeply under the Red spell, there would be no arguing with them. He could wait no longer.

The Apache swung down from a ledge near the valley gate, moved into the open and stood waiting, the alien weapon resting across his forearm. If necessary, he intended to give a demonstration with it for an object lesson.

"*Dar-u-gar!*" The war cry which had once awakened fear across a quarter of Terra. Thin here, and from only a few throats, but just as menacing.

Two of the horsemen aimed lances, preparing to ride him down. Travis sighted a tree midway between them and pressed the firing button. This time there was a flash, a flicker of light, to mark the disappearance of a living thing.

One of the lancers' ponies reared, squealed in fear. The other kept on his course.

"Menlik!" Travis shouted. "Hold up your man! I do not want to kill!"

The shaman called out, but the lancer was already level with the vanished tree, his head half turned on his shoulders to witness the blackened earth where it had stood. Then he dropped his lance, sawed on the reins. A rifle bullet might not have halted his charge, unless it killed or wounded, but what he had just seen was a thing beyond his understanding.

The tribesmen sat their horses, facing Travis, watching him with the feral eyes of the wolves they claimed as forefathers, wolves that possessed the cunning of the wild, cunning enough not to rush breakneck into unknown danger.

Travis walked forward. "Menlik, I would talk—"

There was an outburst from the horsemen, protests from Hulagur and one or two of the others. But the shaman urged his mount into a walking pace toward the Apache until they stood only a few feet from each other—the warrior of the steppes and the Horde facing the warrior of the desert and the People.

"You have taken a woman from our yurts," Menlik said, but his eyes were more on the alien gun than on the man who held it. "Brave are you to come again into our land. He who sets foot in the stirrup must mount into the saddle; he who draws blade free of the scabbard must be prepared to use it."

"The Horde is not here—I see only a handful of people," Travis replied. "Does Menlik propose to go up against the Apaches so? Yet there are those who are his greater enemies."

"A stealer of women is not such a one as needs a regiment under a general to face him."

Suddenly Travis was impatient of the ceremonious talking; there was so little time.

"Listen, and listen well, Shaman!" He spoke curtly now. "I have not your woman. She is already crossing the mountains southward," he pointed with his chin—"leading the Reds into a trap."

Would Menlik believe him? There was no need, Travis decided, to tell him now that Kaydessa's part in this affair was involuntary.

"And you?" The shaman asked the question the Apache had hoped to hear.

"*We,*" Travis emphasized that, "march now against those hiding behind in their ship out there." He indicated the northern plains.

Menlik raised his head, surveying the land about them with disbelieving, contemptuous appraisal.

"You are chief then of an army, an army equipped with magic to overcome machines?"

"One needs no army when he carries this." For the second time Travis displayed the power of the weapon he carried, this time cutting into shifting rubble an outcrop of cliff wall. Menlik's expression did not change, though his eyes narrowed.

The shaman signaled his small company, and they dismounted. Travis was heartened by this sign that Menlik was willing to talk. The Apache made a similar gesture, and Jil-Lee and Buck, their own weapons well in sight, came out to back him. Travis knew that the Tatar had no way of knowing that the three were alone; he well might have believed an unseen troop of Apaches were near-by and so armed.

"You would talk—then talk!" Menlik ordered.

This time Travis outlined events with an absence of word embroidery. "Kaydessa leads the Reds into a trap we have set beyond the peaks—four of them ride with her. How many now remain in the ship near the settlement?"

"There are at least two in the flyer, perhaps eight more in the ship. But there is no getting at them in there."

"No?" Travis laughed softly, shifted the weapon on his arm. "Do you not think that this will crack the shell of that nut so that we can get at the meat?"

Menlik's eyes flickered to the left, to the tree which was no longer a tree but a thin deposit of ash on seared ground.

"They can control us with the caller as they did before. If we go up against them, then we are once more gathered into their net—before we reach their ship."

"That is true for you of the Horde; it does not affect the People," Travis returned. "And suppose we burn out their machines? Then will you not be free?"

"To burn up a tree? Lightning from the skies can do that."

"Can lightning," Buck asked softly, "also make rock as sand of the river?"

Menlik's eyes turned to the second example of the alien weapon's power.

"Give us proof that this will act against their machines!"

"What proof, Shaman?" asked Jil-Lee. "Shall we burn down a mountain that you may believe? This is now a matter of time."

Travis had a sudden inspiration. "You say that the 'copter is out. Suppose we use that as a target?"

"That—that can sweep the flyer from the sky?" Menlik's disbelief was open.

Travis wondered if he had gone too far. But they needed to rid themselves of that spying flyer before they dared to move out into the plain. And to use the destruction of the helicopter as an example, would be the best proof he could give of the invincibility of the new Apache arms.

"Under the right conditions," he replied stoutly, "yes."

"And those conditions?" Menlik demanded.

"That it must be brought within range. Say, below the level of a neighboring peak where a man may lie in wait to fire."

Silent Apaches faced silent Mongols, and Travis had a chance to taste what might be defeat. But the helicopter must be taken before they advanced toward the ship and the settlement.

"And, maker of traps, how do you intend to bait this one?" Menlik's question was an open challenge.

"You know these Reds better than we," Travis counterattacked. "How would you bait it, Son of the Blue Wolf?"

"You say Kaydessa is leading the Reds south; we have but your word for that," Menlik replied. "Though how it would profit you to lie on such a matter—" He shrugged. "If you do speak the truth, then the 'copter will circle about the foothills where they entered."

"And what would bring the pilot nosing farther in?" the Apache asked.

Menlik shrugged again. "Any manner of things. The Reds have never ventured too far south; they are suspicious of the heights—with good cause." His fingers, near the hilt of his tulwar, twitched. "Anything which might suggest that their party is in difficulty would bring them in for a closer look—"

"Say a fire, with much smoke?" Jil-Lee suggested.

Menlik spoke over his shoulder to his own party. There was a babble of answer, two or three of the men raising their voices above those of their companions.

"If set in the right direction, yes," the shaman conceded. "When do you plan to move, Apaches?"

"At once!"

But they did not have wings, and the cross-country march they had to make was a rough journey on foot. Travis' "at once" stretched into night hours filled with scrambling over rocks, and an early morning of preparations, with always the threat that the helicopter might not return to fly its circling mission over the scene of operations. All they had was Menlik's assurance that while any party of the Red overlords was away from their well-defended base, the flyer did just that.

"Might be relaying messages on from a walkie-talkie or something like that," Buck commented.

"They should reach our ship in two days ... three at the most ... if they are pushing," Travis said thoughtfully. "It would be a help—if that flyer is a link in any com unit—to destroy it before its crew picks up and relays any report of what happens back there."

Jil-Lee grunted. He was surveying the heights above the pocket in which Menlik and two of the Mongols were piling brush. "There ... there ... and there...." The Apache's chin made three juts. "If the pilot swoops for a quick look, our cross fire will take out his blades."

They held a last conference with Menlik and then climbed to the perches Jil-Lee had selected. Sentries on lookout reported by mirror flash that Tsoay, Deklay, Lupe, and Nolan were now on the move to join the other three Apaches. If and when Manulito's trap closed its jaws on the Reds at the western ship, the news would pass and the Apaches would move out to storm the enemy fort on the prairie. And should they blast any caller the helicopter might carry, Menlik and his riders would accompany them.

There it was, just as Menlik had foretold: The wasp from the open country was flying into the hills. Menlik, on his knees, struck flint to steel, sparking the fire they hoped would draw the pilot to a closer investigation.

The brush caught, and smoke, thick and white, came first in separate puffs and then gathered into a murky pillar to form a signal no one could overlook. In Travis' hands the grip of the gun was slippery. He rested the end of the barrel on the rock, curbing his rising tension as best he could.

To escape any caller on the flyer, the Tatars had remained in the valley below the Apaches' lookout. And as the helicopter circled in, Travis sighted two men in its cockpit, one wearing a helmet identical to the one they had seen on the Red hunter days ago. The Reds' long undisputed sway over the Mongol forces would make them overconfident. Travis thought that even if they sighted one of the waiting Apaches, they would not take warning until too late.

Menlik's bush fire was performing well and the flyer was heading straight for it. The machine buzzed the smoke once, too high for the Apaches to trust raying its blades. Then the pilot came back in a lower sweep which carried him only yards above the smoldering brush, on a level with the snipers.

Travis pressed the button on the barrel, his target the fast-whirling blades. Momentum carried the helicopter on, but at least one of the marksmen, if not all three, had scored. The machine plowed through the smoke to crack up beyond.

Was their caller working, bringing in the Mongols to aid the Reds trapped in the wreck?

Travis watched Menlik make his way toward the machine, reach the cracked cover of the cockpit. But in the shaman's hand was a bare blade on which the sun glinted. The Mongol wrenched open the sprung door, thrust inward with the tulwar, and the howl of triumph he voiced was as worldless and wild as a wolf's.

More Mongols flooding down ... Hulagur ... a woman ... centering on the helicopter. This time a spear plunged into the interior of the broken flyer. Payment was being extracted for long slavery.

The Apaches dropped from the heights, waiting for Menlik to leave the wild scene. Hulagur had dragged out the body of the helmeted man and the Mongols were stripping off his equipment, smashing it with rocks, still howling their war cry. But the shaman came to the dying smudge fire to meet the Apaches.

He was smiling, his upper lip raised in a curve suggesting the victory purr of a snow tiger. And he saluted with one hand.

"There are two who will not trap men again! We believe you now, *andas*, comrades of battle, when you say you can go up against their fort and make it as nothing!"

Hulagur came up behind the shaman, a modern automatic in his hand. He tossed the weapon into the air, caught it again, laughing—disclaiming something in his own language.

"From the serpents we take two fangs," Menlik translated. "These weapons may not be as dangerous as yours, but they can bite deeper, quicker, and with more force than our arrows."

It did not take the Mongols long to strip the helicopter and the Reds of what they could use, deliberately smashing all the other equipment which had survived the wreck. They had accomplished one important move: The link between the southbound exploring party and the Red headquarters—if that was the role the helicopter had played—was now gone. And the "eyes" operating over the open territory of the plains had ceased to exist. The attacking war party could move against the ship near the Red settlement, knowing they had only controlled Mongol scouts to watch for.

And to penetrate enemy territory under those conditions was an old, old game the Apaches had played for centuries.

While they waited for the signals from the peaks, a camp was established and a Mongol dispatched to bring up the rest of the outlaws and all extra mounts. Menlik carried to the Apaches a portion of the dried meat which had been transported Horde fashion—under the saddle to soften it for eating.

"We do not skulk any longer like rats or city men in dark holes," he told them. "This time we ride, and we shall take an accounting from those out there—a fine accounting!"

"They still have other controllers," Travis pointed out.

"And you have that which is an answer to all their machines," blazed Menlik in return.

"They will send against us your own people if they can," Buck warned.

Menlik pulled at his upper lip. "That is also truth. But now they have no eyes in the sky, and with so many of their men away, they will not patrol too far from camp. I tell you, *andas*, with these weapons of yours a man could rule a world!"

Travis looked at him bleakly. "Which is why they are taboo!"

"Taboo?" Menlik repeated. "In what manner are these forbidden? Do you not carry them openly, use them as you wish? Are they not weapons of your own people?"

Travis shook his head. "These are the weapons of dead men—if we can name them men at all. These we took from a tomb of the star race who held Topaz when our world was only a hunting ground of wild men wearing the skins of beasts and slaying mammoths with stone spears. They are from a tomb and are cursed, a curse we took upon ourselves with their use."

There was a strange light deep in the shaman's eyes. Travis did not know who or what Menlik had been before the Red conditioner had returned him to the role of Horde shaman. He might have been a technician or scientist—and deep within him some remnants of that training could now be dismissing everything Travis said as fantastic superstition.

Yet in another way the Apache spoke the exact truth. There was a curse on these weapons, on every bit of knowledge gathered in that warehouse of the towers. As Menlik had already noted, that curse was power, the power to control Topaz, and then perhaps to reach back across the stars to Terra.

When the shaman spoke again his words were a half whisper. "It will take a powerful curse to keep these out of the hands of men."

"With the Reds gone or powerless," Buck asked, "what need will anyone have for them?"

"And if another ship comes from the skies—to begin all over again?"

"To that we shall have an answer, also, if and when we must find it," Travis replied. That could well be true ... other weapons in the warehouse powerful enough to pluck a spaceship out of the sky, but they did not have to worry about that now.

"Arms from a tomb. Yes, this is truly dead men's magic. I shall say so to my people. When do we move out?"

"When we know whether or not the trap to the south is sprung," Buck answered.

The report came an hour after sunrise the next morning when Tsoay, Nolan, and Deklay padded into camp. The war chief made a slight gesture with one hand.

"It is done?" Travis wanted confirmation in words.

"It is done. The Pinda-lick-o-yi entered the ship eagerly. Then they blew it and themselves up. Manulito did his work well."

"And Kaydessa?"

"The woman is safe. When the Reds saw the ship, they left their machine outside to hold her captive. That mechanical caller was easily destroyed. She is now free and with the *mba'a* she comes across the mountains, Manulito and Eskelta with her also. Now—" he looked from his own people to the Mongols, "why are you here with these?"

"We wait, but the waiting is over," Jil-Lee said. "Now we go north!"

18

They lay along the rim of a vast basin, a scooping out of earth so wide they could not sight its other side. The bed of an ancient lake, Travis speculated, or perhaps even the arm of a long-dried sea. But now the hollow was filled with rolling waves of golden grass, tossing heavy heads under the flowing touch of a breeze with the exception of a space about a mile ahead where round domes—black, gray, brown—broke the yellow in an irregular oval around the globular silver bead of a spacer: a larger ship than that which had brought the Apaches, but of the same shape.

"The horse herd ... to the west." Nolan evaluated the scene with the eyes of an experienced raider. "Tsoay, Deklay, you take the horses!"

They nodded, and began the long crawl which would take them two miles or more from the party to stampede the horses.

To the Mongols in those domelike yurts horses were wealth, life itself. They would come running to investigate any disturbance among the grazing ponies, thus clearing the path to the ship and the Reds there. Travis, Jil-Lee, and Buck, armed with the star guns, would spearhead that attack—cutting into the substance of the ship itself until it was a sieve through which they could shake out the enemy. Only when the installations it contained were destroyed, might the Apaches hope for any assistance from the Mongols, either the outlaw pack waiting well back on the prairie or the people in the yurts.

The grass rippled and Naginlta poked out a nose, parting stems before Travis. The Apache beamed an order, sending the coyotes with the horse-raiding party. He had seen how the animals could drive hunted split-horns; they would do as well with the ponies.

Kaydessa was safe, the coyotes had made that clear by the fact that they had joined the attacking party an hour earlier. With Eskelta and Manulito she was on her way back to the north.

Travis supposed he should be well pleased that their reckless plan had succeeded as well as it had. But when he thought of the Tatar girl, all he could see was her convulsed face close to his in the ship corridor, her raking nails raised to tear his cheek. She had an excellent reason to hate him, yet he hoped....

They continued to watch both horse herd and domes. There were people moving about the yurts, but no signs of life at the ship. Had the Reds shut themselves in there, warned in some way of the two disasters which had whittled down their forces?

"Ah—!" Nolan breathed.

One of the ponies had raised its head and was facing the direction of the camp, suspicion plain to read in its stance. The Apaches must have reached the point between the herd and the domes which had been their goal. And the Mongol guard, who had been sitting cross-legged, the reins of his mount dangling close to his hand, got to his feet.

"Ahhhuuuuu!" The ancient Apache war cry that had sounded across deserts, canyons, and southwestern Terran plains to ice the blood, ripped just as freezingly through the honey-hued air of Topaz.

The horses wheeled, racing upslope away from the settlement. A figure broke from the grass, flapped his arms at one of the mounts, grabbed at flying mane, and pulled himself up on the bare back. Only a master horseman would have done that, but the whooping rider now drove the herd on, assisted by the snapping and snarling coyotes.

"Deklay—" Jil-Lee identified the reckless rider, "that was one of his rodeo tricks."

Among the yurts it was as if someone had ripped up a rotten log to reveal an ants' nest and sent the alarmed insects into a frenzy. Men boiled out of the domes, the majority of them running for the horse pasture. One or two were mounted on ponies that must have been staked out in the settlement. The main war party of Apaches skimmed silently through the grass on their way to the ship.

The three who were armed with the alien weapons had already tested their range by experimentation back in the hills, but the fear of exhausting whatever powered those barrels had curtailed their target practice. Now they snaked to the edge of the bare ground between them and the ladder hatch of the spacer. To cross that open space was to provide targets for lances and arrows—or the superior armament of the Reds.

"A chance we can hit from here." Buck laid his weapon across his bent knee, steadied the long barrel of the burner, and pressed the firing button.

The closed hatch of the ship shimmered, dissolved into a black hole. Behind Travis someone let out the yammer of a war whoop.

"Fire—cut the walls to pieces!"

Travis did not need that order from Jil-Lee. He was already beaming unseen destruction at the best target he could ask for—the side of the sphere. If the globe was armed, there was no weapon which could be depressed far enough to reach the marksmen at ground level.

Holes appeared, irregular gaps and tears in the fabric of the ship. The Apaches were turning the side of the globe into lacework. How far those rays penetrated into the interior they could not guess.

Movement at one of the holes, the chattering burst of machine-gun fire, spatters of soil and gravel into their faces; they could be cut to pieces by that! The hole enlarged, a scream ... cut off....

"They will not be too quick to try that again," Nolan observed with cold calm from behind Travis' post.

Methodically they continued to beam the ship. It would never be space-borne again; there were neither the skills nor materials here to repair such damage.

"It is like laying a knife to fat," Lupe said as he crawled up beside Travis. "Slice, slice—!"

"Move!" Travis reached to the left, pulled at Jil-Lee's shoulder.

Travis did not know whether it was possible or not, but he had a heady vision of their combined fire power cutting the globe in half, slicing it crosswise with the ease Lupe admired.

They scurried through cover just as someone behind yelled a warning. Travis threw himself down, rolled into a new firing position. An arrow sang over his head; the Reds were doing what the Apaches had known they would—calling in the controlled Mongols to fight. The attack on the ship must be stepped up, or the Amerindians would be forced to retreat.

Already a new lacing of holes appeared under their concentrated efforts. With the gun held tight to his middle, Travis found his feet, zigzagged across the bare ground for the nearest of those openings. Another arrow clanged harmlessly against the fabric of the ship a foot from his goal.

He made it in, over jagged metal shards which glowed faintly and reeked of ozone. The weapons' beams had penetrated well past both the outer shell and the wall of insulation webbing. He climbed a second and smaller break into a corridor enough like those of the western ship to be familiar. The Red spacer, based on the general plan of the alien derelict ship as his own had been, could not be very different.

Travis tried to subdue his heavy breathing and listen. He heard a confused shouting and the burr of what might be an alarm system. The ship's brain was the control cabin. Even if the Reds dared not try to lift now, that was the core of their communication lines. He started along the corridor, trying to figure out its orientation in relation to that all-important nerve center.

The Apache shoved open each door he passed with one shoulder, and twice he played a light beam on installations within cabins. He had no idea of their use, but the wholesale destruction of each and every machine was what good sense and logic dictated.

There was a sound behind. Travis whirled, saw Jil-Lee and beyond him Buck.

"Up?" Jil-Lee asked.

"And down," Buck added. "The Tatars say they have hollowed a bunker beneath."

"Separate and do as much damage as you can," Travis suggested.

"Agreed!"

Travis sped on. He passed another door and then backtracked hurriedly as he realized it had given on to an engine room. With the gun he blasted two long lines cutting the fittings into ragged lumps. Abruptly the lights went out; the burr of the alarms was silenced. Part of the ship, if not all, was dead. And now it might come to hunter and hunted in the dark. But that was an advantage as far as the Apaches were concerned.

Back in the corridor again, Travis crept through a curiously lifeless atmosphere. The shouting was stilled as if the sudden failure of the machines had stunned the Reds.

A tiny sound—perhaps the scrape of a boot on a ladder. Travis edged back into a compartment. A flash of light momentarily lighted the corridor; the approaching figure was using a torch. Travis drew his knife with one hand, reversed it so he could use the heavy hilt as a silencer. The other was hurrying now, on his way to investigate the burned-out engine cabin. Travis could hear the rasp of his fast breathing. Now!

The Apache had put down the gun, his left arm closed about a shoulder, and the Red gasped as Travis struck with the knife hilt. Not clean—he had to hit a second time before the struggles of the man were over. Then, using his hands for eyes, he stripped the limp body on the floor of automatic and torch.

With the Red's weapon in the front of his sash, the burner in one hand and the torch in the other, Travis prowled on. There was a good chance that those above might believe him to be their comrade returning. He found the ladder leading to the next level, began to climb, pausing now and then to listen.

Shock preceded sound. Under him the ladder swayed and the globe itself rocked a little. A blast of some kind must have been set off at or under the level of the ground. The bunker Buck had mentioned?

Travis clung to the ladder, waited for the vibrations to subside. There was a shouting above, a questioning.... Hurriedly he ascended to the next level, scrambled out and away from the ladder just in time to avoid the light from another torch flashed down the well. Again that call of inquiry, then a shot—the boom of the explosion loud in the confined space.

To climb into the face of that light with a waiting marksman above was sheer folly. Could there be another way up? Travis retreated down one of the corridors raying out from the ladder well. A quick inspection of the cabins along that route told him he had reached a section of living quarters. The pattern was familiar; the control cabin would be on the next level.

Suddenly the Apache remembered something: On each level there should be an emergency opening giving access to the insulation space between the inner and outer skins of the ship through which repairs could be made. If he could find that and climb up to the next level....

The light shining down the well remained steady, and there was the echoing crack of another shot. But Travis was far enough away from the ladder now to dare use his own torch, seeking the door he needed on the wall surface. With a leap of heart he sighted the outline—his luck was in! The Russian and western ships were alike.

Once the panel was open he flashed his torch up, finding the climbing rungs and, above, the shadow outline of the next level opening. Securing the alien gun in his sash beside the automatic and holding the torch in his mouth, Travis climbed, not daring to think of the deep drop below. Four ... five ... ten rungs, and he could reach the other door.

His fingers slid over it, searching for the release catch. But there was no answering give. Balling his fist, he struck down at an awkward angle and almost lost his balance as the panel fell away beneath his blow. The door swung and he pulled through.

Darkness! Travis snapped on the torch for an instant, saw about him the relays of a com system, and gave it a full spraying as he pivoted, destroying the eyes and ears of the ship—unless the burnout he had effected below had already done that. A flash of automatic fire from his left, a searing burn along his arm an inch or so below the shoulder—

Travis' action was purely reflex. He swung the burner around, even as his mind gave a frantic No! To defend himself with automatic, knife, arrow—yes; but not this way. He huddled against the wall.

An instant earlier there had been a man there, a living, breathing man—one of his own species, if not of his own beliefs. Then because his own muscles had unconsciously obeyed warrior training, there was this. So easy—to deal death without really meaning to. The weapon in his hands was truly the devil gift they were right to fear. Such weapons were not to be put into the hands of men—any men—no matter how well intentioned.

Travis gulped in great mouthfuls of air. He wanted to throw the burner away, hurl it from him. But the task he could rightfully use it for was not yet done.

Somehow he reeled on into the control cabin to render the ship truly a dead thing and free himself of the heavy burden of guilt and terror between his hands. That weight could be laid aside; memory could not. And no one of his kind must ever have to carry such memories again.

  * * * * *

The booming of the drums was like a pulse quickening the blood to a rhythm which bit at the brain, made a man's eyes shine, his muscles tense as if he held an arrow to bow cord or arched his fingers about a knife hilt. A fire blazed high and in its light men leaped and whirled in a mad dance with tulwar blades catching and reflecting the red gleam of flames. Mad, wild, the Mongols were drunk with victory and freedom. Beyond them, the silver globe of the ship showed the black holes of its death, which was also the death of the past—for all of them.

"What now?" Menlik, the dangling of amulets and charms tinkling as he moved, came up to Travis. There was none of the wild fervor in the shaman's face; instead, it was as if he had taken several strides out of the life of the Horde, was emerging into another person, and the question he asked was one they all shared.

Travis felt drained, flattened. They had achieved their purpose. The handful of Red overlords were dead, their machines burned out. There were no controls here any more; men were free in mind and body. What were they to do with that freedom?

"First," the Apache spoke his own thoughts—"we must return these."

The three alien weapons were lashed into a square of Mongol fabric, hidden from sight, although they could not be so easily shut out of mind. Only a few of the others, Apache or Mongol, had seen them; and they must be returned before their power was generally known.

"I wonder if in days to come," Buck mused, "they will not say that we pulled lightning out of the sky, as did the Thunder Slayer, to aid us. But this is right. We must return them and make that valley and what it holds taboo."

"And what if another ship comes—one of *yours?*" Menlik asked shrewdly.

Travis stared beyond the Tatar shaman to the men about the fire. His nightmare dragged into the open.... What if a ship did come in, one with Ashe, Murdock, men he knew and liked, friends on board? What then of his guardianship of the towers and their knowledge? Could he be as sure of what to do then? He rubbed his hand across his forehead and said slowly:

"We shall take steps when—or if—that happens—"

But could they, would they? He began to hope fiercely that it would not happen, at least in his lifetime, and then felt the cold bleakness of the exile they must will themselves into.

"Whether we like it or not," (was he talking to the others or trying to argue down his own rebellion?) "we cannot let what lies under the towers be known ... found ... used ... unless by men who are wiser and more controlled than we are in our time."

Menlik drew his shaman's wand, twiddled it between his fingers, and beneath his drooping lids watched the three Apaches with a new kind of measurement.

"Then I say to you this: Such a guardianship must be a double charge, shared by my people as well. For if they suspect that you alone control these powers and their secret, there will be envy, hatred, fear, a division between us from the first—war ... raids.... This is a large land and neither of our groups numbers many. Shall we split apart fatally from this day when there is room for all? If these ancient things are evil, then let us both guard them with a common taboo."

He was right, of course. And they would have to face the truth squarely. To both Apache and Mongol any off-world ship, no matter from which side, would be a menace. Here was where they would remain and set roots. The sooner they began thinking of themselves as people with a common bond, the better it would be. And Menlik's suggestion provided a tie.

"You speak well," Buck was saying. "This shall be a thing we share. We are three who know. Do you be three also, but choose well, Menlik!"

"Be assured that I will!" the Tatar returned. "We start a new life here; there is no going back. But as I have said: The land is wide. We have no quarrel with one another, and perhaps our two peoples shall become one; after all, we do not differ too greatly...." He smiled and gestured to the fire and the dancers.

Among the Mongols another man had gone into action, his head thrown back as he leaped and twirled, voicing a deep war cry. Travis recognized Deklay. Apache, Mongol—both raiders, horsemen, hunters, fighters when the need arose. No, there was no great difference. Both had been tricked into coming here, and they had no allegiance now for those who had sent them.

Perhaps clan and Horde would combine or perhaps they would drift apart—time would tell. But there would be the bond of the guardianship, the determination that what slept in the towers would not be roused—in their lifetime or many lifetimes!

Travis smiled a bit crookedly. A new religion of sorts, a priesthood with sacred and forbidden knowledge ... in time a whole new life and civilization stemming from this night. The bleak cold of his early thought cut less deep. There was a different kind of adventure here.

He reached out and gathered up the bundle of the burners, glancing from Buck to Jil-Lee to Menlik. Then he stood up, the weight of the burden in his arms, the feeling of a greater weight inside him.

"Shall we go?"

To get the weapons back—that was of first importance. Maybe then he could sleep soundly, to dream of riding across the Arizona range at dawn under a blue sky with a wind in his face, a wind carrying the scent of piñon pine and sage, a wind which would never caress or hearten him again, a wind his sons and sons' sons would never know. To dream troubled dreams, and hope in time those dreams would fade and thin—that a new world would blanket out the old. Better so, Travis told himself with defiance and determination—better so!

KEY OUT OF TIME

CONTENTS

LOTUS WORLD

There was a shading of rose in the pearl arch of sky, deepening at the horizon meeting of sea and air in a rainbow tint of cloud. The lazy swells of the ocean held the same soft color, darkened with crimson veins where spirals of weed drifted. A rose world bathed in soft sunlight, knowing only gentle winds, peace, and—sloth.

Ross Murdock leaned forward over the edge of the rock ledge to peer down at a beach of fine sand, pale pink sand with here and there a glitter of a crystalline "shell"—or were those delicate, fluted ovals shells? Even the waves came in languidly. And the breeze which ruffled his hair, smoothed about his sun-browned, half-bare body, caressed it, did not buffet on its way inland to stir the growths which the Terran settlers called "trees" but which possessed long lacy fronds instead of true branches.

Hawaika—named for the old Polynesian paradise—a world seemingly without flaw except the subtle one of being too perfect, too welcoming, too wooing. Its long, uneventful, unchanging days enticed forgetfulness, offered a life without effort. Except for the mystery....

Because this world was not the one pictured on the tape which had brought the Terran settlement team here. A map, a directing guide, a description all in one, that was the ancient voyage tape. Ross himself had helped to loot a storehouse on an unknown planet for a cargo of such tapes. Once they had been the space-navigation guides for a race or races who had ruled the star lanes ten thousand years in his own world's past, a civilization which had long since sunk again into the dust of its beginning.

Those tapes returned to Terra after their chance discovery, were studied, probed, deciphered by the best brains of his time, shared out by lot between already suspicious Terran powers, bringing into the exploration of space bitter rivalries and old hatreds.

Such a tape had landed their ship on Hawaika, a world of shallow seas and archipelagoes instead of true continents. The settlement team had had all the knowledge contained on that tape crowded into them, only to discover that much they had learned from it was false!

Of course, none of them had expected to discover here still the cities, the civilization the tape had projected as existing in that long-ago period. But no present island string they had visited approximated those on the maps they had seen, and so far they had not found any trace that any intelligent beings had walked, built, lived, on these beautiful, slumberous atolls. So, what had happened to the Hawaika of the tape?

Ross's right hand rubbed across the ridged scars which disfigured his left one, to be carried for the rest of his life as a mark of his meeting with the star voyagers in the past of his own world. He had deliberately seared his own flesh to break the mental control they had asserted. Then the battle had gone to him. But from it he had brought another scar—the unease of that old terror when Ross Murdock, fighter, rebel, outlaw by the conventions of his own era, Ross Murdock who considered himself an exceedingly tough individual, that toughness steeled by the training for Time Agent sorties, had come up against a power he did not understand, instinctively hated and feared.

Now he breathed deeply of the wind—the smell of the sea, the scents of the land growths, strange but pleasant. So easy to relax, to drop into the soft, lulling swing of this world in which they had found no fault, no danger, no irritant. Yet, once those others had been here—the blue-suited, hairless ones he called "Baldies." And what had happened then ... or afterward?

A black head, brown shoulders, slender body, broke the sleepy slip of the waves. A shimmering mask covered the face, catching glitter-fire in the sun. Two hands freed a chin curved yet firmly set, a mouth made more for laughter than sternness, wide dark eyes. Karara Trehern of the Alii, the one-time Hawaiian god-chieftain line, was an exceedingly pretty girl.

But Ross regarded her aloofly, with a coldness which bordered on hostility, as she flipped her mask into its pocket on top of the gill-pack. Below his rocky perch she came to a halt, her feet slightly apart in the sand, an impish twist to her lips as she called mockingly:

"Why not come in? The water's fine."

"Perfect, like all the rest of this." Some of his impatience came out in the sour tone. "No luck, as usual?"

"As usual," Karara conceded. "If there ever was a civilization here, it's been gone so long we'll probably never find any traces. Why don't you just pick out a good place to set up that time-probe and try it blind?"

Ross scowled. "Because"—his patience was exaggerated to the point of insult—"we have only one peep-probe. Once it's set we can't tear it down easily for transport somewhere else, so we want to be sure there's something to look at beyond."

She began to wring the water out of her long hair. "Well, as far as we've explored ... nothing. Come yourself next time. Tino-rau and Taua aren't particular; they like company."

Putting two fingers to her mouth, Karara whistled. Twin heads popped out of the water, facing the shore and her. Projecting noses, mouths with upturned corners so they curved in a lasting pleasant grin at the mammals on the shore—the dolphin pair, mammals whose ancestors had chosen the sea, whistled back in such close counterfeit of the girl's signal that they could be an echo of her call. Years earlier their species' intelligence had surprised, almost shocked, men. Experiments, training, co-operation, had developed a tie which gave the water-limited race of mankind new eyes, ears, minds, to see, evaluate, and report concerning an element in which the bipeds were not free.

Hand in hand with that co-operation had gone other experiments. Just as the clumsy armored diving suits of the early twentieth century had allowed man to begin penetration into a weird new world, so had the frog-man equipment made him still freer in the sea. And now the gill-pack which separated the needed oxygen from the water made even that lighter burden of tanks obsolete. But there remained depths into which man could not descend, whose secrets were closed to him. There the dolphins operated, in a partnership of minds, equal minds—though that last fact had been difficult for man to accept.

Ross's irritation, unjustified as he knew it to be, did not rest on Tino-rau or Taua. He enjoyed the hours when he buckled on gill-pack and took to the sea with those two ten-foot, black-and-silver escorts sharing the action. But Karara ... Karara's presence was a different matter altogether.

The Agents' teams had always been strictly masculine. Two men partnered for an interlocking of abilities and temperaments, going through training together, becoming two halves of a strong and efficient whole. Before being summarily recruited into the Project, Ross had been a loner—living on the ragged edges of the law, an indigestible bit for the civilization which had become too ordered and "adjusted" to absorb his kind. But in the Project he had discovered others like himself—men born out of time, too ruthless, too individualistic for their own age, but able to operate with ease in the dangerous paths of the Time Agents.

And when the time search for the wrecked alien ships had succeeded and the first intact ship found, used, duplicated, the Agents had come from forays into the past to be trained anew for travel to the stars. First there had been Ross Murdock, criminal. Then there had been Ross Murdock and Gordon Ashe, Time Agents. Now there was still Ross and Gordon and a quest as perilous as any they had known. Yet this time they had to depend upon Karara and the dolphins.

"Tomorrow"—Ross was still not sorting out his thoughts, truly aware of the feeling which worked upon him as a thorn in the finger—"I will come."

"Good!" If she recognized his hostility for what it was, that did not bother her. Once more she whistled to the dolphins, waved a casual farewell with one hand, and headed up the beach toward the base camp. Ross chose a more rugged path over the cliff.

Suppose they did not find what they sought near here? Yet the old taped map suggested that this was approximately the site starred upon it. Marking a city? A star port?

Ashe had volunteered for Hawaika, demanded this job after the disastrous Topaz affair when the team of Apache volunteers had been sent out too soon to counter what might have been a Red sneak settlement. Ross was still unhappy over the ensuing months when only Major Kelgarries and maybe, in a lesser part, Ross had kept Gordon Ashe in the Project at all. That Topaz had been a failure was accepted when the settlement ship did not return. And that had added to Ashe's sense of guilt for having recruited and partially trained the lost team.

Among those dispatched over Ashe's vehement protests had been Travis Fox who had shared with Ashe and Ross the first galactic flight in an age-old derelict spaceship. Travis Fox—the Apache archaeologist—had he ever reached Topaz? Or would he and his team wander forever between worlds? Did they set down on a planet where some inimical form of native life or a Red settlement had awaited them? The very uncertainty of their fate continued to ride Ashe.

So he insisted on coming out with the second settlement team, the volunteers of Samoan and Hawaiian descent, to carry on a yet more exciting and hazardous exploration. Just as the Project had probed into the past of Terra, so would Ashe and Ross now attempt to discover what lay in the past of Hawaika, to see this world as it had been at the height of the galactic civilization, and so to learn what they could about their fore-runners into space. And the mystery they had dropped into upon landing added to the necessity for that discovery or discoveries.

Their probe, if fortune favored them, might become a gate through time. The installation was a vast improvement over these passage points they had first devised. Technical information had taken a vast leap forward after Terran engineers and scientists had had access to the tapes of the stellar empire. Adaptations and shortcuts developed, so that a new hybrid technology came into use, woven from the knowledge and experimentation of two civilizations thousands of years apart in time.

If and when he or Ashe—or Karara and her dolphins—discovered the proper site, the two Agents could set up their own equipment. Both Ross and Ashe had had enough drill in the process. All they needed was the brick of discovery; then they could build their wall. But they must find some remainder of the past, the smallest trace of ancient ruin upon which to center their peep-probe. And since landing here the long days had flowed into weeks with no such discovery made.

Ross crossed the ridge of rock which formed a cocks-comb rise on the island's spine and descended to the village. As they had been trained, the Polynesian settlers adapted native products to their own heritage of building and tools. It was necessary that they live off the land, for their transport ship had had storage space only for a limited number of supplies and tools. After it took off to return home they would be wholly on their own for several years. Their ship, a silvery ball, rested on a rock ledge, its pilot and crew having lingered to learn the results of Ashe's search. Four days more and they would have to lift for home even if the Agents still had only negative results to report.

That disappointment was driving Ashe, the way that six months earlier his outrage and guilt feelings over the Topaz affair had driven him. Karara's suggestion carried weight the longer Ross thought about it. With more swimmers hunting, there was just that much increased chance of turning up some clue. So far the dolphins had not reported any dangerous native sea life or any perils except the natural ones any diver always had at his shoulder under the waves.

There were extra gill-packs, and all of the settlers were good swimmers. An organized hunt ought to shake the Polynesians out of their present do-it-tomorrow attitude. As long as they had had definite work before them—the unloading of the ship, the building of the village, all the labors incidental to the establishing of this base—they had shown energy and enthusiasm. It was only during the last couple of weeks that the languor which appeared part of the atmosphere here had crept up on them, so that now they were content to live at a slower and lazier pace. Ross remembered Ashe's comparison made the evening before, likening Hawaika to a legendary Terran island where the inhabitants lived a drugged existence, feeding upon the seeds of a native plant. Hawaika was fast becoming a lotus land for Terrans.

"Through here, then westward...." Ashe hunched over the crate table in the mat-walled house. He did not look up as Ross entered. Karara's still damp head was bowed until those black locks, now sleeked to her round skull, almost touched the man's close-cropped brown hair. They were both studying a map as if they saw not lines on paper but the actual inlets and lagoons which that drawing represented.

"You are sure, Gordon, that this *is* the modern point to match the site on the tape?" The girl brushed back straying hair.

Ashe shrugged. There were tight brackets about his mouth which had not been there six months ago. He moved jerkily, not with the fluid grace of those old days when he had faced the vast distance of time travel with unruffled calm and a self-confidence to steady and support the novice Ross.

"The general outline of these two islands could stand for the capes on this—" He pulled a second map, this on transparent plastic, to fit over the first. The capes marked on the much larger body of land did slip over the modern islands with a surprising fit. The once large island, shattered and broken, could have produced the groups of atolls and islets they now prospected.

"How long—" Karara mused aloud, "and why?"

Ashe shrugged. "Ten thousand years, five, two." He shook his head. "We have no idea. It's apparent that there must have been some world-wide cataclysm here to change the contours of the land masses so much. We may have to wait on a return space flight to bring a 'copter or a hydroplane to explore farther." His hand swept beyond the boundaries of the map to indicate the whole of Hawaika.

"A year, maybe two, before we could hope for that," Ross cut in. "Then we'll have to depend on whether the Council believes this important enough." The contrariness which spiked his tongue whenever Karara was present made him say that without thinking. Then the twitch of Ashe's lip brought home Ross's error. Gordon needed reassurance now, not a recitation of the various ways their mission could be doomed.

"Look here!" Ross came to the table, his hand sweeping past Karara, as he used his forefinger for a pointer. "We know that what we want could be easily overlooked, even with the dolphins helping us to check. This whole area's too big. And you know that it is certain that whatever might be down there would be hidden with sea growths. Suppose ten of us start out in a semi-circle from about here and go as far as this point, heading inland. Video-cameras here and here ... comb the whole sector inch by inch if we have to. After all, we have plenty of time and manpower."

Karara laughed softly. "Manpower—always manpower, Ross? But there is woman-power, too. And we have perhaps even sharper sight. But this is a good idea, Gordon. Let me see—" she began to tell off names on her fingers, "PaKeeKee, Vaeoha, Hori, Liliha, Taema, Ui, Hono'ura—they are the best in the water. Me ... you, Gordon, Ross. That makes ten with keen eyes to look, and always there are Tino-rau and Taua. We will take supplies and camp here on this island which looks so much like a finger crooked to beckon. Yes, somehow that beckoning finger seems to me to promise better fortune. Shall we plan it so?"

Some of the tight look was gone from Ashe's face, and Ross relaxed. This was what Gordon needed—not to be sitting in here going over maps, reports, reworking over and over their scant leads. Ashe had always been a field man; and the settlement work had been stultifying, a laborious chore for him.

When Karara had gone Ross dropped down on the bunk against the side wall.

"What *did* happen here, do you think?" Half was real interest in the mystery they had mulled over and over since they had landed on a Hawaika which diverged so greatly from the maps; the other half, a desire to keep Ashe thinking on a subject removed from immediate worries. "An atomic war?"

"Could be. There are old radiation traces. But these aliens had, I'm sure, progressed beyond atomics. Suppose, just suppose, they could tamper with the weather, with the balance of the planet's crust? We don't know the extent of their powers, how they would use them. They had a colony here once, or there would have been no guide tape. And that is all we are sure of."

"Suppose"—Ross rolled over on his stomach, pillowed his head on his arms—"we could uncover some of that knowledge—"

The twitch was back at Ashe's lips. "That's the risk we have to run now."

"Risk?"

"Would you give a child one of those hand weapons we found in the derelict?"

"Naturally not!" Ross snapped and then saw the point. "You mean—*we* aren't to be trusted?"

The answer was plain to read in Ashe's expression.

"Then why this whole setup, this hunt for what might mean trouble?"

"The old pinch, the bad one. What if the Reds discover something first? They drew some planets in the tape lottery, remember. It's a seesaw between us—we advance here, they there. We have to keep up the race or lose it. They must be combing their stellar colonies for a few answers just as furiously as we are."

"So, we go into the past to hunt if we have to. Well, I think I could do without answers such as the Baldies would know. But I will admit that I would like to know what did happen here—two, five, ten thousand years ago."

Ashe stood up and stretched. For the first time he smiled. "Do you know, I rather like the idea of fishing off Karara's beckoning finger. Maybe she's right about that changing our luck."

Ross kept his face carefully expressionless as he got up to prepare their evening meal.

LAIR OF MANO-NUI

Just under the surface of the water the sea was warm, weird life showed colors Ross could name, shades he could not. The corals, the animals masquerading as plants, the plants disguised as animals which inhabited the oceans of Terra, had their counterparts here. And the settlers had given them the familiar names, though the crabs, the fish, the anemones, and weeds of the shallow lagoons and reefs were not identical with Terran creatures. The trouble was that there was too much, such a wealth of life to attract the eyes, hold attention, that it was difficult to keep to the job at hand—the search for what was not natural, for what had no normal place here.

As the land seduced the senses and bewitched the off-worlder, so did the sea have its enchantment to pull one from duty. Ross resolutely skimmed by a forest of weaving, waving lace which varied from a green which was almost black to a pale tint he could not truly identify. Among those waving fans lurked ghost-fish, finned swimmers transparent enough so that one could sight, through their pallid sides, the evidences of recently ingested meals.

The Terrans had begun their sweep-search a half hour ago, slipping overboard from a ferry canoe, heading in toward the checkpoint of the finger isle, forming an arc of expert divers, men and girls so at home in the ocean that they should be able to make the discovery Ashe needed—if such did exist.

Mystery built upon mystery on Hawaika, Ross thought as he used his spear-gun to push aside a floating banner of weed in order to peer below its curtain. The native life of this world must always have been largely aquatic. The settlers had discovered only a few small animals on the islands. The largest of which was the burrower, a creature not unlike a miniature monkey in that it had hind legs on which it walked erect and forepaws, well clawed for digging purposes, which it used with as much skill and dexterity as a man used hands. Its body was hairless and it was able to assume, chameleon-like, the color of the soil and rocks where it denned. The head was set directly on its bowed shoulders without vestige of neck; and it had round bubbles of eyes near the top of its skull, a nose which was a single vertical slit, and a wide mouth fanged for crushing the shelled creatures on which it fed. All in all, to Terran eyes, it was a vaguely repulsive creature, but as far as the settlers had been able to discover it was the highest form of land life. The smaller rodentlike things, the two species of wingless diving birds, and an odd assortment of reptiles and amphibians sharing the island were all the burrowers' prey.

A world of sea and islands, what type of native intelligent life had it once supported? Or had this been only a galactic colony, with no native population before the coming of the stellar explorers? Ross hovered above a dark pocket where the bottom had suddenly dipped into a saucer-shaped depression. The sea growth about the rim rippled in the water raggedly, but there was something about its general outline....

Ross began a circumference of that hollow. Allowing for the distortion of the growths which had formed lumpy excrescences or reached turrets toward the surface—yes, allowing for those—this was decidedly something out of the ordinary! The depression was too regular, too even, Ross was certain of that. With a thrill of excitement he began a descent into the cup, striving to trace signs which would prove his suspicion correct.

How many years, centuries, had the slow coverage of the sea life gathered there, flourished, died, with other creatures to build anew on the remains? Now there was only a hint that the depression had other than a natural beginning.

Anchoring with a one-handed grip on a spike of Hawaikan coral—smoother than the Terran species—Ross aimed the butt of his spear-gun at the nearest wall of the saucer, striving to reach into a crevice between two lumps of growth and so probe into what might lie behind. The spear rebounded; there was no breaking that crust with such a fragile tool. But perhaps he would have better luck lower down.

The depression was deeper than he had first judged. Now the light which existed in the shallows vanished. Red and yellow as colors went, but Ross was aware of blues and greens in shades and tints which were not visible above. He switched on his diving torch, and color returned within its beam. A swirl of weed, pink in the light, became darkly emerald beyond as if it possessed the chameleon ability of the burrowers.

He was distracted by that phenomenon, and so he transgressed the diver's rule of never becoming so absorbed in surroundings as to forget caution. Just when did Ross become aware of that shadow below? Was it when a school of ghost-fish burst unexpectedly between weed growths, and he turned to follow them with the torch? Then the outer edge of his beam caught the movement of a shape, a flutter in the water of the gloomy depths.

Ross swung around, his back to the wall of the saucer, as he aimed the torch down at what was arising there. The light caught and held for a long moment of horror something which might have come out of the nightmares of his own world. Afterward Ross knew that the monster was not as large as it seemed in that endless minute of fear, perhaps no bigger than the dolphins.

He had had training in shark-infested seas on Terra, been carefully briefed against the danger from such hunters of the deep and ocean jungles. But this kind of thing had only existed before in the fairy tales of his race as the dragon of old lore. A scaled head with wide eyes gleaming in the light beam with cold and sullen hate, a gaping mouth fang-filled, a horn-set muzzle, that long, undulating neck and, below it, the half-seen bulk of a monstrous body.

His spear-gun, the knife at his waist belt, neither were protection against this! Yet to turn his back on that rising head was more than Ross could do. He pulled himself back against the wall of the saucer. The thing before him did not rush to attack. Plainly it had seen him and now it moved with the leisure of a hunter having no fears concerning the eventual outcome of the hunt. But the light appeared to puzzle it and Ross kept the beam shining straight into those evil eyes.

The shock of the encounter was wearing off; now Ross edged his flipper into a crevice to hold him steady while his hand went to the sonic-com at his waist. He tapped out a distress call which the dolphins could relay to the swimmers. The swaying dragon head paused, held rigid on a stiff, scaled column in the center of the saucer. That sonic vibration either surprised or bothered the hunter, made it wary.

Ross tapped again. The belief that if he tried to escape, he was lost, that only while he faced it so had he any chance, grew stronger. The head was only inches below the level of his flippered feet as he held to the weeds.

Again that weaving movement, the rise of head, a tremor along the serpent neck, an agitation in the depths. The dragon was on the move again. Ross aimed the light directly at the head. The scales, as far as he could determine, were not horny plates but lapped, silvery ovals such as a fish possessed. And the underparts of the monster might even be vulnerable to his spear. But knowing the way a Terran shark could absorb the darts of that weapon and survive, Ross feared to attack except as a last resort.

Above and to his left there was a small hollow where in the past some portion of the growths had been ripped away. If he could fit himself into that crevice, perhaps he could keep the dragon at bay until help arrived. Ross moved with all the skill he had. His hand closed upon the edge of the niche and he whirled himself up, just making it into that refuge as the head lashed at him wickedly. His suspicion that the dragon would attack anything on the run was well founded, and he knew he had no hope of winning to the surface above.

Now he stood in the crevice, facing outward, watching the head darting in the water. He had switched off the torch, and the loss of light appeared to bewilder the reptile for some precious seconds. Ross pulled as far back into the niche as he could, until the point of one shoulder touched a surface which was sleek, smooth, and cold. The shock of that contact almost sent him hurtling out again.

Gripping the spear before him in his right hand, Ross cautiously felt behind him with the left. His finger tips glided over a seamless surface where the growths had been torn or peeled away. Though he could not, or dared not, turn his head to see, he was certain that this was his proof that the walls of the saucer had been fashioned and placed there by some intelligent creature.

The dragon had risen, hovering now in the water directly before the entrance to Ross's hole, its neck curled back against its bulk. It had wide flippers moving like planes to hold it poised. The body, sloping from a massive round of shoulders to a tapering rear, was vaguely familiar. If one provided a Terran seal with a gorgon head and scales in place of fur, the effect would be similar. But Ross was assuredly not facing a seal at this moment.

Slight movement of the flippers kept it as stabilized as if it sprawled on a supporting surface. With the neck flattened against the body, the head curved downward until the horn on its snout pointed the tip straight at Ross's middle. The Terran steadied his spear-gun. The dragon's eyes were its most vulnerable targets; if the creature launched the attack, Ross would aim for them.

Both man and dragon were so intent upon their duel that neither was conscious of the sudden swirl overhead. A sleek dark shape struck down, skimming across the humped-back ridge of the dragon. Some of the settlers had empathy with the dolphins to a high degree, but Ross's own powers of contact were relatively feeble.

Only now he was given an assurance of aid, and a suggestion to attack. The dragon head writhed, twisted as the reptile attempted to see above and behind its own length. But the dolphin was only a streak fast disappearing. And that writhing changed the balance the monster had maintained, pushing it toward Ross.

The Terran fired too soon and without proper aim, so the dart snaked past the head. But the harpoon line half hooked about the neck and seemed to confuse the creature. Ross squirmed as far back as he could into his refuge and drew his knife. Against those fangs the weapon was an almost useless toy, but it was all he had.

Again the dolphin dived in attack on the reptile, this time seizing in its mouth the floating cord of the harpoon and giving it a jerk which jolted the dragon even more off balance, pulling it away from Ross's niche and out into the center of the saucer.

There were two dolphins in action now, Ross saw, playing the dragon as matadors might play a bull, keeping the creature disturbed by their agile maneuvers. Whatever prey came naturally to the Hawaikan monster was not of this type, and the creature was not prepared to deal effectively with their teasing, dodging tactics. Neither had touched the beast, but they kept it constantly striving to get at them.

Though it swam in circles attempting to face its teasers, the dragon did not abandon the level before Ross's refuge, and now and then it darted its head at him, unwilling to give up its prey. Only one of the dolphins frisked and dodged above now as the sonic on Ross's belt vibrated against his lower ribs with its message warning to be prepared for further action. Somewhere above, his own kind gathered. Hurriedly he tapped out in code his warning in return.

Two dolphins busy again, their last dive over the dragon pushing the monster down past Ross's niche toward the saucer's depths. Then they flashed up and away. The dragon was rising in turn, but coming to meet the Hawaikan creature was a ball giving off light, bringing sharp vision and color with it.

Ross's arm swung up to shield his eyes. There was a flash; such answering vibration carried through the waves that even his nerves, far less sensitive than those of the life about him, reacted. He blinked behind his mask. A fish floated by, spiraling up, its belly exposed. And about him growths drooped, trailed lifelessly through the water; while there was a now motionless bulk sinking to the obscurity of the depression floor. A weapon perfected on Terra to use against sharks and barracuda had worked here to kill what could have been more formidable prey.

The Terran wriggled out of the niche, rose to meet another swimmer. As Ashe descended, Ross relayed his news via the sonic. The dolphins were already nosing into the depths in pursuit of their late enemy.

"Look here—" Ross guided Ashe to the crevice which had saved him, aimed the torch beam into it. He had been right! There was a long groove in the covering built up by the growths; a vertical strip some six feet long, of a uniform gray, showed. Ashe touched the find and then gave the alert via the sonic code.

"Metal or an alloy, we've found it!"

But what did they have? Even after an hour's exploration by the full company, Ashe's expert search with his knowledge of artifacts and ancient remains, they were still baffled. It would require labor and tools they did not have, to clear the whole of the saucer. They could be sure only of its size and shape, and the fact that its walls were of an unknown substance which the sea could cloak but not erode. For the length of gray surface showed not the slightest pitting or time wear.

Down at its centermost point they found the dragon's den, an arch coated with growth, before which sprawled the body of the creature. That was dragged aloft with the dolphins' aid, to be taken ashore for study. But the arch itself ... was that part of some old installation?

Torches to the fore, they entered its shadow, only to remain baffled. Here and there were patches of the same gray showing in its interior. Ashe dug the butt of his spear-gun into the sand on the flooring to uncover another oval depression. But what it all signified or what had been its purpose, they could not guess.

"Set up the peep-probe here?" Ross asked.

Ashe's head moved in a slow negative. "Look farther ... spread out," the sonic clicked.

Within a matter of minutes the dolphins reported new remains—two more saucers, each larger than the first, set in a line on the ocean floor, pointing directly to Karara's Finger Island. Cautiously explored, these were discovered to be free of any but harmless life; they stirred up no more dragons.

When the Terrans came ashore on Finger Island to rest and eat their midday meal one of the men paced along the beached dragon. Ashore it lost none of its frightening aspect. And seeing it, even beached and dead, Ross wondered at his luck in surviving the encounter without a scratch.

"I think that this one would be alone," PaKeeKee commented. "Where there is an eater of this size, there is usually only one."

"Mano-Nui!" The girl Taema shivered as she gave to this monster the name of the shark demon of her people. "Such a one is truly king shark in these waters! But why have we not sighted its like before? Tino-rau, Taua ... they have not reported such—"

"Probably because, as PaKeeKee says, these things are rare," Ashe returned. "A carnivore of size would have to have a fairly wide hunting range, yet there's evidence that this thing has laired in that den for some time. Which means that it must have a defined hunting territory allowing no trespassing from others of its species."

Karara nodded. "Also it may hunt only at intervals, eat heavily, and lie quiet until that meal is digested. There are large snakes on Terra that follow that pattern. Ross was in its front yard when it came after him—"

"From now on"—Ashe swallowed a quarter of fruit—"we know what to watch for, and the weapon which will finish it off. Don't forget that!"

The delicate mechanisms of their sonics had already registered the vibrations which would warn of a dragon's presence, and the depth globes would then do the rest.

"Big skull, oversize for the body." PaKeeKee squatted on his heels by the head lying on the sand at the end of the now fully extended neck.

Ross had heretofore been more aware of the armament of that head, the fangs set in the powerful jaws, the horn on the snout. But PaKeeKee's comment drew his attention to the fact that the scale-covered skull did dome up above the eye pits in a way to suggest ample brain room. Had the thing been intelligent? Karara put that into words:

"Rule One?" She went over to survey the carcass.

Ross resented her half question, whether it was addressed to him or mere thinking aloud on her part.

Rule One: Conserve native life to the fullest extent. Humanoid form may not be the only evidence of intelligence.

There were the dolphins to prove that point right on Terra. But did Rule One mean that you had to let a monster nibble at you because it might just be a high type of alien intelligence? Let Karara spout Rule One while backed into a crevice under water with that horn stabbing at her mid-section!

"Rule One does not mean to forego self-defense," Ashe commented mildly. "This thing is a hunter, and you can't stop to apply recognition techniques when you are being regarded as legitimate prey. If you are the stronger, or an equal, yes—stop and think before becoming aggressive. But in a situation like this—take no chances."

"Anyway, from now on," Karara pointed out, "it could be possible to shock instead of kill."

"Gordon"—PaKeeKee swung around—"what have we found here—besides this thing?"

"I can't even guess. Except that those depressions were made for a purpose and have been there for a long time. Whether they were originally in the water, or the land sank, that we don't know either. But now we have a site to set up the peep-probe."

"We do that right away?" Ross wanted to know. Impatience bit at him. But Ashe still had a trace of frown. He shook his head.

"Have to make sure of our site, very sure. I don't want to start any chain reaction on the other side of the time wall."

And he was right, Ross was forced to admit, remembering what had happened when the galactics had discovered the Red time gates and traced them forward to their twentieth-century source, ruthlessly destroying each station. The original colonists of Hawaika had been as giants to Terran pygmies when it came to technical knowledge. To use even a peep-probe indiscreetly near one of their outposts might bring swift and terrible retribution.

THE ANCIENT MARINERS

Another map spread out and this time pinned down with small stones on beach gravel.

"Here, here, and here—" Ashe's finger indicated the points marked in a pattern which flared out from three sides of Finger Island. Each marked a set of three undersea depressions in perfect alliance with the land which, according to the galactic map, had once been a cape on a much larger land mass. Though the Terrans had found the ruins, if those saucers in the sea could be so termed, the remains had no meaning for the explorers.

"Do we set up here?" Ross asked. "If we could just get a report to send back...." That might mean the difference between awakening the co-operation of the Project policy makers so that a flood of supplies and personnel would begin to head their way.

"We set up here," Ashe decided.

He had selected a point between two of the lines where a reef would provide them with a secure base. And once that decision was made, the Terrans went into action.

Two days to go, to install the peep-probe and take some shots before the ship had to clear with or without their evidence. Together Ross and Ashe floated the installation out to the reef, Ui and Karara helping to tow the equipment and parts, the dolphins lending pushing noses on occasion. The aquatic mammals were as interested as the human beings they aided. And in water their help was invaluable. Had dolphins developed hands, Ross wondered fleetingly, would they have long ago wrested control of their native world—or at least of its seas—from the human kind?

All the human beings worked with practiced ease, even while masked and submerged, to set the probe in place, aiming it landward at the check point of the Finger's protruding nail of rock. After Ashe made the final adjustments, tested each and every part of the assembly, he gestured them in.

Karara's swift hand movement asked a question, and Ashe's sonic code-clicked in reply: "At twilight."

Yes, dusk was the proper time for using a peep-probe. To see without risk of being sighted in return was their safeguard. Here Ashe had no historical data to guide him. Their search for the former inhabitants might be a long drawn-out process skipping across centuries as the machine was adjusted to Terran time eras.

"When were they here?" Back on shore Karara shook out her hair, spread it over her shoulders to dry. "How many hundred years back will the probe return?"

"More likely thousands," Ross commented. "Where will you start, Gordon?"

Ashe brushed sand from the page of the notebook he had steadied against one bent knee and gazed out at the reef where they had set the probe.

"Ten thousand years—"

"Why?" Karara wanted to know. "Why that exact figure?"

"We know that galactic ships crashed on Terra then. So their commerce and empire—if it was an empire—was far-flung at that time. Perhaps they were at the zenith of their civilization; perhaps they were already on the down slope. I do not think they were near the beginning. So that date is as good a starting place as any. If we don't hit what we're after, then we can move forward until we do."

"Do you think that there ever was a native population here?"

"Might have been."

"But without any large land animals, no modern traces of any," she protested.

"Of people?" Ashe shrugged. "Good answers for both. Suppose there was a world-wide epidemic of proportions to wipe out a species. Or a war in which they used forces beyond our comprehension to alter the whole face of this planet, which did happen—the alteration, I mean. Several things could have removed intelligent life. Then such species as the burrowers could have developed or evolved from smaller, more primitive types."

"Those ape-things we found on the desert planet." Ross thought back to their first voyage on the homing derelict. "Maybe they had once been men and were degenerating. And the winged people, they could have been less than men on their way up—"

"Ape-things ... winged people?" Karara interrupted. "Tell me!"

There was something imperious in her demand, but Ross found himself describing in detail their past adventures, first on the world of sand and sealed structures where the derelict had rested for a purpose its involuntary passengers had never understood, and then of the Terrans' limited exploration of that other planet which might have been the capital world of a far-flung stellar empire. There they had made a pact with a winged people living in the huge buildings of a jungle-choked city.

"But you see"—the Polynesian girl turned to Ashe when Ross had finished—"you did find them—these ape-things and the winged people. But here there are only the dragons and the burrowers. Are they the start or the finish? I want to know—"

"Why?" Ashe asked.

"Not just because I am curious, though I am that also, but because we, too, must have a beginning and an end. Did we come up from the seas, rise to know and feel and think, just to return to such beginning at our end? If your winged people were climbing and your ape-things descending"—she shook her head—"it would be frightening to hold a cord of life, both ends in your hands. Is it good for us to see such things, Gordon?"

"Men have asked that question all their thinking lives, Karara. There have been those who have said no, who have turned aside and tried to halt the growth of knowledge here or there, attempted to make men stand still on one tread of a stairway. Only there is that in us which will not stop, ill-fitted as we may be for the climbing. Perhaps we shall be safe and untroubled here on Hawaika if I do not go out to that reef tonight. By that action I may bring real danger down on all of us. Yet I can not hold back for that. Could you?"

"No, I do not believe that I could," she agreed.

"We are here because we are of those who must know—volunteers. And being of that temperament, it is in us always to take the next step."

"Even if it leads to a fall," she added in a low tone.

Ashe gazed at her, though her own eyes were on the sea where a lace of waves marked the reef. Her words were ordinary enough, but Ross straightened to match Ashe's stare. Why had he felt that odd instant of uneasiness as if his heart had fluttered instead of beating true?

"I know of you Time Agents," Karara continued. "There were plenty of stories about you told while we were in training."

"Tall tales, I can imagine, most of them." Ashe laughed, but his amusement sounded forced to Ross.

"Perhaps. Though I do not believe that many could be any taller than the truth. And so also I have heard of that strict rule you follow, that you must do nothing which might alter the course of history. But suppose, suppose here that the course of history could be altered, that whatever catastrophe occurred might be averted? If that was done, what would happen to our settlement in the here and now?"

"I don't know. That is an experiment which we have never dared to try, which we won't try—"

"Not even if it would mean a chance of life for a whole native race?" she persisted.

"Alternate worlds then, maybe." Ross's imagination caught up that idea. "Two worlds from a change point in history," he elaborated, noting her look of puzzlement. "One stemming from one decision, another from the alternate."

"I've heard of that! But, Gordon, if you could return to the time of decision here and you had it in your power to say, 'Yes—live!' or 'No—die!' to the alien natives, what would you do?"

"I don't know. But neither do I think I shall ever be placed in that position. Why do you ask?"

She was twisting her still damp hair into a pony tail and tying it so with a cord. "Because ... because I feel.... No, I can not really put it into words, Gordon. It is that feeling one has on the eve of some important event—anticipation, fear, excitement. You'll let me go with you tonight, please! I want to see it—not the Hawaika that is, but that other world with another name, the one they saw and knew!"

An instant protest was hot in Ross's throat, but he had no time to voice it. For Ashe was already nodding.

"All right. But we may have no luck at all. Fishing in time is a chancy thing, so don't be disappointed if we don't turn you up that other world. Now, I'm going to pamper these old bones for an hour or two. Amuse yourselves, children." He lay back and closed his eyes.

The past two days had wiped half the shadows from his lean, tanned face. He had dropped two years, three, Ross thought thankfully. Let them be lucky tonight, and Ashe's cure could be nearly complete.

"What do you think happened here?" Karara had moved so that her back was now to the wash of waves, her face more in the shadow.

"How do I know? Could be any of ten different things."

"And will I please shut up and leave you alone?" she countered swiftly. "Do you wish to savor the excitement then, explore a world upon world, or am I saying it right? We have Hawaika One which is a new world for us;

now there is Hawaika Two which is removed in time, not distance. And to explore that—"

"We won't be exploring it really," Ross protested.

"Why? Did your agents not spend days, weeks, even months of time in the past on Terra? What is to prevent your doing the same here?"

"Training. We have no way of learning the drill."

"What do you mean?"

"Well, it wasn't as easy as you seem to think it was back on Terra," he began scornfully. "We didn't just stroll through one of those gates and set up business, say, in Nero's Rome or Montezuma's Mexico. An Agent was physically and psychologically fitted to the era he was to explore. Then he trained, and how he trained!" Ross remembered the weary hours spent learning how to use a bronze sword, the technique of Beaker trading, the hypnotic instruction in a language which was already dead centuries before his own country existed. "You learned the language, the customs, everything you could about your time and your cover. You were letter perfect before you took even a trial run!"

"And here you would have no guides," Karara said, nodding. "Yes, I can see the difficulty. Then you will just use the peep-probe?"

"Probably. Oh, maybe later on we can scout through a gate. We have the material to set one up. But it would be a strictly limited project, allowing no chance of being caught. Maybe the big brains back home can take peep-data and work out some basis of infiltration for us from it."

"But that would take years!"

"I suppose so. Only you begin to swim in the shallows, don't you—not by jumping off a cliff!"

She laughed. "True enough! However, even a look into the past might solve part of the big mystery."

Ross grunted and stretched out to follow Ashe's example. But behind his closed eyes his brain was busy, and he did not cultivate the patience he needed. Peep-probes were all right, but Karara had a point. You wanted more than a small window into a mystery, you wanted a part in solving it.

The setting of the sun deepened rose to red, made a dripping wine-hued banner of most of the sky, so that under it they moved in a crimson sea, looked back at an island where shadows were embers instead of ashes. Three humans, two dolphins, and a machine mounted on a reef which might not even have existed in the time they sought. Ashe made his final adjustments, and then his finger pressed a button and they watched the vista-plate no larger than the palms of two hands.

Nothing, a dull gray nothing! Something must have gone wrong with their assembly work. Ross touched Ashe's shoulder. But now there were shadows gathering on the plate, thickening, to sharpen into a distinct picture.

It was still the sunset hour they watched. But somehow the colors were paler, less red and sullen than the ones about them in the here and now. And they were not seeing the isle toward which the probe had been aimed; they were looking at a rugged coastline where cliffs lifted well above the beach-strand. While on those cliffs—! Ross had not realized Karara had reached out to grasp his arm until her nails bit into his flesh. And even then he was hardly aware of the pain. Because there was a building on the cliff!

Massive walls of native rock reared in outward defenses, culminating in towers. And from the high point of one tower the pointed tail of a banner cracked in the wind. There was a headland of rock reaching out, not toward them but to the north, and rounding that....

"War canoe!" Karara exclaimed, but Ross had another identification: "Longboat!"

In reality, the vessel was neither one nor the other, not the double canoe of the Pacific which had transported warriors on raid from one island to another, or the shield-hung warship of the Vikings. But the Terrans were right in its purpose: That rakish, sharp-prowed ship had been fashioned for swift passage of the seas, for maneuverability as a weapon.

Behind the first nosed another and a third. Their sails were dyed by the sun, but there were devices painted on them, and the lines of those designs glittered as if they had been drawn with a metallic fluid.

"The castle!" Ashe's cry pulled their attention back to land.

There was movement along those walls. Then came a flash, a splash in the water close enough to the lead ship to wet her deck with spray.

"They're fighting!" Karara shouldered against Ross for a better look.

The ships were altering course, swinging away from land, out to sea.

"Moving too fast for sails alone, and I don't see any oars." Ross was puzzled. "How do you suppose...."

The bombardment from the castle continued but did not score any hits. Already the ships were out of range, the lead vessel off the screen of the peep as well. Then there was just the castle in the sunset. Ashe straightened up.

"Rocks!" he repeated wonderingly. "They were throwing rocks!"

"But those ships, they must have had engines. They weren't just depending on sails when they retreated." Ross added his own cause for bewilderment.

Karara looked from one to the other. "There is something here you do not understand. What is wrong?"

"Catapults, yes," Ashe said with a nod. "Those would fit periods corresponding from the Roman Empire into the Middle Ages. But you're right, Ross, those ships had power of some kind to take them offshore that quickly."

"A technically advanced race coming up against a more backward one?" hazarded the younger man.

"Could be. Let's go forward some." The incoming tide was washing well up on the reef. Ashe had to don his mask as he plunged head and shoulders under water to make the necessary adjustment.

Once more he pressed the button. And Ross's gasp was echoed by one from the girl. The cliff again, but there was no castle dominating it, only a ruin, hardly more than rubble. Now, above the sites of the saucer depressions great pylons of silvery metal, warmed into fire brilliance by the sunset, raked into the sky like gaunt, skeleton fingers. There were no ships, no signs of any life. Even the vegetation which had showed on shore had vanished. There was an atmosphere of stark abandonment and death which struck the Terrans forcibly.

Those pylons, Ross studied them. Something familiar in their construction teased his memory. That refuel planet where the derelict ship had set down twice, on the voyage out and on their return. That had been a world of metal structures, and he believed he could trace a kinship between his memory of those and these pylons. Surely they had no connection with the earlier castle on the cliff.

Once more Ashe ducked to reset the probe. And in the fast-fading light they watched a third and last picture. But now they might have been looking at the island of the present, save that it bore no vegetation and there was a rawness about it, a sharpness of rock outline now vanished.

Those pylons, were they the key to the change which had come upon this world? What were they? Who had set them there? For the last Ross thought he had an answer. They were certainly the product of the galactic empire. And the castle ... the ships ... natives ... settlers? Two widely different eras, and the mystery still, lay between them. Would they ever be able to bring the key to it out of time?

They swam for the shore where Ui had a fire blazing and their supper prepared.

"How many years lying between those probes?" Ross pulled broiled fish apart with his fingers.

"That first was ten thousand years ago, the second," Ashe paused, "only two hundred years later."

"But"—Ross stared at his superior—"that means—"

"That there was a war or some drastic form of invasion, yes."

"You mean that the star people arrived and just took over this whole planet?" Karara asked. "But why? And those pylons, what were they for? How much later was that last picture?"

"Five hundred years."

"The pylons were gone, too, then," Ross commented. "But why—?" he echoed Karara's question.

Ashe had taken up his notebook, but he did not open it. "I think"—there was a sharp, grim note in his voice—"we had better find out."

"Put up a gate?"

Ashe broke all the previous rules of their service with his answer:

"Yes, a gate."

STORM MENACE

"We have to know." Ashe leaned back against the crate they had just emptied. "Something was done here—in two hundred years—and then, an empty world."

"Pandora's box." Ross drew a hand across his forehead, smearing sweat and fine sand into a brand.

Ashe nodded. "Maybe we run that risk, loosing all the devils of the aliens. But what if the Reds open the box first on one of their settlement worlds?"

There it was again, the old thorn which prodded them into risks and recklessness. Danger ahead on both paths. Don't risk trying to learn galactic secrets, but don't risk your enemy's learning them either. You held a white-hot iron in both hands in this business. And Ashe was right, they had stumbled on something here which hinted that a whole world had been altered to suit some plan. Suppose the secret of that alteration was discovered by their enemies?

"Were the ship and castle people natives?" Ross wondered aloud.

"Just at a guess they were, or at least settlers who had been established here so long they had developed a local form of civilization which was about on the level of a feudal society."

"You mean because of the castle and the rock bombardment. But what about the ships?"

"Two separate phases of a society at war, perhaps a more progressive against a less technically advanced. American warships paying a visit to the Shogun's Japan, for example."

Ross grinned. "Those warships didn't seem to fancy their welcome. They steered out to sea fast enough when the rocks began to fall."

"Yes, but the ships could exist in the castle pattern; the pylons could not!"

"Which period are you aiming for first—the castle or the pylons?"

"Castle first, I think. Then if we can't pick up any hints, we'll take some jumps forward until we do connect. Only we'll be under severe handicaps. If we could only plant an analyzer somewhere in the castle as a beginning."

Ross did not show his surprise. If Ashe was talking on those terms, then he was intending to do more than just lurk around a little beyond the gate; he was really planning to pick up alien speech patterns, eventually assume an alien agent identity!

"Gordon!" Karara appeared between two of the lace trees. She came so hastily that the contents of the two cups she carried slopped over. "You must hear what Hori has to say—"

The tall Samoan who trailed her spoke quickly. For the first time since Ross had known him he was very serious, a frown line between his eyes. "There is a bad storm coming. Our instruments register it."

"How long away?" Ashe was on his feet.

"A day ... maybe two...."

Ross could see no change in the sky, islands, or sea. They had had idyllic weather for the six weeks since their planeting, no sign of any such trouble in the Hawaikan paradise.

"It's coming," Hori repeated.

"The gate is half up," Ashe thought aloud, "too much of it set to be dismantled again in a hurry."

"If it's completed," Hori wanted to know, "would it ride out a storm?"

"It might, behind that reef where we have it based. To finish it would be a fast job."

Hori flexed his hands. "We're more brawn than brain in these matters, Gordon, but you've all our help, for what it's worth. What about the ship, does it lift on schedule?"

"Check with Rimbault about that. This storm, how will it compare to a Pacific typhoon?"

The Samoan shook his head. "How do we know? We have not yet had to face the local variety."

"The islands are low," Karara commented. "Winds and water could—"

"Yes! We'd better see Rimbault about a shelter if needed."

If the settlement had drowsed, now its inhabitants were busy. It was decided that they could shelter in the spaceship should the storm reach hurricane proportions, but before its coming the gate must be finished. The final fitting was left to Ashe and Ross, and the older agent fastened the last bolt when the waters beyond the reef were already wind ruffled, the sky darkening fast. The dolphins swam back and forth in the lagoon and with them Karara, though Ashe had twice waved her to the shore.

There was no sunlight left, and they worked with torches. Ashe began his inspection of the relatively simple transfer—the two upright bars, the slab of opaque material forming a doorstep between them. This was only a skeleton of the gates Ross had used in the past. But continual experimentation had produced this more easily transported installation.

Piled in a net were several supply containers ready for an exploring run—extra gill-packs, the analyzer, emergency rations, a medical kit, all the basics. Was Ashe going to try now? He had activated the transfer, the rods were glowing faintly, the slab they guarded having an eerie blue glimmer. He probably only wanted to be sure it worked.

What happened at that moment Ross could never find any adequate words to describe, nor was he sure he could remember. The disorientation of the pass-through he had experienced before; this time he was whirled into a vortex of feeling in which his body, his identity, were rift from him and he lost touch with all stability.

Instinctively he lashed out, his reflexes more than his conscious will keeping him above water in the wild rage of a storm-whipped sea. The light was gone; here was only dark and beating water. Then a lightning flash ripped wide the heavens over Ross as his head broke the surface and he saw, with unbelieving eyes, that he was being thrust shoreward—not to the strand of Finger Island—but against a cliff where water pounded an unyielding wall of rock.

Ross comprehended that somehow he had been jerked through the gate, that he was now fronting the land that had been somewhere beneath the heights supporting the castle. Then he fought for his life to escape the hammer of the sea determined to crack him against the surface of the cliff.

A rough surface loomed up before him, and he threw himself in that direction, embracing a rock, striving to cling through the backwash of the wave which had brought him there. His nails grated and broke on the stone, and then the fingers of his right hand caught in a hole, and he held with all the strength in his gasping, beaten body. He had had no preparation, no warning, and only the tough survival will which had been trained and bred into him saved his life.

As the water washed back, Ross strove to pull up farther on his anchorage, to be above the strike of the next wave. Somehow he gained a foot before it came. The mask of the gill-pack saved him from being smothered in that curling torrent as he clung stubbornly, resisting again the pull of the retreating sea.

Inch by inch between waves he fought for footing and stable support. Then he was on the surface of the rock, out of all but the lash of spray. He crouched there, spent and gasping. The thunder roar of the surf, and beyond it the deeper mutter of the rage in the heavens, was deafening, dulling his sense as much as the ordeal through which he had passed. He was content to cling where he was, hardly conscious of his surroundings.

Sparks of light along the shore to the north at last caught Ross's attention. They moved, some clustering along the wave line, a few strung up the cliff. And they were not part of the storm's fireworks. Men here—why at this moment?

Another bolt of lightning showed him the answer. On the reef fringe which ran a tongue of land into the sea hung a ship—two ships—pounded by every hammer wave. Shipwrecks ... and those lights must mark castle dwellers drawn to aid the survivors.

Ross crawled across his rock on his hands and knees, wavered along the cliff wall until he was again faced with angry water. To drop into that would be a mistake. He hesitated—and now more than his own predicament struck home to him.

Ashe! Ashe had been ahead of him at the time gate. If Ross had been jerked through to this past, then somewhere in the water, on the shore, Gordon was here too! But where to find him....

Setting his back to the cliff and holding to the rough stone, Ross got to his feet, trying to see through the welter of foam and water. Not only the sea poured here; now a torrential rain fell into the bargain, streaming down about him, battering his head and shoulders. A chill rain which made him shiver.

He wore gill-pack, weighted belt with its sheathed tool and knife, flippers, and the pair of swimming trunks which had been suitable for the Hawaika he knew; but this was a different world altogether. Dare he use his torch to see the way out of here? Ross watched the lights to the north, deciding they were not too unlike his own beam, and took the chance.

Now he stood on a shelf of rock pitted with depressions, all pools. To his left was a drop into a boiling, whirling caldron from which points of stone fanged. Ross shuddered. At least he had escaped being pulled into that!

To his right, northward, there was another space of sea, a narrow strip, and then a second ledge. He measured the distance between that and the one on which he perched. Staying where he was would not locate Ashe.

Ross stripped off his flippers, made them fast in his belt. Then he leaped and landed painfully, as his feet slipped and he skidded face down on the northern ledge.

As he sat up, rubbing a bruised and scraped knee, he saw lights advancing in his direction. And between them a shadow crawling from water to shore. Ross stumbled along the ledge hastening to reach that figure, who lay still now just out of the waves. Ashe?

Ross's limping pace became a trot. But he was too late; the other lights, two of them, had reached the shadow. A man—or at least a body which was humanoid—sprawled face down. Other men, three of them, gathered over the exhausted swimmer.

Those who held the torches were still partially in the dark, but the third stooped to roll over their find. Ross caught the glint of light on a metallic headcovering, the glisten of wet armor of some type on the fellow's back and shoulders as he made quick examination of the sea's victim.

Then.... Ross halted, his eyes wide. A hand rose and fell with expert precision. There had been a blade in that hand. Already the three were turning away from the man so ruthlessly dispatched. Ashe? Or some survivor of the wrecked ships?

Ross retreated to the end of the ledge. The narrow stream of water dividing it from the rock where he had won ashore washed into a cave in the cliff. Dare he try to work his way into that? Masked, with the gill-pack, he could go under surface if he were not smashed by the waves against some wall.

He glanced back. The lights were very close to the end of his ledge. To withdraw to the second rock would mean being caught in a dead end, for he dared not enter the whirlpool on its far side. There was really no choice: stay and be killed, or try for the cave. Ross fastened on his flippers and lowered his body into the narrow stream. The fact that it was narrow and guarded on either side by the ledges tamed the waves a little, and Ross found the tug against him not so great as he feared it would be.

Keeping hand-holds on the rock, he worked along, head and shoulders often under the wash of rolling water, but winning steadily to the break in the cliff wall. Then he was through, into a space much larger than the opening, water-filled but not with a wild turbulence of waves.

Had he been sighted? Ross kept a handhold to the left of that narrow entrance, his body floating with the rise and fall of the water. He could make out the gleam of light without. It might be that one of those hunters had leaned out over the runnel of the cave entrance, was flashing his torch down into the water there.

Behind mask plate Ross's lips writhed in the snarl of the hunted. In here he would have the advantage. Let one of them, or all three, try to follow through that rock entrance and....

But if he had been sighted at the mouth of the lair, none of his trackers appeared to wish to press the hunt. The light disappeared, and Ross was left in the dark. He counted a hundred slowly and then a second hundred before he dared use his own torch.

For all its slit entrance this was a good-sized hideaway he had chanced upon. And he discovered, when he ventured to release his wall hold and swim out into its middle, the bottom arose in a slope toward its rear.

Moments later Ross pulled out of the water once more, to crouch shivering on a ledge only lapped now and then by wavelets. He had found a temporary refuge, but his good fortune did not quiet his fears. Had that been Ashe on the shore? And why had the swimmer been so summarily executed by the men who found him?

The ships caught on the reef, the castle on the cliff above his head ... enemies ... ships' crews and castle men? But the callous act of the shore patrol argued a state of war carried to fanatic proportions, perhaps inter-racial conflict.

He could not hope to explore until the storm was over. To plunge back into the sea would not find Ashe. And to be hunted along the shore by an unknown enemy was simply asking to die without achieving any good in return. No, he must remain where he was for the present.

Ross unhooked the torch from his belt and used it on this higher portion of the cave. He was perched on a ledge which protruded into the water in the form of a wedge. At his back the wall of the cave was rough, and trails of weed were festooned on its projections. The smell of fishy decay was strong enough to register as Ross pulled off his mask. As far as he could now see there was no exit except by sea.

A movement in the water brought his light flashing down into the dark flood. Then a sleek head arose in the path of that ray. Not a man swimming, but one of the dolphins!

Ross's exclamation of surprise was half gasp, half cry. The second dolphin showed for a moment and between the shadow of their bodies, just under the surface, moved a third form.

"Ashe!" Ross had no idea how the dolphins had come through the time gate, but that they had guided to safety a Terran he did not doubt at all. "Ashe!"

But it was not Ashe who came wading to the ledge where Ross waited with hand outstretched. He had been so sure of the other's identity that he blinked in complete bewilderment as his eyes met Karara's and she half stumbled, half reeled against him.

His arms about her shoulders steadied her, and her shivering body was close to his as she leaned her full weight upon him. Her hands made a feeble movement to her mask, and he pulled it off. Uncovered, her face was pale and drawn, her eyes now closed, and her breath came in ragged, tearing sobs which shook her even more.

"How did you get here?" Ross demanded even as he pushed her down on the ledge.

Her head moved slowly, in a weak gesture of negation.

"I don't know ... we were close to the gate. There was a flash of light ... then—" Her voice sealed up with a note of hysteria in it. "Then ... I was here ... and Taua with me. Tino-rau came ... Ross, Ross ... there was a man swimming. He got ashore; he was getting to his feet and—and they killed him!"

Ross's hold tightened; he stared into her face with fierce demand. "Was it Gordon?"

She blinked, brought her hand up to her mouth, and wiped it back and forth across her chin. There was a small red trickle growing between her fingers, dripping down her arm.

"Gordon?" She repeated it as if she had never heard the name before.

"Yes, did they kill Gordon?"

In his grasp she was swaying back and forth. Then, realizing he was shaking her, Ross got himself under control.

But a measure of understanding had come into her eyes. "No, not Gordon. Where is Gordon?"

"You haven't seen him?" Ross persisted, knowing it was useless.

"Not since we were at the gate." Her words were less slurred. "Weren't you with him?"

"No. I was alone."

"Ross, where are we?"

"Better say—when are we," he replied. "We're through the gate and back in time. And we have to find Gordon!" He did not want to think of what might have happened out on the shore.

TIME WRECKED

"Can we go back?" Karara was herself again, her voice crisp.

"I don't know." Ross gave her the truth. The force which had drawn them through the gate was beyond his experience. As far as he knew, there had never been such an involuntary passage by time gate, and what their trip might mean he did not know.

The main concern was that Ashe must have come through, too, and that he was missing. Just let the storm abate, and, with the dolphins' aid, Ross's chance for finding the missing agent was immeasurably better. He said so now, and Karara nodded.

"Do you suppose there is a war going on here?" She hugged her arms across her breast, her shoulders heaving in the torch light with shudders she could not control. The damp chill was biting, and Ross realized that was also danger.

"Could be." He got to his feet, switched the light from the girl to the walls. That seaweed, could it make them some form of protective covering?

"Hold this—aim it there!" He thrust the torch into her hands and went for one of the loops of kelp.

Ross reeled in lines of the stuff. It was rank-smelling but only slightly damp, and he piled it on the ledge in a kind of nest. At least in the hollow of that mound they would be sheltered after a fashion.

Karara crawled into the center of the mass, and Ross followed her. The smell of the stuff filled his nose, was almost like a visible cloud, but he had been right, the girl stopped shivering, and he felt a measure of warmth in his own shaking body. Ross snapped off the torch, and they lay together in the dark, the half-rotten pile of weed holding them.

He must have slept, Ross guessed, when he stirred, raising his head. His body was stiff, aching, as he braced himself up on his hands and peered over the edge of their kelp nest. There was light in the cave, a pale grayish wash which grew stronger toward the slit opening. It must be day. And that meant they could move.

Ross groped in the weed, his hand falling on a curve of shoulder.

"Wake up!" His voice was hoarse and held the snap of an order.

There was a startled gasp in answer, and the mound beside him heaved as the girl stirred.

"Day out—" Ross pointed.

"And the storm—" she stood up, "I think it is over."

It was true that the level of water within the cave had fallen, that wavelets no longer lapped with the same vigor. Morning ... the storm over ... and somewhere Ashe!

Ross was about to snap his mask into place when Karara caught at his arm.

"Be careful! Remember what I saw—last night they were killing swimmers!"

He shook her off impatiently. "I'm no fool! And with the packs on we do not have to surface. Listen—" he had another thought, one which would provide an excellent excuse for keeping her safely out of his company, reducing his responsibility for her, "you take the dolphins and try to find the gate. We'll want out as soon as I locate Ashe."

"And if you do not find him soon?"

Ross hesitated. She had not said the rest. What if he could not find Gordon at all? But he would—he had to!

"I'll be back here"—he checked his watch, no longer an accurate timekeeper, for Hawaikan days held an hour more than the Terran twenty-four, but the settlers kept the off-world measurement to check on work periods—"in, say, two hours. You should know by then about the gate, and I'll have some idea of the situation along the shore. But listen—" Ross caught her shoulders in a taut grip, pulled her around to face him, his eyes hot and almost angry as they held hers, "don't let yourself be seen—" He repeated the cardinal rule of Agents in new territory. "We don't dare risk discovery."

Karara nodded and he could see that she understood, was aware of the importance of that warning. "Do you want Tino-rau or Taua?"

"No, I'm going to search along the shore first. Ashe would have tried for that last night ... was probably driven in the way we were. He'd go to ground somewhere. And I have this—" Ross touched the sonic on his belt. "I'll set it on his call; you do the same with yours. Then if we get within distance, he'll pick us up. Back here in two hours—"

"Yes." Karara kicked free of the weed, was already wading down to where the dolphins circled in the cave pool waiting for her. Ross followed, and the four swam for the open sea.

It could not be much after dawn, Ross thought, as he clung by one hand to a rock and watched Karara and the dolphins on their way. Then he paddled along the shore northward for his own survey of the coast. There was a rose cast in the sky, warming the silver along the far reaches of the horizon. And about him bobbed storm flotsam, so that he had to pick a careful way through floating debris.

On the reef one of the wrecked ships had vanished entirely. Perhaps it had been battered to death by the waves, ground to splinters against the rocks. The other still held, its prow well out of the now receding waves, jagged holes in its sides through which spurts of water cascaded now and then.

The wreck which had been driven landward was composed of planks, boxes, and containers rolled by the waves' force. Much of this was already free of the sea, and on the beach figures moved examining it. In spite of the danger of chance discovery, Ross edged along rocks, seeking a vantage point from which he could watch that activity.

He was flat against a sea-girt boulder, a swell of floating weed draped about him, when the nearest of the foraging parties moved into good view.

Men ... at least they had the outward appearance of men much like himself, though their skin was dark and their limbs appeared disproportionately long and thin. There were two groups of them, four wearing only a scanty loincloth, busy turning over and hunting through the debris under the direction of the other two.

The workers had thick growths of hair which not only covered their heads, but down their spines and the outer sides of their thin arms and legs to elbow and knee. The hair was a pallid yellow-white in vivid contrast to their dark skins, and their chins protruded sharply, allowing the lower line of their faces to take on a vaguely disturbing likeness to an animal's muzzle.

Their overseers were more fully clothed, wearing not only helmets on their heads, whose helms had a protective visor over the face, but also breast- and back-plates molded to their bodies. Ross thought that these could not be solid metal since they adapted to the movements of the wearers.

Feet and legs were covered with casing combinations of shoe and leggings, colored dull red. They were armed with swords of an odd pattern; their points curved up so that the blade resembled a fishhook. Unsheathed, the blades were clipped to a waist belt by catches which glittered in the weak morning light as if gem set.

Ross could see little of their faces, for the beak visors overhung their features. But their skins were as dusky as those of the laborers, and their arms and legs of the same unusual length ... men of the same race, he deduced.

Under the orders of the armed overseers the laborers were reducing the beach to order, sorting out the flotsam into two piles. Once they gathered about a find, and the sound of excited speech reached Ross as an agitated clicking. The armored men came up, surveyed the discovery. One of them shrugged, and clicked an order.

Ross caught only a half glimpse of the thing two of the workers dragged away. A body! Ashe.... The Terran was about to move closer when he saw the green cloak dragging about the corpse. No, not Gordon, just another victim from the wrecks.

The aliens were working their way toward Ross, and perhaps it was time for him to go. He was pushing aside his well-arranged curtain of weed when he was startled by a shout. For a second he thought he might have been sighted, until resulting action on shore told him otherwise.

The furred workers shrank back against the mound to which they had just dragged the body. While the two guards took up a position before them, curved swords, snapped from their belt hooks, ready in their hands. Again that shout. Was it a warning or a threat? With the language barrier Ross could only wait to see.

Another party approached along the beach from the south. In the lead was a cloaked and hooded figure, so muffled in its covering of silver-gray that Ross had no idea of the form beneath. Silvery-gray—no, now that hue was deepening with blue tones, darkening rapidly. By the time the cloaked newcomer had passed the rock which sheltered the Terran the covering was a rich blue which seemed to glow.

Behind the leader were a dozen armed men. They wore the same beaked helmets, the supple encasing breast- and back-plates, but their leggings were gray. They, too, carried curved swords, but the weapons were still latched to their belts and they made no move to draw them in spite of the very patent hostility of the guards before them.

Blue cloak halted some three feet from the guards. The sea wind pulled at the cloak, wrapping it about the body beneath. But even so, the wearer remained well hidden. From under a flapping edge came a hand. The fingers, long and slender, were curled about an ivory-colored wand which ended in a knob. Sparks flashed from it in a continuous flickering.

Ross clapped his hand to his belt. To his complete amazement the sonic disk he wore was reacting to those flashes, pricking sharply in perfect beat to their blink-blink. The Terran cupped his scarred fingers over the disk as he waited to see what was going to happen, wondering if the holder of that wand might, in return, pick up the broadcast of the code set on Ashe's call.

The hand clasping the wand was not dusky-skinned but had much of the same ivory shade as the rod, so that to Ross the meeting between flesh and wand was hardly distinguishable. Now by one firm thrust the hand planted the rod into the sand, leaving it to stand sentinel between the two parties.

Retreating a step or two, the red-clad guards gave ground. But they did not reclasp their swords. Their attitude, Ross judged, was that of men in some awe of their opponent, but men urged to defiance, either by a belief in the righteousness of their cause, or strengthened by an old hatred.

Now the cloaked one began to speak—or was that speech? Certainly the flow of sound had little in common with the clicking tongue Ross had caught earlier. This trill of notes possessed the rise and fall of a chant or song which could have been a formula of greeting—or a warning. And the lines of warriors escorting the chanter stood to attention, their weapons still undrawn.

Ross caught his lower lip between his teeth and bit down on it. That chanting—it crawled into the mind, set up a pattern! He shook his head vigorously and then was shocked by that recklessness. Not that any of those on shore had glanced in his direction.

The chant ended on a high, broken note. It was followed by a moment of silence through which sounded only the wind and the beat of wave.

Then one of the laborers flung up his head and clicked a word or two. He and his fellows fell face down on the beach, cupping their hands to pour sand over their unkempt heads. One of the guards turned with a sharp yell to boot the nearest of the workers in the ribs.

But his companion cried out. The wand which had stood so erect when it was first planted, now inclined toward the working party, its sparks shooting so swiftly and with such slight break between that they were fast making a single beam. Ross jerked his hand from contact with the sonic; a distinct throb of pain answered that stepping up of the mysterious broadcast.

The laborers broke and ran, or rather crawled on their bellies until they were well away, before they got to their feet and pelted back down the strand. However, the guards were of sterner stuff. They were withdrawing all right, but slowly backing away, their swords held up before them as men might retreat before insurmountable odds.

When they were well gone the robed one took up the wand. Holding it out beyond, the cloaked leader of the second party approached the two piles of salvage the workers had heaped into rough order. There was a detailed inspection of both until the robed one came upon the body.

At a trilled order two of the warriors came up and laid out the corpse. When the robed one nodded they stood well back. The rod moved, the tip rather than the knobbed head being pointed at the body.

Ross's head snapped back. That bolt of light, energy, fire—whatever it was—issuing from the rod had dazzled him into momentary blindness. And a vibration of force through the air was like a blow.

When he was able to see once more there was nothing at all on the sand where the corpse had lain, nothing except a glassy trough from which some spirals of vapor arose. Ross clung to his rock support badly shaken.

Men with swords ... and now this—some form of controlled energy which argued of technical development and science. Just as the cliff castle had bombarded with rocks ships sailing with a speed which argued engine power of an unknown type. A mixture of barbaric and advanced knowledge. To assess this, he needed more experience, more knowledge than he possessed. Now Ashe could....

Ashe!

Ross was jerked back to his own quest. The rod was quiet, no more sparks were flung from its knob. And under Ross's touch his sonic was quiet also. He snapped off the broadcast. If that device had picked up the flickering of the rod, the reverse could well be true.

The cloaked one chose from the pile of goods, and its escort gathered up the designated boxes, a small cask or two. So laden, the party returned south the way they had come. Ross allowed his breath to expel in a sigh of relief.

He worked his way farther north along the coast, watching other parties of the furred workers and their guards. Lines of the former climbed the cliff, hauling their spoil, their destination the castle. But Ross saw no sign of Ashe, received no answer to the sonic code he had reset once the strangers were out of distance. And the Terran began to realize that his present search might well be fruitless, though he fought against accepting it.

When he turned back to the slit cave Ross's fear was ready to be expressed in anger, the anger of frustration over his own helplessness. With no chance of trying to penetrate the castle, he could not learn whether or not Ashe had been taken prisoner. And until the workers left the beach he could not prowl there hunting the grimmer evidence his mind flinched from considering.

Karara waited for him on the inner ledge. There was no sign of the dolphins and as Ross pulled out of the water, pushing aside his mask, her face in the thin light of the cave was deeply troubled.

"You did not find him," she made that a statement rather than a question.

"No."

"And I did not find it—"

Ross used a length of weed from the nest as a towel. But now he stood very still.

"The gate ... no sign of it?"

"Just this—" She reached behind her and brought up a sealed container. Ross recognized one of the supply cans they had had in the cache by the gate. "There are others ... scattered. Taua and Tino-rau seek them now. It is as if all that was on the other side was sucked through with us."

"You are sure you found the right place?"

"Is—is this not part of it?" Again the girl sought for something on the ledge. What she held out to him was a length of metal rod, twisted and broken at one end as if a giant hand had wrenched it loose from the installation.

Ross nodded dully. "Yes," his voice was harsh as if the words were pulled out of him against his will and against all hope—"that's part of a side bar. It—it must have been totally wrecked."

Yet, even though he held that broken length in his hands, Ross could not really believe the gate was gone. He swam out once more, heading for the reef where the dolphins joined him as guides. There was a second piece of broken tube, the scattered containers of supplies, that was all. The Terrans were wrecked in time as surely as those ships had been wrecked on the sea reef the night before!

Ross headed once again for the cave. Their immediate needs were of major importance now. The containers must be all gathered and taken into their hiding place, because upon their contents three human lives could depend.

He paused just at the entrance to adjust the net of containers he transported. And it was that slight chance which brought him knowledge of the intruder.

On the ledge Karara was heaping up the kelp of the nest. But to one side and on a level with the girl's head....

Ross dared not flash his torch, thus betraying his presence. Leaving the net hitched to the rock by its sling, he swam under water along the side of the cave by a route which should bring him out within striking distance of that hunched figure perching above to watch Karara's every move.

LOKETH THE USELESS

The wash of waves covered Ross's advance until he came up against the wall not too far from the spy's perch. Whoever crouched there still leaned forward to watch Karara. And Ross's eyes, having adjusted to the gloom of the cavern, made out the outline of head and shoulders. The next two or three minutes were the critical ones for the Terran. He must emerge on the ledge in the open before he could attack.

Karara might almost have read his mind and given conscious help. For now she went out on the point of the ledge to whistle the dolphins' summons. Tino-rau's sleek head bobbed above water as he answered the girl with a bubbling squeak. Karara knelt and the dolphin came to butt against her out-held hand.

Ross heard a gasp from the watcher, a faint sound of movement. Karara began to sing softly, her voice rippling in one of the liquid chants of her own people, the dolphin interjecting a note or two. Ross had heard them at that before, and it made perfect cover for his move. He sprang.

His grasp tightened on flesh, fingers closed about thin wrists. There was a yell of astonishment and fear from the stranger as the Terran jerked him from his perch to the ledge. Ross had his opponent flattened under him before he realized that the other had offered no struggle, but lay still.

"What is it?" Karara's torch beam caught them both. Ross looked down into a thin brown face not too different from his own. The wide-set eyes were closed, and the mouth gaped open. Though he believed the Hawaikan unconscious, Ross still kept hold on those wrists as he moved from the sprawled body. With the girl's aid he used a length of kelp to secure the captive.

The stranger wore a garment of glistening skintight material which covered body, legs, and feet, but left his lanky arms bare. A belt about his waist had loops for a number of objects, among them a hook-pointed knife which Ross prudently removed.

"Why, he is only a boy," Karara said. "Where did he come from, Ross?"

The Terran pointed to the wall crevice. "He was up there, watching you."

Her eyes were wide and round. "Why?"

Ross dragged his prisoner back against the wall of the cave. After witnessing the fate of those who had swum ashore from the wreck, he did not like to think what motive might have brought the Hawaikan here. Again Karara's thoughts must have matched his, for she added:

"But he did not even draw his knife. What are you going to do with him, Ross?"

That problem already occupied the Terran. The wisest move undoubtedly was to kill the native out of hand. But such ruthlessness was more than he could stomach. And if he could learn anything from the stranger—gain some knowledge of this new world and its ways—he would be twice winner. Why, this encounter might even lead to Ashe!

"Ross ... his leg. See?" The girl pointed.

The tight fit of the alien's clothing made the defect clear; the right leg of the stranger was shrunken and twisted. He was a cripple.

"What of it?" Ross demanded sharply. This was no time for an appeal to the sympathies.

But Karara did not urge any modification of the bonds as he half feared she would. Instead, she sat back cross-legged, an odd, withdrawn expression making her seem remote though he could have put out his hand to touch her.

"His lameness—it could be a bridge," she observed, to Ross's mystification.

"A bridge—what do you mean?"

The girl shook her head. "This is only a feeling, not a true thought. But also it is important. Look, I think he is waking."

The lids above those large eyes were fluttering. Then with a shake of the head, the Hawaikan blinked up at them. Blank bewilderment was all Ross could read in the stranger's expression until the alien saw Karara. Then a flood of clicking speech poured from his lips.

He seemed utterly astounded when they made no answer. And the fluency of his first outburst took on a pleading note, while the expectancy of his first greeting faded away.

Karara spoke to Ross. "He is becoming afraid, very much afraid. At first, I think, he was pleased ... happy."

"But why?"

The girl shook her head. "I do not know; I can only feel. Wait!" Her hand rose in imperious command. She did not rise to her feet, but crawled on hands and knees to the edge of the ledge. Both dolphins were there, raising their heads well out of the water, their actions expressing unusual excitement.

"Ross!" Karara's voice rang loudly. "Ross, they can understand him! Tino-rau and Taua can understand him!"

"You mean, they understand this language?" Ross found that fantastic, awesome as the abilities of the dolphins were.

"No, his mind. It's his mind, Ross. Somehow he thinks in patterns they can pick up and read! They do that, you know, with a few of us, but not in the same way. This is more direct, clearer! They're so excited!"

Ross glanced at the prisoner. The alien had wriggled about, striving to raise his head against the wall as a support. His captor pulled the Hawaikan into a sitting position, but the native accepted that aid almost as if he were not even aware of Ross's hands on his body. He stared with a kind of horrified disbelief at the bobbing dolphin heads.

"He is afraid," Karara reported. "He has never known such communication before."

"Can they ask him questions?" demanded Ross. If this odd mental tie between Terran dolphin and Hawaikan did exist, then there was a chance to learn about this world.

"They can try. Now he only knows fear, and they must break through that."

What followed was the most unusual four-sided conversation Ross could have ever imagined. He put a question to Karara, who relayed it to the dolphins. In turn, they asked it mentally of the Hawaikan and conveyed his answer back via the same route.

It took some time to allay the fears of the stranger. But at last the Hawaikan entered wholeheartedly into the exchange.

"He is the son of the lord ruling the castle above." Karara produced the first rational and complete answer. "But for some reason he is not accepted by his own kind. Perhaps," she added on her own, "it is because he is crippled. The sea is his home, as he expresses it, and he believes me to be some mythical being out of it. He saw me swimming, masked, and with the dolphins, and he is sure I change shape at will."

She hesitated. "Ross, I get something odd here. He does know, or thinks he knows, creatures who can appear and disappear at will. And he is afraid of their powers."

"Gods and goddesses—perfectly natural."

Karara shook her head. "No, this is more concrete than a religious belief."

Ross had a sudden inspiration. Hurriedly he described the cloaked figure who had driven the castle people from the piles of salvage. "Ask him about that one."

She relayed the question. Ross saw the prisoner's head jerk around. The Hawaikan looked from Karara to her companion, a shade of speculation in his expression.

"He wants to know why you ask about the Foanna? Surely you must well know what manner of beings they are."

"Listen—" Ross was sure now that he had made a real discovery, though its importance he could not guess, "tell him we come from where there are no Foanna. That we have powers and must know of their powers."

If he could only carry on this interrogation straight and not have to depend upon a double translation! And could he even be sure his questions reached the alien undistorted?

Wearily Ross sat back on his heels. Then he glanced at Karara with a twinge of concern. If he was tired by their roundabout communication, she must be doubly so. There was a droop to her shoulders, and her last reply had come in a voice hoarse with fatigue. Abruptly he started up.

"That's enough—for now."

Which was true. He had to have time for evaluation, to adjust to what they had learned during the steady stream of questions passed back and forth. And in that moment he was conscious of his hunger, just as his voice was paper dry from lack of drink. The canister of supplies he had left by the cave entrance ...

"We need food and drink." He fumbled with his mask, but Karara motioned him back from the water.

"Taua brings ... Wait!"

The dolphin trailed the net of containers to them. Ross unscrewed one, pulled out a bulb of fresh water. A second box yielded the dry wafers of emergency rations.

Then, after a moment's hesitation, Ross crossed to the prisoner, cut his wrist bonds, and pressed both a bulb and a wafer into his hold. The Hawaikan watched the Terrans eat before he bit into the wafer, chewing it with vigor, turning the bulb around in his fingers with alert interest before he sucked at its contents.

As Ross chewed and swallowed, mechanically and certainly with no relish, he fitted one fact to another to make a picture of this Hawaikan time period in which they were now marooned. Of course, his picture was based on facts they had learned from their captive. Perhaps he had purposely misled them or fogged some essentials. But could he have done that in a mental contact? Ross would simply have to accept everything with a certain amount of cautious skepticism.

Anyway, there were the Wreckers of the castle—petty lordlings setting up their holds along the coasts, preying upon the shipping which was the lifeblood of this island-water world. The Terrans had seen them in action last night and today. And if the captive's information was correct, it was not only the storm's fury which brought the waves' harvest. The Wreckers had some method of attracting ships to crack up on their reefs.

Some method of attraction.... And that force which had pulled the Terrans through the time gate; could there be a connection? However, there remained the Wreckers on the cliff. And their prey, the seafarers of the ocean, with an understandably deep enmity between them.

Those two parties Ross could understand and be prepared to deal with, he thought. But there remained the Foanna. And, from their prisoner's explanation, the Foanna were a very different matter.

They possessed a power which did not depend upon swords or ships or the natural tools and weapons of men. No, they had strengths which were unearthly, to give them superiority in all but one way—numbers. Though the Foanna had their warriors and servants, as Ross had seen on the beach, they, themselves, were of another race—a very old and dying race of which few remained. How many, their enemies could not say, for the Foanna had no separate identities known to the outer world. They appeared, gave their orders, levied their demands, opposed or aided as they wished—always just one or two at a time—always so muffled in their cloaks that even their physical appearances remained a mystery. But there was no mystery about their powers. Ross gathered that no Wrecker lord, no matter how much a leader among his own kind, how ambitious, had yet dared to oppose actively one of the Foanna, though he might make a token protest against some demand from them.

And certainly the captive's description of those powers in action suggested a supernatural origin of Foanna knowledge, or at least for its application. But Ross thought that the answer might be that they possessed the remnants of some almost forgotten technical know-how, the heritage of a very old race. He had tried to learn something of the origin of the Foanna themselves, wondering if the robed ones could be from the galactic empire. But the answer had come that the Foanna were older than recorded time, that they had lived in the great citadel before the race of the Terrans' prisoner had risen from very primitive savagery.

"What do we do now?" Karara broke in upon Ross's thoughts as she refastened the containers.

"These slaves that the Wreckers take upon occasion ... Maybe Ashe...." Ross was catching at very fragile straws; he had to. And the stranger had said that able-bodied men who swam ashore relatively uninjured were taken captive. Several had been the night before.

"Loketh."

Ross and Karara looked around. The prisoner put down the water bulb, and one of his hands made a gesture they could not mistake; he pointed to himself and repeated that word, "Loketh."

The Terran touched his own chest. "Ross Murdock."

Perhaps the other was as impatient as he with their roundabout method of communication and had decided to try and speed it up. The analyzer! Ashe had included the analyzer with the equipment by the gate. If Ross could find that ... why, then the major problem could be behind them. Swiftly he explained to Karara, and with a vigorous nod of assent she called to Taua, ordering the rest of the salvage material from the gate be brought to them.

"Loketh." Ross pointed to the youth. "Ross." That was himself. "Karara." He indicated the girl.

"Rosss." The alien made a clicking hiss of the first name. "Karara—" He did better with the second.

Ross carefully unpacked the box Taua had located. He had only slight knowledge of how the device worked. It was intended to record a strange language, break it down into symbols already familiar to the Time Agents. But could it also be used as a translator with a totally alien tongue? He could only hope that the rough handling of its journey through the gate had not damaged it and that the experiment might possibly work.

Putting the box between them, he explained what he wanted; and Karara took up the small micro-disk, speaking slowly and distinctly the same liquid syllables she had used in the dolphin song. Ross clicked the lever when she was finished, and watched the small screen. The symbols which flashed there had meaning for him right enough; he could translate what she had just taped. The machine still worked to that extent.

Now he pushed the box into place before Loketh and made the visibly reluctant Hawaikan take the disk from Karara. Then through the dolphin link Ross passed on definite instructions. Would it work as well to translate a stellar tongue as it had with languages past and present of his own planet?

Reluctantly Loketh began to talk to the disk, at first in a very rapid mumble and then, as there was no frightening response, with less speed and more confidence. There were symbol lines on the vista-plate in accordance, and some of them made sense! Ross was elated.

"Ask him: Can one enter the castle unseen to check on the slaves?"

"For what reason?"

Ross was sure he had read those symbols correctly.

"Tell him—that one of our kind may be among them."

Loketh did not reply so quickly this time. His eyes, grave and measuring, studied Ross, then Karara, then Ross again.

"There is a way ... discovered by this useless one."

Ross did not pay attention to the odd adjective Loketh chose to describe himself. He pressed to the important matter.

"Can and will he show me that way?"

Again that long moment of appraisal on the part of Loketh before he answered. Ross found himself reading the reply symbols aloud.

"If you dare, then I will lead."

WITCHES MEAT

He might be recklessly endangering all of them, Ross knew. But if Ashe was immured somewhere in that rock pile over their heads, then the risk of trusting Loketh would be worth it. However, because Ross was chancing his own neck did not mean that Karara need be drawn into immediate peril too. With the dolphins at her command and the supplies, scanty as those were, she would have a good chance to hide here safely.

"Holding out for what?" she asked quietly after Ross elaborated on this subject, thus bringing him to silence.

Because her question was just. With the gate gone the Terrans were committed to this time, just as they had earlier been committed to Hawaika when on their home world they had entered the spaceship for the take-off. There was no escape from the past, which had become their present.

"The Foanna," she continued, "these Wreckers, the sea people—all at odds with one another. Do we join any, then their quarrels must also become ours."

Taua nosed the ledge behind the girl, squeaked a demand for attention. Karara looked around at Loketh; her look was as searching as the one the native had earlier turned on her and Ross.

"He"—the girl nodded at the Hawaikan—"wishes to know if you trust him. And he says to tell you this: Because the Shades chose to inflict upon him a twisted leg he is not one with those of the castle, but to them a broken, useless thing. Ross, I gather he thinks we have powers like the Foanna, and that we may be supernatural. But because we did not kill him out of hand and have fed him, he considers himself bound to us."

"Ritual of bread and salt ... could be." Though it might be folly to match alien customs to Terran, Ross thought of that very ancient pact on his own world. Eat a man's food, become his friend, or at least declare a truce between you. Stiff taboos and codes of behavior marked nations on Terra, especially warrior societies, and the same might be true here.

"Ask him," Ross told Karara, "what is the rule for food and drink between friends or enemies!" The more he could learn of such customs the better protection he might be able to weave for them.

Long moments for the relay of that message, and then Loketh spoke into the micro-disk of the analyzer, slowly, with pauses, as if trying to make sure Ross understood every word.

"To give bread into the hands of one you have taken in battle, makes him your man—not as a slave to labor, but as one who draws sword at your bidding. When I took your bread I accepted you as cup-lord. Between such there is no betrayal, for how may a man betray his lord? I, Loketh, am now a sword in your hands, a man in your service. And to me this is doubly good, for as a useless one I have never had a lord, nor one to swear to. Also, with this Sea Maid and her followers to listen to thoughts, how could any man speak with a double tongue were he one who consorted with the Shadow and wore the Cloak of Evil?"

"He's right," Karara added. "His mind is open; he couldn't hide his thoughts from Taua and Tino-rau even if he wished."

"All right, I'll accept that." Ross glanced about the ledge. They had piled the containers at the far end. For Karara to move might be safe. He said so.

"Move where?" she asked flatly. "Those men from the castle are still hunting drift out there. I don't think anyone knows of this cave."

Ross nodded to Loketh. "He did, didn't he? I wouldn't want you trapped here. And I don't want to lose those supplies. What is in those containers may be what saves us all."

"We can sink those over by the wall, weight them down in a net. Then, if we have to move, they will be ready. Do not worry—that is my department." She smiled at him with a slightly mocking lift of lips.

Ross subsided, though he was irritated because she was right. The management of the dolphin team and sea matters were her department. And while he resented her reminder of that point he could not deny the justice of her retort.

In spite of his crippled leg, Loketh displayed an agility which surprised Ross. Freed from his ankle bonds, he beckoned the Terran back to the very niche where he had hidden to watch Karara. Up he swung into that and in a second had vanished from sight.

Ross followed, to discover it was not a niche after all but the opening of a crevice, leading upward as a vent. And it had been used before as a passage. There was no light, but the native guided Ross's hands to the hollow climbing holds cut into the stone. Then Loketh pushed past and went up the crude ladder into the dark.

It was difficult to judge either time or distance in this black tube. Ross counted the holds for some check. His agent training made one part of his mind sharply aware of such things; the need for memorizing a passage which led into the enemy's territory was apparent. What the purpose of this slit had originally been he did not know, but strongholds on Terra had had their hidden ways in and out for use in times of siege, and he was beginning to believe that these aliens had much in common with his own kind.

He had reached twenty in his counting and his senses, alerted by training and instinct, told him there was an opening not too far above. But the darkness remained so thick it fell in tangible folds about his sweating body. Ross almost cried out as fingers clamped about his wrist when he reached for a new hold. Then urged by that grasp, he was up and out, sprawling into a vertical passage. Far ahead was a gray of faint light.

Ross choked and then sneezed as dust puffed up from between his scrabbling hands. The hold which had been on his wrist shifted to his shoulder, and with a surprising strength Loketh hauled the Terran to his feet.

The passage in which they stood was a slit extending in height well above their heads, but narrow, not much wider than Ross's shoulders. Whether it was a natural fault or had been cut he could not tell.

Loketh was ahead again, his rocking limp making the outline of his body a jerky up-and-down shadow. Again his speed and agility amazed the Terran. Loketh might be lame, but he had learned to adapt to his handicap very well.

The light increased and Ross marked slits in the walls to his right, no wider than the breadth of his two fingers. He peered out of one and was looking into empty air while below he heard the murmur of the sea. This way must run in the cliff face above the beach.

A click of impatient whisper drew him on to join Loketh. Here was a flight of stairs, narrow of tread and very steep. Loketh turned back and side against these to climb, his outspread hand flattened on the stone as if it possessed adhesive qualities to steady him. For the first time his twisted leg was a disadvantage.

Ross counted again—ten, fifteen of those steps, bringing them once more into darkness. Then they emerged from a well-like opening into a circular room. A sudden and dazzling flare of light made the Terran shade his eyes. Loketh set a pallid but glowing cone on a wall shelf, and the Terran discovered that the burst of light was only relative to the dark of the passage; indeed it was very weak illumination.

The Hawaikan braced his body against the far wall. The strain of his effort, whatever its purpose, was easy to read in the contorted line of his shoulders. Then the wall slid under Loketh's urging, a slow move as if the weight of the slab he strove to handle was almost too great for his slender arms, or else the need for caution was intensified here.

They now fronted a narrow opening, and the light of the cone shone only a few feet into the space. Loketh beckoned to Ross and they went on. Here the left wall was cut in many places emitting patches of light in a way which bore no resemblance to conventional windows. It was like walking behind a pierced screen which followed no logical pattern in the cutaway portions. Ross gazed out and gasped.

He was standing above the center core of the castle, and the life below and beyond drew his attention. He had seen drawings reproducing the life of a feudal castle. This resembled them and yet, as Ross studied the scene closer, the differences between the Terran past and this became more distinct.

In the first place there were those animals—or were they animals?—being hooked up to a cart. They had six limbs, walking on four, holding the remaining two folded under their necks. Their harness consisted of a network fitted over their shoulders, anchored to the folded limbs. Their grotesque heads, bobbing and weaving on lengthy necks, their bodies, were sleekly scaled. Ross was startled by a resemblance he traced to the sea dragon he had met in the future of this world.

But the creatures were subject to the men harnessing them. And the activity in other respects ... Ross had to fight a wayward and fascinated interest in all he could see, force himself to concentrate on learning what might be pertinent to his own mission. But Loketh did not allow him to watch for long. Instead, his hand on the Terran's arm urged the other down the gallery behind the screen and once more into the bulk of the fortress.

Another narrow way ran through the thickness of the walls. Then a patch of light, not that of outer day, but a reddish gleam from an opening waist high. There Loketh went awkwardly to his good knee, motioning Ross to follow his example.

What lay below was a hall furnished with a barbaric rawness of color and glitter. There were long strips of brightly hued woven stuff on the walls, touched here and there with sparkling glints which were jewel-like. And set at intervals among the hangings were oval objects perhaps Ross's height on which were designs and patterns picked out in paint and metal. Maybe the stylized representation of native plants and animals.

The whole gave an impression of clashing color, just as the garments of those gathered there were garish in turn.

There were three Hawaikans on the two-step dais. All wore robes fitting tightly to the upper portion of their bodies, girded to their waists with elaborate belts, then falling in long points to floor level, the points being finished off with tassels. Their heads were covered with tight caps which were a latticework of decorated strips, glittering as they moved. And the mixture of colors in their apparel was such as to offend Terran eyes with their harsh clash of shade against shade.

Drawn up below the dais were two rows of guards. But the reason for the assembly baffled Ross, since he could not understand the clicking speech.

There came a hollow echoing sound as from a gong. The three on the dais straightened, turned their attention to the other end of the hall. Ross did not need Loketh's gesture to know that something of importance was about to begin.

Down the hall was a somber note in the splash of clashing color. The Terran recognized the gray-blue robe of the Foanna. There were three of the robed ones this time, one slightly in advance of the other two. They came at a gliding pace as if they swept along above that paved flooring, not by planting feet upon it. As they halted below the dais the men there rose.

Ross could read their reluctance to make that concession in the slowness of their movements. They were plainly being compelled to render deference when they longed to refuse it. Then the middle one of the castle lords spoke first.

"Zahur—" Loketh breathed in Ross's ear, his pointed finger indicating the speaker.

Ross longed vainly for the ability to ask questions, a chance to know what was in progress. That the meeting of the two Hawaikan factions was important he did not doubt.

There was an interval of silence after the castle lord finished speaking. To the Terran this spun on and on and he sensed the mounting tension.

This must be a showdown, perhaps even a declaration of open hostilities between Wreckers and the older race. Or perhaps the pause was a subtle weapon of the Foanna, used to throw a less-sophisticated enemy off balance, as a judo fighter might use an opponent's attack as part of his own defense.

When the Foanna did make answer it came in the singsong of chanted words. Ross felt Loketh shiver, felt the crawl of chill along his own spine. The words—if those were words and not just sounds intended to play upon the mind and emotions of a listener—cut into one. Ross wanted to close his ears, thrust his fingers into them to drown out that sound, yet he did not have the power to raise his hands.

It seemed to him that the men on the dais were swaying now as if the chant were a rope leashed about them, pulling them back and forth. There was a clatter; one of the guards had fallen to the floor and lay there, rolling, his hands to his head.

A shout from the dais. The chanting reached a note so high that Ross felt the torment in his ears. Below, the lines of guards had broken. A party of them were heading for the end of the hall, making a wide detour around the Foanna. Loketh gave a small choked cry; his fingers tightened on Ross's forearm with painful intensity as he whispered.

What was about to happen meant something important. To Loketh or to him? Ashe! Was this concerned with Ashe? Ross crowded against the opening, tried to see the direction in which the guards had disappeared.

The wait made him doubly impatient. One of the men on the dais had dropped on the bench there, his head forward on his hands, his shoulders quivering. But the one Loketh had identified as Zahur still fronted the Foanna spokesman, and Ross gave tribute to the strength of will which kept him there.

They were returning, the guards, and herded between their lines three men. Two were Hawaikans, their bare dark bodies easily identifiable. But the third—Ashe! Ross almost shouted his name aloud.

The Terran stumbled along and there was a bandage above his knee. He had been stripped to his swimming trunks, all his equipment taken from him. There was a dark bruise on his left temple, the angry weal of a lash mark on neck and shoulder.

Ross's hands clenched. Never in his life had he so desperately wanted a weapon as he did at that moment. To spray the company below with a machine gun would have given him great satisfaction. But he had nothing but the knife in his belt and he was as cut off from Ashe as if they were in separate cells of some prison.

The caution which had been one of his inborn gifts and which had been fostered by his training, clamped down on his first wild desire for action. There was not the slightest chance of his doing Ashe any good at the present. But he had this much—he knew that Gordon was alive and that he was in the aliens' hands. Faced by those facts Ross could plan his own moves.

The Foanna chant began again, and the three prisoners moved; the two Hawaikans turned, set themselves on either side of Ashe, and gave him support. Their actions had a mechanical quality as if they were directed by a will beyond their own. Ashe gazed about him at the Wreckers and the robed figures. His awareness of them both suggested to Ross that if the natives had come under the control of the Foanna, the Terran resisted their influence. But Ashe did not try to escape the assistance of his two fellow prisoners, and he limped with their aid back down the hall, following the Foanna.

Ross deduced that the captives had been transferred from the lord of the castle to the Foanna. Which meant Ashe was on his way to another destination. The Terran was on his feet and headed back, intent on returning to the sea cave and starting out after Ashe as soon as he could.

"You have found Gordon!" Karara read his news from his face.

"The Wreckers had him prisoner. Now they've turned him over to the Foanna—"

"What will *they* do with him?" the girl demanded of Loketh.

His answer came roundabout as usual as the native squatted by the analyzer and clicked his answer into it.

"They have claimed the wreck survivors for tribute. Your companion will be witches' meat."

"Witches' meat?" repeated Ross, uncomprehending.

Then Karara drew a gagged breath which was a gasp of horror.

"Sacrifice! Ross, he must mean they are going to use Gordon for a sacrifice."

Ross stiffened and then whirled to catch Loketh by the shoulders. The inability to question the native directly was an added disaster now.

"Where are they taking him? Where?" He began that fiercely, and then forced control on himself.

Karara's eyes were half closed, her head back; she was manifestly aiming that inquiry at the dolphins, to be translated to Loketh.

Symbols burned on the analyzer screen.

"The Foanna have their own fortress. It can be entered best by sea. There is a boat ... I can show you, for it is my own secret."

"Tell him—yes, as soon as we can!" Ross broke out. The old feeling that time was all-important worried at him. Witches' meat ... witches' meat ... the words were sharp as a lash.

THE FREE ROVERS

Twilight made a gray world where one could not trace the true meeting of land and water, sea and sky. Surely the haze about them was more than just the normal dusk of coming night.

Ross balanced in the middle of the skiff as it bobbed along the swell of waves inside a barrier reef. To his mind the craft carrying the three of them and their net of supplies was too frail, rode too high. But Karara paddling in the bow, Loketh at the stern seemed to be content, and Ross could not, for pride's sake, question their competency. He comforted himself with the knowledge that no agent was able to absorb every primitive skill, and Karara's people had explored the Pacific in out-rigger canoes hardly more stable than their present vessel, navigating by currents and stars.

Smothering his feeling of helplessness and the slow anger that roused in him, the Terran busied himself with study of a sort. They had had the longer part of the day in the cave before Loketh would agree to venture out of hiding and paddle south. Ross, using the analyzer, had, with Loketh's aid, set about learning what he could of the native tongue.

Now possessed of a working vocabulary of clicked words, he was able to follow Loketh's speech so that translation through the dolphins was not necessary except for complicated directions. Also, he had a more detailed briefing of the present situation on Hawaika.

Enough to know that they might be embarking on a mad venture. The citadel of the Foanna was distinctly forbidden ground, not only for Loketh's people but also for the Foanna's Hawaikan followers who were housed and labored in an outer ring of fortification-cum-village. Those natives were, Ross gathered, a hereditary corps of servants and warriors, born to that status and not recruited from the native population at large. As such, they were armored by the "magic" of their masters.

"If the Foanna are so powerful," Ross had demanded, "why do you go with us against them?" To depend so heavily on the native made him uneasy.

The Hawaikan looked to Karara. One of his hands raised; his fingers sketched a sign toward the girl.

"With the Sea Maid and her magic I do not fear." He paused before adding, "Always has it been said of me—and to me—that I am a useless one, fit only to do women's tasks. No word weaver shall ever chant my battle deeds in the great hall of Zahur. I who am Zahur's true son can not carry my sword in any lord's train. But now you offer me one of the great to-be-remembered quests. If I go, so may I prove that I am a man, even if I go limpingly. There is nothing the Foanna can do to me which is worse than what the Shadow has already done. Choosing to follow you I may stand up to face Zahur in his own hall, show him that the blood of his House has not been drained from my veins because I walk crookedly!"

There was such bitter fire, not only in the sputtering rush of Loketh's words, but in his eyes, his face, the wry twist of his lips, that Ross believed him. The Terran no longer had any doubts that the castle outcast was willing to brave the unknown terrors of the Foanna keep, not just to aid Ross whom he considered himself bound to serve by the customs of his people, but because he saw in this venture a chance to gain what he had never had, a place in his warrior culture.

Shut off from the normal life of his people, he had early turned to the sea. His twisted leg had not proved a handicap in the water, and he stated with confidence that he was the best swimmer in the castle. Not that the men of his father's following had taken greatly to the sea, which they looked upon merely as a way of preying upon the true sea rovers.

The reef on which the ships had been wrecked was a snare of sorts—first by the whim of nature when wind and current piled up the trading ships there. Then, Ross was startled when Loketh elaborated on a later development of that trap.

"So Zahur returned from this meeting and set up a great magic among the rock, according to the spells he was taught. Now ships are drawn there so the wrecks have been many and Zahur becomes an even greater lord with many men coming to take sword oath under him."

"This magic," asked Ross, "of what manner is it and where did Zahur obtain it?"

"It is fashioned so—" Loketh sketched two straight lines in the air, "not curved as a sword. And the color of water under a storm sky, both rods being as tall as a man. There was much care to set them in place, that was done by a man of Glicmas."

"A man of Glicmas?"

"Glicmas is now the high lord of the Iccio. He is blood kin to Zahur, yet Zahur must take sword oath to send to Glicmas a fourth of all his sea-gleanings for a year in payment for this magic."

"And Glicmas, where did he get it? From the Foanna?"

Loketh made an emphatic denial of that. "No, the Foanna have spoken out against their use, making even greater ill feeling between the Old Ones and the coast people. It is said that Glicmas saw a great wonder in the sky and followed it to a high place of his own country. A mountain broke in twain and a voice issued forth from the rent, calling that the lord of the country come and stand to hear it. When Glicmas did so he was told that the magic would be his. Then the mountain closed again and he found many strange things upon the ground. As he uses them they make him akin to the Foanna in power. Some he gives to those who are his blood kin, and together they will be great until they close their fists not only upon the sea rovers, but upon the Foanna also. This they have come to believe."

"But you do not?" Karara asked then.

"I do not know, Sea Maid. The time is coming when perhaps they shall have their chance to prove how strong is their magic. Already the Rovers gather in fleets as they never did before. And it seems that they, too, have found a new magic, for their ships fly through the water, depending no longer on wind-filling sails, or upon strong arms of men at long paddles. There is a struggle before us. But that you must know, being who and what you are, Sea Maid."

"And what do you think I am? What do you think Ross is?"

"If the Foanna dwell on land and hold old knowledge and power beyond our reckoning in their two hands," he replied, "then it is possible that the same could have roots in the sea. It is my belief that you are of the Shades, but not the Shadow. And this warrior is also of your kind—but perhaps in different degree, putting into action your desires and wishes. Thus, if you go up against the Foanna, you shall be well matched, kind to kind."

Nice to be so certain of that, Ross thought. He did not share Loketh's confidence on that subject.

"The Shades ... the Shadow ..." Karara persisted. "What are these, Loketh?"

An odd expression crossed the Hawaikan's face. "Are those not known to you, Sea Maid? Indeed, then you are of a breed different from the men of land. The Shades are those of power who may come to the aid of men should it be their desire to influence the future. And the Shadow ... the Shadow is That Which Ends All—man, hope, good. To Which there is no appeal, and Which holds a vast and enduring hatred for that which has life and full substance."

"So Zahur has this new magic. Is it the gift of Shades or Shadow?" Ross brought them back to the subject which had sparked in him a small warning signal.

"Zahur prospers mightily." Loketh's answer was ambiguous.

"And so the Shadow could not provide such magic?" The Terran pushed.

But before the Hawaikan had a chance to answer, Karara added another question:

"But you believe that it did?"

"I do not know. Only the magic has made Zahur a part of Glicmas, and Glicmas is now perhaps a part of that which spoke from the mountain. It is not well to accept gifts which tie one man to another unless there is from the first a saying of how deep that bond may run."

"I think you are wise in that, Loketh," Karara said.

But the uneasiness had grown in Ross. Alien powers, out of a mountain heart, passed from one lord to another. And on the other hand the Rovers' sudden magic in turn, lending their ships wings. The two facts balanced in an odd way. Back on Terra there had been those sudden and unaccountable jumps in technical knowledge on the part of the enemy, jumps which had set in action the whole Time Travel service of which he had become a part. And these jumps had not been the result of normal research; they had come from the looting of derelict spaceships wrecked on his world in the far past.

Could driblets of the same stellar knowledge have been here deliberately fed to warring communities? He asked Loketh about the possibility of space-borne explorers. But to the Hawaikan that was a totally foreign conception. The stars, for Loketh, were the doorways and windows of the Shades, and he treated the suggestion of space travel as perhaps natural to those all-powerful specters, but certainly not for beings like himself. There was no hint that Hawaika had been openly visited by a galactic ship. Though that did not bar such landings. The planet was, Ross thought, thinly populated. Whole sections of the interiors of the larger islands were wilderness, and this world must be in the same state of only partial occupation as his own earth had been in the Bronze Age when tribes on the march had fanned out into virgin wilderness, great forests, and steppes unwalked by man before their coming.

Now as he balanced in the canoe and tried to keep his mind off the queasiness in his middle and the insecurity of the one thickness of sea-creature hide stretched over a bone framework which made up the craft between his person and the water, Ross still mulled over what might be true. Had the galactic invaders for their own purposes begun to meddle here, leaking weapons or tools to upset what must be a very delicate balance of power? Why? To bring on a conflict which would occupy the native population to the point of exhaustion or depopulation? So they could win a world for their own purposes without effort or risk on their part? Such cold-blooded fishing in carefully troubled waters fitted very well with the persons of the Baldies as he had known them on Terra.

And he could not set aside that memory of this very coast as he had seen it through the peep, the castle in ruins, tall pylons reaching from the land into the sea. Was this the beginning of that change which would end in the Hawaika of his own time, empty of intelligent life, shattered into a loose network of islands?

"This fog is strange." Karara's words startled Ross to return to the here and now.

The haze he had been only half conscious of when they had put out from the tiny secret bay where Loketh kept his boat, was truly a fog, piling up in soft billows and cutting down visibility with speed.

"The Foanna!" Loketh's answer was sharp, a recognition of danger. "Their magic—they hide their place so! There is trouble, trouble on the move!"

"Do we land then?" Ross did not ascribe the present blotting out of the landscape to any real manipulation of nature on the part of the all-powerful Foanna. Too many times the reputations of "medicine men" had been so enhanced by coincidence. But he did doubt the wisdom of trying to bore ahead blindly in this murk.

"Taua and Tino-rau can guide us," Karara reminded him. "Throw out the rope, Ross. What is above water will not confuse them."

He moved cautiously, striving to adapt his actions to the swing of the boat. The line was ready coiled to hand and he tossed the loose end overboard, to feel the cord jerk taut as one of the dolphins caught it up.

They were being towed now, though both paddlers reinforced the forward tug with their efforts. The curtain gathering above the surface of the water did not hamper the swimmers beneath its surface, and Ross felt relief. He turned his head to speak to Loketh.

"How near are we?"

The mist had thickened to the point that, close as the native was, the lines of his body blurred. His clicking answer seemed distorted, too, almost as if the fog had altered not only his form but his personality.

"Maybe very soon now. We must see the sea gate before we are sure."

"And if we aren't able to see that?" challenged Ross.

"The sea gate is above and below the water. Those who obey the Sea Maid, who are able to speak thought to thought, will find it if we can not."

But they were never to reach that goal. Karara gave warning: "There are ships about."

Ross knew that the dolphins had told her. He demanded in turn: "What kind?"

"Larger, much larger than this."

Then Loketh broke in: "A Rover Raider—three of them!"

Ross frowned. He was the cripple here. The other two, with their ability to communicate with the dolphins, were the sighted, he the blind. And he resented his handicap in a burst of bitterness which must have colored his tone as he ordered, "Head inshore—now!"

Once on land, even in the fog, he felt that they had the advantage in any hide-and-seek which might ensue with this superior enemy force. But afloat he was helpless and vulnerable, a state Ross did not accept easily.

"No," Loketh returned as sharply. "There is no place to land along the cliff."

"We are between two of the ships," Karara reported.

"Your paddles—" Ross schooled his voice to a whisper, "hold them—don't use them. Let the dolphins take us on. In the fog, if we make no sound, we may get by the ships."

"Right!" Karara agreed, and he heard an assenting grunt from Loketh.

They were moving very slowly. Strong as the dolphins were, they dared not expend all their strength on towing the skiff too fast. Ross thought furiously. Perhaps the sea could be their way of escape if the need arose. He had no idea why raiding ships were moving under the cover of fog into the vicinity of the Foanna citadel. But the Terran's knowledge of tactics led him to guess that this impending visit was not anticipated by the Foanna, nor was it a friendly one. And, as veteran seamen who should normally be wary of fog as thick as this, the Rovers themselves must have a driving reason, or some safeguard which led them here now.

But dared the three spill out of their boat, trust to their swimming ability and that of the dolphins, and invade the Foanna sea gate so? Could they use the coming Rover attack as a cover for their own invasion of the hold? Ross considered that the odds in their favor were beginning to look better.

He whispered his idea and began to prepare their gear. The boat was still headed for the shore the three could not see. But they could hear sounds out of the white cotton wall which told them how completely they were boxed in by the raiders; creaks, whispers, noises, Ross could not readily identify, carried across the waves.

Before leaving the cave and beginning this voyage they had introduced Loketh to the use of the gill-pack, made him practice in the depths of the cave pool with one of the extras drawn through the gate among the supplies. Now all three were equipped with the water aid, and they could be gone in the sea before the trap closed.

"The supply net—" Ross warned Karara. A moment or two later there was a small bump against the skiff at his left hand. He cautiously raised the collection of containers and eased the burden into the water, knowing that one of the dolphins would take charge of it.

However, he was not prepared for what happened next. Under him the boat lurched first one way and then the other in sharp jerks as if the dolphins were trying to spill them into the sea. Ross heard Karara call out, her voice thin and frightened:

"Taua! Tino-rau! They have gone mad! They will not listen!"

The boat raced in a zigag path. Loketh clutched at Ross, striving to steady him, to keep the boat on an even keel.

"The Foanna—!" Just as Loketh cried out, Karara plunged over the prow of the boat, whether by design or chance Ross did not know.

And then the craft whirled about, smashed side against side with a dark bulk looming out of the fog. Above, Ross heard cries, knew that they had crashed against one of the raiders. He fought to retain his balance, but he had been knocked to the bottom of the boat against Loketh and they struggled together, unable to move during a precious second or two.

Out of the air over their heads dropped a mass of waving strands which enveloped both of them. The stuff was adhesive, slimy. Ross let out a choked cry as the lines tightened about his arms and body, pinioning him.

Those tightened, wove a net. Now he was being drawn up out of the plunging skiff, a helpless captive. His flailing legs, still free of the slimy cords, struck against the side of the larger ship. Then he swung in, over the well of the deck, thudded down on that surface with bruising force, unable to understand anything except that he had been taken prisoner by a very effective device.

Loketh dropped beside him. But Karara was not brought in, and Ross held to that small bit of hope. Had she made it to freedom by dropping into the water before the Rovers netted them? He could see men gathering about him, masked and distorted in the fog. Then he was rolled across the deck, boosted over the edge of a hatch and knew an instant of terror as he fell into the depth below.

How long was he unconscious? It could not have been very long, Ross decided, as he opened his eyes on dark, heard the small sounds of the ship. He lay very still, trying to remember, to gather his wits before he tried to flex his arms. They were held tight to his sides by strands which no longer seemed slimy, but were wrinkling as they dried. There was an odor from them which gagged him. But there was no loosening of those loops in spite of his struggles, which grew more intense as his strength returned. And at last he lay panting, knowing there was no easy way of escape from here.

BATTLE TEST

Babble of speech, cries, sounded muffled to Ross, made a mounting clamor on the deck. Had the raiders' ship been boarded? Was it now under attack? He strove to hear and think through the pain in his head, the bewilderment.

"Loketh?" He was certain that the Hawaikan had been dumped into the same hold.

The only answer was a low moan, a mutter from the dark. Ross began to inch his way in that direction. He was no seaman, but during that worm's progress he realized that the ship itself had changed. The vibration which had carried through the planks on which he lay was stilled. Some engine shut off; one portion of his mind put that into familiar terms. Now the vessel rocked with the waves, did not bore through them.

Ross brought up against another body.

"Loketh!"

"Ahhhhh ... the fire ... the fire—!" The half-intelligible answer held no meaning for the Terran. "It burns in my head ... the fire—"

The rocking of the ship rolled Ross away from his fellow prisoner toward the opposite side of the hold. There was a roar of voice, bull strong above the noise on deck, then the sound of feet back and forth there.

"The fire ... ahhh—" Loketh's voice rose to a scream.

Ross was now wedged between two abutments he could not see and from which his best efforts could not free him. The pitching of the ship was more pronounced. Remembering the two vessels he had seen pounded to bits on the reef, Ross wondered if the same doom loomed for this one. But that disaster had occurred during a storm. And, save for the fog, this had been a calm night, the sea untroubled.

Unless—maybe the shaking his body had received during the past few moments had sharpened his thinking—unless the Foanna had their own means of protection at the sea gate and this was the result. The dolphins.... What had made Tino-rau and Taua react as they did? And if the Rover ship was out of control, it would be a good time to attempt escape.

"Loketh!" Ross dared to call louder. "Loketh!" He struggled against the drying strands which bound him from shoulder to mid thigh. There was no give in them.

More sounds from the upper deck. Now the ship was answering to direction again. The Terran heard sounds he could not identify, and the ship no longer rocked so violently. Loketh moaned.

As far as Ross could judge, they were heading out to sea.

"Loketh!" He wanted information; he must have it! To be so ignorant of what was going on was unbearable frustration. If they were now prisoners in a ship leaving the island behind.... The threat of that was enough to set Ross struggling with his bonds until he lay panting with exhaustion.

"Rossss?" Only a Hawaikan could make that name a hiss.

"Here! Loketh?" But of course it was Loketh.

"I am here." The other's voice sounded oddly weak as if it issued from a man drained by a long illness.

"What happened to you?" Ross demanded.

"The fire ... the fire in my head—eating ... eating...." Loketh's reply came with long pauses between the words.

The Terran was puzzled. What fire? Loketh had certainly reacted to something beyond the unceremonious handling they had received as captives. This whole ship had reacted. And the dolphins.... But what fire was Loketh talking about?

"I did not feel anything," he stated to himself as well as to the Hawaikan.

"Nothing burning in your head? So you could not think—"

"No."

"It must have been the Foanna magic. Fire eating so that a man is nothing, only that which fire feeds upon!"

Karara! Ross's thoughts flashed back to those few seconds when the dolphins had seemed to go crazy. Karara had then called out something about the Foanna. So the dolphins must have felt this, and Karara, and Loketh. Whatever *it* was. But why not Ross Murdock?

Karara possessed an extra, undefinable sense which gave her contact with the dolphins. Loketh had a mind which those could read in turn. But such communication was closed to Ross.

At first that realization carried with it a feeling of shame and loss. That he did not have what these others possessed, a subtle power beyond the body, a part of mind, was humbling. Just as he had felt shut out and crippled when he had been forced to use the analyzer instead of the sense the others had, so did he suffer now.

Then Ross laughed shortly. All right, sometimes insensitivity could be a defense as it had at the sea gate. Suppose his lack could also be a weapon? He had not been knocked out as the others appeared to be. But for the bad luck of having been captured before the raiders had succumbed, Ross could, perhaps, have been master of this ship by now. He did not laugh now; he smiled sardonically at his own grandiose reaction. No use thinking about what might have been, just file this fact for future reference.

A creaking overhead heralded the opening of the hatch. Light lanced down into the cubby, and a figure swung over and down a side ladder, coming to stand over Ross, feet apart for balancing, accommodating to the swing of the vessel with the ease of long practice.

Thus Ross came face to face with his first representative of the third party in the Hawaikan tangle of power—a Rover.

The seaman was tall, with a heavier development of shoulder and upper arms than the landsmen. Like the guards he wore supple armor, but this had been colored or overlaid with a pearly hue in which other tints wove opaline lines. His head was bare except for a broad, scaled band running from the nape of his neck to the mid-point of his forehead, a band supporting a sharply serrated crest not unlike the erect fin of some Terran fish.

Now as he stood, fists planted on hips, the Rover presented a formidable figure, and Ross recognized in him the air of command. This must be one of the ship's officers.

Dark eyes surveyed Ross with interest. The light from the deck focused directly across the raider's shoulder to catch the Terran in its full glare, and Ross fought the need for squinting. But he tried to give back stare for stare, confidence for self-confidence.

On Terra in the past more than one adventurer's life had been saved simply because he had the will and nerve enough to face his captors without any display of anxiety. Such bravado might not hold here and now, but it was the only weapon Ross had to hand and he used it.

"You—" the Rover broke the silence first, "you are not of the Foanna—" He paused as if waiting an answer—denial or protest. Ross provided neither.

"No, not of the Foanna, nor of the scum of the coast either." Again a pause.

"So, what manner of fish has come to the net of Torgul?" He called an order aloft. "A rope here! We'll have this fish and its fellow out—"

Loketh and Ross were jerked up to the outer deck, dumped into the midst of a crowd of seamen. The Hawaikan was left to lie but, at a gesture from the officer, Ross was set on his feet. He could see the nature of his bonds now, a network of dull gray strands, shriveled and stinking, but not giving in the least when he made another try at moving his arms.

"Ho—" The officer grinned. "This fish does not like the net! You have teeth, fish. Use them, slash yourself free."

A murmur of applause from the crew answered that mild taunt. Ross thought it time for a countermove.

"I see you do not come too close to those teeth." He used the most defiant words his limited Hawaikan vocabulary offered.

There was a moment of silence, and then the officer clapped his hands together with a sharp explosion of sound.

"You would use your teeth, fish?" he asked and his tone could be a warning.

This was going it blind with a vengeance, but Ross took the next leap in the dark. He had the feeling, which often came to him in tight quarters, that he was being supplied from some hard core of endurance and determination far within him with the right words, the fortunate guess.

"On which one of you?" He drew his lips tight, displaying those same teeth, wondering for one startled moment if he should take the Rover's query literally.

"Vistur! Vistur!" More than one voice called.

One of the crew took a step or two forward. Like Torgul, he was tall and heavy, his over-long arms well muscled. There were scars on his forearms, the seam of one up his jaw. He looked what he was, a very tough fighting man, one who was judged so by peers as seasoned and dangerous.

"Do you choose to prove your words on Vistur, fish?" Again the officer had a formal note in his question, as if this was all part of some ceremony.

"If he meets with me as he stands—no other weapons." Ross flashed back.

Now he had another reaction from them. There were some jeers, a sprinkling of threats as to Vistur's intentions. But Ross caught also the fact that two or three of them had gone silent and were eyeing him in a new and more searching fashion and that Torgul was one of those.

Vistur laughed. "Well said, fish. So shall it be."

Torgul's hand came out, palm up, facing Ross. In its hollow was a small object the Terran could not see clearly. A new weapon? Only the officer made no move to touch it to Ross, the hand merely moved in a series of waves in mid-air. Then the Rover spoke.

"He carries no unlawful magic."

Vistur nodded. "He's no Foanna. And what need have I to fear the spells of any coast crawler? I am Vistur!"

Again the yells of his supporters arose in hearty answer. The statement held more complete and quiet confidence than any wordy boast.

"And I am Ross Murdock!" The Terran matched the Rover tone for tone. "But does a fish swim with its fins bound to its sides? Or does Vistur fear a free fish too greatly to face one?"

His taunt brought the result Ross wanted. The ties were cut from behind, to flutter down as withered, useless strings. Ross flexed his arms. Tight as those thongs had been they had not constricted circulation, and he was ready to meet Vistur. The Terran did not doubt that the Rover champion was a formidable fighter, but he had not had the advantage of going through one of the Agent training courses. Every trick of unarmed fighting known on his own world had been pounded into Ross long ago. His hands and feet could be as deadly weapons as any crook-bladed sword—or gun—provided he could get close enough to use them properly.

Vistur stripped off his weapon belt, put to one side his helmet, showing that under it his hair was plaited into a braid coiled about the crown of his head to provide what must be an extra padding for that strangely narrowed helm. Then he peeled off his armor, peeled it literally indeed, catching the lower edge of the scaled covering with his hands and pulling it up and over his head and shoulders as one might skin off a knitted garment. Now he stood facing Ross, wearing little more than the Terran's swimming trunks.

Ross had dropped his belt and gill-pack. He moved into the circle the crew had made. From above came a strong light, centering from a point on the mainmast and giving him good sight of his opponent.

Vistur was being urged to make a quick end of the reckless challenger, his supporters shouting directions and encouragement. But if the Rover had confidence, he also possessed the more intelligent and valuable trait of caution in the face of the unknown. He outweighed, apparently outmatched Ross, but he did not rush in rashly as his backers wished him to.

They circled, Ross studying every move of the Rover's muscles, every slight fraction of change in the other's balance. There would be something to telegraph an attack from the other. For he intended to fight purely in defense.

The charge came at last as the crew grew impatient and yelled their impatience to see the prisoner taught a lesson. But Ross did not believe it was that which sent Vistur at him. The Hawaikan simply thought he knew the best way to take the Terran.

Ross ducked so that a hammer blow merely grazed him. But the Terran's stiffened hand swept sidewise in a judo chop. Vistur gave a whooping cry and went to his knees and Ross swung again, sending the Rover flat to the deck. It had been quick but not so vicious as it might have been. The Terran had no desire to kill or even disable Vistur for more than a few minutes. His victim would carry a couple of aching bruises and perhaps a hearty respect for a new mode of fighting from this encounter. He could have as easily been dead had either of those blows landed other than where Ross chose to plant them.

"Ahhhh—"

The Terran swung around, setting his back to the foot of the mast. Had he guessed wrong? With their chosen champion down, would the crew now rush him? He had gambled on the element of fair play which existed in a primitive Terran warrior society after a man-to-man challenge. But he could be wrong. Ross waited, tense. Just let one of them pull a weapon, and it could be his end.

Two of them were aiding Vistur to his feet. The Rover's breath whistled in and out of him with that same whooping, and both of his hands rose unsteadily to his chest. The majority of his fellows stared from him to the slighter Terran as if unable to believe the evidence of their eyes.

Torgul gathered up from the deck the belt and gill-pack Ross had shed in preparation for the fight. He turned the belt around over his forearm until the empty knife sheath was uppermost. One of the crew came forward and slammed back into its proper place the long diver's knife which had been there when Ross was captured. Then the Rover offered belt and gill-pack to Ross. The Terran relaxed. His gamble had paid off; by the present signs he had won his freedom.

"And my swordsman?" As he buckled on the belt Ross nodded at Loketh still lying bound where they had pushed him at the beginning of the fight.

"He is sworn to you?" Torgul asked.

"He is."

"Loose the coast rat then," the Rover ordered. "Now—tell me, stranger, what manner of man are you? Do you come from the Foanna, after all? You have a magic which is not our magic, since the Stone of Phutka did not reveal it on you. Are you from the Shades?"

His fingers moved in the same sign Loketh had once made before Karara. Ross gave his chosen explanation.

"I am from the sea, Captain. As for the Foanna, they are no friend to me, since they hold captive in their keep one who is my brother-kin."

Torgul stared him up and down. "You say you are from the sea. I have been a Rover since I was able to stumble on my two feet across a deck, after the manner and custom of my people, yet I have never seen your like before. Perhaps your coming means ill to me and mine, but by the Law of Battle, you have won your freedom on this ship. I swear to you, however, stranger, that if ill comes from you, then the Law will not hold, and you shall match your magic against the Strength of Phutka. That you shall discover is another thing altogether."

"I will swear any oath you desire of me, Captain, that I have no ill toward you and yours. There is only one wish I hold: to bring him whom I seek out from the Foanna hold before they make him witches' meat."

"That will be a task worthy of any magic you may be able to summon, stranger. We have tasted this night of the power of the sea gate. Though we went in under the Will of Phutka, we were as weeds whirled about on the waves. Who enters that gate must have more force than any we now know."

"And you, too, then have a score to settle with the Foanna?"

"We have a score against the Foanna, or against their magic," Torgul admitted. "Three ships—one island fairing—are gone as if they never were! And those who went with them are of our fleet-clan. There is the work of the Shadow stretching dark and heavy across the sea, new come into these waters. But there remains nothing we can do this night. We have been lucky to win to sea again. Now, stranger, what shall we do with you? Or will you take to the sea again since you name it as home?"

"Not here," Ross countered swiftly. He must gain some idea of where they might be in relation to the island, how far from its shore. Karara and the dolphins—what had happened to them?

"You took no other prisoners?" Ross had to ask.

"There were more of you?" Torgul countered.

"Yes." No need to say how many, Ross decided.

"We saw no others. You ... all of you—" the Captain rounded on the still-clustered crew, "get about your work! We must raise Kyn Add by morning and report to the council."

He walked away and Ross, determined to learn all he could, followed him into the stern cabin. Here again the Terran was faced with barbaric splendor in carvings, hangings, a wealth of plate and furnishing not too different from the display he had seen in the Wreckers' castle. As Ross hesitated just within the doorway Torgul glanced back at him.

"You have your life and that of your man, stranger. Do not ask more of me, unless you have that within your hands to enforce the asking."

"I want nothing, save to be returned to where you took me, Captain."

Torgul smiled grimly. "You are the sea, you yourself said that. The sea is wide, but it is all one. Through it you must have your own paths. Take any you choose. But I do not risk my ship again into what lies in wait before the gates of the Foanna."

"Where do you go then, Captain?"

"To Kyn Add. You have your own choice, stranger—the sea or our fairing."

There would be no way of changing the Rover's decision, Ross thought. And even with the gill-pack he could not swim back to where he had been taken. There were no guideposts in the sea. But a longer acquaintance with Torgul might be helpful.

"Kyn Add then, Captain." He made the next move to prove equality and establish himself with this Rover, seating himself at the table as one who had the right to share the Captain's quarters.

DEATH AT KYN ADD

The hour was close to dawn again and a need for sleep weighted Ross's eyelids, was a craving as strong as hunger. Still restlessness had brought him on deck, sent him to pacing, alert to this vessel and its crew.

He had seen the ships of the Terran Bronze Age traders—small craft compared to those of his own time, depending upon oarsmen when the wind failed their sails, creeping along coasts rather than venturing too far into dangerous seas, sometimes even tying up at the shore each night. There had been other ships, leaner, hardier. Those had plunged into the unknown, touching lands beyond the sea mists, sailed and oared by men plagued by the need to learn what lay beyond the horizon.

And here was such a ship, taut, well kept, larger than the Viking longboats Ross had watched on the tapes of the Project's collection, yet most like those far-faring Terran craft. The prow curved up in a mighty bowsprit where was the carved likeness of the sea dragon Ross had fought in the Hawaika of his own time. The eyes of that monster flashed with a regular blink of light which the Terran did not understand. Was it a signal or merely a device to threaten a possible enemy?

There were sails, now furled as this ship bored on, answering to the steady throb of what could only be an engine. And his puzzlement held. A Viking longboat powered by motor? The mixture was incongruous.

The crew were uniform as to face. All of them wore the flexible pearly armor, the skull-strip helmets. Though there were individual differences in ornaments and the choice of weapons. The majority of the men did carry curve-pointed swords, though those were broader and heavier than those the Terran had seen ashore. But several had axes with sickle-shaped heads, whose points curved so far back that they nearly met to form a circle.

Spaced at regular intervals on deck were boxlike objects fronting what resembled gun ports. And smaller ones of the same type were on the raised deck at the stern and mounted in the prow, their muzzles, if the square fronts might be deemed muzzles, flanking the blinking dragon head. Catapults of some type? Ross wondered.

"Rosss—" His name was given the hiss Loketh used, but it was not the Wrecker youth who joined him now at the stern of the ship. "Ho ... that was strong magic, that fighting knowledge of yours!"

Vistur rubbed his chest reminiscently. "You have big magic, sea man. But then you serve the Maid, do you not? Your swordsman has told us that even the great fish understand and obey her."

"Some fish," qualified Ross.

"Such fish as that, perhaps?" Vistur pointed to the curling wake of foam.

Startled, Ross stared in that direction. Torgul's command was the centermost in a trio of ships, and those cruised in a line, leaving three trails of troubled wave behind them. Coming up now to port in the comparative calm between two wakes was a dark object. In the limited light Ross could be sure of nothing save that it trailed the ships, appeared to rest on or only lightly in the water, and that its speed was less than that of the vessels it doggedly pursued.

"A fish—that?" Ross asked.

"Watch!" Vistur ordered.

But the Hawaikan's sight must have been keener than the Terran's. Had there been a quick movement back there? Ross could not be sure.

"What happened?" He turned to Vistur for enlightenment.

"As a salkar it leaps now and then above the surface. But that is no salkar. Unless, Ross, you who say you are from the sea have servants unlike any finned one we have drawn in by net or line before this day."

The dolphins! Could Tino-rau or Taua or both be in steady pursuit of the ships? But Karara ... Ross leaned against the rail, stared until his eyes began to water from the strain of trying to make out the nature of the black blot. No use, the distance was too great. He brought his fist down against the wood, trying to control his impatience. More than half of him wanted to burst into Torgul's quarters, demand that the Captain bring the ship about to pick up or contact that trailer or trailers.

"Yours?" again Vistur asked.

Ross had tight rein on himself now. "I do not know. It could well be."

It could well be also that the smart thing would be to encourage the Rovers to believe that he had a force of sea dwellers much larger than the four Time castaways. The leader of an army—or a navy—had more prestige in any truce discussion than a member of a lost scouting party. But the thought that the dolphins could be trailing held both promise and worry—promise of allies, and worry over what had happened to Karara. Had she, too, disappeared after Ashe into the hold of the Foanna?

The day did not continue to lighten. Though there was no cottony mist as had enclosed them the night before, there was an odd muting of sea and sky, limiting vision. Shortly Ross was unable to sight the follower or followers. Even Vistur admitted he had lost visual contact. Had the blot been hopelessly outdistanced, or was it still dogging the wakes of the Rover ships?

Ross shared the morning meal with Captain Torgul, a round of leathery substance with a salty, meaty flavor, and a thick mixture of what might be native fruit reduced to a tart paste. Once before he had tasted alien food when in the derelict spaceship it had meant eat or starve. And this was a like circumstance, since their emergency ration supplies had been lost in the net. But though he was apprehensive, no ill effects followed. Torgul had been uncommunicative earlier; now he was looser of tongue, volunteering that they were almost to their port—the fairing of Kyn Add.

The Terran had no idea how far he might question the Hawaikan, yet the fuller his information the better. He discovered that Torgul appeared willing to accept Ross's statement that he was from a distant part of the sea and that local customs differed from those he knew.

Living on and by the sea the Rovers were quick-witted, adaptive, with a highly flexible if loose-knit organization of fleet-clans. Each of these had control over certain islands which served them as "fairings," ports for refitting and anchorage between voyages, usually ruggedly wooded where the sea people could find the raw material for their ships. Colonies of clans took to the sea, not in the slim, swift cruisers like the ship Ross was now on, but in larger, deeper vessels providing living quarters and warehouses afloat. They lived by trade and raiding, spending only a portion of the year ashore to grow fast-sprouting crops on their fairing islands and indulge in some manufacture of articles the inhabitants of the larger and more heavily populated islands were not able to duplicate.

Their main article of commerce was, however, a sea-dwelling creature whose supple and well-tanned hide formed their defensive armor and served manifold other uses. This could only be hunted by men trained and fearless enough to brave more than one danger Torgul did not explain in detail. And a cargo of such skins brought enough in trade to keep a normal-sized fleet-clan for a year.

There was warfare among them. Rival clans tried to jump each other's hunting territories, raid fairings. But until the immediate past, Ross gathered, such encounters were relatively bloodless affairs, depending more upon craft and skillful planning to reduce the enemy to a position of disadvantage in which he was forced to acknowledge defeat, rather than ruthless battle of no quarter.

The shore-side Wrecker lords were always considered fair game, and there was no finesse in Rover raids upon them. Those were conducted with a cold-blooded determination to strike hard at a long-time foe. However, within the past year there had been several raids on fairings with the same blood-bath result of a foray on a Wrecker port. And, since all the fleet-clans denied the sneak-and-strike, kill-and-destroy tactics which had finished those Rover holdings, the seafarers were divided in their opinion as to whether the murderous raids were the work of Wreckers suddenly acting out of character and taking to the sea to bring war back to their enemies, or whether there was a rogue fleet moving against their own kind for some purpose no Rover could yet guess.

"And you believe?" Ross asked as Torgul finished his résumé of the new dangers besetting his people.

Torgul's hand, its long, slender fingers spidery to Terran eyes, rubbed back and forth across his chin before he answered:

"It is very hard for one who has fought them long to believe that suddenly those shore rats are entrusting themselves to the waves, venturing out to stir us with their swords. One does not descend into the depths to kick a salkar in the rump; not if one still has his wits safely encased under his skull braid. As for a rogue fleet ... what would turn brother against brother to the extent of slaying children and women? Raiding for a wife, yes, that is common among our youth. And there have been killings over such matters. But not the killing of a woman—never of a child! We are a people who have never as many women as there are men who wish to bring them into the home cabin. And no clan has as many children as they hope the Shades will send them."

"Then who?"

When Torgul did not answer at once Ross glanced at the Captain, and what the Terran thought he saw showing for an instant in the other's eyes was a revelation of danger. So much so that he blurted out:

"You think that I—we—"

"You have named yourself of the sea, stranger, and you have magic which is not ours. Tell me this in truth: Could you not have killed Vistur easily with those two blows if you had wished it?"

Ross took the bold course. "Yes, but I did not. My people kill no more wantonly than yours."

"The coast rats I know, and the Foanna, as well as any man may know their kind and ways, and my people—But you I do not know, sea stranger. And I say to you as I have said before, make me regret that I suffered you to claim battle rights and I shall speedily correct that mistake!"

"Captain!"

That cry had come from the cabin door behind Ross. Torgul was on his feet with the swift movements of a man called many times in the past for an instant response to emergency.

The Terran was close on the Rover's heels as they reached the deck. A cluster of crewmen gathered on the port side near the narrow bow. That odd misty quality this day held provided a murk hard to pierce, but the men were gesturing at a low-riding object rolling with the waves.

That was near enough for even Ross to be able to distinguish a small boat akin to the one in which he, Karara, and Loketh had dared the sea gate of the Foanna.

Torgul took up a great curved shell hanging by a thong on the mainmast. Setting its narrow end to his lips, he blew. A weird booming note, like the coughing of a sea monster, carried over the waves. But there was no answer from the drifting boat, no sign it carried any passengers.

"Hou, hou, hou—" Torgul's signal was re-echoed by shell calls from the other two cruisers.

"Heave to!" the Captain ordered. "Wakti, Zimmon, Yoana—out and bring that in!"

Three of the crew leaped to the railing, poised there for a moment, and then dived almost as one into the water. A rope end was thrown, caught by one of them. And then they swam with powerful strokes toward the drifting boat. Once the rope was made fast the small craft was drawn toward Torgul's command, the crewmen swimming beside it. Ross longed to know the reason for the tense expectancy of the men around him. It was apparent the skiff had some ominous meaning for them.

Ross caught a glimpse of a body huddled within the craft. Under Torgul's orders a sling was dropped, to rise, weighted with a passenger. The Terran was shouldered back from the rail as the limp body was hurried into the Captain's cabin. Several crewmen slid down to make an examination of the boat itself.

Their heads came up, their eyes searched along the rail and centered on Ross. The hostility was so open the Terran braced himself to meet those cold stares as he would a rush from a challenger.

A slight sound behind sent Ross leaping to the right, wanting to get his back against solid protection. Loketh came up, his limp making him awkward so that he clutched at the rail for support. In his other hand was one of the hooked swords bared and ready.

"Get the murderers!" Someone in the back line of the massing crew yipped that.

Ross drew his diver's knife. Shaken at this sudden change in the crew's attitude, he was warily on the defensive. Loketh was beside him now and the Hawaikan nodded to the sea.

"Better go there," he cried. "Over before they try to gut you!"

"Kill!" The word shrilled into a roar from the Rovers. They started up the deck toward Ross and Loketh. Then someone leaped between, and Vistur fronted his own comrades.

"Stand away—" One of the others ran forward, thrusting at the tall Rover with a stiffened out-held arm to fend him out of their path.

Vistur rolled a shoulder, sending the fellow shunting away. He went down while two more, unable to halt, thudded on him. Vistur stamped on an outstretched hand and sent a sword spinning.

"What goes here!" Torgul's demand was loud enough to be heard. It stopped a few of the crew and two more went down as the Captain struck out with his fists. Then he was facing Ross, and the chill in his eyes was the threat the others had voiced.

"I told you, sea stranger, that if I found you were a danger to me or mine, you would meet the Justice of Phutka!"

"You did," Ross returned. "And in what way am I now a danger, Captain?"

"Kyn Add has been taken by those who are not Wreckers, not Rovers, not those who serve the Foanna—but strangers out of the sea!"

Ross could only stare back, confused. And then the full force of his danger struck home. Who those raiding sea strangers could be, he had no idea, but that he was now condemned out of his own mouth was true and he realized that these men were not going to listen to any argument from him in their present state of mind.

The growl of the crew was that of a hungry animal. Ross saw the wisdom in Loketh's choice. Far better chance the open sea than the mob before them.

But his time for choice had passed. Out of nowhere whirled a lacy gray-white net, slapping him back against a bulkhead to glue him there. Ross tried to twist loose, got his head around in time to see Loketh scramble to the top of the rail, turn as if to launch himself at the men speeding for the now helpless Terran. But the Hawaikan's crippled leg failed him and he toppled back overside.

"No!" Again Torgul's shout halted the crew. "He shall take the Black Curse with him when he goes to meet the Shadow—and only one can speak that curse. Bring him!"

Helpless, reeling under their blows, dragged along, Ross was thrown into the Captain's cabin, confronted by a figure braced up by coverings and cushions in Torgul's own chair.

A woman, her face a drawn death's head of skin pulled tight upon bone, yet a fiery inner strength holding her mind above the suffering of her body, looked at the Terran with narrowed eyes. She nursed a bandaged arm against her, and now and then her mouth quivered as if she could not altogether control some emotion or physical pain.

"Yours is the cursing, Lady Jazia. Make it heavy to bear for him as his kind has laid the burden of pain and remembering on all of us."

She brought her good hand up to her mouth, wiping its back across her lips as if to temper their quiver. And all the time her eyes held upon Ross.

"Why do you bring me this man?" Her voice was strained, high. "He is not of those who brought the Shadow to Kyn Add."

"What—?" Torgul began and then schooled his voice to a more normal tone. "Those were from the sea?" He was gentle in his questioning. "They came out of the sea, using weapons against which we had no defense?"

She nodded. "Yes, they made very sure that only the dead remained. But I had gone to the Shrine of Phutka, since it was my day of duty, and Phutka's power threw its shade over me. So I did not die, but I saw—yes, I saw!"

"Not those like me?" Ross dared to speak to her directly.

"No, not those like you. There were few ... only so many—" She spread out her five fingers. "And they were all of one like as if born in one birth. They had no hair on their heads, and their bodies were of this hue—" She plucked at one of the coverings they had heaped around her; it was a lavender-blue mixture.

Ross sucked in his breath, and Torgul was fast to pounce upon the understanding he read in the Terran's face.

"Not your kind—but still you know them!"

"I know them," Ross agreed. "They are the enemy!"

The Baldies from the ancient spaceships, that wholly alien race with whom he had once fought a desperate encounter on the edge of an unnamed sea in the far past of his own world. The galactic voyagers were here—and in active, if secret, conflict with the natives!

WEAPON FROM THE DEPTHS

Jazia told her story with an attention to time and detail which amazed Ross and won his admiration for her breed. She had witnessed the death and destruction of all which was her life, and yet she had the wit to note and record mentally for possible future use all that she had been able to see of the raiders.

They had come out of the sea at dawn, walking with supreme confidence and lack of any fear. Axes flung when they did not reply to the sentries' challenges had never touched them, and a bombardment of heavier missiles had been turned aside. They proved invulnerable to any weapon the Rovers had. Men who made suicidal rushes to use sword or battle ax hand-to-hand had fallen, before they were in striking distance, under spraying tongues of fire from tubes the aliens carried.

Rovers were not fearful or easily cowed, but in the end they had fled from the five invaders, gone to ground in their halls, tried to reach their beached ships, only to die as they ran and hid. The slaughter had been remorseless and entire, leaving Jazia in the hill shrine as the only survivor. She had hidden for the rest of the day, seen the killing of a few fugitives, and that night had stolen to the shore, launched one of the ship's boats which was in a cove well away from the main harbor of the fairing, heading out to sea in hope of meeting the homing cruisers with her warning.

"They stayed there on the island?" Ross asked. That point of her story puzzled him. If the object of that murderous raid had been only to stir up trouble among the Hawaikan Rovers, perhaps turning one clan against the other, as he had deduced when he had listened to Torgul's report of similar happenings, then the star men should have withdrawn as soon as their mission was complete, leaving the dead to call for vengeance in the wrong direction. There would be no reason to court discovery of their true identity by lingering.

"When the boat was asea there were still lights at the fairing hall, and they were not our lights, nor did the dead carry them," she said slowly. "What have those to fear? They can not be killed!"

"If they are still there, that we can put to the test," Torgul replied grimly, and a murmur from his officers bore out his determination.

"And lose all the rest of you?" Ross retorted coldly. "I have met these before; they can will a man to obey them. Look you—" He slammed his left hand flat on the table. The ridges of scar tissue were plain against his tanned skin. He knew no better way of driving home the dangers of dealing with the star men than providing this graphic example. "I held my own hand in fire so that the hurt of it would work against their pull upon my thoughts, against their willing that I come and be easy meat for their butchering."

Jazia's fingers flickered out, smoothed across his old scars lightly as she gazed into his eyes.

"This, too, is true," she said slowly. "For it was also pain of body which kept me from their last snare. They stood by the hall and I saw Prahad, Okun, Mosaji, come out to them to be killed as if they were in a hold net and were drawn. And there was that which called me also so that I would go to them though I called upon the Power of Phutka to save. And the answer to that plea came in a strange way, for I fell as I went from the shrine and cut my arm on the rocks. The pain of that hurt was as a knife severing the net. Then I crawled for the wood and that calling did not come again—"

"If you know so much about them, tell us what weapons we may use to pull them down!" That demand came from Vistur.

Ross shook his head. "I do not know."

"Yet," Jazia mused, "all things which live must also die sooner or later. And it is in my mind that these have also a fate they dread and fear. Perhaps we may find and use it."

"They came from the sea—by a ship, then?" Ross asked. She shook her head.

"No, there was no ship; they came walking through the breaking waves as if they had followed some road across the sea bottom."

"A sub!"

"What is that?" Torgul demanded.

"A type of ship which goes under the waves, not through them, carrying air within its hull for the breathing of the crew."

Torgul's eyes narrowed. One of the other captains who had been summoned from the two companion cruisers gave a snort of disbelief.

"There are no such ships—" he began, to be silenced by a gesture from Torgul.

"We know of no such ships," the other corrected. "But then we know of no such devices as Jazia saw in operation either. How does one war upon these under-the-seas ships, Ross?"

The Terran hesitated. To describe to men who knew nothing of explosives the classic way of dealing with a sub via depth charges was close to impossible. But he did his best.

"Among my people one imprisons in a container a great power. Then the container is dropped near the sub and—"

"And how," broke in the skeptical captain, "do you know where such a ship lies? Can you see it through the water?"

"In a way—not see, but hear. There is a machine which makes for the captain of the above-seas ship a picture of where the sub lies or moves so that he may follow its course. Then when he is near enough he drops the container and the power breaks free—to also break apart the sub."

"Yet the making of such containers and the imprisoning of the power within them," Torgul said, "this is the result of a knowledge which is greater than any save the Foanna may possess. You do not have it?" His conclusion was half statement, half question.

"No. It took many years and the combined knowledge of many men among my people to make such containers, such a listening device. I do not have it."

"Why then think of what we do not have?" Torgul's return was decisive. "What *do* we have?"

Ross's head came up. He was listening, not to anything in that cabin, but to a sound which had come through the port just behind his head. There—it had come again! He was on his feet.

"What—?" Vistur's hand hovered over the ax at his belt. Ross saw their gaze centered on him.

"We may have reinforcements now!" The Terran was already on his way to the deck.

He hurried to the rail and whistled, the thin, shrill summons he had practiced for weeks before he had ever begun this fantastic adventure.

A sleek dark body broke water and the dolphin grin was exposed as Tino-rau answered his call. Though Ross's communication powers with the two finned scouts was very far from Karara's, he caught the message in part and swung around to face the Rovers who had crowded after him.

"We have a way now of learning more about your enemies."

"A boat—it comes without sail or oars!" One of the crew pointed.

Ross waved vigorously, but no hand replied from the skiff. Though it came steadily onward, the three cruisers its apparent goal.

"Karara!" Ross called.

Then side by side with Tino-rau were two wet heads, two masked faces showing as the swimmers trod water—Karara and Loketh.

"Drop ropes!" Ross gave that order as if he rather than Torgul commanded. And the Captain himself was one of those who moved to obey.

Loketh came out of the sea first and as he scrambled over the rail he had his sword ready, looking from Ross to Torgul. The Terran held up empty hands and smiled.

"No trouble now."

Loketh snapped up his mask. "So the Sea Maid said the finned ones reported. Yet before, these thirsted for your blood on their blades. What magic have you worked?"

"None. Just the truth has been discovered." Ross reached for Karara's hand as she came nimbly up the rope, swung her across the rail to the deck where she stood unmasked, brushing back her hair and looking around with a lively curiosity.

"Karara, this is Captain Torgul," Ross introduced the Rover commander who was staring round-eyed at the girl. "Karara is she who swims with the finned ones, and they obey her." Ross gestured to Tino-rau. "It is Taua who brings the skiff?" he asked the Polynesian.

She nodded. "We followed from the gate. Then Loketh came and said that ... that...." She paused and then added, "But you do not seem to be in danger. What has happened?"

"Much. Listen—this is important. There is trouble at an island ahead. The Baldies were there; they murdered the kin of these men. The odds are they reached there by some form of sub. Send one of the dolphins to see what is happening and if they are still there...."

Karara asked no more questions, but whistled to the dolphin. With a flip of tail Tino-rau took off.

Since they could make no concrete plan of action, the cruiser captains agreed to wait for Tino-rau's report and to cruise well out of sight of the fairing harbor until it came.

"This belief in magic," Ross remarked to Karara, "has one advantage. The natives seem able to take in their stride the fact the dolphins will scout for us."

"They have lived their lives on the sea; for it they must have a vast respect. Perhaps they know, as did my people, that the ocean has many secrets, some of which are never revealed except to the forms of life which claim their homes there. But, even if you discover this Baldy sub, what will the Rovers be able to do about it?"

"I don't know—yet." Ross could not tell why he clung to the idea that they could do anything to strike back at the superior alien force. He only knew that he was not yet willing to relinquish the thought that in some way they could.

"And Ashe?"

Yes, Ashe....

"I don't know." It hurt Ross to admit that.

"Back there, what really happened at the gate?" he asked Karara. "All at once the dolphins seemed to go crazy."

"I think for a moment or two they did. You felt nothing?"

"No."

"It was like a fire slashing through the head. Some protective device of the Foanna, I think."

A mental defense to which he was not sensitive. Which meant that he might be able to breach that gate if none of the others could. But he had to be there first. Suppose, just suppose Torgul could be persuaded that this attack on the gutted Kyn Add was useless. Would the Rover commander take them back to the Foanna keep? Or with the dolphins and the skiff could Ross himself return to make the try?

That he could make it on his own, Ross doubted. Excitement and will power had buoyed him up throughout the past Hawaikan day and night. Now fatigue closed in, past his conditioning and the built-in stimulant of the Terran rations, to enclose him in a groggy haze. He had been warned against this reaction, but that was just another item he had pushed out of his conscious mind. The last thing he remembered now was seeing Karara move through a fuzzy cloud.

Voices argued somewhere beyond, the force of that argument carried more by tone than any words Ross could understand. He was pulled sluggishly out of a slumber too deep for any dream to trouble, and lifted heavy eyelids to see Karara once again. There was a prick in his arm—or was that part of the unreality about him?

"—four—five—six—" she was counting, and Ross found himself joining in:

"—seven—eight—nine—ten!"

On reaching "ten" he was fully awake and knew that she had applied the emergency procedure they had been drilled in using, giving him a pep shot. When Ross sat up on the narrow bunk there was a light in the cabin and no sign of day outside the porthole. Torgul, Vistur, the two other cruiser captains, all there ... and Jazia.

Ross swung his feet to the deck. A pep-shot headache was already beginning, but would wear off soon. There was, however, a concentration of tension in the cabin, and something must have driven Karara to use the drug.

"What is it?"

Karara fitted the medical kit into the compact carrying case.

"Tino-rau has returned. There *is* a sub in the bay. It emits energy waves on a shoreward beam."

"Then they are still there." Ross accepted the dolphin's report without question. Neither of the scouts would make a mistake in those matters. Energy waves beamed shoreward—power for some type of unit the Baldies were using? Suppose the Rovers could find a way of cutting off the power.

"The Sea Maid has told us that this ship sits on the bottom of the harbor. If we could board it—" began Torgul.

"Yes!" Vistur brought his fist down against the end of the bunk on which the Terran still sat, jarring the dull, drug-borne pain in Ross's head. "Take it—then turn it against its crew!"

There was an eagerness in all Rover faces. For that was a game the Hawaikan seafarers understood: Take an enemy ship and turn its armament against its companions in a fleet. But that plan would not work out. Ross had a healthy respect for the technical knowledge of the galactic invaders. Of course he, Karara, even Loketh might be able to reach the sub. Whether they could then board her was an entirely different matter.

Now the Polynesian girl shook her head. "The broadcast there—Tino-rau rates it as lethal. There are dead fish floating in the bay. He had warning at the reef entrance. Without a shield, there will be no way of getting in."

"Might as well wish for a depth bomb," Ross began and then stopped.

"You have thought of something?"

"A shield—" Ross repeated her words. It was so wild this thought of his, and one which might have no chance of working. He knew almost nothing about the resources of the invaders. Could that broadcast which protected the sub and perhaps activated the weapons of the invaders ashore be destroyed? A wall of fish—sea life herded in there as a shield ... wild, yes, even so wild it might work. Ross outlined the idea, speaking more to Karara than to the Rovers.

"I do not know," she said doubtfully. "That would need many fish, too many to herd and drive—"

"Not fish," Torgul cut in, "salkars!"

"Salkars?"

"You have seen the bow carving on this ship. That is a salkar. Such are larger than a hundred fish! Salkars driven in ... they might even wreck this undersea ship with their weight and anger."

"And you can find these salkars near-by?" Ross began to take fire. That dragon which had hunted him—the bulk of the thing was well above any other sea life he had seen here. And to its ferocity he could give testimony.

"At the spawning reefs. We do not hunt at this season which is the time of the taking of mates. Now, too, they are easily angered so they will even attack a cruiser. To slay them at present is a loss, for their skins are not good. But they would be ripe for battle were they to be disturbed."

"And how would you get them from the spawning reefs to Kyn Add?"

"That is not too difficult; the reef lies here." Torgul drew lines with the point of his sword on the table top. "And here is Kyn Add. Salkars have a great hunger at this time. Show them bait and they will follow; especially will they follow swimming bait."

There were a great many holes in the plan which had only a halfway chance of working. But the Rovers seized upon it with enthusiasm, and so it was set up.

Perhaps some two hours later Ross swam toward the land mass of Kyn Add. Gleams of light pricked on the shore well to his left. Those must mark the Rover settlement. And again the Terran wondered why the invaders had remained there. Unless they knew that there had been three cruisers out on a raid and for some reason they were determined to make a complete mop-up.

Karara moved a little to his right, Taua between them, the dolphin's super senses their guide and warning. The swiftest of the cruisers had departed, Loketh on board to communicate with Tino-rau in the water. Since the male dolphin was the best equipped to provide a fox for salkar hounds, he was the bait for this weird fishing expedition.

"No farther!" Ross's sonic pricked a warning against his body. Through that he took a jolt which sent him back, away from the bay entrance.

"On the reef." Karara's tapped code drew him on a new course. Moments later they were both out of the water, though the wash of waves over their flippered feet was constant. The rocks among which they crouched were a rough harborage from which they could see the shore as a dark blot. But they were well away from the break in the reef through which, if their outlandish plan succeeded, the salkars would come.

"A one-in-a-million chance!" Ross commented as he put up his mask.

"Was not the whole Time Agent project founded on just such chances?" Karara asked the right question. This was Ross's kind of venture. Yes, one-in-a-million chances had been pulled off by the Time Agents. Why, it had been close to those odds against their ever finding what they had first sought along the back trails of time—the wrecked spaceships.

Just suppose this could be a rehearsal for another attack? If the salkars could be made to crack the guard of the Baldies, could they also be used against the Foanna gate? Maybe.... But take one fight at a time.

"They come!" Karara's fingers gripped Ross's shoulder. Her hand was hard, bar rigid. He could see nothing, hear nothing. That warning must have come from the dolphins. But so far their plan was working; the monsters of the Hawaikan sea were on their way.

BALDIES

"Ohhhh!" Karara clutched at Ross, her breath coming in little gasps, giving vent to her fear and horror. They had not known what might come from this plan; certainly neither had foreseen the present chaos in the lagoon.

Perhaps the broadcast energy of the enemy whipped the already vicious-tempered salkars into this insane fury. But now the moonlit water was beaten into foam as the creatures fought there, attacking each other with a ferocity neither Terran had witnessed before.

Lights gleamed along the shore where the alien invaders must have been drawn by the clamor of the fighting marine reptiles. Somewhere in the heights above the beach of the lagoon a picked band of Rovers should now be making their way from the opposite side of Kyn Add under strict orders not to go into attack unless signaled. Whether the independent sea warriors would hold to that command was a question which had worried Ross from the first.

Tino-rau and Taua in the waters to the seaward of the reef, the two Terrans on that barrier itself, and between them and the shore the wild melee of maddened salkars. Ross started. The sonic warning which had been pulsing steadily against his skin cut off sharply. The broadcast in the bay had been silenced! This was the time to move, but no swimmer could last in the lagoon itself.

"Along the reef," Karara said.

That would be the long way round, Ross knew, but the only one possible. He studied the cluster of lights ashore. Two or three figures moved there. Seemingly the attention of the aliens was well centered upon the battle still in progress in the lagoon.

"Stay here!" he ordered the girl. Adjusting his mask, Ross dropped into the water, cutting away from the reef and then turning to swim parallel with it. Tino-rau matched him as he went, guiding Ross to a second break in the reef, toward the shore some distance from where the conflict of the salkars still made a hideous din in the night.

The Terran waded in the shallows, stripping off his flippers and snapping them to his belt, letting his mask swing free on his chest. He angled toward the beach where the aliens had been. At least he was better armed for this than he had been when he had fronted the Rovers with only a diver's knife. From the Time Agent supplies he had taken the single hand weapon he had long ago found in the armory of the derelict spaceship. This could only be used sparingly, since they did not know how it could be recharged, and the secret of its beam still remained secret as far as Terran technicians were concerned.

Ross worked his way to a curtain of underbrush from which he had a free view of the beach and the aliens. Three of them he counted, and they were Baldies, all right—taller and thinner than his own species, their bald heads gray-white, the upper dome of their skulls overshadowing the features on their pointed chinned faces. They all wore the skintight blue-purple-green suits of the space voyagers—suits which Ross knew of old were insulated and protective for their wearers, as well as a medium for keeping in touch with one another. Just as he, wearing one, had once been trailed over miles of wilderness.

To him, all three of the invaders looked enough alike to have been stamped out from one pattern. And their movements suggested that they worked or went into action with drilled precision. They all faced seaward, holding tubes aimed at the salkar-infested lagoon. There was no sound of any explosion, but green spears of light struck at the scaled bodies plunging in the water. And where those beams struck, flesh seared. Methodically the trio raked the basin. But, Ross noted, those beams which had been steady at his first sighting, were now interrupted by flickers. One of the Baldies upended his tube, rapped its butt against a rock as if trying to correct a jamming. When the alien went into action once again his weapon flashed and failed. Within a matter of moments the other two were also finished. The lighted rods pushed into the sand, giving a glow to the scene, darkened as a fire might sink to embers. Power fading?

An ungainly shape floundered out of the churned water, lumbered over the shale of the beach, its supple neck outstretched, its horned nose down for a gore-threatening charge. Ross had not realized that the salkars could operate out of what he thought was their natural element, but this wild-eyed dragon was plainly bent on reaching its tormentors.

For a moment or two the Baldies continued to front the creature, almost, Ross thought, as if they could not believe that their weapons had failed them. Then they broke and ran back to the fairing which they had taken with such contemptuous ease. The salkar plowed along in their wake, but its movements grew more labored the farther it advanced, until at last it lay with only its head upraised, darting it back and forth, its fanged jaws well agape, voicing a coughing howl.

Its plaint was answered from the water as a second of its kind wallowed ashore. A terrible wound had torn skin and flesh just behind its neck; yet still it came on, hissing and bubbling a battle challenge. It did not attack its fellow; instead it dragged its bulk past the first comer, on its way after the Baldies.

The salkars continued to come ashore, two more, a third, a fourth, mangled and torn—pulling themselves as far as they could up the beach. To lie, facing inland, their necks weaving, their horned heads bobbing, their cries a frightful din. What had drawn them out of their preoccupation of battle among themselves into this attempt to reach the aliens, Ross could not determine. Unless the intelligence of the beasts was such that they had been able to connect the searing beams which the Baldies had turned on them so tellingly with the men on the beach, and had responded by striving to reach a common enemy.

But no desire could give them the necessary energy to pull far ashore. Almost helplessly beached, they continued to dig into the yielding sand with their flippers in a vain effort to pursue the aliens.

Ross skirted the clamoring barrier of salkars and headed for the fairing. A neck snapped about; a head was lowered in his direction. He smelled the rank stench of reptile combined with burned flesh. The nearest of the brutes must have scented the Terran in turn, as it was now trying vainly to edge around to cut across Ross's path. But it was completely outclassed on land, and the man dodged it easily.

Three Baldies had fled this way. Yet Jazia had reported five had come out of the sea to take Kyn Add. Two were missing. Where? Had they remained in the fairing? Were they now in the sub? And that sub—what had happened to it? The broadcast had been cut off; he had seen the failure of the weapons and the shore lights. Might the sub have suffered from salkar attack? Though Ross could hardly believe that the beasts could wreck it.

The Terran was traveling blindly, keeping well under cover of such brush as he could, knowing only that he must head inland. Under his feet the ground was rising, and he recalled the nature of this territory as Torgul and Jazia had pictured it for him. This had to be part of the ridge wall of the valley in which lay the buildings of the fairing. In these heights was the Shrine of Phutka where Jazia had hidden out. To the west now lay the

Rover village, so he had to work his way left, downhill, in order to reach the hole where the Baldies had gone to ground. Ross made that progress with the stealth of a trained scout.

Hawaika's moon, triple in size to Terra's companion, was up, and the landscape was sharply clear, with shadows well defined. The glow, weird to Terran eyes, added to the effect of being abroad in a nightmare, and the bellowing of the grounded salkars continued a devils' chorus.

When the Rovers had put up the buildings of their fairing, they had cleared a series of small fields radiating outward from those structures. All of these were now covered with crops almost ready to harvest. The grain, if that Terran term could be applied to this Hawaikan product, was housed in long pods which dipped from shoulder-high bushes. And the pods were well equipped with horny projections which tore. A single try at making his way into one of those fields convinced Ross of the folly of such an advance. He sat back to nurse his scratched hands and survey the landscape.

To go down a very tempting lane would be making himself a clear target for anyone in those buildings ahead. He had seen the flamers of the Baldies fail on the beach, but that did not mean the aliens were now weaponless.

His best chance, Ross decided, was to circle north, come back down along the bed of a stream. And he was at the edge of that watercourse when a faint sound brought him to a frozen halt, weapon ready.

"Rosss—"

"Loketh!"

"And Torgul and Vistur."

This was the party from the opposite side of the island, gone expertly to earth. In the moonlight Ross could detect no sign of their presence, yet their voices sounded almost beside him.

"They are in there, in the great hall." That was Torgul. "But no longer are there any lights."

"Now—" An urgent exclamation drew their attention.

Light below. But not the glow of the rods Ross had seen on the beach. This was the warm yellow-red of honest fire, bursting up, the flames growing higher as if being fed with frantic haste.

Three figures were moving down there. Ross began to believe that there were only this trio ashore. He could sight no weapons in their hands, which did not necessarily mean they were unarmed. But the stream ran close behind the rear wall of one of the buildings, and Ross thought its bed could provide cover for a man who knew what he was doing. He pointed out as much to Torgul.

"And if their magic works and you are drawn out to be killed?" The Rover captain came directly to the point.

"That is a chance to be taken. But remember ... the magic of the Foanna at the sea gate did not work against me. Perhaps this won't either. Once, earlier, I won against it."

"Have you then another hand to give to the fire as your defense?" That was Vistur. "But no man has the right to order another's battle challenge."

"Just so," returned Ross sharply. "And this is a thing I have long been trained to do."

He slid down into the stream bed. Approaching from this angle, the structures of the fairing were between him and the fire. So screened he reached a log wall, got to his feet, and edged along it. Then he witnessed a wild scene. The fire raged in great, sky-touching tongues. And already the roof of one of the Rover buildings smoldered. Why the aliens had built up such a conflagration, Ross could not guess. A signal designed to reach some distance?

He did not doubt there was some urgent purpose. For the three were dragging in fuel with almost frenzied haste, bringing out of the Rover buildings bales of cloth to be ripped apart and whirled into the devouring flames, furniture, everything movable which would burn.

There was one satisfaction. The Baldies were so intent upon this destruction that they kept no watch save that now and then one of them would run to the head of the path leading to the lagoon and listen as if he expected a salkar to come pounding up the slope.

"They're ... they're rattled!" Ross could hardly believe it. The Baldies who had always occupied his mind and memory as practically invincible supermen were acting like badly frightened primitives! And when the enemy was so off balance you pushed—you pushed hard.

Ross thumbed the button on the grip of the strange weapon. He sighted with deliberation and fired. The blue figure at the top of the path wilted, and for a long moment neither of his companions noted his collapse. Then one of them whirled and started for the limp body, his colleague running after him. Ross allowed them to reach his first victim before he fired the second and third time.

All three lay quiet, but still Ross did not venture forth until he had counted off a dozen Terran seconds. Then he slipped forward keeping to cover until he came up to the bodies.

The blue-clad shoulder had a flaccid feel under his hand as if the muscles could not control the flesh about them. Ross rolled the alien over, looked down in the bright light of the fire into the Baldy's wide-open eyes. Amazement—the Terran thought he could read that in the dead stare which answered his intent gaze—and then anger, a cold and deadly anger which chilled into ice.

"Kill!"

Ross slewed around, still down on one knee, to face the charge of a Rover. In the firelight the Hawaikan's eyes were blazing with fanatical hatred. He had his hooked sword ready to deliver a finishing stroke. The Terran blocked with a shoulder to meet the Rover's knees, threw him back. Then Ross landed on top of the fighting crewman, trying to pin the fellow to earth and avoid that recklessly slashing blade.

"Loketh! Vistur!" Ross shouted as he struggled.

More of the Rovers appeared from between the buildings, bearing down on the limp aliens and the two fighting men. Ross recognized the limping gait of Loketh using a branch to aid him into a running scuttle across the open.

"Loketh—here!"

The Hawaikan covered the last few feet in a dive which carried him into Ross and the Rover. "Hold him," the Terran ordered and had just time enough to throw himself between the Baldies and the rest of the crew. There was a snarling from the Rovers; and Ross, knowing their temper, was afraid he could not save the captives which they considered, fairly, their legitimate prey. He must depend upon the hope that there were one or two cooler heads among them with enough authority to restrain the would-be avengers. Otherwise he would have to beam them into helplessness.

"Torgul!" he shouted.

There was a break in the line of runners speeding for him. The big man lunging straight across could only be Vistur; the other, yelling orders, was Torgul. It would depend upon how much control the Captain had over his men. Ross scrambled to his feet. He had clicked on the beamer to its lowest frequency. It would not kill, but would render its victim temporarily paralyzed; and how long that state would continue Ross had no way of knowing. Tried on Terran laboratory animals, the time had varied from days to weeks.

Vistur used the flat side of his war ax, clapping it against the foremost runners, setting his own bulk to impose a barrier. And now Torgul's orders appeared to be getting through, more and more of the men slacked, leaving a trio of hotheads, two of whom Vistur sent reeling with his fists.

The Captain came up to Ross. "They are alive then?" He leaned over to inspect the Baldy the Terran had rolled on his back, assessing the alien's frozen stare with thoughtful measurement.

"Yes, but they can not move."

"Well enough." Torgul nodded. "They shall meet the Justice of Phutka after the Law. I think they will wish that they had been left to the boarding axes of angry men."

"They are worth more alive than dead, Captain. Do you not wish to know why they have carried war to your people, how many of them there may yet be to attack—and other things? Also—" Ross nodded at the fire now catching the second building, "why have they built up that blaze? Is it a signal to others of their kind?"

"Very well said. Yes, it would be well for us to learn such things. Nor will Phutka be jealous of the time we take to ask questions and get answers, many answers." He prodded the Baldy with the toe of his sea boot.

"How long will they remain so? Your magic has a bite in it."

Ross smiled. "Not my magic, Captain. This weapon was taken from one of their own ships. As to how long they will remain so—that I do not know."

"Very well, we can take precautions." Under Torgul's orders the aliens were draped with capture nets like those Ross and Loketh had worn. The sea-grown plant adhered instantly, wet strands knitting in perfect restrainers as long as it was uncut.

Having seen to that, Torgul ordered the excavation of Kyn Add.

"As you say," he remarked to Ross, "that fire may well be a signal to bring down more of their kind. I think we have had the Favor of Phutka in this matter, but the prudent man stretches no favor of that kind too far. Also," he looked about him—"we have given to Phutka and the Shades our dead; there is nothing for us here now but hate and sorrow. In one day we have been broken from a clan of pride and ships to a handful of standardless men."

"You will join some other clan?" Karara had come with Jazia to stand on the stone ledge chipped to form a base for a column bearing a strange, brooding-eyed head looking seaward. The Rover woman was superintending the freeing of the head from the column.

At the Terran girl's question the Captain gazed down into the dreadful chaos of the valley. They could yet hear the roars of the dying salkars. The reptiles that had made their way to land had not withdrawn but still lay, some dead now, some with weaving heads reaching inland. And the whole of the fairing was ablaze with fire.

"We are now blood-sworn men, Sea Maid. For such there is no clan. There is only the hunting and the kill. With the magic of Phutka perhaps we shall have a short hunt and a good kill."

"There ... now ... so...." Jazia stepped back. The head which had faced the sea was lowered carefully to a wide strip of crimson-and-gold stuff she had brought from Torgul's ship. With her one usable hand the Rover woman drew the fabric about the carving, muffling it except for the eyes. Those were large ovals deeply carved, and in them Ross saw a glitter. Jewels set there? Yet, he had a queer, shivery feeling that something more than gems occupied those sockets—that he had actually been regarded for an instant of time, assessed and dismissed.

"We go now." Jazia waved and Torgul sent men forward. They lifted the wrapped carving to a board carried between them and started downslope.

Karara cried out and Ross looked around.

The pillar which had supported the head was crumbling away, breaking into a rubble which cascaded across the stone ledge. Ross blinked—this must be an illusion, but he was too tired to be more than dully amazed as he became one of the procession returning to the ships.

THE SEA GATE OF THE FOANNA

Ross raised a shell cup to his lips but hardly sipped the fiery brew it contained. This was a gesture of ceremony, but he wanted a steady head and a quick tongue for any coming argument. Torgul, Afrukta, Ongal—the three commanders of the Rover cruisers; Jazia, who represented the mysterious Power of Phutka; Vistur and some other subordinate officers; Karara; himself, with Loketh hovering behind: a council of war. But summoned against whom?

The Terran had come too far afield from his own purpose—to reach Ashe in the Foanna keep. And to further his own plans was a task he doubted his ability to perform. His attack on the Baldies had made him too important to the Rovers for them to allow him willingly to leave them on a quest of his own.

"These star men"—Ross set down the cup, tried to choose the most telling words in his limited Hawaikan vocabulary—"possess weapons and powers you can not dream of, that you have no defense against. Back at Kyn Add we were lucky. The salkars attacked their sub and halted the broadcast powering their flamers. Otherwise we could not have taken them, even though we were many against their few. Now you talk of hunting them in their own territory—on land and in the mountains where they have their base. That would be folly akin to swimming barehanded to front a salkar."

"So—then we must sit and wait for them to eat us up?" flared Ongal. "I say it is better to die fighting with one's blade wet!"

"Do you not also wish to take at least one of the enemy with you when you fight to that finish?" Ross countered. "These could kill you before you came in blade range."

"You had no trouble with that weapon of yours," Afrukta spoke up.

"I have told you—this weapon was stolen from them. I have only one and I do not know how long it will continue to serve me, or whether they have a defense against it. Those we took were naked to any force, for their broadcast had failed them. But to smash blindly against their main base would be the act of madmen."

"The salkars opened a way for us—" That was Torgul.

"But we can not move a pack of those inland to the mountains," Vistur pointed out reasonably.

Ross studied the Captain. That Torgul was groping for a plan and that it had to be a shrewd one, the Terran guessed. His respect for the Rover commander had been growing steadily since their first meeting. The cruiser-raiders had always been captained by the most daring men of the Rover clans. But Ross was also certain that a successful cruiser commander must possess a level-headed leaven of intelligence and be a strategist of parts.

The Hawaikan force needed a key which would open the Baldy base as the salkars had opened the lagoon. And all they had to aid them was a handful of facts gained from their prisoners.

Oddly enough the picklock to the captives' minds had been produced by the dolphins. Just as Tino-rau and Taua had formed a bridge of communication between the Terran and Loketh, so did they read and translate the thoughts of the galactic invaders. For the Baldies, among their own kind, were telepathic, vocalizing only to give orders to inferiors.

Their capture by these primitive "inferiors" had delivered the first shock, and the mind-probes of the dolphins had sent the "supermen" close to the edge of sanity. To accept an animal form as an equal had been shattering.

But the star men's thoughts and memories had been winnowed at last and the result spread before this impromptu council. Rovers and Terrans were briefed on the invaders' master plan for taking over a world. Why they desired to do so even the dolphins had not been able to discover; perhaps they themselves had not been told by their superiors.

It was a plan almost contemptuous in its simplicity, as if the galactic force had no reason to fear effective opposition. Except in one direction—one single direction.

Ross's fingers tightened on the shell cup. Had Torgul reached that conclusion yet, the belief that the Foanna could be their key? If so, they might be able to achieve their separate purposes in one action.

"It would seem that they are wary of the Foanna," he suggested, alert to any telltale response from Torgul. But it was Jazia who answered the Terran's half question.

"The Foanna have a powerful magic; they can order wind and wave, man and creature—if so be their will. Well might these killers fear the Foanna!"

"Yet now they move against them," Ross pointed out, still eyeing Torgul. The Captain's reply was a small, quiet smile.

"Not directly, as you have heard. It is all a part of their plan to set one of us against the other, letting us fight many small wars and so use up our men while they take no risks. They wait the day when we shall be exhausted and then they will reveal themselves to claim all they wish. So today they stir up trouble between the Wreckers and the Foanna, knowing that the Foanna are few. Also they strive in turn to anger us by raids, allowing us to believe that either the Wreckers or Foanna have attacked. Thus—" he held up his left thumb, made a pincers of right thumb and forefinger to close upon it, "they hope to catch the Foanna, between Wreckers and Rovers. Because the Foanna are those they reckon the most dangerous they move against them now, using us and weakening our forces into the bargain. A plan which is clever, but the plan of men who do not like to fight with their own blades."

"They are worse than the coast scum, these cowards!" Ongal spat.

Torgul smiled again. "That is what they believe we will say, kinsman, and so underrate them. By our customs, yes, they are cowards. But what care they for our judgments? Did we think of the salkars when we used them to force the lagoon? No, they were only beasts to be our tools. So now it is the same with us, except that we know what they intend. And we shall not be such obedient tools. If the Foanna are our answer, then—" He paused, gazing into his cup as if he could read some shadowy future there.

"If the Foanna are the answer, then what?" Ross pushed.

"Instead of fighting the Foanna, we must warm, cherish, try to ally ourselves with them. And do all that while we still have time!"

"Just how do we do these things?" demanded Ongal. "The Foanna you would warn, cherish, claim as allies, are already our enemies. Were we not on the way to force their sea gate only days ago? There is no chance of seeking peace now. And have the finned ones not learned from the women-killers that already there is an army of Wreckers camped about the citadel to which these sons of the Shadow plan to lend certain weapons? Do we throw away three cruisers—all we have left—in a hopeless fight? Such is the council of one struck by loss of wits."

"There is a way—my way," Ross seized the opening. "In the Foanna citadel is my sword-lord, to whose service I am vowed. We were on our way to attempt his freeing when your ship picked us out of the waves. He is learned beyond me in the dealing with strange peoples, and if the Foanna are as clever as you say, they will already have discovered that he is not just a slave they claimed from Lord Zahur."

There it was in the open, his own somewhat tattered hope that Ashe had been able to impress his captors with his knowledge and potential. Trained to act as contact man with other races, there was a chance that Gordon had saved himself from whatever fate had been planned for the prisoners the Foanna had claimed. If that happened, Ashe could be their opening wedge in the Foanna stronghold.

"This also I know: That which guards the gate—which turns your minds whirling and sent you back from your raid—does not affect me. I may be able to win inside and find my clansman, and in that doing treat with the Foanna."

The Baldy prisoners had not underestimated the attack on the Foanna citadel. As the Rover cruisers beat in under the cover of night the fires and torches of both besieged and besiegers made a wild glow across the sky. Only on the sea side of the fortress there was no sign of involvement. Whatever guarded the gate must still be in force.

Ross stood with his feet well apart to balance his body against the swing of the deck. His suggestion had been argued over, protested, but at last carried with the support of Torgul and Jazia, and now he was to make his try. The sum of the Rovers' and Loketh's knowledge of the sea gate had been added for his benefit, but he knew that this venture must depend upon himself alone. Karara, the dolphins, the Hawaikans, were all too sensitive to the barrier.

Torgul moved in the faint light. "We are close; our power is ebbing. If we advance, we shall be drifting soon."

"It is time then." Ross crossed to the rope ladder, but another was there before him. Karara perched on the rail. He regarded her angrily.

"You can't go."

"I know. But we are still safe here. Just because you are free of one defense of the gate, Ross, do not believe that makes it easy."

He was stung by her assumption that he could be so self-assured.

"I know my business."

Ross pushed past her, swinging down the rope ladder, pausing only above water level to snap on flippers, make sure of the set of his weighted belt, and slide his gill-mask over his face. There was a splash beside him as the net containing spare belt, flippers, and mask hit the water and he caught at it. These could provide Ashe's escape from the fortress.

The lights on the shore made a wide arc of radiance across the sea. As Ross headed toward the wave-washed coast he began to hear shouting and other sounds which made him believe that the besiegers were in the midst of an all-out assault. Yet those distant fires and rocketlike blasts into the sky had a wavery blur. And Ross, making his way with the effortless water cleaving of the diver, surfaced now and then to spot film curling up from the surface of the sea between the two standing rock pillars which marked the sea gate.

He was startled by a thunderous crack, rending the air above the small bay. Ross pulled to one of the pillars, steadied himself with one hand against it. Those twists of film rising from the surging surface were thickening. More tendrils grew out from parent stems to creep along above the waves, raising up sprouts and branches in turn. A wall of mist was building between gate and shore.

Again a thunderclap overhead. Involuntarily the Terran ducked. Then he turned his face up to the sky, striving to see any evidence of storm. What hung there sped the growth of the fog on the water. Yet where the fog was gray-white, it was a darkness spouting from the highest point of the citadel. Ross could not explain how he was able to see one shade of darkness against equal dusk, but he did—or did he only sense it? He shook his head, willing himself to look away from the finger. Only it was a finger no longer; now it was a fist aimed at the stars it was fast blotting out. A fist rising to the heavens before it curled back, descended to press the fortress and its surroundings into rock and earth.

Fog curled about Ross, spilled outward through the sea gates. He loosed his grip on the pillar and dived, swimming on through the gap with the fortress of the Foanna before him.

There was a jetty somewhere ahead; that much he knew from Torgul's description. Those who served the Foanna sometimes took sea roads and they had slim, fast cutters for such coastwise travel. Ross surfaced cautiously, to discover there was no visibility to wave level. Here the mist was thick, a smothering cover so bewildering he was confused as to direction. He ducked below again and flippered on.

Was his confusion born of the fog, or was it also in his head? Did he, after all, have this much reaction to the gate defense? Ross ducked that suspicion as he had ducked the moist blanket on the surface. He had come from the gate, which meant that the jetty must lie—there!

A few moments later Ross had proof that his sense of direction had not altogether failed him, when his shoulder grazed against a solid obstruction in the water and his exploring touch told him that he had found one of the jetty piles. He surfaced again and this time he heard not a thunder roll but the singsong chanting of the Foanna.

It was loud, almost directly above his head, but since the cotton mist held he was not afraid of being sighted. The chanter must be on the jetty. And to Ross's right was a dark bulk which he thought was one of the cutters. Was a sortie by the besieged being planned?

Then, out of the night, came a dazzling beam, well above the level of Ross's head where he clung to the piling. It centered on the cutter, slicing into the substance of the vessel with the ease of steel piercing clay. The chanting stopped on mid-note, broken by cries of surprise and alarm. Ross, pressing against the pile, received a jolt from his belt sonic.

There must be a Baldy sub in the basin inside the gate. Perhaps the flame beam now destroying the cutter was to be turned on the walls of the keep in turn.

Foanna chant again, low and clear. Splashes from the water as those on the jetty cast into the sea objects Ross could not define. The Terran's body jerked, his mask smothered a cry of pain. About his legs and middle, immersed in the waves, there was cold so intense that it seared. Fear goaded him to pull up on one of the under beams of the pier. He reached that refuge and rubbed his icy legs with what vigor he could summon.

Moments later he crept along toward the shore. The energy ray had found another target. Ross paused to watch a second cutter sliced. If the counter stroke of the Foanna would rout the invaders, it had not yet begun to work.

The net holding the extra gear brought along in hopes of Ashe's escape weighed the Terran down, but he would not abandon it as he felt his way from one foot- and hand-hold to the next. The waves below gave off an icy exudation which made him shiver uncontrollably. And he knew that as long as that effect lasted he dared not venture into the sea again.

Light ... along with the cold, there was a phosphorescence on the water—white patches floating, dipping, riding the waves. Some of them gathered under the pier, clustering about the pilings. And the fog thinned with their coming, as if those irregular blotches absorbed and fed upon the mist. The Terran could see now he had reached the land end of the jetty. He wedged his flippers into his belt, pulled on over his feet the covers of salkar-hide Torgul had provided.

Save for his belt, his trunks, and the gill-pack, Ross's body was bare and the cold caught at him. But, slinging the carry net over his shoulder, he dropped to the damp sand and stood listening.

The clamor of the attack which had carried all the way offshore to the Rover cruisers had died away. And there were no more claps of thunder. Instead, there was now a thick wash of rain.

No more fire rays as he faced seaward. And the fog was lifting, so Ross could distinguish the settling cutters, their bows still moored to the jetty. There was no movement there. Had those on the pier fled?

Dot ... dash ... dot ...

Ross did not drop the net. But he crouched back in the half protection of the piling. For a moment which stretched beyond Terran time measure he froze so, waiting.

Dot ... dash ... dot ...

Not the prickle induced by the enemy installations, it was a real coded call picked up by his sonic, and one he knew.

Don't rush, he told himself sharply—play it safe. By rights only two people in this time and place would know that call. And one would have no reason to use it. But—a trap? This could be a trap. Awe of the Foanna powers had touched him a little in spite of his off-world skepticism. He could be lured now by someone using Ashe's call.

Ross stripped for action after a fashion, bundling the net and its contents into a hollow he scooped behind a pile well above water level. The alien hand weapon he had left with Karara, not trusting it to the sea. But he had his diver's knife and his two hands which, by training, could be, and had been, deadly weapons.

With the sonic against the bare skin of his middle where it would register strongest, knife in hand, Ross moved into the open. The floating patches did not supply much light, but he was certain the call had come from the jetty.

There was movement there—a flash or two. And the sonic? Ross had to be sure, very sure. The broadcast was certainly stronger when he faced in that direction. Dared he come into the open? Perhaps in the dark he could cut Ashe away from his captors so they could swim for it together.

Ross clicked a code reply. Dot ... dot ... dot ...

The answer was quick, imperative: "Where?"

Surely no one but Ashe could have sent that! Ross did not hesitate.

"Be ready—escape."

"No!" Even more imperative. "Friends here...."

Had he guessed rightly? Had Ashe established friendly relations with the Foanna? But Ross kept to the caution which had been his defense and armor so long. There was one question he thought only Ashe could answer, something out of the past they had shared when they had made their first journey into time disguised as Beaker traders of the Bronze Age. Deliberately he tapped that question.

"What did we kill in Britain?"

Tensely he waited. But when the reply came it did not pulse from the sonic under his fingers; instead, a well-remembered voice called out of the night.

"A white wolf." And the words were Terran English.

"Ashe!" Ross leaped forward, climbed toward the figure he could only dimly see.

THE FOANNA

"Ross!" Ashe's hands gripped his shoulders as if never intending to free him again. "Then you did come through—"

Ross understood. Gordon Ashe must have feared that he was the only one swept through the time door by that freak chance.

"And Karara and the dolphins!"

"Here—now?" In this black bowl of the citadel bay Ashe was only a shadow with voice and hands.

"No, out with the Rover cruisers. Ashe, do you know the Baldies are on Hawaika? They've organized this whole thing—the attack here—trouble all over. Right now they have one of their subs out there. That's what cut those cutters to pieces. Five days ago five of them wiped out a whole Rover fairing, just five of them!"

"Gordoon." Unlike the hissing speech of the Hawaikans, this new voice made a singing, lilting call of Ashe's name. "This is your swordsman in truth?" Another shadow drew near them, and Ross saw the flutter of cloak edge.

"This is my friend." There was a tone of correction in Ashe's reply. "Ross, this is the Guardian of the sea gate."

"And you come," the Foanna continued, "with those who gather to feast at the Shadow's table. But your Rovers will find little loot to their liking—"

"No." Ross hesitated. How did one address the Foanna? He had claimed equality with Torgul. But that approach was not the proper one here; instinct told him that. He fell back on the complete truth uttered simply. "We took three of the Baldy killers. From them we learned they move to wipe out the Foanna first. For you," he addressed himself to the cloaked shape, "they believe to be a threat. We heard that they urged the Wreckers to this attack and so—"

"And so the Rovers come, but not to loot? Then they are something new among their kind." The Foanna's reply was as chill as the sea bay's water.

"Loot does not summon men who want a blood price for their dead kin!" Ross retorted.

"No, and the Rovers are believers in the balance of hurt against hurt," the Foanna conceded. "Do they also believe in the balance of aid against aid? Now that is a thought upon which depends much. Gordoon, it would seem that we may not take to our ships. So let us return to council."

Ashe's hand was on Ross's arm guiding him through the murk. Though the fog which had choked the bay had vanished, thick darkness remained and Ross noted that even the fires and flares were dimmed and fewer. Then they were in a passage where a very faint light clung to the walls.

Robed Foanna, three of them, moved ahead with that particular gliding progress. Then Ashe and Ross, and bringing up the rear, a dozen of the mailed guards. The passageway became a ramp. Ross glanced at Ashe. Like the Foanna, the Terran Agent wore a cloak of gray, but his did not shift color from time to time as did those of the Hawaikan enigmas. And now Gordon shoved back its folds, revealing supple body armor.

Questions gathered in Ross. He wanted to know—needed desperately to know—Ashe's standing with the Foanna. What had happened to raise Gordon from the status of captive in Zahur's hold to familiar companionship with the most dreaded race on this planet?

The ramp's head faced blank wall with a sharp-angled turn to the right of a narrower passage. One of the Foanna made a slight sign to the guards, who turned with drilled precision to march off along the passage. Now the other Foanna held out their wands.

What a moment earlier had been unbroken surface showed an opening. The change had been so instantaneous that Ross had not seen any movement at all.

Beyond that door they passed from one world to another. Ross's senses, already acutely alert to his surroundings, could not supply him with any reason by sight, sound, or smell for his firm conviction that this hold was alien as neither the Wrecker castle nor the Rover ships had been. Surely the Foanna were not the same race, perhaps not even the same species as the other native Hawaikans.

Those robes which he had seen both silver gray and dark blue, now faded, pearled, thinned, until each of the three still gliding before him were opalescent columns without definite form.

Ashe's grasp fell on Ross's arm once more, and his whisper reached the younger man thinly. "They are mistresses of illusion. Be prepared not to believe all that you see."

Mistresses—Ross caught that first. Women, or at least female then. Illusion, yes, already he was convinced that here his eyes could play tricks on him. He could hardly determine what was robe, what was wall, or if more than shades of shades swept before him.

Another blank wall, then an opening, and flowing through it to touch him such a wave of alienness that Ross felt he was buffeted by a storm wind. Yet as he hesitated before it, reluctant in spite of Ashe's hold to go ahead, he also knew that this did not carry with it the cold hostility he had known while facing the Baldies. Alien—yes. Inimical to his kind—no.

"You are right, younger brother."

Spoken those words—or forming in his mind?

Ross was in a place which was sheer wonder. Under his feet dark blue—the blue of a Terran sky at dusk—caught up in it twinkling points of light as if he strode, not equal with stars, but above them! Walls—were there any walls here? Or shifting, swaying blue curtains on which silvery lines ran to form symbols and words which some bemused part of his brain almost understood, but not quite.

Constant motion, no quiet, until he came to a place where those swaying curtains were stilled, where he no longer strode above the sky but on soft surface, a mat of gray living sod where his steps released a spicy fragrance. And there he really saw the Foanna for the first time.

Where had their cloaks gone? Had they tossed them away during that walk or drift across this amazing room, or had the substance which had formed those coverings flowed away by itself? As Ross looked at the three in wonder he knew that he was seeing them as not even their servants and guards ever viewed them. And yet was he seeing them as they really were or as they wished him to see them?

"As we are, younger brother, as we are!" Again an answer which Ross was not sure was thought or speech.

In form they were humanoid, and they were undoubtedly women. The muffling cloaks gone, they wore sleeveless garments of silver which were girded at the waist with belts of blue gems. Only in their hair and their eyes did they betray alien blood. For the hair which flowed and wove about them, cascading down shoulders, rippling about their arms, was silver, too, and it swirled, moved as if it had a separate life of its own. While their eyes.... Ross looked into those golden eyes and was lost for seconds until panic awoke in him, forcing him after sharp struggle to look away.

Laughter? No, he had not heard laughter. But a sense of amusement tinged with respect came to him.

"You are very right, Gordoon. This one is also of your kind. He is not witches' meat." Ross caught the distaste, the kind of haunting unhappiness which colored those words, remnants of an old hurt.

"These are the Foanna," Ashe's voice broke more of the spell. "The Lady Ynlan, The Lady Yngram, the Lady Ynvalda."

The Foanna—these three only?

She whom Ashe had named Ynlan, whose eyes had entrapped and almost held what was Ross Murdock, made a small gesture with her ivory hand. And in that gesture as well as in the words witches' meat the Terran read the unhappiness which was as much a part of this room as the rest of its mystery.

"The Foanna are now but three. They have been only three for many weary years, oh man from another world and time. And soon, if these enemies have their way, they will not be three—but none!"

"But—" Ross was still startled. He knew from Loketh that the Wreckers had deemed the Foanna few in number, an old and dying race. But that there were only three women left was hard to believe.

The response to his unspoken wonder came clear and determined. "We may be but three; however, our power remains. And sometimes power distilled by time becomes the stronger. Now it would seem that time is no longer our servant but perhaps among our enemies. So tell us this tale of yours as to why the Rovers would make one with the Foanna—tell us all, younger brother!"

Ross reported what he had seen, what Tino-rau and Taua had learned from the prisoners taken at Kyn Add. And when he had finished, the three Foanna stood very still, their hands clasped one to the other. Though they were only an arm's distance from him, Ross had the feeling they had withdrawn from his time and world.

So complete was their withdrawal that he dared to ask Ashe one of the many questions which had been boiling inside him.

"Who are they?" But Ross knew he really meant: What are they?

Gordon Ashe shook his head. "I don't really know—the last of a very old race which possesses powers and knowledge different from any we have believed in for centuries. We have heard of witches. In the modern day we discount the legends about them. The Foanna bring those legends alive. And I promise you this—if they turn those powers loose"—he paused—"it will be such a war as this world, perhaps any world has never seen!"

"That is so." The Foanna had returned from the place to which they had withdrawn. "And this is also the truth or one face of the truth. The Rovers are right in their belief that we have kept some measure of balance between one form of change and another on this world. If we were as many as we once were, then against us these invaders could not move at all. But we are three only and also—do we have the right to evoke disaster which will strike not only the enemy but perhaps recoil upon the innocent? There has been enough death here already. And those who are our servants shall no longer be asked to face battle to keep an empty shell inviolate. We would see with our own eyes these invaders, probe what they would do. There is ever change in life, and if a pattern grows too set, then the race caught in it may wither and die. Maybe our pattern has been too long in its old design. We shall make no decision until we see in whose hands the future may rest."

Against such finality of argument there was no appeal. These could not be influenced by words.

"Gordoon, there is much to be done. Do you take with you this younger brother and see to his needs. When all is in readiness we shall come."

One minute Ross had been standing on the carpet of living moss. Then ... he was in a more normal room with four walls, a floor, a ceiling, and light which came from rods set in the corners. He gasped.

"Stunned me, too, the first time they put me through it," he heard Ashe say. "Here, get some of this inside you, it'll steady your head."

There was a cup in his hand, a beautifully carved, rose-red container shaped in the form of a flower. Somehow Ross brought it to his lips with shaking hands, gulped down a good third of its contents. The liquid was a mixture of tart and sweet, cooling his mouth and throat, but warming as it went down, and that glow spread through him.

"What—how did they do that?" he demanded.

Ashe shrugged. "How do they do the hundred and one things I have seen happen here? We've been teleported. How it's done I don't know any more than I did the first time it happened. Simply a part of Foanna 'magic' as far as spectators are concerned." He sat down on a stool, his long legs stretched out before him. "Other worlds, other ways—even if they are confounded queer ones. As far as I know, there's no reason for their power to work, but it does. Now, have you seen the time gate? Is it in working order?"

Ross put down the now empty cup and sat down opposite Ashe. As concisely as he could, he outlined the situation with a quick résumé of all that had happened to him, Karara, and the dolphins since they had been sucked through the gate. Ashe asked no questions, but his expression was that of the Agent Ross had known, evaluating and listing all the younger man had to report. When the other was through he said only two words:

"No return."

So much had happened in so short a time that Ross's initial shock at the destruction of the gate had faded, been well overlaid by all the demands made upon his resources, skill, and strength. Even now, the fact Ashe voiced seemed of little consequence balanced against the struggle in progress.

"Ashe—" Ross rubbed his hands up and down his arms, brushing away grains of sand, "remember those pylons with the empty seacoast behind them? Does that mean the Baldies are going to win?"

"I don't know. No one has ever tried to change the course of history. Maybe it is impossible even if we dared to try." Ashe was on his feet again, pacing back and forth.

"Try what, Gordoon?"

Ross jerked around, Ashe halted. One of the Foanna stood there, her hair playing about her shoulders as if some breeze felt only by her stirred those long strands.

"Dare to try and change the course of the future," Ashe explained, accepting her materialization with the calm of one who had witnessed it before.

"Ah, yes, your traveling in time. And now you think that perhaps this poor world of ours has a choice as to which overlords it will welcome? I do not know either, Gordoon, whether the future may be altered nor if it be wise to try. But also ... well, perhaps we should see our enemy before we are set in any path. Now, it is time that we go. Younger brother, how did you plan to leave this place when you accomplished your mission?"

"By the sea gate. I have extra swimming equipment cached under the jetty."

"And the Rover ships await you at sea?"

"Yes."

"Then we shall take your way, since the cutters are sunk."

"There is only one extra gill-pack—and that Baldy sub is out there, too!"

"So? Then we shall try another road, though it will sap our power temporarily." Her head inclined slightly to the left as if she listened. "Good! Our people are now in the passage which will take them to safety. What those outside will find here when they break in will be of little aid to their plans. Secrets of the Foanna remain secrets past others' prying. Though they shall try, oh, how they shall try to solve them! There is knowledge that only certain types of minds can hold and use, and to others it remains for all time unlearnable. Now—"

Her hand reached out, flattened against Ross's forehead.

"Think of your Rover ship, younger brother, see it in your mind! And see well and clearly for me."

Torgul's cruiser was there; he could picture with details he had not thought he knew or remembered. The deck in the dark of the night with only a shaded light at the mast. The deck ...

Ross gave a choked cry. He did not see this in his mind; he saw it with his eyes! His hand swung out in an involuntary gesture of repudiation and struck painfully against wood. He was on the cruiser!

A startled exclamation from behind him—then a shout. Ashe was here and beyond him three cloaked figures, the Foanna. They had their own road indeed and had taken it.

"You ... Rosss—" Vistur fronted them, his face a mixture of bewilderment and awe. "The Foanna—" said in a half whisper, echoed by crewmen gathering around, but not too close.

"Gordon!" Karara elbowed her way between two of the Hawaikans and ran across the deck. She caught the Agent's both hands as if to assure herself that he was alive and there before her. Then she turned to the three Foanna.

There was an odd expression on the Polynesian girl's face, first of measurement with some fear, and then of dawning wonder. From beneath the cloak of the middle Foanna came the rod of office with its sparking knob. Karara dropped Ashe's hands, took a tentative step forward and then another. The knob was directly before her, breast high. She brought up both hands, cupping them about the knob, but not touching it directly. The sparks it emitted could have been flashing against her flesh, but Karara displayed no awareness of that. Instead, she lifted both hands farther, palm up and cupped, as if she carried some invisible bounty, then flattened them, loosing what she held.

There was a sigh from the crewmen; Karara's gesture had been confident, as if she knew just what she was doing and why. And Ross heard Ashe draw a deep breath also as the Terran girl turned, allying herself with the Foanna.

"These Great Ones stand in peace," she said. "It is their will that no harm comes to this ship and those who sail in her."

"What do the Great Ones want of us?" Torgul advanced but not too near.

"To speak concerning those who are your prisoners."

"So be it." The Captain bowed. "The Great Ones' will is our will; let it be as they wish."

RETURN TO THE BATTLE

Ross lay listening to the even breathing from across the cabin. He had awakened in that quick transference from sleep to consciousness which was always his when on duty, but he made no attempt to move. Ashe was still sleeping.

Ashe, whom he thought or had thought he knew as well as one man could ever know another, who had taken the place of family for Ross Murdock the loner. Years—two ... four of them now since he had made half of that partnership.

His head turned, though he could not see that lean body, that quiet, controlled face. Ashe still looked the same, but ... Ross's sense of loss was hurt and anger mingled. What had they done to Gordon, those three? Bewitched? Tales Terrans had accepted as purest fantasy for centuries came into his mind. Could it be that his own world once had its Foanna?

Ross scowled. You couldn't refute their "magic," call it by what scientific name you wished—hypnotism ... teleporting. They got results, and the results were impressive. Now he remembered the warning the Foanna themselves had delivered hours earlier to the Rovers. There were limits to their abilities; because they were forced to draw on mental and physical energy, they could be exhausted. Thus, they had barriers, too.

Again Ross considered the subject of barriers. Karara had been able to meet the aliens, if not mind-to-mind, then in a closer way even than Ashe. The talent which tied her to the dolphins had in turn been a bond with the Foanna. Ashe and Karara could enter that circle, but not Ross Murdock. Along with his new separation from Ashe came that feeling of inferiority to bite on, and the taste was sour.

"This isn't going to be easy."

So Ashe was awake.

"What can they do?" Ross asked in return.

"I don't know. I don't believe that they can teleport an army into Baldy headquarters the way Torgul expects. And it wouldn't do such an army much good to get there and then be outclassed by the weapons the Baldies might have," Ashe said.

Ross had a moment of warmth and comfort; he knew that tone of old. Ashe was studying the problem, willing to talk out difficulties as he always had before.

"No, outright assault isn't the answer. We'll have to know more about the enemy. One thing puzzles me: Why have the Baldies suddenly stepped up their timing?"

"What makes you think they have?"

"Well, according to the accounts I've heard, it's been about three or four planet years here since some off-world devices have been infiltrating the native civilization—"

"You mean such things as those attractors set up on the reef at Zahur's castle?" Ross remembered Loketh's story.

"Those, and other things. The refinements added to the engine power on these ships.... Torgul said they spread from Rover fleet to fleet; no one's sure where they started. The Baldies began slowly, but they are speeding up now—those fairing attacks have all been recent. And this assault on the Foanna citadel blew up almost overnight on a flimsy excuse. Why the quick push after the slow beginning?"

"Maybe they decided the natives are easy pushovers and they no longer have to worry about any real opposition," Ross suggested.

"Could be. Self-confidence becoming arrogance when they didn't uncover any opponent strong enough to matter. Or else, they may be spurred by some need with a time limit. If we knew the reason for those pylons, we might guess their motives."

"Are you going to try to change the future?"

"That sounds arrogant, too. Can we if we wish to? We never dared to try it on Terra. And the risk may be worse than all our fears. Also, the choice is not ours."

"There's one thing I don't understand," Ross said. "Why did the Foanna walk out of the citadel and leave it undefended for their enemies? What about their guards? Did they just leave them too?" He was willing to make the most of any flaw in the aliens' character.

"Most of their people had already escaped through underground ways. The rest left when they knew the cutters had been sunk," Ashe returned. "As to why they deserted the citadel, I don't know. The decision was theirs."

There—up with the barrier between them again. But Ross refused to accept the cutoff this time, determined to pull Ashe back into the familiar world of the here and now.

"That keep could be a trap, about the best on this planet!" The idea was more than just a gambit to attract Ashe's attention, it was true! A perfect trap to catch Baldies.

"Don't you see," Ross sat up, slapped his feet down on the deck as he leaned forward eagerly. "Don't you see ... if the Baldies know anything at all about the Foanna, and I'm betting they do and want to learn all they can, they'll visit the citadel. They won't want to depend on second- and third-hand reports of the place, especially ones delivered by primitives such as the Wreckers. They had a sub there. I'll bet the crew are in picking over the loot right now!"

"If that's what they're hunting"—there was amusement in Ashe's tone—"they won't find much. The Foanna have better locks than their enemies have keys. You heard Ynlan before we left—any secrets left will remain secrets."

"But there's bait—bait for a trap!" argued Ross.

"You're right!" To the younger man's joy Ashe's enthusiasm was plain. "And if the Baldies could be led to believe that what they wanted was obtainable with just a little more effort, or the right tools—"

"The trap could net bigger catch than just underlings!" Ross's thought matched Ashe's. "Why, it might even pull in the VIP directing the whole operation! How can we set it up, and do we have time?"

"The trap would have to be of Foanna setting; our part would come after it was sprung." Ashe was thoughtful again. "But it is the only move which we can make at present with any hope of success. And it will only work if the Foanna are willing."

"Have to be done quickly," Ross pointed out.

"Yes, I'll see." Ashe was a dark figure against the thin light of the companionway as he slid back the cabin door. "If Ynvalda agrees...." As he went out Ross was right behind him.

The Foanna had been given, by their own choice, quarters on the bow deck of the cruiser where sailcloth had been used to form a tent. Not that any of the awe-stricken Rovers would venture too near them. Ashe reached for the flap of the fabric and a lilting voice called:

"You seek us, Gordoon?"

"This is important."

"Yes, it is important, for the thought which brings you both has merit. Enter then, brothers!"

The flap was looped aside and before them was a swirling of mist? ... light? ... sheets of pale color? Ross could not have described what he saw—save if the Foanna were there, he could not distinguish them from the rippling of their hair, the melting film of their robes.

"So, younger brother, you think that which was our home and our treasure box has now become a trap for the confounding of those who believe we are a threat to them?"

Somehow Ross was not surprised that they knew about his idea before he had said a word, before Ashe had given any explanations. Their omniscience was only a small portion of their other talents.

"Yes."

"And why do you believe so? We swear to you that the coast folk can not be driven into those parts of the castle which mean the most, any more than our sea gate can be breached unless we will it so."

"Yet I swam through the sea gate, and the sub was there also." Ross knew again a flash of—was it pleasure?—at being able to state this fact. There *were* chinks in the Foanna defenses.

"Again the truth. You have that within you, young brother, which is both a lack and a shield. True also that this underseas ship entered after you. Perhaps it has a shield as part of it; perhaps those from the stars have their own protection. But they can not reach the heart of what they wish, not unless we open the doors for them. It is your belief, younger brother, that they still strive to force such doors?"

"Yes. Knowing there is something to be learned, they will try for it. They will not dare not to." Ross was very certain on that point. His encounters with the Baldies had not led to any real understanding. But the way they had wiped out the line of Russian time stations made him sure that they dealt thoroughly with any situation they considered a threat.

From the prisoners taken at Kyn Add they had learned the invaders believed the Foanna their enemies here, even though the Old Ones had not repulsed them or their activities. Therefore, it followed that, having taken the stronghold, the Baldies would endeavor to rip open every one of its secrets.

"A trap with good bait—"

Ross wondered which one of the Foanna said that. To see nothing but the swirls of mist-color, listen to disembodied voices from it, was disconcerting. Part of the stage dressing, he decided, for building their prestige with the other races with whom they dealt. Three women alone would have to buttress their authority with such trappings.

"Ah, younger brother, indeed you are beginning to understand us!" Laughter, soft, but unmistakable.

Ross frowned. He did not feel the touch-go-touch of mental communication which the dolphins used. But he did not doubt that the Foanna read his thoughts, or at least a few of them.

"Some of them," echoed from the mist. "Not all—not as your older brother's or the maiden whose mind meets with ours. With you, younger brother, it is a thought here, a thought there, and only our intuition to connect them into a pattern. But now, there is serious planning to be done. And, knowing this enemy, you believe they will come to search for what they can not find. So you would set a trap. But they have weapons beyond your weapons, have they not, younger brother? Brave as are these Rover kind, they can not use swords against flame, their hands against a killer who may stand apart and slay. What remains, Gordoon? What remains in our favor?"

"You have your weapons, too," Ashe answered.

"Yes, we have our weapons, but long have they been used only in one pattern, and they are atuned to another race. Did our defenses hold against you, Gordoon, when you strove to prove that you were as you claimed to be? And did another repulse younger brother when he dared the sea gate? So can we trust them in turn against these other strangers with different brains? Only at the testing shall we know, and in such learning perhaps we shall also be forced to eat the sourness of defeat. To risk all may be to lose all."

"That may be true," Ashe assented.

"You mean the sight you have had into our future says that this happens? Yes, to stake all and to lose—not only for ourselves, but for all others here—that is a weighty decision to make, Gordoon. But the trap promises. Let us think on it for a space. Do you also consult with the Rovers if they wish to take part in what may be desperate folly."

Torgul paced the afterdeck, well away from the tent which sheltered the Foanna, but with his eyes turning to it as Ross explained what might be a good attack.

"Those women-killers would have no fear of Foanna magic, rather would they come to seek it out? It would be a chance to catch leaders in a trap?"

"You have heard what the prisoners said or thought. Yes, they would seek out such knowledge and we would have this chance to capture them—"

"With what?" Torgul demanded. "I am not Ongal to argue that it is better to die in pursuit of blood payment than to take an enemy or enemies with me! What chance have we against their powers?"

"Ask that of them!" Ross nodded toward the still silent tent.

Even as he spoke the three cloaked Foanna emerged, pacing down to mid-ship where Torgul and his lieutenants, Ross and Ashe came to meet them.

"We have thought on this." The lilting half chant which the Foanna used for ordinary communication was a song in the dawn wind. "It was in our minds to retreat, to wait out this troubling of the land, since we are few and that which we hold within us is worth the guarding. But now, what profit such guardianship when there may be none to whom we may pass it after us? And if you have seen the truth, elder brother"—the cowled heads swung to Ashe—"then there may be no future for any of us. But still there are our limitations. Rover," now they spoke directly to Torgul, "we can not put your men within the citadel by desiring—not without certain aids which lie sealed there now. No, we, ourselves, must win inside bodily and then ... then, perhaps, we can pull tight the lines of our net!"

"To run a cruiser through the gate—" Torgul began.

"No, not a ship, Captain. A handful of warriors in the water can risk the gate, but not a ship."

Ashe broke in, "How many gill-packs do we have?"

Ross counted hurriedly. "I left one cached ashore. But there's mine and Karara's and Loketh's—also two more—"

"To pass the gates," that was the Foanna, "we ourselves shall not need your underwater aids."

"You," Ross said to Ashe, "and I with Karara's pack—"

"For Karara!"

Both the Terrans looked around. The Polynesian girl stood close to the Foanna, smiling faintly.

"This venture is mine also," she spoke with conviction. "As it is Tino-rau's and Taua's. Is that not so, Daughters of the Alii of this world?"

"Yes, Sea Maid. There are weapons of many sorts, and not all of them fit into a warrior's hand or can be swung with the force of a man's arm and shoulder. Yes, this venture is yours, also, sister."

Ross's protests bubbled unspoken; he had to accept the finality of the Foanna decree. It seemed now that the make-up of their task force depended upon the whims of the three rather than the experience of those trained to such risks. And Ashe was apparently willing to accept their leadership.

So it was an odd company that took to the water just as dawn colored the sky. Loketh had clung fiercely to his pack, insisted that he be one of the swimmers, and the Foanna accepted him as well. Ross and Ashe, Loketh, and Baleku, a young under-officer of Ongal's, accorded the best swimmer of the fleet, Karara and the dolphins. And with them those three others, shapes sliding smoothly through the water, as difficult to define in this new element as they had been in their tent. Before them frisked the dolphins. Tino-rau and Taua played about the Foanna in an ecstatic joy and when all were in the sea they shot off shoreward.

That sub within the sea gate, had it unleashed the same lethal broadcast as the one at Kyn Add? But the dolphins could give warning if that were so.

Ross swam easily, Ashe next, Loketh on his left, Baleku a little behind and Karara to the fore as if in vain pursuit of the dolphins—the Foanna well to the left. A queer invasion party, even queerer when one totaled up the odds which might lie ahead.

There was no mist or storm this morning to hide the headlands where the Foanna citadel stood. And the promontories of the sea gate were starkly clear in the growing light. The same drive which always was a part of Ross when he was committed to action sustained him now, though he was visited by a small prick of doubt when he thought that the leadership did not lie with Ashe but with the Foanna.

No warning of any trouble ahead as they passed between the mighty, sea-sunk bases of the gate pillars. Ross depended upon his sonic, but there was no adverse report from the sensitive recorder. The terrible chill of the water during the night attack had been dissipated, but here and there dead sea things floated, being torn and devoured by hunters of the waves.

They were well past the pillars when Ross was aware that Loketh had changed place in the line, spurting ahead. After him went Baleku. They caught up with Karara, flashed past her.

Ross looked to Ashe, on to the Foanna, but saw nothing to explain the action of the two Hawaikans. Then his sonic beat out a signal from Ashe.

"Danger ... follow the Foanna ... left."

Karara had already changed course to head in that direction. Ahead of her he could see Loketh and Baleku both still bound for the mid-point of the shore where the jetty and the sunken cutters were. Ashe passed before him, and Ross reluctantly followed orders.

A shelf of rock reached out from the cliff wall, under it a dark opening. The Foanna sought this without hesitation, Ashe, Karara, and Ross following. Moments later they were out of the water where footing sloped back and up. Below them Tino-rau and Taua nosed the rise, their heads lifting out of the water as they "spoke." And Karara hastened to reply.

"Loketh ... Baleku ..." Ross began when he caught a mental stroke of anger so deadly that it was a chill lance into his brain. He faced the Foanna, startled and a little frightened.

"They will not come—now." A knob-crowned wand stretched out in the air, pointing to the upper reaches of the slope. "Nor can any of their blood—unless we win."

"What is wrong?" Ashe asked.

"You were right, very right, men out of time! These invaders are not to be lightly dismissed. They have turned one of our own defenses against us. Loketh, Baleku, all of their kind, can be made into tools for a master. They belong to the enemy now."

"And we have failed so early?" Karara wanted to know.

Again that piercing thrust of anger so vivid that it was no mere emotion but seemed a tangible force.

"Failed? No, not yet have we even begun to fight! You were very right; this is such an evil as must be faced and fought, even if we lose all in battle! Now we must do that which none of our own race has done for generations—we must open three locks, throw wide the Great Door, and seek out the Keeper of the Closed Knowledge!"

Light, a sharp ray sighting from the tip of the wand. And the Foanna following that beam, the three Terrans coming after ... into the unknown.

THE OPENING OF THE GREAT DOOR

It was not the general airlessness of the long-closed passage which wore on Ross's nerves, made Karara suddenly reach out and clasp fingers about the wrists of the two men she walked between; it was a crushing sensation of age, of a toll of years so long, so heavy, as to make time itself into a turgid flood which tugged at their bodies, mired their feet as they trudged after the Foanna. This sense of age, of a dead and heavy past, was so stifling that all three Terrans breathed in gasps.

Karara's breaths became sobs. Yet she matched her pace to Ashe and Ross, kept going. Ross himself had little idea of their surroundings, but one small portion of his brain asked answerless questions. The foremost being: Why did the past crush in on him here? He had traveled time, but never before had he been beaten with the feel of countless dead and dying years.

"Going back—" That hoarse whisper came from Ashe, and Ross thought he understood.

"A time gate!" He was eager to accept such an explanation. Time gates he could understand, but that the Foanna used one....

"Not our kind," Ashe replied.

But his words had pulled Ross out of a spell which had been as quicksand about him. And he began to fight back with a determination not to be sucked into what filled this place. In spite of Ross's efforts, his eyes could supply him with no definite impression of where they were. The ramp had led them out of the sea, but where they walked now, linked hand to hand, Ross could not say. He could see the glimmer of the Foanna; turning his head he could see his companions as shadows, but all beyond that was utter dark.

"Ahhhh—" Karara's sobs gave way to a whisper which was half moan. "This is a way of gods, old gods, gods who never dealt with men! It is not well to walk the road of the gods!"

Her fear lapped to Ross. He faced that emotion as he had faced so many different kinds of fear all his life. Sure, he felt that pressure on him, not the pressure of past centuries now—but a power beyond his ability to describe.

"Not our gods!" Ross put his stubborn defiance into words, more as a shield against his own wavering. "No power where there is no belief!" From what half-forgotten bit of reading had he dredged that knowledge? "No being without belief!" he repeated.

To his vast amazement he heard Ashe laugh, though the sound bordered on hysteria.

"No belief, no power," the older man replied. "You've speared the right fish, Ross! No gods of ours dwell here, Karara, and whatever god does has no rights over us. Hold to that, girl, hold tight!"

"Ah, ye forty thousand gods,　Ye gods of sea, of sky, of woods,　Of mountains, of valleys,　Ye assemblies of gods,　Ye elder brothers of the gods that are,　Ye gods that once were,　Ye that whisper. Ye that watch by night,　Ye that show your gleaming eyes,　Come down, awake, stir,　Walk this road, walk this road!"

She was singing, first softly and then more strongly, the liquid words of her own tongue repeated in English as if what she strove to call she would share with her companions. Now there was triumph in her singing and Ross found himself echoing her, "Walk this road!" as a demand.

It was still there, all of it, the crushing weight of the past, and that which brooded within that past, which had reached out for them, to possess or to alter. Only they were free of that reaching now. And they could see too! The fuzzy darkness was lighter and there were normal walls about them. Ross put out his free hand and rubbed finger tips along rough stone.

Once more their senses were assaulted by a stealthy attack from beyond the bounds of space and time as the walls fell away and they came out into a wide space whose boundaries they could not see. Here that which brooded was strong, a mighty weight poised aloft to strike them down.

"Come down, awake, stir...." Karara's pleading sank again to a whisper, her voice sounded hoarse as if her mouth were dry, her words formed by a shrunken tongue, issued from a parched throat.

Light spreading in channels along the floor, making a fiery pattern—patterns within patterns, intricate designs within designs. Ross jerked his eyes away from those patterns. To study them was danger, he knew without being warned. Karara's nails bit into his flesh and he welcomed that pain; it kept him alert, conscious of what was Ross Murdock, holding him safely apart from something greater than he, but entirely alien.

The designs and patterns were lines on a pavement. And now the three Foanna, swaying as if yielding to unseen winds, began to follow those patterns with small dancing steps. But the Terrans remained where they were, holding to one another for the sustaining strength their contact offered.

Back, forth, the Foanna danced—and once more their cloaks vanished or were discarded, so their silver-bright figures advanced, retreated, weaving a way from one arabesque to another. First about the outer rim and then in, by spirals and circles. No light except the crimson glowing rivulets on the floor, the silver bodies of the Foanna moving back and forth, in and out.

Then, suddenly, the three dancers halted, huddled together in an open space between the designs. And Ross was startled by the impression of confusion, doubt, almost despair wafted from them to the Terrans. Back across the patterned floor they came, their hands clasped even as the Terrans stood together, and now they fronted the three out of time.

"Too few ... we are too few...." she who was the mid one of the trio said. "We can not open the Great Door."

"How many do you need?" Karara's voice was no longer parched, frightened. She might have traveled through fear to a new serenity.

Why did he think that, Ross wondered fleetingly. Was it because he, too, had had the same release?

The Polynesian girl loosed her grip on her companions' hands, taking a step closer to the Foanna.

"Three can be four—"

"Or five." Ashe moved up beside her. "If we suit your purpose."

Was Gordon Ashe crazy? Or had he fallen victim to whatever filled this place? Yet it was Ashe's voice, sane, serene, as Ross had always heard it. The younger Agent wet his lips; it was his turn to have a dry mouth. This was not his game; it could not be. Yet he summoned voice enough to add in turn:

"Six—"

When it came the Foanna answer was a warning:

"To aid us you must cast aside your shields, allow your identities to become one with our forces. Having done so, it may be that you shall never be as you are now but changed."

"Changed...."

The word echoed, perhaps not in the place where they stood, but in Ross's head. This was a risk such as he had never taken before. His chances in the past had been matters of action where his own strength and wits were matched against the problem. Here, he would open a door to forces he and his kind should not meet—expose himself to danger such as did not exist on the plane where weapons and strength of arm could decide victory or defeat.

And this was not really his fight at all. What did it matter to Terrans ten thousand years or so in the future what happened to Hawaikans in this past? He was a fool; they were all fools to become embroiled in this. The Baldies and their stellar empire—if that ever had existed as the Terrans surmised—was long gone before his breed entered space.

"If you accomplish this with our aid," said Ashe, "will you be able to defeat the invaders?"

Again a lengthening moment of silence before the Foanna replied:

"We can not tell. We only know that there is a force laid up here, set behind certain gates in the far past, upon which we may call for some supreme effort. But this much we also know: The Evil of the Shadow reaches out from here now, and where that darkness falls men will no longer be men but things in the guise of men who obey and follow as mindless creatures. As yet this shadow of the Shadow is a small one. But it will spread, for that is the nature of those who have spawned it. They have chanced upon and corrupted a thing we know. Such power feeds upon the will to power. Having turned it to their bidding, they will not be able to resist using it, for it is so easy to do and the results exult the nature of those who employ it.

"You have said that you and those like you who travel the time trails fear to change the past. Here the first steps have been taken to alter the future, but unless we complete the defense it will be ill for all of us."

"And this is your only weapon?" Ashe asked once more.

"The only one strong enough to stand against that which is now unleashed."

In the pavement the fiery lines were bright and glowing. Even when Ross shut his eyes, parts of those designs were still visible against his eyelids.

"We don't know how." He made a last feeble protest on the side of prudence. "We couldn't move as you did."

"Apart, no—together, yes."

The silvery figures were once more swaying, the mist which was their hair flowing about them. Karara's hands went out, and the slender fingers of one of the Foanna lifted, closed about firm, brown Terran flesh. Ashe was doing the same!

Ross thought he cried out, but he could not be sure, as he watched Karara's head begin to sway in concert with her Foanna partner, her black hair springing out from her shoulders to rival the rippling strands of the alien's. Ashe was consciously matching steps with the companion who also drew him along a flowing line of fire.

In this last instant Ross realized the time for retreat was past—there was no place left to go. His hands went out, though he had to force that invitation because in him there was a shrinking horror of this surrender. But he could not let the others go without him.

The Foanna's touch was cool, and yet it seemed that flesh met his flesh, fingers as normal as his met fingers in that grasp. And when that hold was complete he gave a small gasp. For his horror was wiped away; he knew in its place a burst of energy which could be disciplined to use as a weapon or a tool in concentrated and complicated action. His feet so ... and then so.... Did those directions flow without words from the Foanna's fingers to his and then along his nerves to his brain? He only knew which was the proper next step, and the next, and the next, as they wove their way along the pattern lines, with their going adding a necessary thread to a design.

Forward four steps, backward one—in and out. Did Ross actually hear that sweet thrumming, akin to the lilting speech of the Foanna, or was it a throbbing in his blood? In and out.... What had become of the others he did not know; he was aware only of his own path, of the hand in his, of the silvery shape at his side to whom he was now tied as if one of the Rover capture nets enclosed them both.

The fiery lines under his feet were smoking, tendrils rising and twisting as the hair of the Foanna rippled and twisted. And the smoke clung, wreathed his body. They moved in a cocoon of smoke, thicker and thicker, until Ross could not even see the Foanna who accompanied him, was only assured of her presence by the hand which grasped his.

And a small part of him clung desperately to the awareness of that clasp as an anchorage against what might come, a tie between the world of reality and the place into which he was passing.

How did one find words to describe this? Ross wondered with that part of him which remained stubbornly Ross Murdock, Terran Time Agent. He thought that he did not see with his eyes, hear with his ears but used other senses his own kind did not recognize nor acknowledge.

Space ... not a room ... a cave-anything made by normal nature. Space which held something.

Pure energy? His Terran mind strove to give name to that which was nameless. Perhaps it was that spark of memory and consciousness which gave him that instant of "Seeing." Was it a throne? And on it a shimmering figure? He was regarded intently, measured, and—set aside.

There were questions or a question he could not hear, and perhaps an answer he would never be able to understand. Or had any of this happened at all?

Ross crouched on a cold floor, his head hanging, drained of energy, of all that feeling of power and well-being he had had when they had begun their dance across the symbols. About him those designs still glowed dully. When he looked at them too intently his head ached. He could almost understand, but the struggle was so exhausting he winced at the effort.

"Gordon—?"

There was no clasp on his hand; he was alone, alone between two glowing arabesques. That loneliness struck at him with the sharpness of a blow. His head came up; frantically he stared about him in search of his companions. "Gordon!" His plea and demand in one was answered:

"Ross?"

On his hands and knees, Ross used the rags of his strength to crawl in that direction, stopping now and then to shade his eyes with his hands, to peer through the cracks between his fingers for some sight of Ashe.

There he was, sitting quietly, his head up as if he were listening, or striving to listen. His cheeks were sunken; he had the drained, worn look of a man strained to the limit of physical energy. Yet there was a quiet peace in his face. Ross crawled on, put out a hand to Ashe's arm as if only by touching the other could he be sure he was not an illusion. And Ashe's fingers came up to cover the younger man's in a grasp as tight as the Foanna's hold had been.

"We did it; together we did it," Ashe said. "But where—why—?"

Those questions were not aimed at him, Ross knew. And at that moment the younger man did not care where they had been, what they had done. It was enough that his terrible loneliness was gone, that Ashe was here.

Still keeping his hold on Ross, Ashe turned his head and called into the wilderness of the symbol-glowing space about them, "Karara?"

She came to them, not crawling, not wrung almost dry of spirit and strength, but on her two feet. About her shoulders her dark hair waved and spun—or was it dark now? Along those strands there seemed to be threaded motes of light, giving a silvery sheen which was a faint echo of the Foanna's tresses. And was it only his bemused and bewildered sight, Ross mused, or was her skin fairer?

Karara smiled down at them and held out her hands, offering one to each. When they took them Ross knew again that surge of energy he had felt when he had followed the Foanna into the maze dance.

"Come! There is much to do."

He could not be mistaken; her voice held the singing lilt of the Foanna. Somehow she had crossed some barrier to become a paler, perhaps a lesser, but still a copy of the three aliens. Was this what they had meant when they warned of a change which might come to those who followed them into the ritual of this place?

Ross looked from the girl to Ashe with searching intensity. No, he could see no outward change in Gordon. And he felt none within himself.

"Come!" Some of Karara's old impetuousness returned as she tugged at them, urging them to their feet and drawing them with her. She appeared to know where they must go, and both men followed her guidance.

Once more they came out of the weird and alien into the normal, for here were the rock walls of a passage running up at an angle which became so steep they were forced to pull along by handholds hollowed in the walls.

"Where are we going?" Ashe asked.

"To cleanse." Karara's answer was ambiguous, and she sped along hardly touching the handholds. "But hurry!"

They finished their climb and were in another corridor where patches of sunlight came through a pierced wall to dazzle their eyes. This was similar to the way which had run beside the courtyard in Zahur's castle.

Ross looked out of the first opening down into a courtyard. But where Zahur's had held the busy life of a castle, this was silent. Silent, but not deserted. There were men below, armed, helmed. He recognized the uniform of the Wrecker warriors, saw one or two who wore the gray of the Foanna servants. They stood in lines, unmoving, without speech among themselves, men who might have been frozen into immobility and arranged so for some game in which they were the voiceless, will-less pieces.

And their immobility was a thing to arouse fear. Were they dead and still standing?

"Come!" Karara's voice had sunk to a whisper and her hand pulled at the men.

"What—?" began Ross.

Ashe shook his head. Those rows below drawn up as if in order to march, unliving rows. They could not be alive as the Terrans knew life!

Ross left his vantage point, ready to follow Karara. But he could not blot from his mind the picture of those lines, nor forget the terrible blankness which made their faces more unhuman, more frightenly alien than those of the Foanna.

SHADES AGAINST SHADOW

The corridor ended in a narrow slit of room, and the wall before them was not the worked stone of the citadel but a single slab of what appeared to be glass curdled into creamy ridges and depressions.

Here were the Foanna, their robes once more cloaking them. Each held, point out, one of the rods. They moved slowly but with the precise gestures of those about a demanding and very important task as they traced each depression in the wall before them with the wand points. Down, up, around ... as their feet had moved in the dance pattern, so now their wands moved to cover each line.

"Now!"

The wands dropped points to the floor. The Foanna moved equidistant from one another. Then, as one, the rods were lifted vertically, brought down together with a single loud tap.

On the wall the blue lines they had traced with such care darkened, melted. The glassy slab shivered, shattered, fell outward in a lace of fragments. So the narrow room became a balcony above a large chamber.

Below a platform ran the full length of that hall, and on it were mounted a line of oval disks. These had been turned to different angles and each reflected light, a ray beam directed at them from a machine whose metallic casing, projecting antennae, was oddly out of place here.

Once more the three staffs of the Foanna raised as one in the air. This time, from the knobs held out over the hall blazed, not the usual whirl of small sparks, but strong beams of light—blue light darkening as it pierced downward until it became thrusting lines of almost tangible substance.

When those blue beams struck the nearest ovals they webbed with lines which cracked wide open. Shattered bits tinkled down to the platform. There was a stir at the end of the hall where the machine stood. Figures ran into plain sight. Baldies! Ross cried out a warning as he saw those star men raise weapon tubes aimed at the perch on which the Foanna stood.

Fire crackling with the speed and sound of lightning lashed up at the balcony. The lances of light met the spears of dark, and there was a flash which blinded Ross, a sound which split open the whole world.

The Terran's eyes opened, not upon darkness but on dazzling light, flashes of it which tore over him in great sweeping arcs. Dazed, sick, he tried to press his prone body into the unyielding surface on which he lay. But there was no way of burrowing out of this wild storm of light and clashing sound. Now under him the very fabric of the floor rocked and quivered as if it were being shaken apart into crumbling rubble.

All the will and ability to move was gone. Ross could only lie there and endure. What had happened, he did not know save that what raged about him now was a warring of inimical forces, perhaps both feeding on each other even as they strove for mastery.

The play of rays resembled sword blades crossing, fencing. Ross threw his arm over his eyes to shut out the intolerable brilliance of that thrust and counter. His body tingled and winced as the whirlwind of energy clashed and reclashed. He was beaten, stupid, as a man pinned down too long under a heavy shelling.

How did it end? In one terrific thunderclap of sound and blasting power? And when did it end—hours … days later? Time was a thing set apart from this. Ross lay in the quiet which his body welcomed thirstily. Then he was conscious of the touch of wind on his face, wind carrying the hint of sea salt.

He opened his eyes and saw above him a patch of clouded sky. Shakily he levered himself up on his elbows. There were no complete walls any more, just jagged points of masonry, broken teeth set in a skull's jawbone. Open sky, dark clouds spattering rain.

"Gordon? Karara?" Ross's voice was a thin whisper. He licked his lips and tried again:

"Gordon!"

Had there been an answering whimper? Ross crawled into a hollow between two fallen blocks. A pool of water? No, it was the cloak of one of the Foanna spread out across the flooring in this fragment of room. Then Ross saw that Ashe was there, the cloaked figure braced against the Terran's shoulder as he half supported, half embraced the Foanna.

"Ynvalda!" Ashe called that with an urgency which was demanding. Now the Foanna moved, raising an arm in the cloak's flowing sleeve.

Ross sat back on his heels.

"Ross—Ashe?" He turned his head. Karara stood here, then came forward, planting her feet with care, her hands outstretched, her eyes wide and unseeing. Ross pulled himself up and went to her, finding that the once solid floor seemed to dip and sway under him, until he, too, must balance and creep. His hands closed on her shoulders and he pulled her to him in mutual support.

"Gordon?"

"Over there. You all right?"

"I think so." Her voice was weak. "The Foanna ... Ynlan ... Ynvalda—"
Steadying herself against him, she tried to look around.

The place which had once been a narrow room, then a balcony, was now
a perch above stomach-turning space. The hall of the oval mirrors was
gone, having disappeared into a hollow the depths of which were veiled by
a vapor which boiled and bubbled as if, far below, some huge caldron hung
above a blazing fire.

Karara cried out and Ross drew her back from that drop. He was
clearer-headed now and looked about for some way down from this
doubtful perch. Of the other two Foanna there was no sign. Had they been
sucked up and out in the inferno they had created with their unleashing of
energy against the Baldies' installation?

"Ross—look!" Karara's cry, her upflung arm directed his attention aloft.

Under the sullen gathering of the storm a sphere arose as a bubble might
seek the surface of a pool before breaking. A ship—a Baldy ship taking off
from the ruined citadel! So some of the enemy had survived that trial of
strength!

The globe was small, a scout used for within-atmosphere exploration,
Ross judged. It arose first, and then moved inland, fleeing the gathering
storm, to be out of sight in moments. Inland, where the mountain base of
the invaders was reputed to be. Retreating? Or bound to gather
reinforcements?

"Baldies?" Karara asked.

"Yes."

She wiped her hand across her face, smearing dust and grime on her
cheeks. As raindrops pattered about them, Ross drew the girl with him into
the alcove where Ashe sheltered with the Foanna. The cowled alien was
sitting up, her hand still gripping one of the wands, now a half-melted ruin.

Ashe glanced at them as if for the first time he remembered they might
be there.

"Baldy ship just took off inland," Ross told him. "We didn't see either
of the other Foanna."

"They have gone to do what is to be done," Ashe's companion replied.
"So some of the enemy fled. Well, perhaps they have learned one lesson,

not to meddle with others' devices. Ahh, so much gone which will never come again! Never again—"

She held up the half-melted wand, turning it back and forth before her, before she cast it away. It flew out, up, then dropped into the caldron of the hall which had been. A gust of rain, cold, chilling the lightly clad Terrans, swept across them.

The Foanna was helped to her feet by Ashe. For a moment she turned slowly, giving a lingering look to the ruins. Then she spoke: "Broken stone holds no value. Take hands, my brothers, my sister, it is time we go hence."

Karara's hand in Ross's right, Ashe's in his left, and both linked to Ynvalda in turn. Then—they were indeed elsewhere, in a courtyard where bodies lay flaccid under the drenching downpour of the rain. And moving among those bodies were the two other Foanna, bending to examine one man after another. Perhaps over one in three they so inspected they held consultation before a wand was used in tracing certain portions of the body between them. When they were finished, that man stirred, moaned, showed signs of life once more.

"Rosss—!" From behind a tumbled wall crept a Hawaikan who did not wear the guard armor of the others. Gill-pack, flippers, diver's belt, had been stripped from him. There was a bleeding gash down the side of his face, and he held his left arm against his body, supported by his right hand.

"Baleku!"

The Rover pulled himself up to his feet and stood swaying. Ross reached him quickly to catch him as he slumped forward.

"Loketh?" the Terran asked.

"The women-killers took him." Somehow the Rover got that out as Ross half supported, half led him to where the Foanna were gathering those they had been able to revive. "They wanted to learn"—Baleku was obviously making a great effort to tell his story—"about ... about where we came from ... where we got the packs."

"So now they will know of us, or will if they get the story out of Loketh." Ashe worked with Ross to splint the Rover's broken arm. "How many of them were here, Baleku?"

The Rover's head moved slowly from side to side. "I do not know in truth. It is—was—like a dream. I was in the water swimming through the sea gate. Then suddenly I was in another place where those from the stars waited about me. They had our packs and belts and these they showed us, demanding to know whereof these were. Loketh was like one deep in sleep and they left him so when they questioned me. Then there came a great noise and the floor under us shook, lightning flashed through the air. Two of the women-killers ran from the room and all of them were greatly excited. They took up Loketh and carried him away, with him the packs and other things. And I was left alone, though I could not move—as if they had left me in a net I could not see.

"More and more were the flashes. Then one of those slayers of women stood in the doorway. He raised his hand, and my feet were free, but I could not move otherwise than to follow after him. We came along a hall and into this court where men stood unstirring, although stones fell from the walls upon some of them and the ground shook—"

Baleku's voice grew shriller, his words ran together. "The one who pulled me after him by his will—he cried out and put his hands to his head. Back and forth he ran, bumping into the standing men, and once running into a wall as if he were blinded. And then he was gone and I was alone. There was more falling stone and one struck my shoulder so I was thrown to the ground. There I lay until you came."

"So few—out of many so few—" One of the Foanna stood beside them, her cloak streaming with the falling rain. "And for these"—she faced the lines of those they had not revived—"there was no chance. They died as helplessly as if they went into a meeting of swords with their arms bound to their sides! Evil have we wrought here."

Ashe shook his head. "Evil has been wrought here, Ynlan, but not by your seeking. And those who died here helplessly may be only a small portion of those yet to be sacrificed. Have you forgotten the slaughter at Kyn Add and those other fairings where women and children were also struck down to serve some purpose we do not even yet know?"

"Lady, Great One—" Baleku struggled to sit up and Ross slipped an arm behind him in aid. "She for whom I made a bride-cup was meat for them at Kyn Add, along with many others. If these slayers are not put to the sword's edge, there will be other fairings so used. And these Shadow ones possess a magic to draw men to them helplessly to be killed. Great One, you have powers; all men know that wind and wave obey your call. Do you now use your magic! It is better to fall with a power we know, than answer such spells as those killers have netted about the men here!"

"This is one weapon which they shall not use again." Ynvalda rose from a stone block where she had been sitting. "And perhaps in its way it was one of the most dangerous. But in defeating it we have by so much weakened ourselves also. And the strong place of these star men lies not on the coast, but inland. They will be warned by those who fled this place. Wind and wave, yes, those have served our purpose in the past. But now perhaps we have found that which our power will not best! Only—for this"—her gesture was for the ruins of the citadel and the dead—"there shall be a payment exacted—to the height of our desire!"

Whether the Foanna did have any control over the storm winds or not, the present deluge appeared not to accommodate them. The dazed, injured survivors of the courtyard were brought to shelter in some of the underground passages.

There appeared to be no other reminders of the Wrecker force which had earlier besieged the keep than those survivors. But within hours some of those who had served the Foanna for generations returned. And the Foanna themselves opened the sea gates so that the Rover cruisers anchored in the small bay below their ruined walls.

A small force, and one ill-equipped to go up against the Baldies. Some five star men's bodies had been found in the citadel, but the ship had gone off to warn their base. To Ross's thinking the advantage still lay with the invaders.

But the Hawaikans refused to accept the idea that the odds were against them. As soon as the storm blew out its force Ongal's cruiser headed northwest to other clan fairings where the Rovers could claim kinship. And Afrukta sailed on the same errand south. While some of the Wreckers were released to carry the warning to their lords. Just how great a force could be gathered through such means and how effective it would be, was a question to make the Terrans uneasy.

Karara disappeared with the Foanna into the surviving inner cliff-burrows below the citadel. But Ashe and Ross remained with Torgul and his officers, striving to bring organization out of the chaos about them.

"We must know just where their lair lies," Torgul stated the obvious. "The mountains you believe, and they can fly in sky ships to and from that point. Well"—he spread out a chart—"here are the mountains on this island, running so. An army marching hither could be sighted from sky ships. Also, there are many mountains. Which is the one or ones we must seek? It may take many tens of days to find that place, while they will always know where we are, watch us from above, prepare for our coming—"

Again Ross mentally paid tribute to the Captain's quick grasp of essentials.

"You have a solution, Captain?" Ashe asked.

"There is the river—here—" Torgul said reflectively. "Perhaps I think in terms of water because I am a sailor. But here it does run, and for this far along it our cruisers may ascend." He pointed with his finger tip. "This lies, however, in Glicmas's land, and he is now the mightiest of the Wrecker lords, his sword always drawn against us. I do not believe that we could talk him into—"

"Glicmas!" Ross interrupted. They both looked at him inquiringly, and he repeated Loketh's story of the Wrecker lord who had had dealings with a "voice from the mountain" and so gained the wrecking devices to make him the dominant lord of the district.

"So!" Torgul exclaimed. "That is the evil of this Shadow in the mountains! No, under those circumstances I do not think we shall talk Glicmas into furthering any raid against those who have made him great over his fellows. Rather will he turn against us in their cause."

"And if we do not use the cruisers up the river"—Ashe conned the map—"then perhaps a small party or parties working overland could strike the stream here, nearer to the uplands."

Torgul frowned at the map. "I do not think so. Even small parties moving in that direction would be sighted by Glicmas's people. The more so if they headed inland. He will not wish to share his secrets with others."

"But, say—a party of Foanna."

The Captain glanced up swiftly to favor Ashe with a keen regard. "Then he would not dare. No, I am sure he would not dare to interfere. Not yet has he risen high enough to turn the hook of his sword against them. But would the Foanna do so?"

"If not the Foanna, then others wearing like robes," Ashe said slowly.

"Others wearing like robes?" repeated Torgul. Now his frown was heavy. "No man would take on the guise of the Foanna; he would be blasted by their power for so doing. If the Foanna will lead us in their persons, then we shall follow gladly, knowing that their magic will be with us."

"There is also this," Ross broke in. "The Baldies have the gill-packs they took from Baleku and Loketh, and they have Loketh. They will want to learn more about us. We hoped that the citadel would provide bait to draw them and it did. That our plan for a trap there was spoiled was ill fortune. But I am sure that if the Baldies believe we are coming to them, they will hold off an all-out attack against our march, hoping to gather us in intact. They'd risk that."

Ashe nodded. "I agree. We are the unknown they must solve now. And this much I am sure of—the future of this world and her people balances on a very narrow line of choice. It is my hope that such a choice is still to be made."

Torgul smiled thinly. "We live in perilous times when the Shades require our swords to go up against the Shadow!"

WORLD IN DOUBT?

The day was dully overcast as all days had been since they had begun this sulk-and-march penetration into the mountain territory. Ross could not accept the idea that the Foanna might actually command wind and wave, storm and sun, as the Hawaikans firmly believed, but the gloomy weather *had* favored them so far. And now they had reached the last breathing point before they took the plunge into the heart of the enemy country. About the way in which they were to make that plunge, Ross had his own plan. One he did not intend to share with either Ashe or Karara. Though he had had to outline it to the one now waiting here with him.

"This is still your mind, younger brother?"

He did not turn his head to look at the cloaked figure. "It is still my mind!" Ross could be firm on that point.

The Terran backed out of the vantage place from which he had been studying the canyonlike valley cupping the Baldy spaceship. Now he got to his feet and faced Ynlan, his own gray cloak billowing out in the wind to reveal the Rover scale armor underneath.

"You can do it for me?" he asked in turn. During the past days the Foanna had admitted that the weird battle within the citadel had weakened and limited their "magic." Last night they had detected a force barrier ahead and to transport the whole party through that by teleporting was impossible.

"Yes, you alone. Then my wand would be drained for a space. But what can you do within their hold, save be meat for their taking?"

"There can not be too many of them left there. That's a small ship. They lost five at the citadel, and the Rovers have three prisoners. No sign of the scout ship we know they have—so more of them must be gone in it. I won't be facing an army. And what they have in the way of weapons may be powered by installations in the ship. A lot of damage done there. Or even if the ship lifted—" He was not sure of what he could do; this was a venture depending largely on improvisation at the last moment.

"You propose to send off the ship?"

"I don't know whether that is possible. No, perhaps I can only attract their attention, break through the force shield so the rest may attack."

Ross knew that he must attempt this independent action, that in order to remain the Ross Murdock he had always been, he must be an actor not a spectator.

The Foanna did not argue with him now. "Where—?" Her long sleeve rippled as she gestured to the canyon. Dull as the skies were overhead, there was light here—too much of it for his purpose as the ground about the ship was open. To appear there might be fatal.

Ross was grasped by another and much more promising idea. The Foanna had transported them all to the deck of Torgul's cruiser after asking him to picture it for her mentally. And to all outward appearances the Baldy ship before them now was twin to the one which had taken him once on a fantastic voyage across a long-vanished stellar empire. Such a ship he knew!

"Can you put me in the ship?"

"If you have a good memory of it, yes. But how know you these ships?"

"I was in one once for many days. If these are alike, then I know it well!"

"And if this is unlike, to try such may mean your death."

He had to accept her warning. Yet outwardly this ship was a duplicate. And before he had voyaged on the derelict he had also explored a Wrecker freighter on his own world thousands of years before his own race had evolved. There was one portion of both ships which had been identical—save for size—and that part was the best for his purpose.

"Send me—here!"

With closed eyes, Ross produced a mental picture of the control cabin. Those seats which were not really seats but webbing support swinging before banks of buttons and levers; all the other installations he had watched, studied, until they were as known to him as the plate bulkheads of the cabin below in which he had slept. Very vivid, that memory. He felt the touch of the Foanna's cool fingers on his forehead—then it was gone. He opened his eyes.

No more wind and gloom, he stood directly behind the pilot's web-sling, facing a vista-plate and rows of controls, just as he had stood so many times in the derelict. He had made it! This was the control cabin of the spacer. And it was alive—the faint thrumming in the air, the play of lights on the boards.

Ross pulled the cowl of his Foanna cloak up over his head. He had had days to accustom himself to the bulk of the robe, but still its swathings were sometimes a hindrance rather than a help. Slowly he turned. There were no Baldies here, but the well door to the lower levels was open, and from it came small sounds echoing up the communication ladder. The ship was occupied.

Not for the first time since he had started on this venture Ross wished for more complete information. Doubtless several of those buttons or levers before him controlled devices which could be the greatest aid to him now. But which and how he did not know. Once in just such a cabin he had meddled and, in activating a long silent installation, had called the attention of the Baldies to their wrecked ship, to the Terrans looting it. Only by the merest chance had the vengeance of the stellar spacemen fallen then on the Russian investigators and not on his own people.

He knew better than to touch anything before the pilot's station, but the banks of controls to one side were concerned with the inner well-being of the ship—and they tempted him. To go it blind was, however, more of a risk than he dared take. There was one future precaution for him.

From a very familiar case beside the pilot's seat Ross gathered up a collection of disks, sorted through them hastily for one which bore a certain symbol on its covering. There was only one of those. Slapping the rest back into their container, Ross pressed a button on the control board.

Again his guess paid off! Another disk was exposed as a small panel slid back. Ross clawed that out of the holder, put in its place the one he had found. Now, if his choice had been correct, the crew who took off in this ship, unless they checked their route tape first, would find themselves heading to another primitive planet and not returning to base. Perhaps exhaustion of fuel might ground them past hope of ever regaining their home port again. Next to damaging the ship, which he could not do, this was the best thing to assure that any enemy leaving Hawaika would not speedily return with a second expeditionary force.

Ross dropped the route disk he had taken out into a pocket on his belt, to be destroyed when he had the chance. Now he catfooted across the deck to look into the well and listen.

The walls glowed with a diffused light. From here the Terran could count at least four levels under him, with perhaps another. The bottom two ought to be supplies and general storage. Then the engine room, tech labs above, and next to the control cabin the living quarters.

Through the fabric of the ship, shivering up his body from the soles of his feet, he could feel the vibration of engines at work. One such must control the force field which ringed this canyon, perhaps even powered the weapons the invaders could turn against any assault.

Ross whirled about, his Foanna cloak in a wide swing. There was one control which he knew. Yes, again the board was the same as the one he was familiar with. His hand plunged out and down, raking the lever from one measure point to the very end of the slit in which it moved. Then he planted himself with his back to the wall. Whoever came up the well hunting the cause for the failure would be facing the other way. Ross crouched a little, pushing the cape well back on his shoulders to free his arms. There was a feline suppleness in his stance just as a jungle cat might wait coming of its prey.

What he heard was a shout below, the click of foot-gear on the rungs of the level ladder. Ross's lips drew back in a snarl which was also feline. He thought that would do it! Spacemen were ultra-sensitive to any failure in air flow.

White head, bare of any hair, thin shoulders a little hunched under the blue-green-lavender stuff of the Baldies' uniforms.... Head turning now so that the eyes could see the necessary switch. An exclamation from the alien and—

But the Baldy never had a chance to complete that turn, look behind him. Ross sprang and struck with the side of his hand. The hairless head snapped forward. His hands already hooked in the other's armpits, the Terran heaved the alien up and over onto the deck of the control cabin. It was only when he was about to bind his captive that Ross discovered the Baldy was dead. A blow calculated to stun the alien had been too severe. Breathing a little faster, the Terran rolled the body back and hoisted it into the navigator's swing-seat, fastening it with the take-off belts. One down—how many left?

He had little time to wonder, for before he could reach the well once again there was a call from below—sharp and demanding. The Terran searched his victim, but the Baldy was unarmed.

Again a shout. Then silence—too complete a silence. How could they have guessed trouble so quickly. Unless, unless the Baldies' mental communication had been at work ... they might even now know their fellow was dead.

But not how he died. Ross was prepared to grant the Baldies super-Terran abilities, but he did not see how they could know what had happened here.

They could only suspect danger, not know the form it had taken. And sooner or later one of them must come to adjust the switch. This could be a duel of patience.

Ross squatted at the edge of the well, trying to make his ears supply him with hints of what might be happening below. Had there been an alteration in the volume of vibration? He set his palm flat to the deck, tried to deduce the truth. But he could not be sure. That there had been some slight change he was certain.

They could not wait much longer without making an attempt to reopen the air-supply regulator, or could they? Again Ross was hampered by lack of information. Perhaps the Baldies did not need the same amount of oxygen his own kind depended upon. And if that were true, Ross could be the first to suffer in playing a waiting game. Well, air was not the only thing he could cut off from here, though it had been the first and most important to his mind. Ross hesitated. Two-edged weapons cut in both directions. But he had to force a countermove from them. He pulled another switch. The control cabin, the whole of the ship, was plunged into darkness.

No sound from below this time. Ross pictured the interior layout of the ships he had known. Two levels down to reach the engine room. Could he descend undetected? There was only one way to test that—try it.

He pulled the Foanna cloak about him, was several rungs down on the ladder when the glow in the walls came on. An emergency switch? With a forward scramble, Ross swung into one of the radiating side corridors. The sliding-door panels along it were all closed; he could detect no sounds behind them. But the vibration in the ship's walls had returned to its steady beat.

Now the Terran realized the folly of his move. He was more securely trapped here than he had been in the control cabin. There was only one way out, up or down the ladder, and the enemy could have that under observation from below. All they would need to do was to use a flamer or a paralyzing ray such as the one he had turned over to Ashe several days ago.

Ross inched along to the stairwell. A faint pad of movement, a shadow of sound from the ladder. Someone on the way up. Could they mentally detect him, know him for an alien intruder by the broadcast of his thoughts? The Baldies had a certain respect for the Foanna and might desire to take one alive. He drew the robe about him, used it to muffle his figure completely as the true wearers did.

But the figure pulling painfully up from rung to rung was no Baldy. The lean Hawaikan arms, the thin Hawaikan face, drawn of feature, painfully blank of expression—Loketh—under the same dread spell as had held the warriors in the citadel courtyard. Could the aliens be using this Hawaikan captive as a defense shield, moving up behind him?

Loketh's head turned, those blank eyes regarded Ross. And their depths were troubled, recognition of a sort returning. The Hawaikan threw up one hand in a beseeching gesture and then went to his knees in the corridor.

"Great One! Great One!" The words came from his lips in a breathy hiss as he groveled. Then his body went flaccid, and he sprawled face down, his twisted leg drawn up as if he would run but could not.

"Foanna!" The one word came out of the walls themselves, or so it seemed.

"Foanna—the wise learn what lies before them when they walk alone in the dark." The Hawaikan speech was stilted, accented, but understandable.

Ross stood motionless. Had they somehow seen him through Loketh's eyes? Or had they been alerted merely by the Hawaikan's call? They believed he was one of the Foanna. Well, he would play that role.

"Foanna!" Sharper this time, demanding. "You lie in our hand. Let us clasp the fingers tightly and you shall be naught."

Out of somewhere the words Karara had chanted in the Foanna temple came to Ross—not in her Polynesian tongue but in the English she had repeated. And softening his voice to his best approximation of the Foanna singsong Ross sang:

"Ye forty thousand gods,
    Ye gods of sea, of sky—of stars," he improvised.
"Ye elders of the gods that are,
    Ye gods that once were,
    Ye that whisper, yet that watch by night,
    Ye that show your gleaming eyes."

"Foanna!" The summons was on the ragged edge of patience. "Your tricks will not move our mountains!"

"Ye gods of mountains," Ross returned, "of valleys, of Shades and not the Shadow," he wove in the beliefs of this world, too. "Walk now this world, between the stars!" His confidence was growing. And there was no use in remaining pent in this corridor. He would have to chance that they were not prepared to kill summarily one of the Foanna.

Ross went to the well, went down the ladder slowly, keeping his robe about him. Here at the next level there was a wider space about the opening, and three door panels. Behind one must be those he sought. He was buoyed up by a curious belief in himself, almost as if wearing this robe did give him in part the power attributed to the Foanna.

He laid his hand on the door to his right and sent it snapping back into its frame, stepped inside as if he entered here by right.

There were three Baldies. To his Terran eyes they were all superficially alike, but the one seated on a control stool had a cold arrogance in his expression, a pitiless half smile which made Ross face him squarely. The Terran longed for one of the Foanna staffs and the ability to use it. To spray that energy about this cabin might reduce the Baldy defenses to nothing. But now two of the paralyzing tubes were trained on him.

"You have come to us, Foanna, what have you to offer?" demanded the commander, if that was his rank.

"Offer?" For the first time Ross spoke. "There is no reason for the Foanna to make any offer, slayer of women and children. You have come from the stars to take, but that does not mean we choose to give."

He felt it now, that inner pulling, twisting in his mind, the willing which was their more subtle weapon. Once they had almost bent him with that willing because then he had worn their livery, a spacesuit taken from the wrecked freighter. Now he did not have that chink in his defense. And all that stubborn independence and determination to be himself alone resisted the influence with a fierce inner fire.

"We offer life to you, Foanna, freedom of the stars. These other dirt creepers are nothing to you, why take you weapons in their cause? You are not of the same race."

"Nor are you!" Ross's hands moved under the envelope of the robe, unloosing the two hidden clasps which held it. That bank of controls before which the commander sat—to silence that would cause trouble. And he depended upon Ynlan. The Rovers should now be massed at either end of the canyon waiting for the force field to fail and let them in.

Ross steadied himself, poised for action. "We have something for you, star men—" he tried to hold their attention with words, "have you not heard of the power of the Foanna—that they can command wind and wave?

That they can be where they were not in a single movement of the eyelid? And this is so—behold!"

It was the oldest trick in the world, perhaps on any planet. But because it was so old maybe it had been forgotten by the aliens. For, as Ross pointed, those heads did turn for an instant.

He was in the air, the robe gathered in his arms wide spread as bat wings. And then they crashed in a tangle which bore them all back against the controls. Ross strove to enmesh them in the robe, using the pressure of his body to slam them all on the buttons and levers of the board. Whether that battering would accomplish his purpose, he could not tell. But that he had only these few seconds torn out of time to try, he knew, and determined to use them as best he could.

One of the Baldies had slithered down to the floor and another was aiming strangely ineffectual blows at him. But the third had wriggled free to bring up a paralyzer. Ross slewed around, dragging the alien he held across his body just as the other fired. But though the fighter went limp and heavy in Ross's hold, the Terran's own right arm fell to his side, his upper chest was numb, and his head felt as if one of the Rover's boarding axes had clipped it. Ross reeled back and fell, his left hand raking down the controls as he went. Then he lay on the cabin floor and saw the convulsed face of the commander above him, a paralyzer aiming at his middle.

To breathe was an effort Ross found torture to endure. The red haze in his head filled all the world. Pain—he strove to flee the pain but was held captive in it. And always the pressure on him kept that agony steady.

"Let ... be...." He wanted to scream that. Perhaps he had, but the pressure continued. Then he forced his eyes open. Ashe—Ashe and one of the Foanna bending over him, Ashe's hands on his chest, pressing, relaxing, pressing again.

"It is good—" He knew Ynvalda's voice. Her hand rested lightly on his forehead and from that touch Ross drew again the quickening of body and spirit he had felt on the dancing floor.

"How—?" He began and then changed to—"Where—?" For this was not the engine room of the spacer. He lay in the open, with sweet, rain-wet wind filling his starved lungs now without Ashe's force aid.

"It is over," Ashe told him, "all over—for now."

But not until the sun reached the canyon hours later and they sat in council, did Ross learn all the tale. Just as he had made his own plan for reaching the spacer, so had Ashe, Karara, and the dolphins worked on a similar attempt. The river running deep in those mountain gorges had provided a road for the dolphins and they found beneath its surface an entrance past the force barrier.

"The Baldies were so sure of their superiority on this primitive world they set no guards save that field," Ashe explained. "We slipped through five swimmers to reach the ship. And then the field went down, thanks to you."

"So I did help—that much." Ross grinned wryly. What had he proven by his sortie? Nothing much. But he was not sorry he had made it. For the very fact he had done it on his own had eased in part that small ache which was in him now when he looked at Ashe and remembered how it had once been. Ashe might be—always would be—his friend, but the old tight-locking comradeship of the Project was behind them, vanished like the time gate.

"And what will you do with them?" Ross nodded toward the captives, the three from the ship, two more taken from the small scouting globe which had homed to find their enemies ready for them.

"We wait," Ynvalda said, "for those on the Rover ship to be brought hither. By our laws they deserve death."

The Rovers at that council nodded vigorously, all save Torgul and Jazia. The Rover woman spoke first.

"They bear the Curse of Phutka heavy on them. To live under such a curse is worse than a clean, quick dying. Listen, it has come upon me that better this curse not only eat them up but be carried by them to rot those who sent them—"

Together the Foanna nodded. "There has been enough of killing," said Ynlan. "No, warriors, we do not say this because we shrink from rightful deaths. But Jazia speaks the truth in this matter. Let these depart. Perhaps they will bear that with them which will convince their leaders that this is not a world they may squeeze in their hands as one crushes a ripe quaya to eat its seeds. You believe in your cursing, Rovers, then let the fruit of it be made plain beyond the stars!"

Was this the time to speak of the switched tapes, Ross wondered. No, he did not really believe that the Rover curse or their treatment of the captives would, either one, influence the star leaders. But, if the invaders did not return to their base, their vanishing might also work to keep another expedition from invading Hawaikan skies. Leave it to chance, a curse, and time....

So it was decided.

"Have we won?" Ross asked Ashe later.

"Do you mean, have we changed the future? Who can answer that? They may return in force, this may have been a step which was taken before. Those pylons may still stand in the future above a deserted sea and island. We shall probably never know."

That was also their own truth. For them also there had been a substitution of journey tapes by Fate, and this was now their Hawaika. Ross Murdock, Gordon Ashe, Karara Trehern, Tino-rau, Taua—five Terrans forever lost in time—in the past with a dubious future. Would this be the barren, lotus world, or another now? Yes, no—either. They had found their key to the mystery out of time, but they could not turn it, and there was no key to the gate which had ceased to exist. Grasp tight the present. Ross looked about him. Yes, the present, which might be very satisfying after all....

www.ingramcontent.com/pod-product-compliance
Lightning Source LLC
Chambersburg PA
CBHW030756260626
47169CB00001B/80